He couldn't be Neil March!

He just couldn't!

He'd said his name was Rory. But…he hadn't admitted his last name.

Maddie's mind screamed for a logical explanation. Anything but the truth. Anything that would make this nightmare go away.

Neil March. The kind, gentle man named Rory who had been romancing her and little Nicky was Neil March, her sworn enemy.

She had very nearly given her heart to this man. Her foolish, foolish heart. Maddie couldn't bear to face the truth. The man who had given life and laughter back to her and her son was Neil March.

How could it be?

A *Publishers Weekly* bestselling and award-winning author with over 1.5 million books in print, **Deb Kastner** writes stories of faith, family and community in a small-town Western setting. She lives in Colorado with her husband and a pack of miscreant mutts, and is blessed with three daughters and two grandchildren. She enjoys spoiling her grandkids, movies, music (The Texas Tenors!), singing in the church choir and exploring Colorado on horseback.

New York Times bestselling author **Janet Tronstad** grew up on her family's farm in central Montana and now lives in Turlock, California, where she is always at work on her next book. She has written more than thirty books, many of them set in the fictitious town of Dry Creek, Montana, where the men spend the winters gathered around the potbellied stove in the hardware store and the women make jelly in the fall.

A Holiday Prayer

Deb Kastner

&

An Angel
for Dry Creek

New York Times Bestselling Author

Janet Tronstad

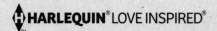

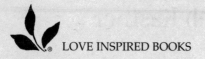

LOVE INSPIRED BOOKS

Recycling programs for this product may not exist in your area.

ISBN-13: 978-1-335-97115-9

A Holiday Prayer & An Angel for Dry Creek

Copyright © 2019 by Harlequin Books S.A.

A Holiday Prayer
First published in 1998. This edition published in 2019.
Copyright © 1998 by Debra Kastner

An Angel for Dry Creek
First published in 1999. This edition published in 2019.
Copyright © 1999 by Janet Tronstad

CONTENTS

A HOLIDAY PRAYER

Deb Kastner

To my three precious daughters, Annie, Kimberly and Katie, who have brought so much joy and meaning to my life. Thank you for showing me every day what it means to have faith as a child.

And to Keith and Dena Rice, for the blessing and inspiration your music and acting have been to me. Keith was the first, and best, Phantom I've ever had the privilege of seeing. Thanks to you both, and to Mark Vogel, for granting me the honor of using your song in this book.

As in water face answereth to face,
so the heart of man to man.
—*Proverbs* 27:19

Prologue

Have I not commanded you?
Be strong and courageous.
Do not be terrified; do not be discouraged,
for the Lord your God will be with you
wherever you go.

—Joshua 1:9

"Why won't they just leave me alone?"

Maddie Carlton glared at the offensive pile of gilt-edged invitations crammed through the mail slot of her town house, then shook her head at her bulldog, Max. "Don't they have anyone else to bother?" Max lifted his soulful eyes to her and shook his jowls.

"Yeah, that's what I thought," she mumbled. With a tired sigh, she bent down and retrieved her mail, tucking it under her arm as she shuffled into the kitchen. She hadn't bothered dressing for the day, and was still in a frayed gray terry-cloth bathrobe and matted slippers.

It was her mourning outfit.

She usually dressed and showered before waking her six-year-old son, Nicky, but today it was too much effort.

Christmas. Her first Christmas without Peter. And the

anniversary of his death. All wrapped up in one mor-
bid package.

The first months of grieving. Peter's birthday. Their
wedding anniversary. Each date came and went, the sun
rose and set, and Maddie was still walking and breathing, still cleaning and cooking—though sometimes it
amazed her.

Life went on. But it was always a struggle.

It was Nicky who kept her rising every morning, moving through the day. For Nicky's sake she would do anything. Even get dressed when she felt like staying in bed,
her head buried under mounds of covers.

With a cup of coffee to increase her fortitude, she
slumped at the kitchen table, spreading her mail before
her. Invitations, mostly. Every charity this side of the
Mississippi River had heard of her tragedy, and every
one of them wanted to partake of her monetary settle-
ment, the flower that they believed grew from the ashes.

Maddie snorted aloud, causing Max, who was trying
to nap at her feet, to sniff and give her his best doggy
put-down for disturbing his rest. If he could, Maddie
thought, he'd be rolling his eyes. As it was, he groaned,
rolled to his feet, turned his back on her and flopped to
the floor again.

"Sorry, Max." She took a handful of envelopes and
flipped through them. Who wanted her money today?

She was about to toss the whole unopened lot into
"file thirteen" when a bright green envelope caught her
eye. Usually the invitations and pleas came in fancy silver or burgundy, or at the very least in a crisp business
envelope.

In addition to being a merry Christmas green, this
envelope had a child's drawing of Santa and his reindeer.
Children's Hospital.

Even the name made her tremble. The other envelopes dropped unnoticed to the floor as she ran a quivering finger across the seal.

For Children's Hospital, she would at least take a look.

Chapter One

Father, I cannot see tomorrow,
Father, I find it hard to pray,
Father, feeling these tears of sorrow,
Carry this weight... Show me the way.
Open up my eyes, Open up my ears,
Open up my heart.
Father, hear my prayer.

—Heartfelt

An ocean of masked partygoers washed toward the Brown Palace Hotel, their laughter echoing in the cold evening air. Maddie closed her eyes, trying to recall the feeling of gurgling laughter caught in her chest, bubbling up into her throat.

Her heart felt void of any emotion but a sense of apprehension at being in the public eye, of being recognized as the Wealthy Widow, as the newspapers had dubbed her.

Country-bred bumpkin was more like it, party clothes or no party clothes.

She stared in awe at the majestic exterior of the his-

toric Brown Palace Hotel, a landmark sandwiched between office buildings in the heart of downtown Denver.

God help me. She sent up a silent prayer. *This isn't
going to work without Your intervention.* She reached inside herself, searching for a snippet of peace that would
make this night easier, but found nothing. Nothing. She
was little more than an empty shell.

It had taken her years to adjust to being a suburban
housewife on the outskirts of a big city, used as she was
to her small hometown in eastern Colorado. No way
would she ever fit in among an ostentatious crowd of
silver-lined philanthropists. Even *with* a mask she was
bound to give away her small-town roots.

Happily-ever-after storybook endings didn't exist. She
was hard proof of that. Perhaps her sparkling Cinderella
satin gown and glass slippers were more appropriate than
she'd imagined. That irony crowned her, just as sure as
the faux-diamond tiara she wore.

She wasn't looking for Prince Charming. She'd already had her one true love. Memories would have to
be enough to bolster her through the remainder of life.

She ought to turn right around and go home where she
belonged. She glanced back at the street, but the taxicab
that had dropped her off in front of the hotel had long
since vanished.

Maddie decided to walk back to 16th Street, where
she could catch a bus back to her own neighborhood. She
didn't really want to be alone in a crowd. Alone at home
was easier to handle. She was still too used to having
Peter by her side. Single was not her style.

And maybe it never would be.

She was looking at her see-through, plastic "glass"
pumps, and didn't see the crowd approaching her until
it was too late. A festive jumble of costumed people

whirled her into their midst and, seeing she was also incognito, whisked her along with them into the hotel.

She fought to be released, but an older woman with a dozen glittering rings on one hand looped her arm through Maddie's, giving her little choice but to follow the others into the dark, panel-floored atrium. She sighed. "'Nothing ventured, nothing gained,'" she quoted to herself.

"Exactly, dear," said the old woman with the rings, who stood at Maddie's side. Maddie had forgot that she wasn't alone, or she certainly wouldn't have spoken aloud. The gray-haired woman put a hand to Maddie's back and gave her a gentle nudge in the direction of the music. "Might as well take a peek, dear heart, since you've come this far."

The voice was filled with such authority that Maddie swiveled to catch her expression, but the woman was already tottering toward a group of friends, waving her arms enthusiastically at a big black bear.

She could see the second floor of the hotel through broad arches, and again felt a quiver of dismay at finding herself among a class of people who would frequent such a place. She felt like a church mouse in a grand cathedral.

Courage, Maddie, she mentally coaxed herself. *These people put their pants on the same way you do. Get a grip on it.*

She wandered tentatively into the ballroom, which had been transformed into a winter wonderland. Billowy cotton clouds hung from the ceiling, sequins glittering from their depths, and many-faceted paper snowflakes graced the walls. Pillarlike lamps wrapped with festive, pungent pine boughs surrounded the dance floor, giving the room a candlelit kind of glow. A twelve-piece orchestra played a lively Chopin waltz in one corner of the ballroom. Already, couples were whirling around the dance floor in time to the music.

The effect was magical, and Maddie experienced the temporary giddy feeling that she'd been transported to another time and place. Was this how Cinderella felt when she walked into the prince's palace? She took a deep breath and smoothed down the satiny folds of her opaque silver gown. *Cinderella.* Would it hurt to pretend? Just a little? And just this once?

Just for tonight, she promised herself. She was in a mask, after all, and had her hair and face made up. No one would recognize her. If the night went well, she might not even recognize herself.

Groups of chattering people mingled around the perimeter of the hall, while others sat at tables before plates mounded with food from the buffet in the next room. Everyone she saw was lavishly costumed—from a portly lion and his chair-wielding lion-tamer wife to Santa and Mrs. Claus.

What if one of the masked men in the room is Neil March? The unspoken question hit her with such sudden force that she nearly reeled. Her stomach tightened as she fought the nausea she felt every time she saw or heard his name.

It was Neil March's fault that she was here tonight. Alone.

Irrational though it might be, Maddie blamed Neil March for Peter's death. There was so much anger, so much pain. It had to be channeled somewhere and Maddie had, whether consciously or not, transferred her negative feelings to Neil March. He was, after all, the owner of the department store, and in her mind, that made him responsible.

The report by the fire department had cleared March's

of any wrongdoing, but she clung stubbornly to her own suspicions. Authorities could be paid off to keep their findings a secret, and if there was one thing Neil March had plenty of, it was money. Hadn't he tried to buy her off, as well?

Her stomach clenched and she scanned the room in earnest.

What if he *was* here? Maddie gasped, fighting the waves of panic.

No. Neil March wouldn't be here. He was a playboy, not a philanthropist. What he'd paid her at Peter's untimely death had been nothing less than blood money. Not offered out of generosity. And definitely not offered out of compassion. Of that she was certain.

Though she knew him to be a practiced businessman, she pictured Neil as a young, arrogant preppy, complete with khaki pants and a designer polo shirt with the collar flipped up on his neck. He'd have a tennis racket slung over one arm and a gorgeous blonde on the other.

She didn't recall seeing any preppy tennis players here tonight mingling among the guests.

She snorted at her own joke. It was the closest she'd come to laughing since Peter had died. The sober thought dropped the smile from her lips.

Neil March was certainly nothing to laugh about.

"Excuse me." She flagged down a passing waiter. "Do you have water?" She realized she sounded like a dehydrated camel after days in the desert, but the waiter remained straight-faced. "Of course, madam."

Moments later she was gulping down a glass of water, coughing and sputtering when it went down wrong. She pounded a fist against her chest to dislodge what felt like a boulder. "Maddie, you *have* to relax!" she muttered under her breath.

"Hey! Check it out. Now *that's* a costume and a half!" a young blonde in a tennis outfit said, grabbing Maddie by the elbow.

There went her theory that there were no tennis players here tonight. The young woman was the gorgeous blonde half of her Neil March scenario, with white culottes that put the *short* in shorts. Bleach-blond hair and a knockout tan in the dead of winter?

Intrigued, Maddie looked to where the blonde was pointing her tennis racket. Something had clearly captured her attention.

Standing in the doorway, his feet braced and hands on his hips, was the Phantom of the Opera, handsome despite the fact that the upper half of his face was masked in stark white.

She was immediately struck by his impressive bearing and thick, broad shoulders. His black cutaway tuxedo was covered with a many-caped greatcoat, fastened at the neck amid snowy-white ruffles. His presence was intense and powerful, and Maddie could see that she wasn't the only woman inexplicably drawn to his mask and the thick black hair curling down around his collar.

He appeared to be looking for someone, his strong, thin lips turned down at the corners in just the shadow of a frown.

His gaze passed where she stood, then moved back again, as if he were taking a second look. No doubt he was, since Ms. Short-shorts was still holding on to Maddie's elbow. She was exactly the sort of woman to make a man do a double take.

Maddie wasn't surprised when he strode toward them. The young woman dropped her tennis racket to her side and stood with one hand on her hip, greeting the Phantom with a brilliant smile.

Oddly enough, Maddie had the peculiar sensation that he was watching *her,* coming for *her,* as if he'd picked an old friend's face from a crowd. And it sent shivers down her spine. But of course that was nonsense. He was coming for the blonde.

With unconscious grace, he unhooked the cape and swung it around, folding it across a chair. Maddie's heart leaped to her throat, and she nearly dropped the water glass that she held in her hand. This man was *definitely* not an old friend.

She would have remembered such a compelling gaze, the way his dark eyes burned through the stark whiteness of the mask…and especially that confident swagger that caught the attention of every woman he passed.

Her head spun as the man grew nearer. She was vaguely aware of the sound of her own breath heavy in her ears, the pounding of her heart in her head.

Now he was in front of her, looking straight at her. As if he knew her. But there was no way he could recognize her through her mask. And even if he could see her face, it was improbable that he'd know her. How could he? She wasn't part of this crowd.

Perhaps that was the problem. Did she stick out like a weed among orchids? Maybe she looked like the grungy suburban housewife that she was, as out of place as a child at a grown-up party.

He grinned then, the smile starting at his lips and emanating from his obsidian-black eyes behind the mask. His smile encompassed both Maddie and the primping blonde at her side.

So that was it. He was being polite, figuring Maddie was Ms. Short-shorts's friend. And he was probably wondering how to get rid of her.

Well, she'd make it easy for him. She didn't know why

Goldilocks had latched on to her in the first place, and she had no qualms about bowing out when she wasn't wanted. She dislodged her elbow from the blonde's grasp just as the Phantom held out his hand and gestured toward the dance floor.

Let's move it, sweetie. He's obviously asking you to dance, and he isn't going to wait forever, Maddie thought uncharitably, wondering why the woman's grip on her elbow had tightened. What was this woman's problem? *Not* a tough decision, especially for one as used to society charity balls as this girl seemed to be.

She glanced to her side. The young woman stared at Maddie with a mixture of disbelief and pique, then glanced at the Phantom. She swung her astonished gaze to Maddie and, with an unladylike snort, flounced away in a huff.

Either the woman was crazy, or a complete idiot. And the Phantom had just been jilted. She turned to the man and offered a regretful shrug and a tentative smile.

The dark-haired man combed his fingers through the curls at the back of his neck. "Well?"

Maddie cocked her head. "Well?" she repeated.

"Dance with me."

His voice was as low and rich as she'd imagined it would be. And she had definitely imagined the words.

Dance?

His eyes lit with amusement at her hesitation.

"Weren't you asking Goldilocks to dance?" she blurted.

"Who?" The Phantom looked genuinely perplexed.

"You know." Maddie tipped her head in the direction the blonde had disappeared. "The tennis player."

The Phantom chuckled. "Not a chance. She's a little

young. And definitely not my type. I was asking *you* to dance."

He was asking her to dance. And the orchestra was breaking into a slow ballad even as they spoke.

She nodded and took the hand he extended.

She felt a twinge of guilt when he swept her into his arms. It felt awkward. She hadn't danced in ages. And for so many years it had only been Peter.

Peter's arms. Peter's whisper.

She felt the electric heat of the Phantom's hand on her hip and her mind clicked into gear. A wave of panic surged over her.

Oh, Lord, what have I gotten into now?

She'd come here to support Children's Hospital, not to dance. It was too much, too fast. To be dancing in another man's arms, feeling another man's heartbeat against her palm. Guilt turned the screw. Was she betraying Peter's memory?

But Peter was gone. The Phantom was here, and his light embrace was not unpleasant. Besides, it was only one dance.

While Peter couldn't dance to save his life, the Phantom was clearly a dancer, swaying easily in time to the music. Peter had been lean and lank, but her fingers now burned with the feel of the Phantom's thick, rippling biceps. And he was shorter than Peter had been, though still a good head taller than Maddie. She would, she thought with an uncomfortable flutter of her stomach, fit right into the crook of the man's shoulder.

As if he read her thoughts, he smiled at her.

At last, an imperfection. She was beginning to think that he was perfect in form and face—or at least what she could see of it. But his smile was crooked and little-boy adorable.

He chuckled low in his chest and his dark eyes sparkled with mirth. He lowered his head until his warm breath tickled the sensitive skin of her neck, sending shivers of delight down her spine. "You're staring at me."

Maddie felt as if he'd jolted her with a white-hot bolt of electricity. With a whimper of dismay, she attempted to shrug out of his arms.

His hand on her hip tightened in response. "Don't run," he implored in a throaty whisper. "Please. I was only kidding."

She grimaced and tittered nervously. "I apologize. It's just that I…"

He lifted his hand from her hip and gently placed his forefinger over her lips. "No. You don't have to explain. Just dance with me."

She nodded, losing track of her thoughts in liquid black eyes reminiscent of some Native American ancestor and confirmed by his angular features and aquiline nose.

He shifted slightly, pulling her into his chest so that his hand now rested at the small of her back. It was a modest gesture, but enough for her to feel the rock-hard ripples of his shoulder under her cheek.

She inhaled deeply, then fought the sense of guilt assaulting her even as the faint spice of the Phantom's aftershave made her nostrils tingle.

Oh, God, she prayed as grief washed over her. How she missed Peter.

Deep inside her heart, the part of her that had agonized through every lonely night, mourning Peter's death, facing the achingly empty king-size bed alone, struggling through empty days, needed to move closer into the embrace of her Phantom gentleman.

She was relieved that he wasn't trying to make idle

conversation. She didn't want to talk. She just wanted to be held. If only for a moment. To feel the brush of warm breath tickle her ear. To revel in strong arms encircling her waist.

But how could she?

She pulled back, opening the space between them. She should turn around and walk away. This instant, while she still had the strength to do so.

The Phantom's warm hand lightly resting on her back sent shivers up her spine that had nothing to do with cold. Her spirit soared.

With a deep inner sigh, she allowed him to draw her closer. Being in his arms felt good and right. She would face her regrets tomorrow.

For tonight, she was going to dance.

Chapter Two

The Phantom leaned back to study the petite woman in his arms. Her face, framed by cinnamon-brown hair, was rosy with color. In her silvery ball gown and glass slippers she made a perfect Cinderella.

Though he still wasn't certain why, she'd caught his eye the moment he had entered the ballroom. Perhaps it was because she looked small, and shy, and completely ill at ease.

He suspected that there was a latent fireman in him someplace, because she looked just like a little lost kitten stranded in a treetop. He felt like grabbing a ladder and rescuing her. Putting a smile on her heart-shaped face, a sparkle in her shadowed brown eyes.

He shifted forward so he could feel the satin softness of her cheek against his. Immediately, he felt her muscles bunch as if she were preparing to spring from his grasp.

She seemed as jumpy as a jackrabbit being chased by a fox. But if she wanted to run away, he couldn't bring himself to let her go. There was something familiar about her—something he couldn't name, but which compelled him to keep her close.

He hadn't even planned to come to the benefit in the first place. He rarely went out anymore.

And he *never* danced. What had drawn him onto the dance floor was as much a mystery to him as was the woman in his arms.

It didn't matter, anyway. He was here now. And he didn't plan to leave. Or to let her go.

His face lingered near her bare shoulder, inhaling her light, musky fragrance. She wasn't smothered in expensive perfume like most women of his acquaintance. No. She smelled like...

Moonlight.

If there were any way to blot out the nightmare of thoughts haunting him, it would be this beautiful woman.

He leaned back and smiled down at her, feeling her body stiffen when his gaze met hers.

Why was she so afraid?

His throat tightened at the look of utter helplessness in her huge brown eyes, and he became suddenly determined to change the course of her evening.

Before the night was through, he vowed to himself, he would hear the sweet sound of her laughter.

Maddie expected him to release her after the song ended, but he continued to sway back and forth as if the orchestra continued to play. She glanced around the room, terrified that she was making a spectacle of herself, but no one seemed to notice the still-dancing couple.

Moments later she heard the shrill wail of a saxophone and sagged with relief as the Phantom adjusted their steps to the beat of the new song. He was obviously determined to enjoy the evening. With her.

Well, so was she. With him.

"What's your name?" he whispered into her ear.

Maddie stepped back and curtsied playfully. "I thought you would have guessed by now," she teased. "Cinderella, of course!"

The Phantom let out a full-bodied laugh that caused those dancing around them to peer at them curiously.

"We're going to play games, are we?" He took a step back and gave an elegant bow. "I guess that would make me your Phantom."

Maddie was more than content to leave the introductions at that. They would all unmask at midnight, after all. If she stayed that long....

She had a sneaking suspicion she just might.

For the moment she was content just to remain in his arms and lose herself in the music. It was pure magic, and she didn't intend to waste a single moment.

The song came to a close and the orchestra's lead violist surprised everyone by breaking out in a fiddling tune. In moments a country line dance was formed.

Her Phantom chuckled and drew her to the edge of the floor. "Sorry, love. I don't do country."

Maddie shrugged. It wasn't hard to smile. Country wasn't her style, either. "I'm ready for a break."

The Phantom indicated a chair and held it for her, while she gathered her skirts and sat. "Are you thirsty? Why don't I get you some..." His sentence trailed off.

She looked up, surprised. His eyes were cloudy and unreadable. He seemed to be sidetracked by something at the far corner of the ballroom.

She followed his gaze but saw nothing out of the ordinary. Unless it was one of a number of beautiful young women over there.

She replied, "No, that's okay. I'm not thirsty."

But the Phantom was not listening. He was already walking away from her, his mind obviously elsewhere.

As if with great effort, he tossed one quick glance back at her. "Excuse me. I'll just…"

And then he was gone.

Maddie sighed and crossed her arms over her chest, though she could feel a hesitant smile still hovering on her lips.

Her fantasy was over. And she really should be angry with the man for abandoning her so abruptly. But the lovely warmth, telling her that she still had a heart, lingered. She felt alive, really alive, for the first time in years.

There would be no regrets. It didn't matter that she'd been deserted for fresher prey. She was more than content just to sit here and watch wildly costumed dancers wiggling to some latest craze in line dancing.

One young man, dressed most appropriately as a rooster, was crowing loudly and shaking his tail feathers in wild abandon. The music did sound rather like a clucking chicken.

She felt a small rumble building deep in her chest, growing promptly into full-fledged laughter. She clapped a hand over her mouth to keep from appearing rude.

But not to stem the flow of laughter. It felt so good— better even than whirling around on the dance floor. She felt like leaping up and shaking her own tail feathers.

Laughter scoured her insides clean. Maybe she'd get really brave and find a partner for one last dance.

"That chicken is really something." The rich, soft, unmistakable baritone came from behind her, next to her ear. Her Phantom was back.

Her heart leaped into her throat, her head buzzing with excitement and the purely female thrill of attracting a handsome man. Not once, but twice. "Yes, he is, isn't he?"

The Phantom chuckled. "I meant the music. It's called 'The Chicken.' I guess 'cause it sounds like a chicken clucking."

Maddie grinned. "I noticed."

"What do you say we get out of here for a while?" he whispered.

It had been a few years, but his words sounded distinctly like a come-on. She cocked her eyebrow. "Out?"

He grinned and held up his hands as if to ward off her unspoken accusation. "Just out for a breath of air and some peace and quiet. That's all. I promise. Promise."

"Oh, but they're going to unmask at midnight!" she protested, though it sounded weak, even to her. She was being worn down, and his wink told her that he knew it. But she really did want to dance again before she left. Desperately.

"Never fear. We'll be back before then. Come on, let's get some air."

Maddie cast one last disappointed glance at the dance floor, then shrugged. It wouldn't hurt to leave for a few minutes. And he'd promised to be back before they unmasked. She hoped they'd have one more dance together before the night ended.

He led her to the door and assisted her with her coat. "I've got a surprise for you."

"Surprise?" she repeated lamely, and then wondered at the wisdom of following an unknown man onto the streets of downtown Denver. A woman couldn't be too careful. And she was no innocent child.

She searched his eyes for some sign of his intentions, but found only a gleam of humor lurking in their black depths. He wasn't giving anything away.

At least not yet. But he wasn't the least bit threatening.

He raised a questioning eyebrow over the top of the mask.

The decision was hers. She glanced back into the ballroom and the safety it represented.

The Phantom stood patiently, arms crossed over his thick chest and a half smile lingering on his lips. She had the niggling impression that he sensed the dilemma she was working through and was certain of the outcome.

She stood undecided for a moment more, knowing what she would do and waiting for the rational part of her brain to call her an impulsive fool. She instinctively trusted her Phantom. He was strong, but gentle. If she were going to gamble with her safety, she would bet on this man.

She nodded slowly. "All right. Let's go."

A gust of crisp Christmas air hit them as they stepped out of the hotel, causing Maddie's lungs to burn. It was a pleasant sensation, she decided. She carefully watched her steps on the icy pavement. Glass slippers weren't exactly winter-weather gear, and she found herself wishing she'd worn her thick leather snow boots.

She slipped and giggled. The Phantom quickly clasped her arm, but not fast enough to keep her from sliding unceremoniously to the ground in a heap. The picture of herself in a satin dress and snow boots sent her into another fit of giggles.

It felt good. Very good.

"Your surprise…." the Phantom reminded her.

He reached a hand to help her to her feet, then pointed at the curb. Her heart pounded as she got her first hint of the Phantom's scheme, which was at that moment stomping its impatience into the pavement. She clapped a hand over her mouth and exclaimed in delight over the slick white horse-drawn carriage, complete with a liveried driver.

"Oh, it's lovely!" she exclaimed as he settled her on the seat and wrapped a wool blanket around her legs. "But aren't we going to freeze?"

The Phantom chuckled and draped an arm around her shoulders. "No chance of that. We'll just take a short ride down the 16th Street Mall. Have you seen the Christmas lights yet? They're gorgeous this time of night."

Maddie shook her head. This was truly a night she would remember for a long time to come. If she believed in fairy tales, she'd think she stepped right into one. Even the crisp air couldn't dull the heat warming her cheeks.

Motioning for the driver to stop, her Phantom gestured at the forty-three-foot Christmas tree in Larimer Square, the largest to be found in Denver.

"Didn't I tell you it was beautiful?" he whispered, his breath fanning her cheek.

She turned her face toward him, expecting him to be watching the Christmas display, hoping to be able to study his masked face. His eyes met hers, and she suddenly realized that he'd been watching her, seeing the wonders of Christmas in downtown Denver through her, sharing in her delight.

Her breath mingled with his, their lips only inches apart. His dark, intense gaze probed hers. It would take only the merest action on her part…just a shimmer of movement and their lips would meet.

Dragging in a breath, she turned away. How could she even consider…? But she had. She did. Guilt ripped through her like a rudder blade on the snow.

She had no right. And even less sense.

"Drive on," her Phantom commanded, leaning back in the seat. She was afraid to look at him, afraid of what she would see in his eyes.

If only he would take that blasted mask off and she

could see him as a real human being instead of the larger-than-life Phantom of the Opera. It was just that fairy-tale feeling again, getting the best of her. He was only a man underneath that mask. A plain, ordinary man. Maybe even disguising some hidden flaw.

The corner of her lips quivered into a smile.

"A penny for your thoughts," he whispered. On the inside of her wrist, he planted a tiny kiss that radiated heat up the entire length of her arm.

She tried to ignore the sensation. "As if I'd sell them so cheap."

The Phantom lifted an eyebrow. He was intrigued by this bright-eyed Cinderella, more so than he wanted to put a value to. "A million dollars, then."

She stiffened.

"What? What did I say?" He'd been teasing, but by the look on her face, he could tell he'd said the wrong thing. She went as hot and then cold as a kitchen tap.

"Nothing."

Nothing. No more than she had told him all evening. And why should it matter? He wasn't in the market for a relationship. He should be glad she wasn't pressing him.

But he wasn't glad.

Who *was* this woman? He'd been stretching his mind for the answer, but the mask continued to throw him. He'd seen her somewhere—he knew he had.

But how to coax her from her shell? Flattery didn't work. With a teasing lilt to his voice, he appealed. "Tell me your name."

Maddie's brown eyes sparkled mischievously. "Not just yet. You'll find out soon enough, in any case." She gently removed her arm from his grasp and laced her fingers together on her lap. "Tell me about you."

"Okay," he agreed easily, leaning back into the cushion and laying his arm over the back of the seat. Perhaps if he opened up, she would feel more comfortable revealing something about herself. He barely dared to hope.

"I work for a large company in the area. I play racquetball and golf. I like pizza and Pepsi. Anything else you want to know?"

"My, my," Maddie bantered. "Vague, aren't we? A large company in the area? That hardly narrows it down. What kind of business?"

"Enough about me," he countered, combing his fingers through the curls on his neck. "Tell me about you."

Maddie didn't want to talk about herself. Not tonight. She lifted her chin. If he could be stubborn, so could she.

The Phantom chuckled again. "We all have secrets, don't we?" he said before tapping the driver on the shoulder. "A rose for the lady, please."

The driver nodded and pulled to the side of the road, gesturing to one of the many corner flower vendors peddling their wares to the late-night Christmas shoppers. "I need a rose," he rasped.

The Phantom presented the single, long-stemmed red rose to Maddie with an endearingly crooked grin. "A beautiful flower for a beautiful lady."

Maddie's breath caught in her throat. "I… I…"

The Phantom frowned and he rolled his eyes.

"What?" Maddie asked in surprise.

"I think I've just blurted out the most inane line in history. And it's all your fault. One look at you and my mind gets all mixed up."

He was teasing her, she knew, but nonetheless she could feel the heat staining her cheeks crimson. She took refuge in inhaling the rose's intoxicating scent. The petals still had moisture on them, and they glistened in the dull light of the streetlamps.

"Won't you tell me your name?" he pleaded quietly, his rich baritone rolling over each syllable. "We're going to unmask soon, anyway. What difference will a few minutes make?"

She stared at her hands clasped in her lap. Maybe he was right. What was the difference? She glanced over at him, but he was staring off into the distance. "Maddie Carlton," she whispered, her breath misting the air.

His gaze snapped to hers, boring into her with such intensity that Maddie felt suffocated.

"You've heard of me," she said quietly, removing the now unnecessary mask from her face. "I lost my husband in the March's Department Store fiasco last Christmas. My only claim to fame is that Neil March settled me with a ridiculous amount of money."

The Phantom's jaw tightened and he looked away. She could see the tension lining his face, causing the muscles in his neck to strain against his cravat.

Maddie unconsciously leaned away from him, wondering what she'd said that had set him off.

He obviously didn't like what he heard. He probably expected her to be some debutante from old money, not a widow with a tragic past and a son to boot.

Well, the truth had to come out sooner or later. There was nothing she could do about it if he was disappointed. None of this was real, anyway.

His eyes became dull and shaded, the fire in his eyes extinguished as effectively as if it had been doused with water.

The fairy tale was over, blown sky-high by her own big mouth. She should have kept her identity a secret, she silently reprimanded herself. She should have extended the fantasy—for what it was worth—as long as possible.

She stared out onto the darkened street and sighed

deeply, remembering. She hadn't even threatened March with a lawsuit or anything. She hadn't wanted a penny of his money. It had just showed up in the mail one day—a certified check for half a million dollars. The first of six checks! Even now she found it hard to comprehend.

She turned back to face him, wondering at his silence.

His dark eyes were full of a mixture of regret and— What was it? Pain? Anger?

She never had the opportunity to find out.

Tapping the driver on the shoulder, he demanded the carriage be stopped. "I've got to go." The words were softly spoken but cut into Maddie's heart as if he'd screamed.

He cleared his throat, then shook his head as if he had decided against explaining further. Tentatively, he reached forward, brushing the inside of his thumb along her cheek in a featherlight caress.

"I…" he said, his voice husky. He leaned forward, his eyes never leaving hers. For Maddie, time moved in slow motion as she waited breathlessly for his lips to meet hers.

When the moment came, she closed her eyes, savoring every touch, every sensation, storing up for the long, empty nights ahead. His lips were cool and firm, but his breath was warm.

With a sigh, he leaned forward, deepening the kiss, just for a moment.

Maddie wanted to cling to him, but she clenched her hands in her lap, willing them not to betray her, shaking so hard that she was sure he could feel it.

"Oh, Maddie," he whispered against her lips, the words deep and razor-sharp.

She opened her eyes when he abruptly pushed away

Chapter Three

Maddie sighed and brushed a stray tendril of hair from her forehead. She felt hot and sweaty and her muscles ached from carrying boxes up from the basement. Yet she hadn't ventured to open a single one of the cartons that now filled her living room.

It was the handwriting scribbled in wide, black marker ink that stopped her.

Peter's handwriting.

Christmas. The boxes set aside for the happiest time of year, laden with bright and glittering decorations that she knew would delight her young son.

But the sight of the festive decorations had no effect on her, except maybe to tighten the vise around her heart.

She wasn't happy. And she didn't know if she could fake it, even for Nicky. Could she really put together a six-foot artificial tree by herself? Never mind lift Nicky to place the angel on top—a tradition formerly and laughingly performed by Peter.

She muttered a prayer for help, but it smacked against the ceiling of her apartment and came showering down again in thousands of tiny pieces. Or at least that's how it felt to her.

She was living in a tiny wooden crate with no air and no light. She'd been abandoned. First by her father. Then by Peter. And now, it seemed, even God had left her to flounder on her own.

Madelaine Anne! She could hear her mother's voice as if it were yesterday. *If you can't find God, it's because you've backed off. He hasn't gone anywhere.*

She toyed with the idea of making a phone call. Mom always knew what to say. But Maddie's faith wasn't as strong as her mother's. In fact, she wasn't sure if she had faith at all. Would someone with real faith question what God had done?

Maddie did. Every single day. Peter's death didn't make any more sense to her now than it had a year ago. Even the newspapers had called it a senseless tragedy.

God is in control.

If that was true, why hadn't she even been able to find a crack in the woodwork of this crate of hers?

Except, perhaps, last night. Last night, for one brief, shining moment, she had remembered what it was like to laugh. The deep melodic voice of her Phantom rang through her memory, and she smiled. He had given her a precious gift. He had helped her laugh again. She would always be grateful to him for that.

Her smile faded. Last night it had been easy to think about celebrating Christmas again. Last night she'd even believed she might enjoy the festive spirit, revel in the preparations.

But not now. Not with all these boxes as glaring reminders of the love she and Peter had shared, love that had brought her dear Nicky into the world.

She would not cry.

And she would *not* let Nicky down. He deserved a

memorable Christmas. And if God *was* here, she was going to give Nicky the best Christmas of his life.

She gritted her teeth against the waves of nausea in her stomach and the ferocious pounding in her head. The huge box containing the Christmas tree was waiting for her attention. With a deep breath for courage, she plunged her arms in, triumphantly emerging with an armful of tree limbs in various shapes and sizes.

After five minutes of work, she'd managed to find the tree base, and had buried herself knee-deep in branches.

She'd never paid the least attention to Peter when he put the tree together, but if he could do it, so could she. Didn't the dumb tree come with instructions?

She burst into frustrated tears. What a stupid thing to cry over, she reprimanded herself. But she didn't try to brush the tears away. If it wasn't this, it would be something else. She hadn't realized how much she depended on Peter.

And now she was alone.

"Why did you leave me, Peter? Why? I never was good enough for you, was I?" The words echoed in the empty room, an echo answered in her empty heart.

She scrubbed a determined hand down her face, resolving to divide and conquer. No stupid artificial tree would get the best of her, even if it took her all day to assemble.

Her lips pinched with determination, she leaned into the box until she felt as though she were being swallowed. She groped around the bottom, her fingers nimbly searching for anything resembling paper, but found nothing but a stray line of garland.

What might Peter have done with the instructions? *Tossed them.*

The thought caught her by surprise and she barked

out a laugh. Of course. That's *exactly* what her handy-
man husband would have done. In his opinion, written
instructions were the bane of a "real" man's existence,
to be scoffed at and referred to only as a last resort.

Which left her with a gigantic tree-size problem.
Hands on her hips, she surveyed the limb-strewn room.

Christmas music. She'd throw on a CD of favorite
Christmas tunes for a little holiday spirit. Maybe all she
needed was to set the mood. Though she thought it highly
improbable that the tree would put itself together even
with the proper ambience.

"Oh, Mama!" Nicky exclaimed, scuffling sleepily
from his bedroom. He was still clad in his superhero
pajamas, his white-blond hair rumpled from sleep. "A
Christmas tree!"

Her heart warmed at the sight of her son's glowing
eyes. It was worth any amount of pain to give her son
some joy in his life. And perhaps—if God were merci-
ful—she could partake in a moment or two of Christmas joy herself.

She wanted to wrap her arms around him in a bear
hug, but knew he would take that as a personal assault on
his big-boy dignity. Instead, she ruffled his hair. "Well,
it's supposed to be."

She laughed as Nicky threw himself into a pile of
limbs as if it were a mountain of crisp autumn leaves.

"As you can see, Mom's having a little bit of trouble
putting this thing together."

Nicky's expression became serious, his brows knit
together. "I'll help."

The look was so much his father's that Maddie's throat
tightened.

Nicky began gathering limbs in his stout little arms.
"Look, Mom. They have colors on the ends."

Hmm. So they did. How had she missed something so patently obvious? She couldn't say, but she felt the heat rising in her cheeks. Leave it to her six-year-old son to solve the problem before she did.

She picked up one of the smaller branches, marked with yellow paint on the end that stuck into the base. "These yellow ones must go on top."

Humming along with "Jingle Bells," she began poking the metal end into the top of the base. They'd have a Christmas tree yet. And maybe even before the new year hit!

"No, Mama. The big branches first. That's how Daddy always used to do it."

Tears sprang again to her eyes, and she quickly brushed them away before her son could see. How could he possibly remember Peter putting up the Christmas tree? It had been two years—two achingly painful years—since there'd been no tree last year. Last year they'd celebrated Christmas in Children's Hospital.

How could Nicky possibly remember that far back? He would have been four, watching Peter with wide-eyed wonder and the universal childhood belief that Daddy could do anything.

But somehow, he remembered.

She cleared her throat against the pain choking the breath from her lungs. The picture of flames engulfing the Santa's workshop display overwhelmed her, as if she were trapped in a theater, forced to watch the same movie over and over. She could smell the acrid smoke... hear her son screaming.

Daddy. Daddy. Daddy!

"Mom?" Nicky pulled on the sleeve of her sweatshirt. "Mom? Are you okay?"

She shook her head to clear the memories. "We're

going to the zoo tonight," she said a little too brightly, forcing her mind to shift gears.

"Will we get to see the elephants?" Nicky asked, excitement brimming from his eyes and voice.

Maddie nodded. "Yes, honey. We'll get to see some very special elephants. They're opening the new Pachyderm Pavilion tonight, and we get to be the first ones to see it."

"What's a pack-eee-drum?"

She laughed and hugged her bouncing, squirming child to her chest. "It means elephants, I think. And maybe rhinos, too. Can you guess why the Pachyderm Pavilion is so special?"

Nicky nodded solemnly. "My teacher told us at school. It has Daddy's name on it, right, Mom?"

"Right, sweetheart. And that's why we get to be the first ones to go inside!"

"Do you think I can feed one of the elephants?"

"I don't know about that. But it wouldn't hurt to ask. You're Peter Carlton's son, after all."

"Yesss!" Nicky bunched his fist and brought his elbow into his hip.

"I think I can safely promise you can feed the ducks. Now, why don't we try and get this Christmas tree up before Christmas has come and gone. Can you help me sort the branches into piles?"

Neil March pulled his wool coat more tightly around his chest and stared dully at the pond where ducks quacked and vied for his attention. The bridge he stood on elevated his contact with the biting wind, and he shivered.

He shouldn't be here. It was too risky. What if she saw him? Then she would know....

But he could no more keep himself from coming tonight than he could stop his heart from beating. He had to see her. At least one more time.

He'd stay well hidden. She'd be busy with the press. There was no way she'd spot him in the crowd. And it wasn't as if she would recognize his face.

She would never have to know the truth.

The air was bitterly cold. He glanced up at the sky, wondering idly if it was going to snow.

He didn't know why anyone would want to come to see the Denver Zoo's Wildlights in this nasty weather— but the park was crowded. Probably the grand opening of the elephant exhibit lured them in. It had been well publicized.

As for him…he was here for her. There was no sense denying it. He was here because he couldn't stand the thought of going through life without looking once more into those sparkling brown eyes.

He wanted so much more, but that was impossible for him. For them. They had barriers between them that made the Great Wall of China pale in comparison. Walls of which she knew nothing, and of which he knew too much.

His life was spiraling from painful to unbearable since meeting Maddie face-to-face, and he could do nothing to stop it. How could he? He deserved to suffer.

He was, after all, responsible for the accident, for the fire, for his store going up in flames. And ultimately, for Peter Carlton's death. He'd have to live with that knowledge for the rest of his life.

With all the strength of his will, he pushed his mind from the future. And from the past. Brooding wouldn't help matters.

At least he had tonight. Another chance to look at her.

To see her shining eyes and glowing face. To listen to the sultry hum of her voice.

Even if she didn't know he was there.

He wondered why she had given so much money to the zoo. Not that he begrudged her the money. He was glad she was spending it, remembering all too well her refusal to sully her hands with his pathetic attempt at atonement. As if anything could make her life better.

It was his fault that she was alone, and the guilt pierced his heart like a lance.

Why had she chosen elephants? They had been his childhood favorite, both at the zoo and the circus. Perhaps her son had chosen where the money went.

Or had they been Peter Carlton's favorite, too?

A mallard swam up to the bridge and quacked loudly, flapping his wings for attention.

Neil glanced at his watch. He had a few minutes left before he needed to join the crowd heading toward the pavilion for the grand opening.

Fishing in his pocket for change, Neil smiled. "You're in luck, Duck. I happen to have a quarter. And I happen to be in a good mood."

It wasn't exactly the truth. But it would have to do. He put the coin in the machine dispensing duck pellets and cranked the handle.

He didn't have much to offer. But at least he could feed the ducks.

Chapter Four

"Mom, look! The polar bear is going for a swim!" Wildlights at the Zoo was a yearly tradition for the Carltons. Adults and children alike enjoyed seeing the animals at night, and the zoo blazing with Christmas color.

Maddie shivered. That polar bear was clean out of his mind, lumbering into the icy water as if he were taking a cool dip in summertime. Give or take a few hours and he might be able to ice-skate on his pool.

If it wasn't so cold, she might really be enjoying herself. But the nip of the wind stole away any pleasure she might have had. Nicky, bouncing with energy, didn't seem to notice, and dashed away to the next display. It was all she could do to keep up with the boy.

She followed him halfheartedly, her mind wandering back to the previous evening.

Last night. What had she been doing at this time last night?

She glanced at her watch.

Dancing. She'd been dancing with her Phantom.

A deep sigh escaped her lips. All she had left of the night was the rose, carefully pressed and drying between the pages of her journal. Were it not for that, Maddie might have thought that it had all been some incredible romantic dream. Like Cinderella's glass slipper, the rose was a memento to remember the occasion by.

She wished she'd given him something, as well. It would be nice to think that there was a man out there somewhere who remembered her as glamorous Cinderella, and not as a pain-stricken widow.

It was just as well that he'd forever remain a Phantom, she reflected as she led her son to the next zoo display. Any more time in the company of the masked man would no doubt have revealed some all-too-real faults that would have brought her crashing back to reality.

He was much better left a dream.

With gigantic effort, she thrust her thoughts back into the present. "Do you want to feed the ducks?" Maddie asked, ruffling her son's white-blond locks. "We've still got a few minutes before we need to head for the elephants."

Loaded with a pocketful of quarters, Nicky shouted and raced for the bridge, and to the machine offering duck pellets. He was tossing them by the fistful at the ducks when Maddie strolled up, breathing heavily of the crisp winter air.

Silently watching Nicky calling to the ducks, a man leaned out over the bridge. His dark hair and the set of his broad shoulders seemed achingly familiar, making butterflies dance in Maddie's stomach.

She stopped short. It couldn't be him. The thought was utterly ridiculous. What would a wealthy businessman be doing at the zoo, and alone at that? She chastised her fickle mind for betraying her.

She was going crazy, that's what it was. She'd spent one pleasant evening with a man, and now that she had returned to reality, and was alone once again, she was conjuring him up from the depths of her mind and projecting him onto a stranger.

Desperation at its ugliest. She needed to get a grip on her emotions. And concentrate on her son.

She gave the man one last glance, hoping that by doing so she could prove to her flighty emotions that she was making something out of nothing. It wasn't him. It couldn't be him. And her eyes would prove it.

As the ducks clamored around Nicky, she heard the rich sound of the man's chuckle. And then he combed his fingers through the curls at his neck.

Her heart quavered and dropped into her toes. Her mind screamed, both in elation and disbelief. It was the one gesture that would forever be etched in her mind— the heart-stopping idiosyncrasy of her Phantom.

Unbidden, anger welled in her chest. He'd abandoned her, and he had never let her see his face. How dare he disappear without a word?

Well, she had some words for him! Persuading her to unmask, and then refusing to do the same. Running off on her without even saying goodbye. Who was it that said women were fickle? It must have been a *man*.

She stomped forward and yanked on the wool of his coat, pulling him around to face her.

When her gaze met his intense, flaming eyes, she gasped. The tiny, niggling voice still whispering that it might not be the same man died a quick and silent death as recognition lit his dark eyes and a crooked smile replaced his frown.

It was her Phantom.

She hadn't even considered the fact that he wouldn't be wearing a mask, or given a thought to what he might look like without it. In her spontaneous rush of anger, she'd approached him without thinking, both dreading and anticipating the confrontation.

She stepped back in shock at what she saw. His strong cheekbones, which had been hidden by the mask, gave even more depth to the planes of his face. He was, as she had known he would be, strikingly handsome.

But that wasn't what made her gasp. His mask had indeed been hiding the truth.

The right side of his face, around the temple, forehead and eye, was covered with very real bandages.

Surprise registered only momentarily on his face before he grinned and shrugged. "I see you caught me. Your Phantom is more like the real Phantom of the Opera than you anticipated, huh?"

Maddie tried to speak, but her mouth was dry. "I... uh..."

"I'm sorry. I can see I startled you. I—"

"Mom! I fed *all* of the ducks!" Nicky bounded between them, bouncing on his toes.

"He did, too!" her Phantom confirmed, smiling in a way that made Maddie's heart turn over. Something about those lips. Perhaps it was the bandages that shadowed the rest of his face, just as the Phantom's mask had. Or maybe she was remembering the sweet tenderness of his kiss.

She shook her head, trying to dispel the thought. Nicky latched on to her arm and peered timidly at the bandage-faced man. "It's okay, Nicky. This man is my—" she hesitated over the word "—friend."

"I'm Mr. M..." His sentence trailed. "Um, Nicky, do you want to ride the train?"

That was all it took to make a fast friend of the young boy, who grabbed the man's hand and pulled him toward the train.

The Phantom scooped Nicky into his arms, placing the boy on his broad shoulders. "Look, there, Nicky! You're as tall as the giraffes, now!"

He was a natural with children, Maddie thought as they headed for the train, and Nicky was eating up his attention, squealing with glee. Warning bells rang in Maddie's mind, and she quickly installed mental barriers. The more she knew of this man, the more there was to like. But fairy tales didn't translate into reality, and she was setting herself up to be left with a crushed pumpkin and a couple of mice for company.

Something she definitely could do without. She'd have to be more careful.

Maddie's eyes met the Phantom's and he smiled, sharing with her in Nicky's delight. It was a small gesture, yet it warmed her heart like a woodstove on a brisk morning.

"I didn't quite catch your name," she reminded him as he planted Nicky on the train, waving as the locomotive powered up.

A surprised look crossed his face, but was quickly shadowed. "Hmm?" he asked, as if he hadn't heard her question.

"Your *name*. You know, what people call you to get your attention. I can't keep calling you Phantom all the time. It would be embarrassing for me and humiliating for you."

Neil glanced at his watch, stalling for time. He hadn't anticipated seeing her again—or rather, having her see him. And now she was demanding his name.

What was he supposed to say? *Hi, my name is Neil March, the man responsible for your husband's death.*

"I…um," he mumbled, looking right and left, wishing desperately that a gap in the earth would open up and give him an escape route. Swallow him whole. He couldn't tell her the truth, though he knew she deserved to hear it.

"Rory," he said, making a split-second decision. "My friends call me Rory."

It wasn't exactly a lie. He had, in fact, been raised as Rory. Neil Rory March III. His father was already Neil Jr., so adding another Neil to the family clan had seemed a bit confusing. Neil had gone by his middle name until he graduated from college and claimed his inheritance.

"Rory," Maddie repeated, running her low, melodic voice over the syllables. The sound was like a balm to his soul.

"Mrs. Carlton!" The master of ceremonies for the grand opening of the Pachyderm Pavilion rushed upon them, startling Neil. He took a step backward and turned his face away from any who might recognize him. "It's time. We've been looking all over for you. Everyone is waiting."

A tumult of confusion ensued as Maddie gathered Nicky under her arm and muttered about not noticing the time. Several others in charge of seeing the grand opening go off without a hitch converged on her, giving her instructions on speaking and wishing her luck.

Neil slipped quietly away into the night, away from Maddie, feeling the cold closing around him with every step he took. His hands clenched into fists, trying to force from his mind the lie still ringing in his ears.

My friends call me Rory.

Chapter Five

Keeping to the shadows of the makeshift tent, Neil adjusted the collar of his knee-length wool coat high around his neck. From his pocket he pulled a Colorado Rockies baseball cap, which he placed low over his brow, shadowing his ravaged face from the crowd.

He couldn't afford to have anyone recognize him and uncover his deception.

It was the very same reason that, up until last night, he never went out in public: to keep the world from finding out the truth about that one accursed night. Finding out the truth about *him*.

Until Maddie.

She forced him out of his self-imposed solitude, though she was the last person on earth with whom he wanted to come face-to-face. The irony of his situation cut him like a razor.

He watched her approach the podium nervously, hesitating before the clamoring crowd. From his vantage point near the front and to the right, he could see her hand shaking as she stepped before the microphone. She tapped it gently with her forefinger, then stepped back when the speakers crackled. Neil couldn't help chuckling.

He tamped down the desire to rescue her. She was putting on a good show for the crowd, but he could see the lines of strain around her mouth, the fear shining in her eyes. He wanted to burst forward, take over the situation, put her at ease. He was good with people, had no trouble speaking in public. He could stand by her side, make things easier for her.

But this was her night. As tough as speaking before this crowd was, it was something she needed to do. He couldn't rush in and take her place, not only because it wouldn't be fair to Maddie, but because he'd be recognized. He needed to stay under the cover of darkness.

Clearing her throat, she began again, quietly at first, and then with growing passion, to tell the agonizing story that began and ended with March's Department Store.

She was so beautiful, even with her features laced with pain and sadness. She looked like an angel from heaven under the stage lights, glowing with a warmth and purity that pervaded even the pain.

Neil's chest tightened. If only it were another place, another time. If he could erase the past, he would be in grave danger of losing his heart.

But the past could never be changed. He would forever live in the cold shadow of Peter Carlton's death.

The chill of the night air enveloped him, the dampness of the light snowfall weighing him down as surely as the guilt burdening his shoulders.

The crowd applauded and Maddie stepped away from the microphone. She grasped Nicky's hand and then wandered through the throng, looking for a familiar face.

Looking for him.

He stepped out of the shadows and turned quickly to leave. He was a coward. His mind berated him even as he walked away. But he couldn't play the game anymore.

He wouldn't. The truth might show in his eyes.

And if she didn't find out…if her big brown eyes met his, he might throw caution to the wind and act on his feelings. He didn't know which was worse. And he didn't want to find out.

He increased his stride and pushed through the crowds, making good his escape.

"Rory, wait!"

She'd seen him. His shoulders stiffened and he slackened his pace. Her words burned inside his chest, but he couldn't help smiling when he looked into her shining eyes. "How did it feel to be up there in front of everyone?" he asked around the guilt clogging his throat.

"I can't believe it. I was so nervous, but once I got up there I just forgot about everything except telling the story. My adrenaline's pumping a mile a minute. It was so…invigorating!"

She reached up and swiped the cap from his head, swatting him playfully in the chest with it.

Neil chuckled and wrenched the cap away from her, tapping her lightly on top of her head before placing the cap in his coat pocket.

With an offended screech, she tried to retrieve it, but he shifted back and forth, always just out of her grasp. "Missed me, Missed me. Now ya gotta kiss me!" he whispered in her ear, hugging her to his chest.

Laughing and sputtering, they both fell into a heap in a cold, wet snowbank. Suddenly her smile faded and self-doubt flooded her expression. "But I— How did I do? Really?"

"You were wonderful, Maddie. Born to be a public speaker."

Maddie grinned. "Now there's hogwash if I've ever heard it. But please—don't stop!" It had been so long since she'd heard a compliment from a man. She felt her cheeks flaming with heat, but she didn't care. Right now she was willing to beg for a compliment from this handsome stranger.

He made her laugh. He made her feel. He made the night light up with thousands of brilliant colors that put the Wildlights to shame.

He pulled her into the curve of his arm, the palm of her hand against his chest. She could feel his heart pounding, and her own heartbeat rose in challenge.

She glanced at her son, hoping the boy was not upset by the sight of this unknown man with his arm around her shoulders. But Nicky seemed oblivious, running ahead with wild abandon from one display to the next. He exclaimed over the lights, bounced excitedly over every new animal he discovered. And when he glanced back at his mother, he only smiled to see her in Rory's arms.

"Shall I tell you how beautiful you are?" Rory whispered as they followed the path her son had taken. "How your brown eyes sparkle in the moonlight?"

"Mmm," Maddie answered, allowing her emotions to be led as her feet were being led. Far from reality and deeply into a dream.

"You can't be serious," she whispered.

"Ah, but I am." He grasped her shoulders and turned her to face him, forcing her to meet his gaze.

"You can feel it," he continued, "here." He placed her palm over his heart. "And you can see it...."

She *could* see into the depths of his blazing dark eyes, see a flicker of untamed emotion so intense that it heated her insides. She couldn't have been married for eight years without recognizing what was happening to her, knowing what she was feeling. Understanding what she'd been missing.

It wasn't just a kiss or a touch that she lacked. She missed the intimacy of two souls meeting, and bonding. She missed this amazing instant and uncanny rapport they shared.

It was what he longed for, as well. She could feel it in her heart. He wasn't playing games with her. The intensity in his eyes left no doubt that he was serious.

And this time, she didn't want to run away.

She knew the moment he read her answer in her eyes. She couldn't have spoken if she had wanted to—except with her heart. And she hoped that was enough for Rory.

He cupped her chin in his palm and shook his head ever so slightly. His dark eyes clouded, but Maddie was beyond being able to do more than lean into him, asking for his affection the only way she could.

"Maddie, I—"

"Rory."

A muffled groan rose from the depths of his chest as he gave in to the longing in his eyes. The unspoken question remained as his gaze locked with hers, and slowly, slowly, he bent his head toward her.

Maddie's senses heightened until she was sure she could feel the crackling of tension in the air between them. His featherlight caress of her cheek, sliding gently to the back of her neck to pull her closer, became the focus of her world.

And those eyes. Those *eyes*.

She wanted to cling to him, to share one breath and heartbeat.

But they both knew this was neither the right time, nor the right place.

Reluctantly, he broke away. "We need to catch up

with Nicky," he murmured, and wrapped his arm around her shoulder, holding her so tightly that he could easily have crushed her, yet so gently that she felt surrounded by the strength of a fortress, safe and protected from the fears haunting her.

She closed her eyes, content for the moment to rest her head against his solid shoulder, to extend the shimmering bliss for as long as possible.

Suddenly his muscles tensed beneath her cheek. Her eyes snapped open to see what was wrong, but Rory wasn't looking at her.

Jaw clenched, he scanned the throng of people nearby. "Where'd he go?" he asked. His voice was crisp with authority.

"Nicky?" She pointed toward the predatory-bird display. "Why, he was right over there when—" She stopped midsentence, her eyes searching the area for her son's familiar face. "Where's Nicky?"

He was gone.

Her stomach lurched into her throat. Where was he? He'd been exclaiming over the eagles not a minute before. Before she'd lost herself in Rory's arms.

"Where is he?" she cried, wresting herself from Rory's embrace. "Where's my son? Oh, if anything happens to Nicky…"

"Maddie." Rory's voice was low and controlled.

"I'll never forgive myself. Oh, God, please let him be safe," she prayed aloud.

"Maddie!"

"This was a terrible, terrible mistake. If I hadn't—"

"Maddie!" Rory took her by the shoulders and gently shook her. "You've got to snap out of it. Take some deep breaths and try to calm down. We'll find him."

The even tenor of his words had the needed effect,

soothing her soul with steady, reassuring waves. His eyes blazed into hers, transferring his strength to her.

She scrubbed at the tears streaking down her face. "You're right. Let's not panic. He can't be far."

"We need to put this together piece by piece. A minute ago, Nicky was in front of the eagle cage. Where would he go from there?" Rory took her hand and began backtracking the way they'd come, his eyes alert.

"I don't know!" she wailed, and burst into a fresh round of tears. "He knows not to wander off. He could be anywhere."

"He could be. But he isn't. He's *somewhere*. We've just got to figure out where." His words were firm, almost harsh, but the hand stroking the tears on her cheek was gentle and reassuring.

Maddie strained to think of where her son might be, but she couldn't get past the wild waves of panic in her mind.

She paused as the answer floated just above her consciousness. "The elephants!"

"Didn't he see the elephants earlier?"

"We didn't get a chance. We were too busy with the program. And they've always been his favorite." Her voice caught. "I promised him. And then I was so preoccupied with my stupid speech, and finding you—I forgot all about it."

"Come on, then." He reached for her hand, then sprinted toward the lights of the pavilion, glancing back from time to time to be sure that she was keeping pace.

She was. She held her breath, hoping against hope that her son was safe. The lights from the Pachyderm Pavilion blazed brightly, beckoning visitors. Nicky would have had no trouble finding his way.

Tears streamed from her eyes, though she fought to

keep them back. "God, please," she whispered quietly and fervently. "Please. Don't take Nicky, too."

She didn't even realize that she spoke aloud until Rory looked back, his brow furrowed. "He won't," he ground out through clenched teeth. "He can't."

"No?" she yelled, her body quivering with rage. She didn't care that she was making a scene, that others were staring at the couple racing helter-skelter through the zoo. Fury threatened to overwhelm her, and she focused on the anger. It gave her strength. It was easier to be angry than afraid. "Why not? He took Peter."

"Maddie, don't."

Rory's voice was laced with pain, as if her words had been directed toward him. She wasn't angry with him. Rory had distracted her, but only because she let him.

She was mad at herself. And at God.

But most of all at Neil March. It was all *his* fault that she was alone. Neil March was responsible for everything bad that had happened to her—even Nicky's disappearance. If Peter was still alive…

But it wasn't Neil March that she was hurting with her cutting words. It was Rory. Dear, kind Rory, who appeared just as upset by Nicky's disappearance as she was.

She didn't know why it should matter to him, why *she* should matter to him. But somehow she knew that Rory's affection for her and Nicky was real. Her anger subsided, leaving her shoulders in tight knots and her stomach unnervingly empty.

Rory stopped as they reached the pavilion and pulled her to him, his breath coming in short gasps that clouded in the crisp air.

Suddenly his embraced tightened. "Maddie, look. There!"

Chapter Six

A chuckle erupted from Rory's throat.

Maddie looked to where he pointed, then sagged against him in relief. If he hadn't been holding her so tightly, she was certain her legs would have folded beneath her.

Nicky was hanging from the guardrail, leaning as far as his gangly body would let him, straining to touch a friendly elephant's trunk. He was talking animatedly to the beast, and didn't even seem to notice that he'd left his mother far behind.

He's growing up, Maddie thought, the realization pinching her heart. But she knew that Nicky would indeed have panicked once he lost interest in the elephants and realized that he was alone.

Just as she and every other child, at some point in their young lives, had done. She remembered the shocking revelation in her own life—that she was nothing more than a tiny dot on the huge map of civilization. And that she was totally and completely alone.

She'd been shopping in a department store with her father, and begging to be able to stop and look at a colorful rack of books. Her father, thinking he'd give his daughter a moment to browse, had stepped two aisles over to look at hand tools—well within earshot, but completely out of Maddie's sight.

How she'd screamed, her little heart frantic. She'd been completely terrified.

And had felt utterly alone.

It had happened again when Peter died, and then again for this brief period when she thought she'd lost Nicky. Fortunately, she'd found him before he'd suffered any trauma over the incident. In fact, she was relatively positive he didn't even know there had *been* an incident.

If only her own heart was so strong.

"Thank God we found him," Rory said, echoing the silent prayer in her own thoughts.

He marched up to the boy and picked him off the rail by the waist. Nicky yelled and squirmed, but Rory held him tightly until he'd calmed.

"You little scamp!" he chastised gently but firmly. "You gave your mother and me a healthy scare."

Nicky started to protest, then looked at Maddie. She knew she couldn't hide her tear-streaked face, and a fresh wave of tears already threatened to engulf her.

"Young man!" she said in her best mother's voice. "Don't you *ever* wander off on me again. Is that understood?"

Nicky's bottom lip quivered endearingly. Maddie gave him a moment, then opened her arms to him. He dashed to her, and she held him tight, squeezing her eyes tight against the tears. Her dear little man. And he was safe. *Thank You, God,* she silently prayed. *Forgive me for my anger. I know I should have trusted You.*

"I'm okay, Mom," Nicky assured, wiggling out of her embrace. "I got kinda lost, but an old lady helped me find the elephants. She told me to stay here till you got here. And she helped me feed that big guy in the middle!"

Maddie touched his shoulder, reassuring herself once again that he was here. He was safe.

"I think we could all use a nice hot cup of cocoa," Rory said, lightly embracing both Maddie and her son. "What do you say we head up to the front gate? There's a restaurant where we can get in out of the cold for a bit." He ruffled Nicky's hair. "I think it's called Elephant something."

"Cool!" Nicky exclaimed, undaunted by his near-trauma.

Smiling at her son's enthusiasm, Maddie agreed, and moments later the three of them were settled in a cozy corner booth with steaming mugs of whipped-cream-topped cocoa.

Neil stared at Maddie, trying to memorize every line and plane of her delicately beautiful face. He was living a precious dream, just being with her, but he knew the night would soon end.

And though it tore him inside to acknowledge it, there wouldn't be any more nights with Maddie. There couldn't be. He was her worst nightmare come to life, worse by far than the Phantom he'd been when he first met her.

If only she knew.

Maddie picked up her mug and toasted. "To happy endings."

Neil's breath caught in his throat. He couldn't speak. Instead, he lifted his own mug and nodded.

She took a tentative sip of the cocoa, then licked at the whipped cream on top, not realizing that a small dollop of cream dotted her nose.

Neil smiled and leaned toward her, wiping off the

cream with the tip of his finger. The brief contact was electric. Their eyes met and held.

His hand traveled lightly down her arm until he'd reached her fingers, which he laced through his own. "You're trembling," he murmured.

Maddie pulled back and crossed her arms. She looked away and took a deep breath, then looked back at him. "I'm just so *angry*."

"Do you want to talk about it?"

She shook her head, then appeared to think better of it. She put an arm around Nicky's shoulders and gave him a squeeze. "Son, since you're done with your cocoa, why don't you go play with those toys over in the Kids' Corner?" She gestured to a corner full of stuffed animals and building blocks. "I think I see an elephant."

Nicky's eyes brightened, and he scrambled over his mother to make a beeline for the toys.

Maddie blew out a breath, squared her shoulders, and locked eyes with Neil's. "Yeah. I do want to talk about it."

Neil nodded.

"I can't help it. I know God wants me to forgive him, and I've tried and tried, but then something like this happens and I get mad all over again."

"Who are you angry at?" He braced himself for the answer he already knew.

"Neil March."

He hadn't prepared well enough to shield himself from hearing his own name thrown like a javelin. To hear his condemnation from her own mouth was almost more than he could bear. Then again, maybe he deserved the pain he was feeling.

"Why?" He croaked the word from a dry mouth, then sought solace in the dregs of his mug. The bitter chocolate taste was fitting, somehow.

"It's his fault I'm in this predicament." She took a deep breath and clasped her mug with whitened knuckles. "I've…never told anyone this before. I don't know if…"

"You don't have to tell me," Neil murmured, relieved by the reprieve she offered.

She looked him in the eye and smiled wearily. "I believe I do. I've been carrying this around with me so long that I… I just want to share it with someone. Do you mind?" Tentatively, she reached for his hand.

Neil's chest constricted until he thought his heart would burst. "No." He forced the words from reluctant lips. "Of course I don't mind."

"Peter and I—" she looked away "—we were having…problems. I… He… We weren't the happy couple we appeared to be. I think he…"

She stopped, her face crumpling with pain.

"You think he…?" Neil prompted gently.

Maddie straightened her shoulders and met his eyes. "I think he was going to leave me. For another woman."

Neil shut his eyes and gulped for air, unable to stand the swirls of pain clouding her eyes. How could a man even consider leaving Maddie? He knew enough about her to know she would be devoted to her marriage, as she was devoted to her child. A wave of anger rose in Neil. Anger at Peter Carlton for hurting Maddie.

His desire to protect her surprised him, and he fought to keep astonishment from registering on his face.

For the first time in his life, he was looking beyond himself, wondering what sharing his life with another person would be like. Maddie wasn't like the glitz-and-glamour women he was accustomed to.

He could fall in love with a woman like Maddie. She sparked powerful feelings in him—feelings that started the first time he saw her, the first time he held her in his arms. And every moment since then—with every look, every touch—the feeling had grown deeper. Stronger.

For all the good it did him. God must have a strange sense of humor, for Neil could never act on his feelings. *Never.*

"What does this have to do with Neil March?" he asked after a lengthy silence.

"Nothing. And everything. Peter and I were fighting, as usual. He took Nicky in to look at the Santa's workshop display to get away from me. I was furious. I was going to—" She paused. "I felt like walking out of that store and just walking, as far away from him as I could. I…wasn't even going to take Nicky. I can't even imagine how I—"

A sob escaped her throat, and she clapped a hand over her mouth to stifle any further display of emotion.

After taking a moment to regain her composure, she continued. "Suddenly, the whole thing went up in flames. It was so fast. So final."

She paused and swiped a hand down her face. "Someone ran into the fire and rescued Nicky, but it was too late for Peter."

"That must have been terrible for you." He squeezed her hand, wishing with all his heart that he could take her in his arms and shield her from any more hurt.

"We never got a chance to make up. We were *fighting* when he died. I think I could have handled it better if he *had* left me for another woman. But this way… nothing's resolved."

"And until it is, you can't go on with your own life?"

"Yes, I suppose that's true. But what can I do? I'm a prisoner of the past, unable to resolve my feelings, to accept what I must and move on."

"That's not true," Neil denied.

Maddie snorted. "No? Then why am I in such bad shape after a year? You'd think I could at least talk about it."

"You *are* talking about it. And a year isn't so very long to grieve."

"Is that what you call it? Grieving? I don't think I've got to grieving yet. I'm still too angry."

"At Neil." It wasn't a question, and Neil braced himself for the answer.

"At Neil. I've heard about him, you know."

Neil laughed without mirth. "What have you heard?"

"He's a playboy. An arrogant rich kid with more money than brains. Proved it, too, after Peter died."

"How so?" He could almost hear the heavy thud of another block of guilt dropping onto his already burdened shoulders. Every word she spoke, every pained glance, added further weight to the millstone dragging him down.

The only thing that kept him from bolting from the table was the knowledge that he deserved her words, and more. He had no defense. He was guilty as charged on all counts.

"By sending me that money. As if money could right the wrong. Erase the past and tie everything up in a neat little bow." Her voice raised an octave. "Well, it doesn't work that way. And sometimes I wish I could tell Mr. High-and-Mighty Neil March that to his face."

You just have, Neil thought, taking a deep breath to steady his nerves. The only thing that kept him from laughing bitterly was the knowledge that such an exclamation would give his masquerade away. He felt like tipping the table, thrusting his fist through the glass window through which he stared into the darkness of night. "You've never seen Neil March, have you?"

"No. And frankly, I don't want to. I'd probably spit in his face. It's blood money, that's what it is. A guilt offering."

Blood money. The accusation rang in his ears, temporarily blinding him with its intensity. And its truth.

It *was* blood money. Because he could do no less. And because he could do no more. Though he wished with all his heart and soul that he could trade places with the dead man. Give Peter back to her.

Peter didn't deserve her, but Maddie was suffering so. Neil felt that he would do anything to relieve her pain. Pain she didn't ask for, and shouldn't have had.

If only he could.

Neil attempted a smile. A pathetic attempt, he thought, wondering if she could see his lips quivering with effort. "Aren't you afraid you're going to run into Neil March now that you are out in society?"

"I'm *not* out in society. The masquerade ball was a fluke. The only reason I went is because it was a benefit for Children's Hospital."

That was the reason he had gone, too. He tightened his lips to a straight line to keep himself from frowning.

"Nicky suffered severe smoke inhalation through that fire. Thank God he wasn't burned. Children's Hospital got him through it."

"Thank God," Neil murmured, and squeezed her hand.

"Yes. I don't think I would have made it if God had taken Nicky, too. That's why I panicked tonight."

He glanced toward the Kids' Corner, where Nicky was playing with large, stuffed zoo animals. Something clinched his heart at the sight of the happy young boy whose life had been spared.

"As for Neil March," Maddie continued, drawing his attention back to her face, "I'll admit the thought crossed my mind that I might run into him at the ball. Fortunately, I didn't. And I'm sure he would never dare show his miserable hide here."

Neil shook his head.

"He knows I'm the major benefactor for this event. How could he not? It's his money I'm spending. But it would take a much bigger man than Neil March to face me down—to come to terms with what he's done."

"You're probably right." Neil ran a finger around the top of his empty mug. His thoughts were racing, and guilt stabbed at his soul.

It would take a much bigger man than Neil March to face me down—to come to terms with what he's done.

It was true. Neil rued the day he was born, but there was no way he would ever come to terms with what he'd done.

And now he'd gone and made things worse. He should have ripped his mask off the moment Maddie had revealed her identity that night on the carriage. He should have declared his name, taken responsibility for his actions right there and then. Apologized and begged her forgiveness.

He should have...

But it was too late for that. He'd wound his web of lies so tightly around himself that he couldn't escape even if he wanted to.

How was he going to tell her now? How could he explain why, after discovering her identity, he had purposefully sought her out again. How he had concealed his identity, even when she mentioned his name. How he'd spent not one, but *two* evenings with her—all the while knowing that he was the bane of her existence. He'd deceived her, when all she deserved was kindness, love and truth.

If she found out now, she would despise him even more, if that were possible. Could he find the strength to tell her the truth? To face the consequences?

He had to find that strength. Maddie deserved the truth. And he deserved to suffer alone with his guilty burden and the memory of the hatred in her eyes when she spoke his name.

"Do you not want to talk about it?"

"What?" Neil asked vaguely, his mind still turning over the possibilities.

"I asked," Maddie said gently, meeting his eyes, "what happened to your face. But if you don't want to talk about it, I'll understand." Rory had grown so silent that she wondered if she had hit a sore spot with him.

His looks didn't matter to her. Not with his kind heart and gentle ways. But that was beside the point, for he was strikingly handsome on the side of his face she could see.

Whatever he was hiding...whatever sort of scar marred the right side of his face, could only intensify the almost ethereal beauty of his countenance. His dark complexion and angular features would only be enhanced by a scar, making him appear even more rugged and virile.

"It doesn't matter to me," she whispered, reaching up to stroke the bandage with the tip of her finger. "I was just curious."

Rory's eyes clouded and he looked away. She had obviously touched a nerve, and she regretted the impulse that had made her ask.

She floundered for a way to redeem herself, stuttering to several false starts while Rory stared moodily out the window.

After several minutes of silence, he said, "I think we should go."

His voice was so gruff, so angry. Everything was falling apart, and she hadn't the slightest idea how to fix it. Oh, *why* had she opened her big mouth?

"Oh. Okay," she said finally, removing her hand from his grasp and clutching her purse. "We can leave. Let me get Nicky bundled up and we're out of here."

Rory nodded vaguely and continued staring out the window.

"Rory, would you mind walking me out to my car? I don't like walking alone in a parking lot this late at night." It sounded juvenile to her own ears, but she was desperate, grasping for anything that might keep her in his company for a few minutes longer. At least until she could find a way to straighten out the mess she'd created, bring a smile back to his handsome face.

"Hmm? Sure." Rory called Nicky over and helped her with the boy's coat, hat and mittens. He thrust a baseball cap on his own head and pulled the brim low over his brow.

He held the door for her, then walked off ahead of her, his collar up against the wind and his hands stuffed deeply in the pockets of his coat. Like a man who didn't want to be disturbed, Maddie thought.

He was going to leave her again, just the way he had the night before. Without a word. Without a trace. Without any way for her to discover his last name. She knew it with a certainty that permeated her entire being.

And she was just as certain that she couldn't let that happen.

"Rory, wait!" she called, rushing to his side.

He turned, a gentle smile on his lips.

She wasn't sure what she'd say when she reached him; she only knew that she had to try. His smile erased her fear, gave her courage to continue.

Until she had met Rory, she had expected to spend the rest of her life alone. But now, looking into the eyes of this kind, gentle man, sharing small moments of joy with him, she was starting to think she could recover from the wounds she nursed. Her Phantom might not be the man she could share the rest of her life with, but he was a beginning.

"I want to see you again," she blurted out before she lost her nerve. She placed an imploring hand on his sleeve, her eyes begging him not to leave, not to run out on her again.

His jaw tightened and he looked away.

Rejecting her in the kindest way he knew, she thought. Her throat tightened until she thought she would choke. She coughed for a breath, then whirled around and walked away, trying to keep her steps slow and even, trying not to reveal how deeply his silent rebuff had hurt her.

"Come on, Nicky, let's go!" she said harshly, turning to see if her son followed.

"Maddie." Rory was at her side, matching his pace to hers. He wouldn't look at her, even now.

"I'm sorry," she muttered. "I'm not usually so forward. It's just that I thought… Well, it doesn't matter what I thought. Forget I said anything."

"No," her Phantom said firmly, engulfing her small hand in his. His voice sounded strained and unnaturally deep. "Don't apologize."

They walked in silence for a moment, their fingers

laced. Maddie tried to still her heart at his touch, tried not to hope that he had changed his mind.

Suddenly he stopped and turned her by the shoulders to face him. "More than anything in this world, I want to see you again. It's just that you don't know—"

"What you look like?" Maddie interrupted. "That doesn't matter to me. You're a good man. It's what's inside that counts."

Rory laughed, but his smile didn't reach his dark, clouded eyes. "Thanks for the vote of confidence, but that wasn't what I was going to say. I—"

A group of reporters appeared as if from nowhere, shining lights in their eyes and thrusting microphones at their mouths.

"Mrs. Carlton, do you plan to…"

"Is this man your new significant other?"

"And you, sir…"

"Of all the—" he began, a hunted look in his eyes. He pushed the microphones away, pulled his cap even lower over his eyes.

"Mrs. Carlton, do you plan to remarry?" A pale, wide-eyed woman concluded her sentence with several thrusts of the tip of her pencil.

Maddie batted it away and flashed Rory a beseeching look. *Get us out of here!* she begged with her gaze.

Rory elbowed his way forward until he was able to slip a stabilizing hand around Maddie's waist. She breathed a sigh of relief as he leaned his head toward hers.

"Maddie, I've got to go," he whispered coarsely in her ear. "Come to the Parade of Lights. I'll find you."

She stiffened. Instead of rescuing her from this swarm of poisonous media personnel, he was leaving. Again. And without her.

A particularly aggressive young man grabbed the sleeve of her jacket and whirled her around, thrusting a microphone under her chin.

"If you would care to comment on—"

Rory! She wrenched her arm from the reporter's grasp and held out her hands to Rory. He had to stay. She hadn't even asked him his last name!

With an apologetic shake of his head he stepped forward, taking her by the shoulders and sweeping a gentle kiss across her cheek. And then he was gone, pushing his way through the cameras with his head bent low.

"Wait!" Maddie called, but he had already disappeared.

"Mrs. Carlton? Can you please tell us why you…"

Maddie put her arm around Nicky and guided him away from the reporters, following the path Rory had taken. She couldn't deal with reporters, not when her heart was rocking harder than a ship in a storm.

Why had the reporters scared him away? Was he so afraid of revealing his scars that he had to run and hide? Reporters were fast becoming a natural, if annoying, part of her life. But she wanted *Rory* to be a part of her life, too.

"I don't even know your last name. How will I find you?" she whispered into the biting night air.

Come to the Parade of Lights. I'll find you.

His words echoed in her mind. She didn't know how Rory would pick her out of the crowd, but deep in her heart she knew it would happen.

Somehow, someway, her Phantom would find her.

Chapter Seven

Maddie sighed in relief as she pulled off the two-lane highway into the small, eastern town of Benton, Colorado. She didn't make the trip as often as she should, she thought with a stab of guilt. Her mother, Celia, and her stepfather, Davis, were only a three-hour drive from Denver.

Nicky would have wanted to be with her today, but she purposely picked a time when he was in school, so she could spend some time alone with her mother.

As for her son's disappointment when he discovered what he'd missed, she promised herself she'd make it up to him, maybe take him up for a visit during his Christmas vacation.

She had more important things to worry about. Like what to do about Rory. He made her heart feel things she was sure she'd never feel again. How could a person be elated with joy and scared to death at the same time? But that's what Rory did to her.

But was she ready for a relationship?

When she was with Rory, the question seemed to answer itself. It felt so natural to be around him, to confide in him, to melt into his embrace. He made her laugh, and feel the sheer joy of being alive again. The sensation even clung for a few extra hours, hovering around Maddie like a warm, welcome cocoon. But by the next morning, back came all the fears and doubts.

And guilt. She gripped the steering wheel with her fist, easing into the slower, small-town traffic. How could she go on with her life when Peter was still hovering in the corner of her thoughts? With nothing resolved, it was difficult to consider moving on.

And even if she could put her past with Peter to rest, there was still Nicky. The boy seemed to like Rory, but there was a gigantic chasm of difference between liking a man who took him riding on the zoo train and accepting a man who consistently took his mother's time and stole away some of her attentiveness—attention Nicky was used to having for himself.

She pulled into the driveway of her mother's ranch-style house and shut down the engine, but didn't make a move to open the door. Instead she sat staring at the friendly redbrick exterior of the house, remembering her own happy childhood there.

She'd learned to roller-skate and bicycle on this driveway. She'd pinched her fingers in the front door. She'd helped her mother plant the now-hibernating rosebushes that lined the front of the house.

She'd experienced her first kiss on the front-porch swing, had her prom pictures taken under the towering maple tree.

Maddie smiled wistfully. She'd had a wonderful, happy childhood here in this home. At least until her father had run out on her mother and her.

She pulled the key from the ignition and tossed it in her purse. She was surprised at how much her father's leaving still hurt. But having a parent desert you when you were twelve—a blossom just beginning to open and flower—wasn't something you ever got over. Not completely.

She could picture the scene as if it were yesterday, her mother down on her knees at the bedside, clutching a hastily scrawled note in her hand. Celia's red-rimmed eyes had filled with compassion as she embraced her only daughter and quietly spoke the words that changed Maddie's world.

He's gone, Maddie. Your father's not coming back.

No explanation. No excuse. Just goodbye.

Maddie didn't know how her mother had survived. Celia was the strongest, most resilient person Maddie knew. Her faith in the goodness of God never wavered, not even when she was faced with raising a child alone in a society not yet ready to accept single mothers.

No one blinked an eye at the fact that Maddie was raising Nicky alone, but Maddie knew her mother hadn't been so lucky. In a small town like Benton, news traveled fast, and opinions, once formed, were difficult to alter. People had turned their backs on the abandoned mother and child.

She could still remember overhearing people speak in low tones about "that woman," as if her mother had done something to run her father out of town. In some bizarre, twisted way, Paul Myers's desertion had fallen squarely on Celia's shoulders.

But Celia had just smiled and continued to think the best of people, starting her own greenhouse to provide for her daughter. No one in Benton would buy anything from her, but there were plenty of vendors in Denver anxious to purchase her mother's hothouse plants. Between working her greenhouse in the daytime and waitressing at night, Celia made enough for both of them to live comfortably and put a little aside for the future. It was Celia's strongest wish that her daughter attend college, have the opportunity to go beyond herself, to be a part of something bigger.

And then Davis Winthrow entered their lives, throwing a man-size wrench into their plans. Her mother had welcomed Davis's commitment and love. Maddie had hated it. Hated *him*. She was too old to favor a replacement father, and why should she want one anyway? No one, most especially Davis Winthrow, could convince her otherwise.

From a twelve-year-old's limited viewpoint, Davis was stealing her mother's love—attention Maddie coveted. She couldn't see that Davis made her mother happy, didn't understand that the human heart could expand to give limitless love to all it embraced.

In her mind, she'd been replaced, removed from Celia's heart to make room for Davis. She'd been hurt, but mostly she'd been angry. And she'd spent the next six years doing her best to make Davis regret marrying her mother.

She slammed her hands hard against the steering wheel. No way would she do that to Nicky. She wasn't about to risk losing him to a love that might well be all in her mind. She wouldn't make the same mistake Celia had, however well-intended her mother's actions had been. But she didn't want to give Rory up, either, which left her at an impasse—a gap impossible to bridge.

Unless her mother could help her work things out. She let herself out of the car and went around the side of the house, through a picket-fence gate and into the backyard, to the hand-built hothouse where she knew her mother would be.

"Mom?" Her call echoed into the steamy, sunshine-filled room.

"Madelaine?" Her mother sounded surprised, sending another tiny dart of guilt into Maddie's chest. Celia Winthrow, pleasantly plump from years of home cooking, stepped from behind a potted palm, brushing fresh soil from her hands.

Maddie gave her mother a hug, and they both retreated to the house. The tiny country kitchen smelled of fresh-baked chocolate-chip cookies, Maddie's favorite.

Her mother washed the dirt from her hands, then set a tray of cookies in front of Maddie and poured two tall glasses of milk. Maddie chuckled at the old-fashioned gesture that was so much her mother.

"What's wrong?" Celia asked, scooting a chair close to Maddie's and sneaking a cookie for herself.

"I didn't say anything was wrong," Maddie protested, also biting into one of the delightfully sweet cookies. "I didn't even say hello yet."

"Hello to you, too. But you don't come all the way to Benton to say hello."

Maddie grimaced. "You've got me there. I'm sorry, Mom. It's been a rough year."

"It has," her mother agreed, patting her on the hand. "But you'll never be a burden to me, you know."

"I know." Maddie went silent as she considered what to say. Four hours ago it had seemed like the only alternative: seeking her mother's advice. But now she didn't know how to begin, what to say. Her mother and stepfather had loved Peter. He'd healed the breach in their family, made things right again.

Whatever Maddie's doubts, her fears about their marriage, Peter had been a Godsend to her family. And now he was gone.

And Maddie was floundering. Her parents loved Peter like a son. His peacemaking shoes were impossible to fill. She wasn't about to tell Celia that she suspected Peter of cheating on her, that she believed he was about to desert Maddie as Paul Myers had once deserted Celia. It would break her mother's heart, a heart that had suffered more than a lifetime's worth of pain.

No, Peter's memory was going to remain sparkling white and pure as a gentle smile. He would continue to remain the son her mother never had.

She felt a quiver of dismay creep up her back as she considered telling them about Rory. How would Celia take to hearing about a new man in Maddie's life?

"Best way is just to spit it out." Celia reached for another cookie.

Maddie sighed. "Do you remember how it felt when you... How did you meet Davis?"

"Davis?" Her mother's white eyebrows rose and her cheeks colored a pleasant pink. "Why, he came into the restaurant where I was waitressing."

"And?" Celia's cheeks went from pink to a fiery red. Her mother was actually blushing! Maddie couldn't remember ever having seen that before.

"He said I poured the meanest cup of coffee he'd ever seen, and would I go out to a movie with him."

Maddie pressed down the distrust that talking about Davis aroused. Years of fighting with the man, of disliking him because of his place in her mother's life, was hard to ignore. Her chest filled with anger.

You're acting like a pigheaded, stubborn teenager! Peter's voice rang in her ears as if he sat on her shoulder— her nagging conscience. *Davis Winthrow has reached out to you every way he knows how. Now it's up to you to do the reaching.*

"How did you feel?" she asked at last, trying to put a damper on her emotions. She must be overtired, she decided, for her mood to be fluctuating so drastically. She and Davis had been getting along for years now. Her initial reaction had to be the result of being stressed out.

"Flattered." Celia bit into her cookie and washed the bite down with milk. "Maddie, what are we talking about here?"

"Me." Maddie sighed again and met her mother's kind, pale eyes. "I've…met someone."

Her mother squeezed her hand. "Maddie, that's wonderful!"

"It is?" Whatever she had imagined her mother's reaction to be—reserve, distrust, antagonism—this wasn't it. There was joy radiating from her mother's face.

"Yes, ma'am, it is! This is Hallelujah and dance-on-the-tables news, and make no mistaking!"

"I thought you'd be…upset," Maddie admitted, smiling in spite of herself. Celia was literally bouncing in her chair, looking as if she might well act on her words and bound onto the table.

"Upset? Why would I be…?"

Maddie grimaced.

"Peter was a good man, Maddie." Celia nodded her understanding. "But he's gone. And you've got a lot of living left to do. I'm *glad* you're ready to move on."

Peter was a good man. Maddie's heart twisted. She wished with all her heart she could believe that, and remember only the good times with Peter. But there were too many unanswered questions for her to rest easy on that score. "I don't *feel* ready. Because—"

"Because Peter's memory keeps lurking in the back of your mind."

Maddie bit the edge of her lip and nodded. "I don't

want to sound like I'm whining or complaining. I've hibernated for a year doing just that—feeling sorry for myself and refusing to acknowledge that I have a life beyond what I had with Peter."

"He'd want you to be happy, you know."

"I know. Everyone keeps telling me that, but it seems like a pat answer. I feel so awkward, like a baby just learning to walk."

"Or like an adult trying to learn to walk again after being paralyzed? That's what's happened to you, you know."

Paralyzed. That's exactly how her heart had felt until Rory had set it back in motion. "How did you get over—" Maddie cleared her throat, trying to force the last word from her lips "—Daddy?"

Celia's eyes clouded with pain, and Maddie regretted the impulsive question, however important the answer was.

"I didn't *get over* him."

Celia's answer rocked Maddie to the core of her soul. How could her mother harbor feelings for a man who'd abandoned her?

"Paul was my first love, as Peter is to you. Yes, Paul deserted me. I struggle with a sense of anger and betrayal to this day on that account. But whatever his faults, I loved Paul, and that love will always be part of me."

Whatever his faults. A cold knot formed in Maddie's stomach and began churning.

"It took me a long time, but I forgave your father for running out on us, and forgave myself, as well. I felt like a complete fool, falling in love with a man who didn't care enough for me to stick around through the hard times. I was angry at myself for misjudging him, for trusting him. I might as well have branded the word *stupid* on my forehead for all to see."

She paused and took a sip of milk. "I had to accept myself. And my love for Paul. It was the only way I could clear my mind, release the hate and anger, and learn to love again."

Maddie wanted to comfort her mother, to apologize for reopening old wounds, unearthing emotions best left buried in the past. Instead, it was Celia reaching out a comforting hand to Maddie.

"You don't need to feel guilty about loving Peter," she whispered, stroking her daughter's temple with the back of her hand. "The amazing thing about the human heart is that there is always room for more love. You don't have to replace one love with another. You don't have to abandon your feelings for Peter to move on with your life. I love Davis with all my heart, but in a different way from the way I loved Paul."

Yes. That's how it was with Rory. Her feelings for Rory were as different from her feelings for Peter as black from white. But they weren't any less real, any less powerful, for being different.

When her mother explained it, everything made sense. The puzzle pieces slid into place. If she and Peter hadn't been fighting…

And then there was Nicky. "I hated Davis for taking you away from me," she blurted, then clapped a hand over her mouth in dismay.

Celia just chuckled. "Don't I know it. You made his life pretty miserable for a few years."

Maddie winced. "Think he'll ever forgive me?"

"He loves you. He always has."

"I guess I knew that." Maddie swallowed hard. "I was

wrong. But that doesn't change the way it was for me—for us. How can I do the same thing to Nicky?"

"Your circumstances are different," Celia gently reminded. "Nicky is only six. He needs a father figure, be it the man you've met, or someone else." She patted her palm against her ample bosom. "I know in my heart you weren't meant to be alone, Maddie. You are a beautiful woman both inside and out. And I'm not the least bit surprised that a nice young man has noticed. Don't keep your life on hold any longer."

"But Nicky—"

"Nicky will adjust. And he'll be happier because *you* are happier. Peter didn't leave you, Maddie. He didn't make a choice to walk out the door and never return. He was nothing at all like your father."

Wasn't he? Maddie didn't know. Those last moments were a blur. But her mother was right in one regard: Peter didn't choose to die. Whether or not he *would* have left her was another question, one to which Maddie didn't have an answer. She wasn't even sure she *wanted* an answer. Maybe she was better off not knowing.

"What's his name, dear?"

"Hmm?" Maddie stopped twirling the cookie on her plate and met her mother's kind gaze. "Oh. Sorry. I was zoning out. His name is Rory."

"Rory what?"

Maddie felt her cheeks warm. She should have known her mother would ask. "I don't know," she reluctantly admitted. "I've never been able to wriggle it out of him."

"Sounds intriguing." Her mother laughed.

"Intriguing. And exasperating." Maddie blew out a labored breath. "Frankly, I'm scared to death. Not of Rory. He seems a gem. But having a relationship after Peter…"

Her mother's face drew closed, her eyes sobered and

her brow puckered. "I remember—" she sighed "—all too well. You don't feel right with another man, but you don't feel right without him."

"Exactly." Maddie closed her eyes, savoring the wave of relief that washed through her. Somehow, just knowing that her mother understood, and had been through something similar to what Maddie was facing, helped more than a bookshelf full of advice.

Been there. Done that. Bought the T-shirt. Maybe she wasn't crazy, after all. And maybe things would work out between her and Rory.

"It will get easier," Celia said as if reading her thoughts. "Don't rush it. But don't run from it, either. Enjoy your mystery man for today, and let tomorrow take care of itself. That's what The Good Book says to do."

"Loosely translated by Mom," Maddie said with a grin.

"What'd Mom do now?" Davis asked, entering the kitchen and leaning over Maddie's shoulder to snatch a handful of cookies. He welcomed Maddie, ruffling her hair affectionately, then leaned his thick shoulder against the door frame.

Davis Winthrow was a handsome, barrel-chested man in his late fifties, with hair as black as the day he'd first walked into their lives, albeit a little thinner on top. His brown eyes twinkled with merriment as he winked at his stepdaughter.

Maddie forced herself to relax under his friendly gaze. Anger had no place in their relationship now.

It wouldn't take a genius to know Davis was a good man, and that he loved her mother to distraction. Maddie couldn't deny it. She didn't even want to.

But it was still hard. Hard to trust. Hard to love.

She turned her smile on Davis. "Mom's just giving me some words of wisdom."

Davis rolled his eyes. "Quotin' Scripture at you again, eh, Maddie? Now you know what I have to put up with," he teased, his gaze pausing for one loving second on Celia's profile.

Maddie couldn't help but smile.

"Oh, sit down, you big oaf!" Celia bantered, winking at Maddie. "And you can get your own milk."

"It's okay," said Maddie with a laugh. "Advice is what I came for."

"Brave woman," Davis muttered before he ducked under the wet tea towel Celia pelted at him.

Maddie laughed again and reached for another cookie. This was the most comfortable she'd felt around her mom—around her parents—in many years. Even when Peter was around, she couldn't quite lift the burden of hurt from her shoulders. But now, for once, she felt relaxed, at home in the house she'd grown up in.

Celia lifted a questioning eyebrow at Maddie. She wouldn't say a word without Maddie's consent.

Maddie felt her face flush with heat, feeling like a teenager getting ready for her first date. Well, she wasn't a teenager anymore, however awkward she felt. She nodded slightly. "You can tell him."

"She's met a young man," Celia informed Davis, a sparkle in her eye.

"That so?" He stroked a hand down his chin and pinched one eye closed. "And when do we get to meet this here feller?"

Maddie rolled her eyes at Davis's put-on country speech. He was a small-town man, but not a hillbilly. "I don't even know if *I'm* going to see him again."

"Why not?" Celia rolled a finger through one of the curls set in her snow-white hair.

"She's just afraid I'll scare him off," Davis grunted.

"You couldn't scare a fly, ya ol' fool. Maddie, dear, what's wrong?"

Maddie quickly wiped away the traces of tears that sprang to her eyes.

The animosity she'd once felt toward Davis was gone and with it the heavy burden of guilt she carried. She'd been unfair to him when she'd accused him of stealing her mother's affection from her. He'd wanted to add his in. Why had it taken her this long to realize what a good man he was, how happy he made her mother?

And he'd never held it against her. She sighed, half in regret, half in shame.

Nothing was wrong, for a change. She felt like laughing and crying and singing, all at once. She squeezed her eyes tightly shut, savoring the refreshing jumble of feelings.

When she opened her eyes, it was to two perplexed, if humor-laced, stares.

"What?" she asked, stifling a giggle.

"You okay?" Davis queried.

"Fine. Never been better."

Celia smiled, then giggled along with her daughter.

Davis grunted and rolled his eyes. "Females. Cry when they're distressed, cry when they're angry, cry when they're happy. Go figure."

Maddie hugged Davis and her mother close, and they all burst into happy laughter.

Neil winced as the cold steel of the surgeon's scissors slid against the tender flesh of his cheek.

The doctor paused.

"Do it," Neil grumbled, closing his eyes and forcing the muscles in his shoulders to slacken. "Just do it."

However loose his shoulder muscles were, he knew he wasn't fooling Doc Ryan. His white-knuckled grip on the armrests of the medical chair was a red flag.

Doc Ryan patted him on the shoulder. "This shouldn't hurt, Neil. Your wounds are fully healed."

Neil grunted noncommittally.

"Of course, you can always elect further reconstructive surgery if what we've done here isn't enough for you."

"Just get the bandage off," Neil barked, then flinched at the unnecessarily rough tenor of his voice. It wasn't Doc's fault that he had these scars.

Today would be the first time in over a year that he would see his face without a bandage. The thought wasn't cheerful.

"There, now," Doc said, removing the last of the bandages. "That wasn't so bad, now, was it, son?"

Neil shook his head, then reached up to touch the unusually soft, puckered skin around his right temple. It felt like the skin of a newborn baby. He clenched his teeth as his gut twisted and turned.

"Look bad, Doc?"

Doc Ryan set his hands on his hips, pursed his lips and raised one gray, bushy eyebrow. "Nah," he said after a short perusal. "I've seen a lot worse mugs than yours, and they ain't been through the trauma you've seen."

"Yeah?" Neil asked, unable to keep relief from flooding into his voice. Life as a deformed man hadn't bothered him a month ago. Now he wished with all his heart that his scars—both those his reflection would reveal and those buried deep in his soul—would disappear. For Maddie. *Because* of Maddie.

"Yeah," Doc Ryan said firmly. "You've still got a scar, and no mistaking. But hey, ladies go for them rough-and-tough, mysterious men. More of a mark of distinction than a scar, really."

Neil chuckled. There was only one lady he wanted to impress, and he wasn't nearly as confident as was Doc Ryan that she would look on his scar in a positive light.

Especially once she knew the truth.

But Maddie definitely liked mysterious men. She'd been attracted to his Phantom's mask. At least he had that in his favor. For now.

"So can I see it?" His voice was a good octave lower than normal, and he paused to clear his throat and run a hand across the stubble on his jawline.

"Of course." Doc Ryan passed him a handheld mirror. "Not the best image, I'm afraid, but it'll give you a general idea how you look."

Neil held his breath as he raised the mirror to eye level. He forced himself to keep his face neutral, his eyes open, to remain steady no matter what he saw in the mirror.

He breathed a sigh of relief as he realized it wasn't some deformed beast staring back at him. It was his own countenance, the face that had graced countless newspaper advertisements before the accident.

He drew the mirror closer and peered anxiously at his right temple. The skin was lighter, and pulled slightly around the faint outline of his scar. A single finger of scarred flesh trailed down his cheek, nipping into his five-o'clock shadow.

Setting the mirror on a nearby tray, he rubbed his palms across his knees. "Not bad, Doc. Not bad at all."

"I'm glad you think so," Doc said wryly. "I wouldn't

want my best customer to think I'd done a shoddy job on him. Bad for business."

"Harrumph." Neil shook his head. "With what you charge, you can live for a year off one patient."

Doc Ryan crossed his arms over his chest. "And I'm well worth every penny," he countered with a grin.

"That you are," Neil agreed easily. "Wouldn't find me saying otherwise."

Doc rubbed his palms together like a crook about to cash in on a landslide. "That's it for you, then, March. Find a pretty woman and celebrate our success with a night on the town." He paused and waggled his bushy brows. "I know that's what I'm going to do."

A pretty woman. If only it were that simple.

Neil thanked the doctor and set off determinedly for his office. There was something he needed to do, something he'd been putting off. And it had nothing to do with celebrating.

He had nothing to celebrate.

"Jason," he announced to his startled secretary as he strode off the elevator into his penthouse office. "Get on the phone with Pattie in PR and tell her to meet me in my office in ten minutes. You come, too."

Jason nodded, politely averting his gaze to the files in his arms.

But his slack jaw was reminiscent of gawking, however courteous his eyes were being, and Neil tensed. "It's okay, Jas. You can look."

Jason mumbled an apology and jabbed his index finger several times at the elevator's down button.

Neil sighed and took a seat behind his desk. He'd better get used to that kind of reaction. Those who didn't know him would no doubt wonder at his scars; those who did, those who knew the whole story—or at least what he'd made known of it—thought the subject was too touchy to bring up in his presence.

For a brief moment he wished he had someone to talk to, someone to unload on. But opening up his feelings to another person wasn't an option. It was a completely foreign notion to the heart of this hardened businessman.

Once, he thought with a wisp of nostalgia, he had that kind of relationship with God. There was a time when his every care went straight to the Father's willing ears—but not now.

Now he felt God must turn a deaf ear to his cries. It was impossible to consider that God might forgive him for Peter Carlton's death. Just as Maddie was unable to forgive.

Neil shook his head to clear his thoughts. Now was not the time to be dwelling on his inner torment. He had business to attend to.

With a discreet knock, Jason and Pattie entered the room, each carrying a steno pad and a pen.

Neil stood and gestured them to chairs. "Have a seat. We've got a lot of ground to cover this afternoon."

The two practically scrambled into their chairs, making Neil feel like an ogre. He'd always treated his co-workers with respect, though recently he'd become distant and broody.

But he knew instinctively that it wouldn't help to apologize, so he cut to the chase. He gave Pattie a direct look, and when she returned it with the quiet confidence born from years of working under him, he asked, "What have you got lined up for the Parade of Lights?"

"Meaning?" she asked, wriggling her pen between her fingers.

"Have you finished planning the float? What's the theme? Have you begun preparations?"

"Everything's done," Pattie said, efficiently brushing a speck of lint from the hem of her green velvet skirt. "Down to the last twinkling light."

Neil swung his chair away from them, staring unseeing at the high-rise across the way. His stomach was in knots. In the back of his mind, he'd hoped nothing had been done yet. But it was really no surprise. The Parade of Lights was an annual event for March's. He had anticipated problems. He'd just hoped beyond hope to avoid them. He blew out a breath and continued. "And the theme is…?"

"In keeping with the Christmas season," Jason piped up. "You know, Santa and the elves. We've even got a pair of real reindeer. That ought to be a hit."

Neil swiveled back to face his colleagues and steepled his fingers thoughtfully. "Isn't there a Santa Claus finale in this parade?"

"Well," stammered Jason, "yes. But—"

"And aren't we going to confuse the kiddies by presenting more than one Santa?"

Even Pattie's face blanched at Neil's grim statement. She hazarded a worried glance at Jason, who frowned back.

"We've clearly made an error in judgment here," Jason began hesitantly. "But I don't think we can change anything this late in the game."

"I do." Neil stood and paced the carpet, combing his fingers through the curls at the back of his neck. "You've got lots of glitter and snow, right?"

"Yes," came Pattie's prompt reply.

"Great." Neil felt the smallest tremor of enthusiasm pierce his quavering insides. He wondered if the others noticed how his voice lightened. "Then it's simple, really."

Pattie and Jason waited silently, their pens poised.

Neil's mind flashed briefly to Maddie. When he revealed himself, he wanted at least a small element of fantasy to cushion the blow. "This parade is for the kids, right?"

Jason nodded and gripped the corners of his steno pad. Pattie tapped her pen against her teeth.

"And what was the top children's movie of the season?"

"The remake of Cinderella," the two chorused.

"And the top-selling toy this Christmas?"

"The talking Cinderella doll!" Pattie announced, bounding from the chair in her excitement.

"Yes!" Neil exclaimed. He was having *fun* planning a parade for children. The thought surprised and amazed him. All this time he had had the opportunity to do something for others, and he'd been too lost in his own dull business world, brooding over his secret pain.

Though if he were honest, his plans were as much for Maddie and Nicky as they were for the other children. His pulse increased with the thought of the pleasure he might bring them. At first, anyway.

Pattie's eyes began to glitter. "I see this!" She nodded slowly, holding up her hands as if framing a picture. "We've got the fluffy clouds and glitter—"

"Right," Neil cut in, warming to his spur-of-the-moment solution. "We add lots of gold and silver. Can we get plenty of flashing lights?"

"Done," said Jason, slapping a palm on his notebook with a crack that reverberated through the office.

"And Cinderella?" Neil queried.

"I'll contact the costumer immediately." Pattie scribbled furiously in her notebook. "Nix the elves. Enter Cinderella."

"There's a real nice gal who works the cosmetic counter. Maybe she could... That is..." Jason's sentence trailed off as he adjusted his tie.

Neil was amused by the flush that rose on the young man's cheeks. He cocked an eyebrow and grinned. "She could...?" he prompted.

"Er...make a pretty Cinderella?" Jason finished in a rush of breath.

"Sign her up," said Neil decisively, regaining his seat behind the desk. "Pattie?"

"Sir?"

"I can trust you to all the details, yes?"

"Of course." She and Jason moved to exit the office.

"Oh, and Pattie..." Neil called as if remembering a last-minute thought.

"Yes?"

"Be sure and order a costume for Prince Charming while you're at it."

"Prince Charming?" Jason repeated, looking vaguely alarmed.

Neil chuckled. "Of course. Can't have Cinderella without Prince Charming."

"And...who would that be?" Pattie asked tentatively.

Neil winked and smiled broadly. "I already have someone in mind."

Chapter Eight

Rory.

Even the thought of his name sent warm fuzzies skittering around her heart and paradoxical shivers of delight trailing down her spine. Maddie couldn't wait to be with him again, to inhale the scent of his spicy cologne, to gaze into his velvety dark eyes.

But how was she ever going to find him? How would he ever find her?

The crowds, lured by an unusually warm winter's evening, had come out in droves for the first night of the Parade of Lights. Elbowing and jostling one another for the best spots to view the spectacle, they swarmed the sidewalks and street corners.

Chances of finding Rory in this mess were slim to none. She strained to recognize his dark head of hair and broad shoulders, searched face after face for her bandaged Phantom—but with no success.

She and Nicky had only covered one city block. The parade route was over a mile. Compounding the problem was the fact that the parade went on for a full seven days.

Meet me at the Parade of Lights.

She ground her teeth in frustration. Why hadn't he told her something more specific? Where? When?

What if she never saw him again?

"Mom? Is it starting yet?" Nicky pulled at her sleeve and gestured to the street, his eyes glowing in childish delight.

It wasn't a cold night, but she'd bundled Nicky and herself in their long johns and goose-down parkas anyway, certain that as the night deepened they'd need them. Right now, though, she was feeling sticky and hot.

And frustrated.

If she *did* find Rory, the first order of business would be getting his last name and a phone number. After she strangled him for putting her through this, that is. Would it have been that difficult for him to name a specific night? A street corner? This was utter madness. She didn't need the extra stress.

What she *did* need was to find out once and for all who Rory was, and why he was being so mysterious about his identity. Again, she scanned the crowds for his tall, broad form and bandaged face.

Where is he? her mind screamed. What if he wasn't here? What if she'd come on the wrong night? If she had to, she thought, clenching her fists, she'd come back every night for a week.

Not that it would make any difference. She would never find Rory in this sea of faces.

A marching band proclaimed the start of the parade and Nicky dragged her to the street corner. "Look, Mom!" A fluorescent blue-and-gold banner held by four young band members announced that the event was sponsored by March's Department Store.

Maddie's stomach turned queasy. Even the slightest reminder of that man could still set her off, and she fought against the angry tears that threatened in the corners of her eyes.

Why was it that she couldn't even read the name of the department store without breaking down? She'd always considered herself stronger than that.

She *was* stronger than that. She bit the inside of her lip. She had to get over it. So what if Neil March sponsored the event? She was here to find Rory.

Or rather, for him to find her. He'd *promised*. And somehow, despite the rational side of her brain telling her that it could never happen, she believed him.

She settled back on the edge of the sidewalk, pulling Nicky over her crossed legs, wrapping her arms tightly around him and giving him a sound kiss on the cheek.

"Mom!" he protested, squirming at the personal affront to his dignity.

She chuckled as he wiggled away from her with a scowl. "Look, Nick. Clowns!"

The boy was instantly entranced, forgetting all about his mother's outrageous and offensive public display of affection. Maddie sighed and wrapped her arms around her knees. She might as well enjoy the parade, though she might be seeing a lot of it in the next week.

A clown riding a stuffed camel that he manipulated with his hands approached her, nuzzling the camel's nose into her neck.

Maddie searched the man's eyes, but they were a pale blue, not the obsidian-black eyes she sought.

She was getting desperate, looking for Rory's face even in a painted clown's. She laughed at herself and slapped the stuffed animal away. The clown shrugged and moved on, allowing Nicky to pat the camel's head.

She didn't know how Rory might be disguised, or

even *if* he'd be disguised, much less *in* the parade. But if he were, he wouldn't be a clown.

Her mind flashed to the sexy, dark Phantom of the Opera she'd first met. The image fit him splendidly. The tall, broad-shouldered man with smoldering dark eyes. A mystery man who moved silently and unexpectedly into her life, sweeping her into a romantic fairy tale and then disappearing once again into the darkness of the night.

I'll find you. She smiled at the echo of the words, his rich baritone laughter haunting the corridors of her mind.

She pulled her thoughts back to the present as a large, glittering float arrived, flashing with hundreds of tiny colored lights. Gaily wrapped presents topped the float, along with several friendly elves, waving, smiling and tossing handfuls of candy to eager children.

Her eyes shifted to Nicky, and her hand snaked out to grab the back of his parka. The boy knew better than to run into the street, but other children were diving for candy, and she was afraid that in his excitement Nicky would forget the rules.

The float passed, followed by a marching band. Another glittery float was on its way. Taking a deep breath, Maddie stretched back on her hands and closed her eyes.

A shower of cellophane-wrapped candy landed directly in her lap. Startled, she looked up onto the float, into the familiar, haunting dark eyes of her Phantom.

His smile faded when she stiffened, reading the banner that proclaimed the float to be compliments of March's Department Store. What was he doing on *that* float?

She realized with a start that his face was no longer bandaged or masked. And he was costumed as Prince Charming, his thick shoulders covered with a familiar black cape, though the rest of the outfit was new.

Why was he on March's float? She'd known he was a wealthy businessman. An upper-level executive. Everything about him reeked power and affluence.

Her mind fled from the obvious answer, the answer she read in his dark, expressive eyes. Eyes that burned with pain. And truth.

He wasn't hiding from cameras and reporters now. He wasn't trying to hide from her probing gaze, either. He was on center stage, and she knew instinctively that he meant himself to be there, and for Maddie to see him.

Prince Charming. Was it a fluke, or a message?

It was clear that the others on the float deferred to him, though he was beaming his customary kind smile at everyone. It was equally clear she'd made a terrible mistake.

He couldn't be Neil March. He just *couldn't*. He had said his name was Rory.

But he hadn't admitted his last name.

He's March's CEO, she thought. *And he was too embarrassed to tell me.* Her mind screamed for a logical explanation. Anything but the truth. Anything that would make her nightmare go away, make the knot in the pit of her stomach loosen, make her throat stop constricting before it strangled her.

Neil March.

Her Phantom, the kind, gentle man who had been romancing her was Neil March.

The spiked realization hit her with all the fury of an ice storm, and she wondered for an agonizing moment if she were going to be sick, right here in front of all these people.

She glared at him, daring him to deny the silent accusation in her eyes.

His jaw tightened and he nodded, his eyes pleading

with her to understand. The glow from the lights on
the float wasn't enough for her to distinguish the features he'd hidden—first with the mask, and then with
the bandage. But even in the shadows, he was strikingly
handsome, his beautiful, compelling dark eyes even now
luring her, causing her heart to soften under his gaze.

She turned away, wrapping her arms tightly around
her rib cage. Willing herself not to fall apart. Not now.
Not in front of him.

She forced herself to take slow, even breaths, though
her lungs were screaming for more oxygen and she felt
dizzy with confusion.

Neil March. How could it be?

Neil waited, willing her to turn back, his soul begging hers to understand. He'd taken a huge risk tonight,
going public—not only with her, but with the world—
for the first time since his accident.

If only she would turn back. That first look, when
shock had given way to recognition, had nearly top-
pled him from the float, so intense, so angry was the
glare. Hatred sparked from her eyes, as he had known
it would—though he had prayed desperately that it
wouldn't.

But that was nothing compared to the emptiness he
felt when she turned away. His chest was so hollow he
wasn't even certain his heart continued to beat.

Why wouldn't she turn around, confront him with her
anger? He was ready to hop down from the float right
now, face whatever he had coming to him.

He shouldn't have come tonight. He should have figured out some way to tell her, to explain. He was an idiot,
displaying himself on March's float. He'd taken a risk
and it had backfired on him.

She'd never understand. And how could he explain?

He clamped his jaw until his teeth hurt. His beautiful, fiery Maddie. He expected her to fight, to yell, to pummel his chest with her fists. But not this. Never this. Why had she turned away?

Neil thrust both hands into the bucket of candy and tossed them blindly to the clamoring children. He couldn't make out faces anymore. His vision had blurred.

He swiped a hand down his face, willing himself to face the crowds, the reporters, the questions.

Eventually, he would have to find Maddie. And *try* to undo the damage that his hollow chest told him was beyond repair. If only he could.

He glanced behind him, hoping beyond hope that his gaze would meet hers, that she would beckon to him. But she was looking in the other direction, staring fiercely through a marching band.

His arms felt suddenly heavy, so heavy he could barely lift the candy from the bucket. He couldn't do this anymore: play the happy, benevolent executive. The thought made him sick to his stomach.

He'd had enough pretending—for one lifetime and then some. With a tired sigh, he jumped from the float and disappeared into the darkness.

Maddie refused to turn back until she was certain the March float was long gone. Nicky was exclaiming over the little cars driven by fez-topped men.

"Nicky, let's go," she ground out from between clenched teeth, but her son didn't hear. He crowed in delight over another marching band, pointing and laughing at the crashing cymbals.

Maddie tightened her fists. She'd just have to wait it out.

She shivered in apprehension. What if Rory...if *Neil* came to see her? How could she face him after...

He had *kissed* her, she recalled suddenly. Even after he knew who she was. They'd become close, emotionally tied to each other. At least she'd thought they had. She had very nearly given her heart to this man. Her foolish heart.

Scrubbing her lips with the sleeve of her coat, she cursed the man who had given life back to her, only to rip it cruelly from her again.

She felt violated. Polluted by a man with a heart of ice.

He didn't know who you were the night you met, her fickle mind whispered. Maddie swallowed hard.

No wonder he'd run away when he found out who she was. He'd been just as shocked as she to discover the paradox of their relationship.

Or had he? Was this all some kind of game to him? Had he known who she was from the beginning? Had he been using her for his own amusement?

Her mind flashed back to the ball, to the way her Phantom had picked her from the crowd as if he'd been waiting just for her. Had he known? Was he laughing at her vulnerability, making sport of her?

But *Rory,* her Rory. He was so kind, so gentle. She could see it in his dark eyes. He put others' needs before his own. The concern in his eyes when Nicky was lost—could any man feign that?

He had shown her how to laugh again.

He *cared* for her. And for Nicky.

But Rory was Neil. Neil was Rory. Her mind seesawed, trying to make the two balance. But it was impossible—completely irreconcilable.

"Maddie." The low, rich baritone whispered on the wind behind her.

She whirled, wondering if her mind was playing tricks on her.

He looked regal, if chilly, in sparkling gold tights and a snow-white tunic. Rory was every inch Prince Charming, from the top of his crowned head to the toes of his soft leather, knee-high boots.

It was a crime for a man to be so blatantly handsome, Maddie thought uncharitably. Especially when that man was Neil March. She looked away, trying to gather her unruly thoughts together again.

Dragging in a breath for courage, she scanned his face, which was now free of any bandages. *She* wasn't the one who should be squirming here. If he had come looking for a fight, he was going to get one—and good! She wasn't about to back down. *She* was the offended party, and he wasn't going to intimidate her with his good looks and charm.

Her eyes met his and held. If it were possible, his eyes were even more piercing unmasked and unbandaged, though the skin around his right eye was lighter than the rest of his face, and a scar arched over his right temple.

On another man, the scar would have marred his perfection, but if anything, it enhanced Rory's features. *Neil's* features.

"You know who I am," he rasped, sounding as if his breath was being cut off.

Maddie nodded, fighting to control the anger that surged in furious waves into her head and extremities until she thought she might burst from rage. It was cold. *So cold.* Cascades of anger felt like warm water on frostbitten fingers. It hurt, terribly, but the alternative was so much worse. She embraced her anger, nurturing it, allowing it to warm her.

"How could you?" she exclaimed, crossing her arms

in front of her to keep from pounding his chest. "What kind of game are you playing, Rory? Or Neil? Or whatever your name is?"

He stood silently, his jaw clenched.

"What? You can't even answer me now? You had all the answers before. Knew just what to do, just what to say to make poor, stupid Maddie Carlton buy the whole act. You must be laughing now."

His dark eyes clouded and he shook his head. "Maddie, I'm—"

"You're a liar. And a cheat, you piece of trash. And if I ever lay eyes on you again it will be too soon."

Nicky turned around, evidently distracted by his mother's harsh tone. He stood in surprise when he saw Neil, who hunkered down to the boy's size. "Mommy, it's the Fireman!" he exclaimed, rushing into Neil's outstretched arm.

"No, honey," Maddie ground out. "Mr. March isn't a fireman. This is Rory, the man we saw at the zoo the other day."

Neil ruffled the boy's parka hood and stood, smiling briefly when the boy patted his leg affectionately.

Maddie, her blood still pulsing in her veins, mentally coaxed herself to calm down. She was an adult, after all, and Neil March couldn't hurt her any more than he already had. She had nothing in her chest but a resounding emptiness. He had taken her heart and trampled it into the dust. She had nothing more to fear from him.

He stood silently, his hands hanging loosely at his sides. She could see the tension in his neck and jaw, but his eyes had cleared.

"Let me explain—" he said finally, his voice low and even.

"You've got nothing to say that I want to hear. Just get away from me."

He stepped forward and grasped her elbow, holding fast when she tried to pull away from his grasp. "Not until you hear what I have to say."

Maddie fought with the urge to clamp her hands over her ears and scream, "La, la, la, la, la!" the way she had when she was a child and didn't want to hear what was being said. Instead she just glared at him.

He raised a dark eyebrow.

"Be my guest, Rory. *Neil,*" she corrected sarcastically.

"You don't have to call me Neil," he said quietly. "I went by Rory as a child. Neil Rory March III. Already had a Senior and Junior, so I was relegated to my middle name."

She didn't want to call him his pet name from childhood. She didn't want to call him anything. She just wanted to run away. But he still had a tight grip on the sleeve of her parka and was planted firmly, legs braced, on the street corner.

She could scream, make a scene, but she dropped that notion the moment it entered her head. She was in the public light too much as it was. The best idea was to give him the silent treatment—a regular dose of his own medicine. She lifted her chin and looked away.

"I never meant to hurt you."

"No? Funny, that's not the way I see it." So much for her silent treatment. Rory had a way of nudging her out of her shell even when she was belligerently refusing to cooperate. "I think you had all this planned from the beginning. I think you set me up. I think you're the lowest slimeball ever to call himself a human being."

He laughed dryly. "You can't call me anything I haven't already called myself."

Pain veiled his expression, and for one brief moment, Maddie felt her heart capitulating. She almost felt sorry for him. Almost believed his pleading, flaming eyes. They were Rory's eyes. Gentle, loving eyes. Eyes a woman could lose herself in. *Almost.*

"Okay, so supposing—and I find it hard to believe—but just supposing you are telling the truth. You didn't know who I was when you waltzed in the door of the ballroom. That you picked me out of the crowd was just some strange coincidence." She paused and hammered her finger into his chest. "You still could have told me the truth. When I took off my mask, you *knew.* And you didn't say a word."

He nodded. "I knew." He brushed his fingers over the back of her hand—a tender, intimate caress. "And I should have faced up to you then. I should have revealed the truth behind my mask."

He forced himself to meet her angry gaze, dragging a deep breath of air to will courage into his lungs. The crisp air stung and he took another gulp. Any feeling, even pain, was better than emptiness. "But, Maddie, I couldn't help myself. That night was like magic for me. It was the first time since…"

He paused and cleared his throat. "I don't go out in public much. Then I saw you, looking so small and alone, so lovely and clearly out of your element. I just had to rescue you. And when we danced, and talked, it opened up a part of me that I didn't even know still existed. You made me laugh again, think about the future without cringing. I never wanted that moment to end. I never wanted *us* to end."

"Harrumph." Her bitter laugh sounded almost like a snort.

"That's right. Once I knew who you were, I knew it could never happen. I ran away, pure and simple."

"No, you didn't," Maddie said, her voice a low monotone and her gaze piercing him with accusation. "Are you going to tell me you didn't know I'd be there at the grand opening of the Pachyderm Pavilion? That you hadn't come specifically to see me? Are you going to lie again, Rory?"

"No. You don't understand." He thrust both hands through his hair. She wasn't listening. She'd worked it all out in her head, thought she knew all the answers.

But she didn't. She couldn't.

How could he tell her…?

"No? Astonish me." Her tone was acerbic, colder than the ice forming on the streets.

"I wish I could," he bit back. "What do you want me to say, Maddie? That I went to the zoo looking for you? Okay, I did. But I didn't plan for you to see me. I didn't plan—" His sentence dropped into silence. *To kiss you. To fall in love with you.*

Her cheeks were flaming. Even angry, she was the most beautiful, desirable woman Neil had ever known. He stamped down the urge to kiss the pretty pout off her lips. It would only make matters worse. Even more to the point, he had no right.

"You manipulated me! You—you made me talk about—"

"About me. Yes. But not for the reason you think. I was trying to figure out how to tell you." He stopped and glanced at a passing float, but it blurred before his eyes. "I know you hate me, Maddie. I know I should have revealed my identity that first night we met. But I didn't. And then I couldn't. And then…"

He paused and reached for her, caressing the satiny skin of her cheek with his thumb.

She didn't pull away, though he could feel the tension pulsing through her muscles. "And then," he repeated, "I didn't want to. I wanted to be anyone in the world but Neil March. I wanted to be…your Rory."

Maddie stood transfixed. His touch was so light, so gentle, yet it sent waves of electricity into her heart. These weren't the enemy's hands cupping her cheek, stroking her hair. They were Rory's hands. It was Rory's face drawing near, Rory's mouth covering her own.

"Rory," she whispered as her arms slipped around his waist.

"Maddie." His voice was tortured.

She stiffened as if hit by a bolt of lightning. It wasn't Rory kissing her. It was *Neil March*. They were one and the same. How could she have forgotten, even for a moment? This was the man responsible for Peter's death.

With a strangled sob, she pushed him away. "Get away from me," she rasped through a closed throat. "Just get away from me. I don't ever want to see you again." She turned away from him, focusing on the parade.

"If you'd just give me a chance to make it up to you. To prove myself."

His breath was warm on her neck, but she would not, *could not* respond. Suddenly the cacophony of voices around them swelled. She glanced around, aware that more than one spectator was caught up in *their* spectacle instead of the parade.

She was making a scene. And it was his fault. "Go away," she snapped.

"Okay." His voice was more than resigned, it was devoid of feeling. But the flame in his eyes when he turned her around by the shoulders was anything but empty. "But I want you to know something before I go."

She gasped for air. Though his hands were on her

shoulders, she felt that she was strangling. She tried to speak—to scream her hatred, her contempt—but nothing came from her dry throat but a small whimper of protest.

"You are the most magnificent woman I've ever met, Maddie Carlton. You have so much to live for. Grab on to life and experience it for all it's worth." His voice was low. "You deserve it."

His gaze probed hers for a moment longer, then he swiveled away from her and strode into the shadows. She stood silently and watched him go. Not knowing what to feel. Not wanting to feel at all.

"And, Maddie?"

His rich baritone came from the darkness. She didn't answer, but waited—her fingernails biting into the soft flesh of her palm—for his final words.

"That wasn't blood money I sent you. Not some form of penance. I know there's no salvation for me. I haven't shied away from my responsibilities. I wear them around my neck like a noose."

She heard his footsteps as he strode away. It was over, and a part of her was glad.

But another, deeper part of her grieved. Grieved for what was…for what might have been.

Why couldn't Neil March have been the savage beast she had imagined him to be? Why did he have to be so…human?

And why did she care?

Chapter Nine

"*Do you want to tell me what's going on?*"

"*Hmm?*" *Peter replied absently, looking through a rack of ties.*

Maddie felt her pulse pounding against her temples, drowning out the sound of bustling Christmas shoppers looking for last-minute gifts.

Why was he playing dumb? Did he think she was a fool?

He must. He'd been staying out late, sneaking around. And once…once a woman had phoned and promptly hung up when she discovered Peter wasn't available.

She swallowed, grimacing as her throat tightened. Her stomach churned. She could still remember the tinkle of the woman's laugh, and it grated like salt in a wound.

Her blood pressure rose a notch as she observed Peter moving nonchalantly from aisle to aisle as if he hadn't a care in the world. Out on a jaunt with his wife and his son, and happy to be there.

Except that it was a lie.

Maddie couldn't put her finger on it, but something in their relationship had changed.

Tiny drops of perspiration beaded on her forehead. "You're hiding something, Peter," she said, latching on to the sleeve of his jacket. "And don't you even try to deny it."

Peter stopped walking and whirled to confront her, his face grim. His eyes, usually so warm and friendly, turned to crystal-blue ice, entirely erasing the congenial laugh lines that ordinarily spoke volumes about his personality.

The mall blurred around her until all she could focus on was Peter's angry face. She squeezed her son's hand, a last-ditch effort to cling to her sanity. She was drifting off the edge, and had no idea how far she would fall.

"Don't go there, Maddie," he said, his voice low and severe. "Just don't. It won't do anyone any good."

Maddie barely restrained herself from pummeling his chest. She wanted to claw his heart out with her hands, because that's exactly what she felt he was doing with his cold, callous words.

She dropped Nicky's hand and squeezed her fists tightly until she could feel her fingernails biting into her palms. The pain was reassuring in a world that was going topsy-turvy.

He hadn't even bothered to deny her unspoken accusation.

"So I'm just supposed to smile and drop it?" she asked in her most cutting tone.

Peter actually smiled, his laugh lines reappearing as if by magic. He beseeched her with his gigantic blue eyes—the little-boy look he used to get his way with her. "I wish you would."

Maddie's mouth dropped open in astonishment. She'd practically accused him of cheating on her, of betraying their sacred vows, and he had the gall to smile at her as if there was nothing amiss between them.

"I don't think so," Maddie exclaimed, causing Nicky to cling to her leg. She reached down and patted his back, wishing she could be likewise comforted.

If only Peter would deny everything, take her in his arms and reassure her of his love...but he'd turned his attention to a display of leather wallets.

"I think," Maddie said through clenched teeth, "that we'll talk about it now.*"*

"Maddie, we're in the middle of a mall," Peter said calmly. "Now is not the time." He paused and rubbed his jaw. "But I can see that I've upset you. Perhaps I've made an error in judgment. I guess I'd better 'fess up— but I'm not going to do it in a mall."

An error in judgment? Choosing the wrong restaurant was an error in judgment. What Peter had done—what he'd practically admitted out loud—went far beyond an error in judgment. He had betrayed the woman he had promised in front of God and witnesses to love, honor and cherish.

Till death do us part.

Maddie rolled over, clutching her pillow.

"You call what you've done to me an error in judgment?" Maddie exclaimed, unable even now to voice the words.

Cheating. Adultery.

Her pulse pounded in her head. Only belatedly did she realize that she had shouted, when several nearby shoppers stopped to gape openmouthed at her, then turn expectantly toward the object of her wrath.

"What I've done to you?" Peter repeated softly. His

*eyes met hers, and then his face blanched to a deathly
white as understanding dawned on him.*

*Anger crossed his face, then disappointment. "Nicky,
come here," Peter said in a low, firm voice, which the
little boy immediately interpreted and obeyed.*

*Nicky willingly detached himself from his mother's
leg and, with a yelp of excitement, threw himself into
his father's waiting arms.*

*"We," he said to Nicky, but met Maddie's eyes over
their son's head, "are going to visit Santa's Workshop."*

The message in his eyes was clear. She was not invited.

*"What do you say to that, champ?" he asked when
Nicky began wriggling in his arms. "Want to go visit
the elves?"*

*He set the boy on the floor and laughingly followed
as Nicky pulled him toward the sparkling exhibit.*

He didn't look back.

*"Guess I'll be shopping," Maddie said to herself as
her two boys, as she'd once affectionately thought of
them, disappeared into the snow-white cotton drifts that
marked the entrance to the workshop.*

*She'd no sooner turned her back on the display than
she heard a deafening* whoosh. *Moments later she was
nearly knocked from her feet by a scorching heat.*

*Terror closed in around her. Her stomach knotted.
She stopped breathing.*

"No," she moaned, startling herself into half wake-
fulness. She punched her pillow and curled back into a
ball, her eyes fluttering shut as sleep once again washed
over her.

*In what felt like slow motion, she turned to see what
she already pictured in her mind.*

She could hear someone screaming as if from a distance.

It was her own voice.

"Nicky! Peter!"

The entrance to the workshop was a wall of flame. The cotton clouds of snow and glitter welcomed the blaze.

She stood transfixed, her heart and her mind numb. This couldn't be happening.

It couldn't be.

It seemed like torturous hours, but it must have been only moments later when someone knocked into her from behind, nearly sending her sprawling.

Stripping his shirt from his back, the man didn't stop to apologize, but dived into the flame-encased workshop. His shirt, placed haphazardly over his nose and mouth, seemed meager protection from the smoke, but it was clear the man was bent on being a hero.

That brief contact, when the man knocked into her, was all Maddie needed to be spurred into action. Following the man's lead, she dashed toward the flames, not bothering to find any measure of protection for herself. She was thinking with her heart, and her heart said that her beloved husband and little boy were in there.

How she would rescue them she didn't know. She only knew that she must try.

Just as she was poised to throw herself into the flames, someone dived for her heels and sent her tumbling. She was quickly and ungraciously pulled away by her feet, but not without protest. She fought and wriggled and scratched, but the old woman she battled with had a bruising grip on her ankles.

Maddie knew she was screaming and crying, but she didn't care. Tears blurred her vision.

"You don't understand," she begged her well-intentioned assailant. "My son! My husband! They are in that inferno! Oh, God help them, please," she prayed aloud.

The woman helped Maddie prop herself against a wall, leaving a firm hand on Maddie's shoulder—whether to comfort or restrain her Maddie couldn't tell.

"They are doing all they can," she said before Maddie could protest further. "The firemen just arrived," the woman continued. "It's going to be okay."

Maddie tried to speak, tried to ask about her husband and son, but nothing came out of her mouth except a pathetic whimper.

The woman looked at Maddie, and in her faded gray eyes Maddie could see the warmth of love, the pain of loss and the years of struggle.

And the light of hope and faith.

Maddie clung to that light as she clung to the woman's gnarled hand. Her faith in God had seen her through difficulties before. Life was wrought with storms. She would simply ride this one out.

Maddie closed her eyes.

When she opened them, the woman was gone.

Maddie leaped to her feet and searched frantically through the thick crowd that had gathered. She knew in her heart the next hours could hold countless agony. She could not do it alone.

Somehow she had believed the woman would be there for her, to hold her hand through the ordeal.

But she was nothing more than a kind stranger. She probably had her own family to get home to.

What had the woman said? It's going to be okay. But how?

Maddie sucked in a deep breath and searched inside of herself for that still, small voice that reassured her that she was not alone. Shoulders set and jaw clenched in grim determination, she turned toward the burning display.

People swirled around her, jostled into her in their rush to evacuate the building. The smoke alarm was blaring its shrill warning. Maddie ignored the people, ignored the warning to escape. She had to reach her son, her husband. No matter what.

A shirtless, soot-covered man stumbled from the inferno, a small, drooping form in his arms.

"Nicky!" Maddie choked out the name.

Paramedics swept the boy from the man's arms just as Maddie rushed forward.

Oh, God, no! Her soul cried out to heaven as she approached the still, charcoal-dusted form of her son.

They were wrapping him in sterile bandages, gently coaxing an oxygen mask over his nose and mouth.

"Is he...?" Maddie stammered, touching the shoulder of a waiting paramedic. "I'm his mother."

"He's alive," the man said crisply.

Maddie's shoulders slumped in relief.

"But we're taking him to Children's Hospital. You can ride with him if you like." The man turned a grave face toward her. "He's hurt pretty badly, ma'am."

Maddie's breath caught in her throat. "Will he...?" she began again.

The paramedic's eyes clouded with compassion as he shook his head. "You'll have to wait until we get to the hospital."

"Of course," Maddie agreed dully, her voice nothing more than a squeak.

But what about Peter? He was still inside the blaze. How could she go with Nicky when Peter had yet to be rescued?

Her mind pulled for an answer while her heart pumped furiously.

Just as suddenly, she was enveloped with calm, and she reached for it, embraced it. She knew what to do.

Peter would want her to go with their son.

She turned toward the ambulance.

"Let me go!" The man's voice was low and threatening.

The sudden commotion momentarily distracted Maddie. She glanced over to see the soot-covered man who had rescued her son struggling between two uniformed firemen, who were holding him by his arms.

"Let me go!" the man demanded again, his voice coarse from smoke. He wrenched this way and that, clearly trying to dislodge himself from their grasp.

All Maddie could make out of the man was his broad shoulders and coal-black hair. Or was that soot?

But when he turned his face toward her, she gasped in shock. One whole side of his face had been burned.

"I've got to go back in there!" the man insisted, seemingly unaware of his injury.

"You've been burned," one of the firemen reasoned, keeping his voice at a low, even timbre. "We're taking you to the hospital."

"No!" the man yelled, loud enough—despite the crowd—for the sound to echo off the walls. "I must go back! There's still a man in there!"

The firemen continued to restrain him.

As the ceiling of the workshop collapsed, there was a rushing sound and a billow of flame.

"No-o-o-o!" the soot-covered rescuer screamed, echoing the agony of her own heart.

"Peter!" Maddie cried simultaneously, reaching her arms out in a powerless gesture.

* * *

"P-e-e-e-t-e-r-r!"

Maddie sat bolt upright in bed, her spine ramrod straight and her hands clenched around sweat-soaked temples. Her feet thrashed around the blankets encasing her legs like a mummy.

It was only a dream. For a moment, her body sagged in relief.

That dream again.

Her muscles tightened as her mind wakened. The horrible nightmare was all too real. She hadn't dreamed the flames, the screaming. If only she really could wake up and make it all disappear.

She huddled into the twisted mound of bedcovers, rubbing her arms against the chill and fear-induced quivering. Coaching herself to take slow, even breaths, she offered a silent prayer that she hadn't wakened Nicky.

It wouldn't be the first time the small boy had stumbled sleepy-eyed into Mommy's bedroom to find out why she had screamed. She usually allowed him to crawl into bed with her, a soft, sweet warmth against the cold depths of her heart. She enjoyed tucking his sweet, downy head into her chest, hearing the smooth incantation of his breathing—a prayer without words.

But tonight she couldn't be strong for him, couldn't comfort him.

For once, *she* wanted to be the child.

No. Not a child, exactly. She wanted a man's thick, strong arms to wrap around her, protecting her from the world's angry darts. She wanted a firm chest to rest against, a broad shoulder to cry on.

She wanted Rory.

The memory of his dark, compassion-filled eyes

flooded her mind, bringing with it a bittersweet combination of tension and relief.

Funny how her heart refused to acknowledge the truth about that man. He was, and always would be, Rory to her, however strongly her mind protested that the flame-eyed Phantom was none other than the despicable Neil March.

She couldn't—wouldn't—analyze the warmth that the mere thought of Rory brought to her insides, the way the memory of his voice soothed her churning emotions. To think of Rory was to tread on dangerous ground.

Squeezing her eyes shut, she curled tightly into a ball, her forehead tucked into her knees. A single sob escaped her throat, and she clenched her teeth against the avalanche of emotion threatening to consume her.

Nights were always the worst.

Why did God allow this to happen? To have lost Peter, and to struggle daily with the unanswered questions, was bad enough. But now to fall in love with the man responsible for her husband's death…

She hiccuped, gulping for air with the high squeak of hyperventilation. It was as if all the oxygen had been squeezed from the room. Her lungs felt ready to collapse from overexertion.

"Why?" she whispered into her pillow. "Why did You make this happen?"

Once the words were uttered, she could no longer hold back the storm in her chest. She began to sob, brokenly at first, then in huge, heartrending wails barely muffled by her down pillow.

For the first time since she had met Rory, she let herself cry—really *cry* for her loss.

For what might have been, and never could be.

For Peter. For Nicky.

For Rory.

And though she thought she ought to be struck down by lightning for lashing out at God, she felt as though He had given her permission to vent, given her the opening she needed to grieve.

As her sobs wound down to an occasional hiccup, she closed her eyes, relaxing into the pillow. Crying had forced her muscles to loosen, even those testy shoulder muscles that were ordinarily rock-hard expressions of her tension.

She drifted into half sleep, marveling at the wonder of a good cry. Bits of Scripture she'd learned as a child washed into her head, comforting her like a gentle hand stroking her sweat-soaked brow.

"'For My thoughts are not your thoughts, neither are your ways My ways,' declares the Lord."

"Trust in the Lord with all your heart, and lean not on your own understanding."

"He gathers the lambs in His arms and carries them close to His heart."

The darkness wrapped around Maddie like a home-made quilt.

Oh, to be a child again…. To know the security of a father watching over his beloved daughter. Maddie longed for safety. Ached for comfort.

With a tiny sigh, she squeezed her eyes shut and imagined a winged warrior in each corner of the bedroom, watching over her, guarding her against hurt and pain.

She could almost see her mother's face, young and fine-boned, whispering softly about how God sent his angels to watch over His children. Remembering the angels often helped her as a child; the thought of an angel in every corner was like a slew of night-lights piercing the darkness.

Even as a parent, it helped to remember the angels. Whenever she feared for Nicky's safety. Whenever life got beyond her control. They were there, watching over her, protecting her from the darkness of the night. She breathed a deep sigh of relief.

Maddie opened her eyes, half expecting the bright shimmer of angel swords around her bed. But of course there was nothing.

And yet…

As she had so often done as a child, Maddie fancied she drifted off to sleep to the soft whir of angel wings.

Chapter Ten

He was stalking her.

What else could you say about a man who lingered in the shadows, hoping to discover where she ate, where she shopped, where she went to relax and have a good time.

There might be prettier ways to describe it, but the truth was that Neil was following Maddie around almost as close as her own shadow.

Except that Maddie Carlton rarely left the house. Which left Neil standing on a cold street corner a good deal of the time.

The evening was crisp, and cold enough to turn his cowboy-boot-encased toes numb. He blew into his fingers, trying to restore circulation.

If he had the brains of an amoeba, he thought, he'd forget about Maddie and go home where it was warm.

And empty.

Ever since he'd met Maddie, his house hadn't been the same. It hadn't been home. His servants couldn't give his house or his heart the warmth of love.

For that he needed Maddie. Someone to tend the fire in his hearth, bank the coals regularly. Someone to share with. Live with. Love with.

Maddie.

His heart jumped into his throat as he saw her slip out the front door, followed by an enthusiastic Nicky. His chest warmed at the sight of the boy. It was bad enough to be separated from Maddie, but he found himself wanting to spend time with Nicky, too.

He wanted them to be a family.

Stamping his feet against the cold, he watched as she drove her car out of the driveway. Then he pulled a helmet over his head, making sure the darkly shaded visor was firmly in place. He didn't want her to recognize him until he could approach her on his terms.

A moment later, he was on his motorcycle. Fortunately, the roads were free of ice, making his Harley a cold but convenient ride. At least on a motorcycle he could easily follow Maddie wherever she was going, weaving in and out of traffic, even taking shortcuts through back alleys if it became necessary. His lips closed in a straight, hard line. He was determined to speak to her.

To make her listen.

He'd considered putting his thoughts down in a letter and sending it to her, but rejected the idea, knowing she'd probably tear it to pieces without reading it once she realized it was from him.

If she could just get past her anger. She had felt something for him—Neil knew she had. At least she felt something for *Rory,* he thought with a grimace.

But he *was* Rory. He just had to make her understand that.

He paused, surprised, when she pulled into a dead-end street that ended at the local elementary school. Neil thought Nicky was old enough to attend school, though he wasn't certain. Was Maddie out for a parent-teacher

conference or something? But Nicky was only in kinder-
garten. Did they even *have* parent-teacher conferences
for kindergarteners?

He took a quick spin around the block to give Maddie
time to go inside the building. By the time he pulled into
the parking lot, it was jam-packed with cars.

Clearly he was mistaken about her intentions, but it
was to his advantage, he decided instantly. He could hide
in the crowd and plan his strategy, wait to approach her
when the time was right. It would be a good sight easier than barging in on a one-on-one meeting. Which he
would have done, had circumstances been different. He
would see Maddie tonight…if he had to buy a ladder and
climb up to her balcony to do so.

He smiled. Romeo, he was not. He wasn't even sure
which window was hers, though he could hazard an ed-
ucated guess from his nights standing watch over her.

He chuckled at the thought, and found himself whistling as he entered the main doors to the school. Perhaps
Nicky was in a performance of some sort. He wanted
to be there for the boy—prove himself to both Nicky
and Maddie.

Prove he would always be there.

He followed the noisy crowd into the gym and discovered some sort of carnival in progress. Booths were set
up in a circular pattern along the outside, with a smaller
circle in the middle facing out. Bright lights and fluorescent colors beckoned onlookers to try their luck, spend
their money to benefit the school. Children were laughing, parents were talking. It was a family scene, and it
warmed Neil's heart just to be there, however tenuous
his current relationship might be.

This was what he wanted. To experience life with the

uncorrupted joy of a child. To coach Little League. To come home to warm, happy nights in Maddie's arms.

He shoved his hands into the pockets of his jeans and began strolling from booth to booth. He kept one eye on the displays, and the other eye on the lookout for Maddie and her son.

As he stopped to purchase a bag of caramel corn from a vendor, he spotted them across the room. Nicky was leaning far into a booth, swinging a magnet-laden fishing pole into a pool of magnetic fish.

"Here," said Neil gruffly, handing the vendor a twenty-dollar bill. "Keep the change."

The man gawked at him openmouthed before recovering with a surprised, "Yes, sir!" The caramel corn was a fifty-cent treat.

Neil strode through the crowd, his eyes never leaving Maddie's back. "For you," he said, thrusting the bag of popcorn into her hands.

Maddie looked startled.

Then angry.

"What are you—" she began, but Nicky turned around, having heard Neil's voice, and squealed excitedly.

"Hello, Mr. Fireman. Can you help me catch a fish?" the boy asked immediately. "Mommy can't fish."

Neil winked at Maddie, who continued to scowl. "Ah. I think she's exaggerating. I'll bet she's a natural." He plunked a dollar onto the counter and was promptly rewarded with a fishing pole, which he extended to Maddie.

"I'm *not* going to—" Maddie began again, but then appeared to back down at the sight of her son's fallen expression. "Oh, all right. But you can't say I didn't warn you!"

She stood with her arms crossed over her chest, holding the fishing pole at an awkward angle, while Neil leaned over Nicky, coaching him on the best way to catch a magnetic fish.

"Wait until you see his mouth beginning to open," he whispered in the boy's ear. "Keep your pole low and steady."

Nicky, his face scrunched in concentration, did just as Neil said.

"Good, good. Now, here it comes…easy…easy…"

"I got him!" Nicky crowed triumphantly, yanking on the pole to reveal a red plastic fish. "I really got him!"

"Of course you did, sport!" Neil said affectionately, slapping Nicky a high five. "I knew you'd be a great fisherman. Just like your mother," he concluded with a pointed look toward Maddie.

"Of all the—" she muttered, leaning against the counter of the display. With a harrumph, she slung her fishing pole over her shoulder. "I can't believe I let you talk me into this," she said, shaking her head at her son.

"And *you!*" Neil felt her glare pierce him. "There are no words to tell you how despicable, how—"

Neil glanced behind her and raised his eyebrows. Dangling from the fishing line she had inadvertently tossed into a pond was a fluorescent-pink magnetic fish.

"I'm going to wipe that grin off your face with my… popcorn," she finished lamely.

"Before you do that," Neil said with a wry grin, "you might want to remove that fish from your pole." He wiggled his index finger at the glaring pink fish.

Nicky clapped his hands in delight. "Way to go, Mom. You caught a fish!"

"I *what?*" Maddie exclaimed, glancing over her shoulder. "I…but I only…"

"I happen to know," said Neil in a conspiratorial stage whisper, laying a gentle arm across the boy's shoulder, "that your mother is an excellent fisherwoman!"

"You happen to know *nothing,*" she barked, grabbing for Nicky's wrist and yanking him to the next display.

Neil sighed. For a moment he'd thought things were going relatively well. Better than he had expected, even.

But now—again—she was turning hostile.

"Maddie, wait!" Neil called, waving his arm. "I need to talk to you." He strode to where she stood glaring at the display of balloons in the next booth.

"We have nothing to talk about," she snapped. "Why don't you just leave me alone!"

Neil took a step back, wounded by her words.

He felt a raging need to justify himself warring in his chest with the dampening reminder that he couldn't justify himself even if he wanted to. He was guilty. It was his fault that Maddie's husband had died.

Maybe Maddie was right. He should turn around, walk away and never return. Become a recluse on some deserted island. Or at the very least hole himself up in his office.

But he couldn't let it go, and the anger surging through his veins made him reckless. If he couldn't beg and plead his way into her life, maybe a shock tactic would work.

"You had more than a few words about Neil March when you thought I was Rory. Why can't you say them to my face?"

Her cheeks blanched, then shaded with anger. She opened her mouth as if to speak, then slammed it closed again and bulldozed past him without a word.

He hadn't really expected her to blow up at him. She was too kind for that. Whatever she thought about him privately, she wouldn't air their dirty laundry in public.

He wasn't even sure that she would confront him if it were just the two of them.

And if he didn't get her to release her anger toward him, he could never make her love him.

It was crazy. Two years ago Neil had lived without a care, wallowing in the jet-set lifestyle that was his heritage. Marrying and starting a family had been the furthest thing from his mind.

And now here was a ready-made family: a family he had neither earned nor deserved, yet he wanted them more than he'd ever wanted anything in his life. He wanted his arms, his heart, his *life,* full of Maddie Carlton and her son.

His gaze followed her profile as she escorted Nicky to a booth on the opposite corner of the gym. The woman would drive him insane! He plowed his fingers through the curls at the back of his neck, massaging the tension from his muscles.

After a moment of indecision, he shrugged his coat over his shoulders. He wasn't accomplishing anything by standing around staring at her.

Except perhaps stirring the flames of his own misery.

He threaded his way through the crowd, intent on his exit. A shrill scream stopped him in his tracks.

The scream was immediately followed by a loud splash and a round of applause. The rescuer in Neil relaxed. He turned just in time to see a soaking wet, gray-haired old woman emerge laughing and huffing from a four-foot pool of water.

The sight of the old-fashioned dunking booth brought a smile to Neil's face as he recalled his own childhood. He remembered an especially fond incident when his sharp aim and strong arm had landed his junior-high principal in the water and Neil on the baseball team.

He'd bet his last dollar that the woman cheerfully climbing from the pool was the principal of the school. A chuckle emerged from his lips as he stepped forward, rummaging through his pockets for some small change.

Just for old times' sake, he'd nail this principal a good one.

He tossed the boy behind the counter a handful of change and hefted a softball, tossing it into the air with a grin. The red-and-black target was only about ten feet away and was at least the size of a paper plate. It would be an easy mark. The booth was really set up for kids around Nicky's age.

Suddenly an idea came to Neil with such unexpected clarity that he nearly dropped his softball. Instead, he slammed the shot into the bull's-eye, sending a flailing, wet principal down for another dunk in the pool.

He ignored the cheerful crowd and moved around to the back of the booth, knocking on the makeshift door he found there. A portly, balding man answered, his curiosity giving way to jovial laughter as Neil explained his intentions.

With half an eye, Maddie watched her son throwing darts at water balloons. Her mind was whirling in tormented circles.

Why was Rory here? What did he want?

There was only one logical answer to the first question: he had followed her here. As to *why* he had followed her, Maddie couldn't begin to guess. The man was as much a mystery to her now as when he had been wearing his Phantom's mask.

Try as she might, she could not make her impression of Rory into Neil March. It just couldn't be done. One of those men was an illusion, and Maddie was simply too gun-shy to make the discovery on her own. If she risked her heart and bet on Rory, and it turned out there was no Rory...

It had already happened—once with Rory and once with Peter. Why were all the men in her life deceitful? Could she not be attracted to anything but lies?

No, it was better to keep her guard up. Trust no one and she wouldn't get hurt.

"Mommy!" Nicky exclaimed, waving a piece of paper in the air. "Look at what I just won!"

It was a certificate for a free throw at the dunking booth. "You won this playing darts?"

"No. A boy came up to me and gave it to me just now. He said I won it."

Maddie shrugged and smiled at her son. "Must be some sort of door prize. C'mon, kiddo. Let's go dunk somebody."

Nicky saw Rory at the exact same moment that Maddie did. She wanted to turn and run, but knew it was too late for that. Her gaze met Rory's, and her heart flamed to life even as she realized that this must be some sort of setup.

"Excuse me," she said to the wet-haired woman behind the counter, "but could you please tell me how many of these door prizes you've handed out today?"

"There are no door prizes," the woman said, but firmly plucked the certificate from Maddie's hand nevertheless. "Give the boy a round of balls," she called to the operator.

Maddie had been conned again, and the familiar flush of anger replaced the warmth pervading her heart.

The sign stuck to the side of the booth confirmed it: Dunk Neil March, Owner of March's Department Store.

Boy, would she like to dunk *him*.

"It's the Fireman!" Nicky exclaimed, waving at Rory.

Rory smiled and waved back to the boy. He looked genuinely happy, dangling his stockinged feet off the edge of a makeshift diving board and calling friendly taunts to Nicky. Maddie felt her throat constrict, then quickly repressed the emotion with another surge of anger.

Anger, she found, was stronger than her less predictable emotions, and right now she needed all the bolstering she could get.

His white-blond hair falling loosely over his forehead, Nicky took the first of three balls, aimed carefully and let loose.

It dropped just short of the target.

"You missed me, sport. But I'll bet I take a dive next time around!" Rory called cheerfully. "C'mon, big guy. Throw me that ball!"

Nicky, his brow furrowed in concentration, threw the second ball high and to the left. His shoulders slumped in defeat. "Aw, I can't do this," he mumbled.

Maddie's heart tightened at her son's fallen look. "It's okay, Nicky. You don't have to throw that last ball if you don't want to."

"Yes. He does," Rory said from the platform, his dark eyes boring into hers.

"Who asked you?" she snapped, aware of the crowd lingering around the booth.

"Nicky, pick up the ball." Rory's voice was low but forceful, and the boy immediately obeyed.

Maddie felt her blood pressure rise, until she was certain that she must have steam escaping from her ears. How *dare* the man override her instructions to her son? How *dare* he believe that he knew what was best for Nicky?

Now Nicky would be hurt and Neil March was to blame.

So what was new? The man had a distinct talent for ruining her life. She shot him a mind-your-own-business glare and crossed her arms over her chest.

Waiting. Watching.

"Now here's the thing, sport," Rory instructed quietly. "You don't have to win, but you do have to try. So give that third throw all you've got, and either way you'll be a winner."

Nicky wiped the frown from his face and nodded at Rory. "Yes, sir!"

Maddie felt a cloud of self-doubt hover over her. Suddenly she could see herself as if from a distance, stepping in to play the protective mother hen when what her son really needed was a man's advice, a chance to prove himself.

It's not whether you win or lose, but how you play the game. A wise old adage Maddie would have completely ignored had Rory not stepped in.

She was always the one calling "Be careful!" to her tree-climbing son, while Peter had always hollered "How high can you climb?"

Not that one was better than the other, she mentally amended. A boy needed both. But now, with only his mother giving counsel, he was being coddled, however unintentionally. She was sheltering him from real life. Overprotecting him when what he really needed was a firm push forward. Like Rory was giving him now.

Nicky took aim and let loose, slamming the ball into the target.

With a whoop, Rory went into the pool, hollering nearly as loudly as was Nicky until his head was submerged.

"Did you see that, Mom? I did it!" Nicky exclaimed, hugging Maddie around the waist and dancing her around.

"Yes, you did!" she agreed, trying to gently wriggle herself free from her son's overenthusiastic embrace.

Rory stood, shaking the water out of his face with a flick of his head. "Way to go, sport! See what can happen if you just keep trying?"

Over Nicky's head, Maddie met Rory's flaming gaze and her heartbeat quickened. His gaze always affected her like that, and she wondered why no one else seemed to notice the way his eyes blazed, how he spoke volumes with those obsidian orbs.

She sent him a silent "thank you," which he acknowledged with a nod. Not a smug or I-told-you-so gesture, but a simple nod of acceptance mixed with a trace of gratitude.

Maddie wondered what he had to be grateful for. He was now sopping wet, and she doubted that he had a change of clothes. It was freezing outside. He was bound to catch a cold, if not something worse.

Oh, what do I care, she scolded herself. But in her heart she knew she did care. Very much.

"Your turn," Rory said, causing her to jerk from her thoughts. She coughed to dislodge the lump in her throat. With his dark hair slicked back, his bold features looked more compelling than she could ever have imagined.

She found herself gaping at Rory like a teenager in love with a rock star. She hoped the trail of her thoughts hadn't been obvious to others, especially to Rory, but from the glimmer of laughter in his eyes, she doubted her luck in *that* department.

"What?" she asked in dismay. He was staring at her,

and was clearly amused by what he saw. He cocked a dark wet eyebrow, the ghost of a smile hovering on his lips.

"I said—" Rory tossed a softball at her "—it's your turn."

His eyes darkened and his smile disappeared. Suddenly it was no game they played, but what felt like a battle—a battle between two strong wills.

"Do it, Maddie." His eyes challenged her, a smirk of amusement in the corner of his mouth giving her every reason in the world to want to knock it off with a softball.

And she was good. Very good. He had no way of knowing that. She was the pitcher on her church softball league. And she could hit the smirk right off his face if she wanted to.

But that's what he wanted her to do. And because it was his game, she no longer wanted to play. Or at least that's what she told herself as she felt her cheeks warm with embarrassment.

People—complete strangers—were laughing and staring at her, caught up in her bickering with Rory and apparently waiting for her to do who-knew-what with the softball.

As if she would stoop to such a juvenile level as to dunk Rory in the pool, worthy of that honor though he might be. An *ice* pool, if she had her way.

But there was nothing on earth that could convince her to play Rory's game. She was not about to give in to aka Neil March. She tossed the softball on the counter with what she hoped was an aloof flick of her hand. "I'm fresh out of tickets."

Rory's eyebrows set in a line over his eyes, which had darkened to midnight-black. "It's free today."

"Not for me, it's not," Maddie countered, her voice

squeaking from the catch in her throat. "Come on, Nicky, let's go home."

Nicky, who was swinging the plastic baseball bat he'd won from dunking Rory, groaned in protest.

"You want to see your mom try to dunk me, don't you, sport?" Rory asked, summoning his reinforcements.

"Yeah, Mom. Do it!"

"Yeah, Mom," Rory repeated with a grim smile, "do it."

She glared at him, but he matched her stare for stare, refusing to blink, move or otherwise break away. How *dare* he pit her son against her that way? What was the man's problem, anyway?

"Are you afraid to try?" He singsonged through a line of "Scaredy-Cat," his eyes gleaming as he intentionally broke their eye contact.

He was trying to provoke her, and in front of strangers, no less! She clenched her fists, fighting to maintain the fine line of control that kept her from diving over the counter and dunking him personally.

She took a deep, steadying breath. His ploy wasn't going to work. She was good and mad, but she wouldn't be manipulated into a water fight. Especially not in front of people she didn't know.

"You couldn't hit the side of a barn. Your aim is so bad you probably couldn't hit me if I were right in front of your nose."

Watch me, you bag of hot air. She eyed him as he took his seat on the latched board and began flutter-kicking the water at his feet.

Juvenile. Infantile. She rolled her eyes. *Sticks and stones and all that stuff,* she reminded her right hand, which curled around a softball on the counter.

Just one throw. That's all it would take to knock that windbag off his perch. And oh, would that feel good.

She gripped the ball and fought for control. Part of her really wanted to take him out. An almost irresistible part of her.

But she wouldn't play his game. She wouldn't. No matter what he called her.

Her eyes locked with his as she set the ball on the counter with a thud, then brushed her hands together in the universal gesture of completion. Finally, forcing a smile that didn't reach her heart, she turned away from him.

He chuckled. "If that isn't just like a woman. Turn and run. Give up before you even start. I didn't peg you as a quitter, but hey, you win some, you lose some. And some games you don't even have the guts to play."

She tensed at his words. Give up? Maddie Carlton, *give up?*

Not in this lifetime.

She had fought a galaxy of battles in the past year. She'd won some, and had come perilously close to losing others.

But she never, *ever* quit.

She whirled so quickly that she couldn't focus on the counter, never mind the target, but nonetheless her hand made contact with a softball. The crowds faded to a dull outline of faces and colors as she scooped the ball into her grasp.

Without even bothering to aim, she slung her arm with every bit of her strength. And missed the mark completely. She hadn't even hit the background, but had sent the ball flying pell-mell into the side of the tent.

Rory had the gall to laugh. "Told you. I knew you couldn't throw a ball."

"Yeah?" Maddie ground out. "Watch me." Her anger was rushing in spurts down her arm, giving her extra throwing power. She knew she could hit the target, and she coaxed herself to relax as she pulled her arm back for another try.

The ball hit the target with a refreshing clang of metal.

"Yes!" She punched a fist of triumph in the air as the man dropped sprawling into the water.

He came up sputtering and laughing. "Not bad. For a girl." He swiped a hand down his face. In moments he had reset the latch and was climbing back on the board. "Now do it again."

As if summoned by a force beyond her control, fury consumed her. She snatched a ball from a waiting attendant and hurled it at the target.

This one's for you, Neil March! her mind screamed as the ball once again made contact with the target and dumped the shivering man into the water.

She didn't even question it when Rory rose from the water and said, "Again."

She grabbed another softball and threw it at the target. Her insides were burning, her head pounding. She was no longer cognizant of the people gathered around the booth, or even of the dripping, dark-eyed man. She only knew her anger, her frustration.

Her pain.

The pounding fury subsided as quickly as it had come, leaving her weak-kneed and breathing heavily. Dazed, she staggered away, leaving Nicky to help Rory towel his clothes off at the front of the booth. She found a quiet place to slump to the floor, leaning her back against a wall.

Her heart fluttered in her throat as her blood pressure returned to normal.

She began to shiver, her body shaking so hard that her teeth chattered. As if *she* had been the one repeatedly dumped into a pool of ice water.

But it wasn't a chill that was making her quake. Maddie recognized the hard knot in her stomach...the queasiness making her head spin...for what it was.

She was frightened. Of herself.

It wasn't Neil March and his deceit that she had been lashing out at as she'd thrown those balls in fury. It wasn't even Peter, who had abandoned her with his death.

No, neither man was the object of her wrath.

Chapter Eleven

The cold gray marble headstone shimmered in the morning mist. Maddie wrapped her parka more firmly around her waist and dropped to her knees beside the well-tended grave. With trembling fingers, she reached out and touched the engraving, fingering the letters almost as if reading braille: Peter Carlton. Faithful Husband. Loving Father.

The words burned into her heart. She hadn't chosen the inscription, couldn't have instructed what she considered a bald-faced lie to be carved indelibly into the marble reminder of Peter's existence.

It was enough to make the old hurt start showing through. Today, though, she didn't feel like crying, at least not in pain. A few *angry* tears might fall before the day was through.

"I met someone," she said aloud, glancing around the vacant cemetery to make certain that she was alone. She didn't want others to hear her. She'd made enough of a spectacle of herself over the past two weeks to last a lifetime. And Rory March was the cause of it all.

No, that wasn't right, either. She'd been placing blame anywhere she could to keep from dealing with her grief.

Peter. Neil March. Even God. But now she realized she'd
made a choice, however unconscious, to fly a holding
pattern, to avoid anything that might cause her pain.
Ironically, she'd ended up being hurt more from hiding
than from facing life head-on.

Now, more than anything, she wanted her life back.
She was determined to end the pity party and confront
whatever she needed to confront.

And the first place her resolution had taken her was to
Peter's grave. She'd asked her mother to watch Nicky so
that she might have some time alone, time to visit Peter.
The two of them had unfinished business between them.
And she wanted to say the words aloud.

She arranged the assortment of roses she had brought
about the headstone, a shock of red and white against the
dreary gray backdrop. When she finished, she sat back
on her heels, observing her work.

"His name is Rory." The name sounded so sweet on
her lips that she said it again. "Rory."

She stood and brushed dirt from the knees of her
blue jeans. Her heart lapped calmly like waves against
the shore. She wondered at the way even the thought of
Rory could bring such peace. And yet such turmoil. His
gentle smile made her feel safe, secure. But his dark,
flashing eyes made her heart leap wildly.

Had Peter ever evoked such polar reactions? All she
could remember was the hurt, the anger. There had been
a time when she'd fancied herself in love, and maybe
what she felt for Peter *was* love. But it was certainly different from what she felt for Rory.

"He's nothing like you." It sounded like an accusation. Maddie was surprised by her own bitter tone. Time
had erased at least some of the pain, but too much still
lurked just underneath the surface.

She closed her eyes and willed Peter's image into her mind. He had been tall, lithe and very blond. But at this very moment, try as she might, his face remained a blur.

In some ways it was a welcome blur, but another part of her wanted to panic. Peter's memory was all she had left of him. And though they had been arguing before he died, their life together hadn't always been that way.

Once upon a time, they'd promised each other the world, shared the same youthful idealism, their hopes and dreams for the future. Peter had been cocky and sure of himself, and Maddie had thought the world turned on his smile. She would have risked anything for his love. She did, in fact, throw her own career choices away to pursue *his* dreams.

At the time it hadn't seemed such a great sacrifice. Now…

Now she was alone with a son to support. Much as she hated to admit it, if it weren't for Neil March's money, they might have starved.

No. That wasn't true. Maddie might not have a college education, but she was determined, and a determined woman couldn't be stopped. She would have made a life for her son even without March's blood money.

She plucked a delicate red rose from the arrangement, looking blankly at her finger when a thorn pierced her skin, causing a tiny droplet of blood to fall on her jeans.

Slowly she began picking the petals from the flower, one by one.

He loves me. He loves me not.

The children's game jumped unbidden to her mind, and her shoulders tensed. "Did you love me?" she whispered at the headstone. "Did you ever love me, Peter?"

How well she remembered walking down the aisle to

become his bride. He had been so happy then, so proud to have her on his arm, to call her his wife.

They'd been young. Full of dreams. But like most young couples, life hadn't been the carefree ride they had anticipated. Bills began to mount. Peter wasn't able to pursue his dream of owning his own tax firm. Instead, he worked indecent hours for ridiculously small wages, caught in the vicious trap of middle management, left with nowhere to go, no ladder of success to climb.

He'd become bitter. Angry. He never complained, but Maddie knew he hated his job, and resented her for tying him down.

The man who used to burst in the door with humorous stories about his day began dragging in after hours, flopping on the couch in front of a blaring television. Not willing to share his day. Never asking about hers.

And then she'd discovered she was pregnant. Nicky had been an accident that she had soon seen as a blessing. The intimacy she lacked with Peter, she found in Nicky, and her son became the center of her world.

She and Peter had drawn further and further apart. To Peter, Nicky had represented another ball and chain, another bleak responsibility keeping him from his dreams. Maddie had resented Peter's attitude and had become withdrawn, distant.

And he'd sought comfort elsewhere. She'd seen it with her own eyes. Peter meeting a woman over lunch. Laughing with her. Whispering to her and sharing secrets that had once been for Maddie's ears alone.

She'd strained to see the face of this nameless woman, but she'd been too far away, and the woman's back had been turned toward Maddie. Instead, she lived with the memory of Peter's joy-filled face as he looked at the other woman.

Her thoughts snapped back to the present with all the ferocity of a bullwhip. The past was past. She couldn't change what had happened, however much she might wish she could. Perhaps if she'd been more understanding…

But it was too late for that. It was time to face the future.

Peter's death had been the key that locked her in, trapping her in the past with nothing but her memories for company.

Rory had changed all that. She had no trouble bringing *his* face to mind: the dominant chin, strong cheekbones and aquiline nose. His piercing black eyes and charming, ready smile.

That smile had broken her prison doors wide-open, allowed her to see the future. To laugh again. To live again.

Her heart swelled as she plucked the final petal from the rose stem. "He loves me," she whispered, and smiled.

She turned toward her car, then stopped abruptly and turned back toward the marble headstone. "And I," she said clearly, her voice sounding like the lilting tinkle of a bell on the wind, "just may love him, too."

Chapter Twelve

Maddie stuffed a handful of popcorn in her mouth and slid farther down into the chair, her eyes never leaving the movie screen. She could feel Rory's eyes on her, but she'd intentionally chosen a seat between two strangers. She didn't want to chance being alone with Rory.

Above all, she didn't want to be alone with herself. Her house—once a safe haven, a fortress to keep others out—now felt like a huge trash compactor. The walls were closing in on her, and there was no one to trigger the release.

After seeing Nicky off to school each morning, she tried to lose herself. She wanted to be where there were crowds. The noisier, the better.

Anything to drown out her thoughts. She spent an extra half hour in the morning reading the Bible, trying to find answers to her dilemma.

Until that day at the dunking booth, she had thought her biggest problems were her hatred of Neil March and her inability to deal with Peter's death. But she had no idea that she possessed the kind of violent emotion that had displayed itself that day. It was black, and ugly, and she didn't want to dwell on it.

As if that weren't bad enough, her conflicting feelings for Rory March never left her whirling mind. It was too much to sort out. She wished she could just forget about it for a while—take a vacation from her thoughts.

But that, she discovered, was impossible, thanks to Rory. Everywhere she went, he was there: the dry cleaner's, the grocery store, even the bank. He was tailing her like a bodyguard—never speaking to her, but never letting her out of his sight. Just when she would feel the comfort of being lost in a crowd, she'd sense that dark gaze on her, and her distress would begin once again.

For all she knew, he had staked out her house. The man must never sleep, she thought. It didn't matter what time of day or night she tried to seek a few minutes' respite from the agony of her thoughts... Rory was there.

He never tried to approach her, but his continued presence was like a thorn in her side. She couldn't deal with Rory yet. She couldn't even deal with herself, and she had a lifetime's worth of baggage to unload before she could begin to consider what to do with Mr. Neil Rory March III.

This afternoon, she had wanted to take in a movie, some gut-wrenching sob story. The cover of darkness was tempting. She'd be able to hide there, lose herself and her problems.

Or so she thought. But Rory's gaze pierced into her back from his seat directly behind her. Even without turning around, she knew he was there, could feel him watching her. Reaching out to her.

And she wasn't ready. What's more, she was sick and tired of trying to avoid him.

She hadn't the slightest idea what the movie was about, though she'd been staring at the screen for a good half hour. That was Rory's fault, too.

"I've had it." She turned and whispered at Rory, momentarily forgetting her usual rule not to make a scene in front of strangers. "You're driving me crazy."

He grinned, as if he were pleased.

Would the man never learn? He was the most incorrigible human being she'd ever had the misfortune to know. "Now, you listen, and listen good. I'm walking out of this theater, and if you so much as *budge* from that seat, you're going to regret it."

He cocked an amused eyebrow. "That so?"

"That's *so*," she affirmed, punctuating her sentence by dumping half a bucket of popcorn on his lap. "Besides, you've got a mess to clean up."

Without waiting for his reaction, she spun away from him and marched up the aisle toward the exit, ignoring the applause and catcalls from amused patrons. Anger burned on her cheeks. And that was *all* it was. She wouldn't let herself be embarrassed for putting Rory in his place. The man deserved what he got and more.

There must be somewhere she could hide from both Rory and her feelings at the same time, she thought as she stepped out into the sunlight. But where would he *not* go?

A women's health club? Maybe. But Maddie didn't feel like working out. And knowing Rory, he'd think nothing of bursting into the women's locker room and demanding her attention. Especially after what she'd just done to him.

Penelope's. Of course! Why hadn't she thought of that sooner? Neil March would never dare set foot in his greatest rival's department store.

She would go to the mall and shop until she dropped, comfortably surrounded by the humming mill of Christmas shoppers. She would forget about Rory, and herself, for a while. And she would use Neil March's money to do it.

Funny, but it was easier to spend the money now that she knew it was Rory's. *His* money didn't seem as tarnished as the elusive Neil March's.

A glance at her watch told her it was time to pick Nicky up from school. Perfect. They'd make a day of it, maybe take in a burger and a thick, chocolate milk shake afterward. And Nicky hadn't been to see Santa yet. Tonight would be the perfect night.

She could finish up her Christmas shopping, spend quality time with her son and escape her nagging conscience—all in one fell swoop.

"When are we gonna see Santa?" Nicky asked the moment she pulled her car into Eastlake Mall. The two anchor stores for the mall were Penelope's and March's. There was absolutely no way Rory would follow her into the competing store with his own store weighing in at the other end, she reassured her quavering heart. Not when he might be recognized. He probably knew Penelope personally.

"Soon, Nicky," she said, adjusting the boy's hood over his head to protect him from the frigid wind. "I have a bit of shopping to do first."

And a bit of forgetting. She would need more than a shopping expedition to erase a lifetime of hurt. But it was a start.

With an occasional furtive glance backward, she crossed the parking lot with Nicky in tow. She half expected Rory to tackle her in the lot, or at least to hover near the entrance, those dark, speaking eyes of his making her feel guilty for shopping the competition.

But there was no sign of him.

With an audible sigh, she relaxed, the tension draining from her shoulders. When her heart tugged gently in disappointment, she ignored it, refusing to analyze the significance. Rory was a heavy burden to bear when she had so much else on her mind. Her feelings for him were becoming more and more obvious. The harder she tried to fight, the stronger they insisted on being heard.

She *had* to force Rory from her mind—at least until she'd dealt with the other issues haunting her. She couldn't go on with her life unless she closed the chapter on her past. But was she really ready to do that? Could she face her suspicions and forgive Peter for what he might or might not have done—for the fact that he'd deserted her, just as her father had once done? Could she honestly forgive and forget?

She didn't know the answer to any of those questions, and her head was beginning to ache from thinking about it.

She sorted through a row of boy's pajamas, looking for Nicky's favorite cartoon characters.

"You'll get a far better deal at March's," advised a deep voice from behind her left shoulder, the rich vibrancy of his tone sending a tendril of delight up her spine.

A chocolate voice, Maddie thought. Smooth and rich. A voice that could make her knees turn to jelly and her heartbeat skip erratically.

"Rory, what are you doing here?" she demanded, spinning to face him.

"You really should shop around, you know. You'll save a good dollar on that product at my store." He made a sweeping gesture with his hand. "Come to think of it, I don't know why you're in Penelope's at all. Take it from someone who knows—everything in this place is overpriced and understocked."

"I came here to get away from you," Maddie said bluntly, unable to contain the jolt of her heart when he crooked a smile.

He placed a hand over his heart. "You wound me. And here I thought you were getting fond of this ugly mug of mine."

Maddie nearly laughed aloud. Ugly mug, indeed. Rory March's striking good looks would stand out in any crowd, the puckered scar on his temple notwithstanding.

But it was his compassionate, dark eyes that attracted her most. Especially when they burned as they were when he looked at her as he was doing now. As if she were the only woman in the world. As if he were right where he wanted to be. By her side. She felt alive. Attractive. The way he had made her feel the night they met.

Put a clamp on it, she reminded herself harshly. He'll only hurt you.

"Don't you have someplace to be?" she snapped, angry with herself at how easily she capitulated.

Taking her gently by the shoulders, he leaned in until his mouth was brushing her earlobe. "Only with you."

Her blood was pulsating so rapidly through her limbs she was certain Rory could feel it in her shoulders. She made a pretense of guiding Nicky down the toy aisle, using the time to reel in her whimsical emotions. "Aren't you afraid Penelope will see you?" she asked, seeing that Rory remained at her elbow.

He barked out a laugh. "Penelope has a plush office in LoDo. I don't think she's even *been* to this store. Except maybe for a press conference or something."

Maddie chewed the side of her lip. "Oh." There went her small-town, middle-class roots showing themselves again. Silly her, to imagine the owner of a store might actually *work* there. She felt like a fool, and couldn't contain the betraying blush rushing to her face.

Neil noticed the color that stained her cheeks a kissable pink. "I'm not laughing at you, Maddie," he said quietly, hoping to reassure her. "I work in *my* store. I believe that I shouldn't ask my employees to do anything I'm not willing to do myself, and that goes all the way down to putting up displays and taking out the trash."

"Oh," said Maddie again, looking small, and vulnerable, and absolutely adorable. Neil wanted to wrap her in his arms and promise her that she'd never be hurt again.

Instead, he reached out a finger to stroke her cheek. To his surprise, she didn't pull away, though he felt her jaw tense at his touch. He continued his monologue in an effort to distract her. "It's a sound business philosophy. March's has a reputation for low employee turnover. Almost unheard of in retail."

Her eyes widened and she pulled away from his hand. Neil shoved his hands in his pockets to keep from reaching for her. The need to touch her, to comfort her, was almost overwhelming, but he knew she would run if he touched her again. She was as skittish as a kitten. And with good reason. She had every right to want to run from him.

"Penelope, on the other hand," he continued, trying to hold her with his words, "wouldn't be caught dead in her store, never mind doing menial labor. She might break a nail."

"Oh."

He could see a question in her eyes, but she remained silent. "What is it, Maddie?" he asked gently.

She spoke so quietly that he almost didn't hear her words. "I can't shop in March's. I can't go back in there."

The pain in her words lanced him. Like her, he had

memories haunting him, but he had been able to overcome them, to rebuild. Or at least to pretend that he had.

Something she was obviously not ready to do.

"I wasn't thinking," he apologized tightly. "Of course you'd feel uncomfortable there."

He turned and strode off, afraid to look back, afraid of what he would see written on Maddie's countenance. Every time he made progress, his past would slap him in the face. It was always there, hovering in the background, waiting to jump out if Neil got too close.

And it would always be there. He'd done everything he could think of to make things right, but it obviously wasn't enough. He was made to endure continued torture, the noose around his neck tightening slowly, choking the life out of him.

What did God expect of him? He thrust his fingers through the curls at his neck, attempting to massage away the lines of tension shooting darts into his head.

He'd do it—whatever *it* was—if he could be with Maddie.

He had to be with Maddie.

"Mr. March!" Jason approached wearing a frantic expression. He took Neil by the arm as he exited Penelope's and entered the mall. "We've been looking all over for you!"

Surprised, Neil allowed Jason to lead him down the mall.

"Are you going to tell me what this is all about?" he asked, humor underlying his tone, "or am I supposed to guess? Offhand," he continued, glancing down at the viselike hold Jason had on his upper arm, "I'd have to guess it must involve some sort of emergency."

Jason's face reddened under his mop of brown curls and he dropped his hold on Neil. "I beg your pardon, sir," he apologized with a groan that indicated he'd realized he'd overstepped his boundaries.

"No offense taken," Neil assured his young secretary.

"It's just that, well, sir, you're late for your appointment as—"

Jason's words were cut off by the approach of the store's publicity agent, Pattie. "It's about time you showed up, Santa. Your stint begins in five minutes. Not a lot of time to get into your suit."

"Santa?" Neil repeated with a blank look.

"Surely you didn't forget you promised the mall to play Santa for some much-needed publicity? Something to distract people from remembering the fire?"

He took a deep breath, then slowly released it. The last thing he wanted right now was to be surrounded by crowds and cameras. "Reschedule," he said, sounding more gruff than he'd intended.

"I'm sorry, sir, but we can't do that. It's too close to Christmas and the press is already here in droves."

Neil rubbed a hand across his pounding forehead. "Then cancel."

He turned to walk away when Pattie's words stopped him short.

"You'll be responsible for disappointing all those children, then? You'll give them a year with no Santa?"

With a sigh, he turned around. "Oh, for crying out loud. Bring on the beard and the big red suit."

Pattie's frown turned to a luminous smile. "I knew it. I just knew it."

Minutes later, Jason was adjusting the belt around Neil's red-clad, pillow-stuffed waist. Fortunately, he thought wryly, the fluffy white beard that covered his cheeks and chin also hid his scar. He didn't want his scars to scare any of the children.

"Hmm," Jason mumbled with a frown, putting the finishing touches on Neil's beard. "This thing won't stay straight."

"Leave it," Neil replied.

Pattie took a step back and looked him over, from the tip of his fur-trimmed cap to the toes of his black boots.

He struggled not to squirm under her inspection, which made him feel like a first-grade kid on class picture day.

"Yes, I think you'll do very nicely," she said at last, tapping her fingers on her chin. "Quite nicely indeed."

Neil looked down at his blaring red, portly figure and grinned. "I'm not certain I agree."

Her blond eyebrows puckered. "You may be right. Let's hear it."

"Hear…what?" Neil croaked, wishing he'd left good enough alone.

"Why your laugh, of course. Give me something loud and jovial. Deep and hearty. Oh, and don't forget to shake your stomach like a bowl full of jelly."

He was getting acting lessons. Santa acting lessons from a totally serious and professional female executive? He couldn't help but burst out laughing.

She shook her head vigorously. "No, no! That's not it at all. My word, do I have to coach you on your lines, as well? The correct version is 'Ho, ho, ho.' I hope you can remember that."

"Ho, ho, ho," Neil repeated, tempering her sarcasm with his own blandness. "I think I can remember that."

"You'd better." Then she turned him around by the shoulders and, with an audible grunt, pushed him out of the dressing room and into a mall packed with waiting children.

"Santa! It's Santa!" a young girl exclaimed, enthusiastically tugging on Neil's pant leg.

Moments later he was surrounded by children of all ages and their harried-looking parents. Some of the younger kids clamored for his attention, latching their fists on to his clothing or shyly holding his hand.

One preteen boy even attempted to yank on his beard, but Neil deftly maneuvered himself out of the boy's grasp.

Stifling an un-Santa-like laugh, he looked back for his publicity elf's assistance, but she was nowhere to be seen.

"Ho, ho, ho," he bellowed, doing his best to sound robust, as much for Pattie, wherever she had disappeared to, as for the children who howled in delight when he spoke.

He knew Eastlake Mall intimately from his many years at March's, so he began moving toward the sleigh in the center of the mall that usually held Santa Claus.

It was slow going, with children attached to each leg and everyone talking at once. He was immediately taken in by the eager innocence in the children's adoring gazes.

He could almost remember a time when he believed in Santa Claus himself. But it wasn't that reminiscence that stung him.

He'd been about Nicky's age, if memory served, when his wisecracking father had spilled the beans and left a devastated six-year-old boy vowing never to believe in anyone again.

Not Santa. Not his father. Not even Jesus.

The only one he could believe in was himself.

Neil's throat tightened. He didn't know exactly how he had come to play Santa Claus in the chaos he called a life. But whatever the reason, he was determined to be the best Santa Claus the media, the mall and the children, had ever seen.

Chapter Thirteen

"Now, Mom?" Nicky asked for the twentieth time in as many minutes.

Maddie glanced at her watch. Had Rory been gone for twenty minutes? It seemed an eternity.

Out of sight, out of mind. Oh, if only it were that easy. But for Maddie, Rory's being out of sight only meant that he plagued her mind, not that he left her in peace. Where was he? What was he doing? And why was he no longer following her around?

He'd been her constant shadow for weeks. And now he had disappeared. That she'd given him the royal brush-off was beside the point. He'd never taken the hint before. Why now?

And why was she feeling anxious rather than relieved? She'd come here to escape Rory, after all. But somehow being alone seemed worse than having Rory's gaze perpetually upon her.

"Yeah, sure, honey. We can go see Santa Claus." And then go home. A steaming bubble bath was definitely in order. Maybe a long soak and a good book would rid her mind of her pesky Phantom.

The line for Santa was unusually long, curling around the back side of the display.

Maddie sighed. It would be a long wait, and she was tired, emotionally as much as physically. "Do you want a soda or something before we get in line?" she asked her son.

Nicky shook his head vigorously and pointed to the display. "Look, Mom. Reindeer!"

The glistening cotton snow and the mechanical elves, reindeer and forest creatures looked so much like March's display that it gave Maddie shivers. She slanted a look at her son, wondering if he noticed the resemblance. But he was leaning far over the rail, his little arms flailing in a futile attempt to touch the bobbing head of the nearest reindeer. Apparently, that part of his past was forgotten. Just as well forgotten, as far as Maddie was concerned. The less poor Nicky had to remember and suffer, the better.

She pointed out a bunny and raccoon wrapping a present, and listened with half an ear as he exclaimed over the display, glad that she could give him back the childhood joy of Christmas.

She only wished she could give herself the same simple happiness. But she wasn't as pliable as she'd been as a child. She still harbored too many doubts to be truly happy. This year, her son's happiness would have to be enough for her.

The couple in front of her bounced a chubby infant between them. The tiny girl was, Maddie noticed with a small flutter of her heart, dressed for the season in a green velvet gown, shiny black shoes and an adorable curly bow fastened to a lock of downy black hair.

Maddie smiled, wondering not for the first time what it would be like to have a daughter of her own. Someone to dress up, do up her hair, share jewelry with. A little girl who would play with Maddie's makeup and who would want to emulate Mommy.

Her throat caught around the scratchy feeling of welling emotion. She'd always wanted more children. She and Peter had planned to have another baby when the time was right, but with Peter's work schedule and the demands placed on Maddie by her rambunctious son, that time never came.

And now it never would.

Bittersweet longing filled her. The baby girl was so precious, even when she went from gurgling and cooing to fussing and fuming. And she shared the turmoil of the small girl's parents who, embarrassed by their baby's wailing, tried a pacifier, and then a bottle in an attempt to soothe her. Nothing seemed to quiet the girl, not even being steadily rocked in her mother's arms.

Maddie recognized the desperate look that passed between the parents as, without words, they struggled to decide whether or not to keep their place in the line, which was getting slowly shorter. She remembered when Nicky had been that age, how helpless she had felt when he refused to respond to her gentle care.

Finally, the tiny girl stopped wailing and settled in her mother's arms. The baby's father tickled and cooed and made silly faces until he brought a dimpled smile to his daughter's face. Just in time for Santa.

"Ho, ho, ho."

Maddie's spine stiffened at the familiar rich baritone, and she whirled to see what could not possibly be true, but which was instantly confirmed. Her gaze met Santa's warm, dark eyes.

Rory March was playing Santa Claus.

And it was far too late for Maddie to back out now. If

the long line of anxious children and parents thought the wailing baby had been loud, it was nothing to the uproar Nicky would make should she choose to drag him kicking and screaming out of the mall without seeing Santa. A six-year-old boy could throw fits that could put a baby's fussing to shame.

Besides, she *wanted* Nicky to see Santa—to put to rest any nightmares that lingered in his dreams. He had to move beyond his fear if he was to heal completely. That meant seeing Santa Claus, even if the jolly old elf happened to be Rory March. She'd just have to deal with it the best she could, for her son's sake and that alone. She would not, she reminded her fluttering heart, allow herself to get flustered over the man. Even if he did look adorable as Santa Claus.

The baby in front of them renewed her screaming fit the moment she laid eyes on the plump, bearded stranger reaching for her. The girl's mom looked mortified. Her dad wore a frustrated scowl, looking as if he was ready to snatch the fussy baby from Santa's arms and forget the whole thing.

And Santa? Rory looked…

Happy.

She'd seen his eyes light up with joy before, and there was no mistaking the pleasure he was taking from his role.

With soft, calm words he quieted the baby, bouncing her gently on one of his red-clad knees. He didn't get her to stop crying, but at least he was able to tone the decibels down a few notches.

He took immediate control with the gentle authority that was so completely Rory, suggesting the mother crouch down by her child for the photo.

With a wavering smile of gratitude, she complied,

kneeling by Santa's side and putting a comforting hand around her daughter. The infant, seeing her mother comfortable with the stranger, became excited and began babbling, eventually cracking a smile that was quickly snapped by the waiting photographer-elf. As Rory smiled for the camera, looking as if he played Santa every day of the week, Maddie had no trouble speculating why he volunteered for the job.

If that's what it was…. For all she knew, the mall required its store owners to take turns as Santa.

Whatever misplaced sense of philanthropy led Rory to don the red suit and play the jolly old elf, watching him in action was another blatant reminder that Rory March was not the coldhearted playboy she once believed him to be.

He gave of *himself*—not just his money or his time.

And he liked children.

"Next!" the efficient little photographer-elf announced in a singsong voice.

Nicky bounded up the stairs, then came to a dead halt, his eyes wide and glistening before the bearded stranger. His bottom lip began quivering as his eyes met Santa's, and even the man's jolly "Ho, ho, ho" didn't wipe the look of distress from the boy's face.

Maddie stood, wavering, uncertain of what to do. How could she rescue her son without damaging his fragile little-boy ego and embarrassing him in front of strangers? How could she let him know that he wasn't facing his fear alone, that his mother's heart was with him every step of the way?

Nicky was oblivious to his surroundings, his attention focused completely on Santa. His eyes darted to the cotton snow behind and around him, and then back to Santa and all he represented.

Then he turned and ran back to Maddie, hugging her legs and burying his face in her stomach. Tamping down her own emotions to respond to her son's anguish, she gently placed an arm around his shoulders and stroked the back of his head with her other hand, murmuring soft words of encouragement.

She hazarded a glance at Rory, who returned her look of concern. She thought he might try to approach the boy, but he remained seated, his brow furrowed and his hands gripping the armrests of his chair.

When Nicky shivered, she dropped to one knee and cupped his chin with her palm. "What's wrong?" she whispered for his ears only. "I thought you *wanted* to see Santa Claus."

Nicky nodded vigorously, tears making his big blue eyes shine in a way that nearly broke Maddie's heart.

She bit her tongue to keep from asking him if he was scared. Of course he was scared. He was in just such a display when he lost his father. But how could she help him get over the trauma?

Her mind spun, examining and discarding option after option, while an impatient crowd began to murmur behind her. Whatever action she chose, it would have to be fast.

"Santa took my daddy away," Nicky admitted, his bottom lip resuming its heart-wrenching quiver.

"Oh, Nicky, no!" Maddie exclaimed, hugging her son to her chest. "No. Santa Claus didn't take your father away. Santa is a good man. He brings toys and gifts to good little children, remember?"

Nicky frowned and shook his head furiously.

She knew Rory could hear their conversation. The pained look in his eyes was a clear indication that he was hurting right along with Nicky.

"It was an accident, son," Maddie continued, struggling to keep her voice reassuringly calm. "Nobody is to blame, especially not Santa Claus."

Nicky's mouth twisted as he considered her words.

Rory gestured with his white-gloved hands. He wanted her to come to him—for them to come to him. Compassion filled his gaze, and suddenly Maddie was glad Santa had turned out to be Rory March.

She tried another tactic, hoping to convince her son to give Santa a chance to redeem himself. It was a tall order, but if anyone could do the job, it would be Rory. Maddie sent up a silent prayer of thanks.

"Maybe you can ask him for something really special this Christmas. To make up for last Christmas, you know?" At least she could do that much for her son, thanks to Rory's money.

"Anything?" Nicky asked, his eyes beginning to sparkle with enthusiasm.

Maddie chuckled. "Well, almost anything. I don't think Santa will bring you a car. At least not for another ten years or so."

Nicky smiled and nodded. "I know what I want."

"Great!" she said, encouraged by his eagerness. "Do you think you can tell Santa Claus about it?"

Nicky eyed Santa with a combination of suspicion and reverence, then nodded. He took a step forward but faltered, looking back at his mother. "Can you come with me? Please?"

Maddie looked up at Rory, who smiled back at her. "Sure, honey. I can come with you if you want me to."

Taking her son's hand, she marched him up the stairs. Rory held out his hands to Nicky. The boy slid a glance to Maddie, who nodded her encouragement. After a moment of hesitation, Nicky stepped into Rory's arms and took a seat on the man's lap.

There was a moment of panic when she realized Nicky might recognize Rory from the time they'd spent together. It hadn't taken Maddie more than a second to recognize Rory's voice. What if her son discovered that Santa was only Rory in disguise?

Her fears were quickly put to rest as Rory winked at her over Nicky's shoulder and lowered his voice an octave. "Have you been a good boy this year, spo—uh, son?"

The combination of profound adoration and sober earnestness that graced her son's face brought a lump to Maddie's throat. Her little man had been so brave, had tried so hard. He deserved the best Christmas ever—and then some.

"Yes, sir," Nicky answered gravely, without smiling.

"Ho, ho, ho. Seems to me you've been extra good this year. Now, what can I put on my list to bring you for Christmas?"

"Well, sir," Nicky began hesitantly, then stopped and wriggled his feet.

"What is it?" Rory asked gently.

"I… I'd like to have a model airplane. One of those kinds you glue together? But—" He hesitated and looked imploringly at Maddie.

She smiled her encouragement and nodded for him to continue.

"But what, son?" Rory prompted. His dark eyes brimmed with so much compassion and—*love*—for the boy that Maddie's heart welled until she was sure it would burst.

She held her breath, waiting for Nicky's other request. She hoped that it would be something a little larger than a model airplane. She wanted to go all out this Christmas, grant him his every wish.

"I, um…" Nicky's voice trailed off. He gave Santa a hard, probing stare, which Rory returned with his own strong, clear gaze. The boy pressed his lips together and nodded. "Can you bring my mom something that will make her happy again?"

Maddie heard a buzzing sound in her ears and her head began to spin. Her sight began to fade to tunnel vision. She gripped the armrest of Rory's chair, fighting for control.

Rory placed a warm hand over hers and gave it a gentle squeeze. Immediately, the spots faded and oxygen streamed into her lungs. She turned her hand over and gave Rory's an answering, grateful squeeze.

Nicky licked his lips and swallowed twice, refusing to meet Santa's eyes.

Rory nodded for him to continue. "It's okay," he assured the boy. "You can ask for anything you want. What do you think will make your mom happy?"

"I dunno," Nicky admitted miserably, staring at his swinging feet. "She's like a normal mom in the daytime," he confided, propping himself up next to Rory's ear.

Maddie strained to hear her son's whisper over her rapid heartbeat.

"But sometimes I hear her crying at night. Daddy died, and she doesn't like to talk about it."

Maddie's stomach twisted into a hard knot. That she was strong enough not to burst into hysterical weeping amazed her. Her poor, suffering son, stifling his own fear and doubts because he had to be the "man" for his mommy.

She barely restrained herself from throwing herself onto Rory's lap and hugging them both. Instead, she stood uncertain, her hands clenched tightly together against the waves of emotion washing through her.

"What is it you are asking for?" Rory questioned softly.

Nicky's eyes lit with enthusiasm as an idea took him. "The Fireman made her laugh. Can you— Yeah! Can you make Mommy fall in love with the Fireman?"

Maddie watched Rory's eyes widen and the corner of his mouth quiver. He must be alarmed by such a request, made doubly potent by the fact that *he* was the man to whom Nicky referred.

Maddie almost smiled despite her own discomfort. Rory was in a pickle if ever she'd seen one. There was no easy out, not even for a man who had made disappearing an art form.

Rory raised his eyebrows at her, his gaze warm and sparkling with mirth. No confusion lurked there—only joy. She felt her cheeks flush under his probing eye.

Rory turned back to the child, his smile fading. "I can't—" He stopped and cleared his throat. "I'm afraid I can't do that, spo—uh, son. Remember, I can only bring things that will fit into my sleigh. I can't make people fall in love."

"But you're Santa Claus!" Nicky protested, bringing a gurgle of laughter to Maddie's throat—despite her distress. "You can do anything!"

"No, son. Not everything. Your mother will have to make her own choice about who to love." Neil wasn't about to let Nicky make the same mistake he'd made as a child. "Have you told God about it?"

"Every night," the boy said with a solemn nod.

"Well, then, that's the best you can do." Neil pressed his lips together tightly, unsure of the storm of emotion in his gut. The little boy and his stubborn, beautiful mother were making his heart ache. He had to consciously remind himself that he was Santa Claus, not Neil March. Santa Claus didn't need a family, what with Mrs. Claus waiting back at the North Pole for him.

Santa couldn't allow Neil March's persistent desire for a wife and son to interfere with what was happening here. He clamped down hard on his jaw, resolute in his determination to play St. Nick to the best of his ability.

"I can't make your mom fall in love," he repeated slowly, "but maybe I can bring her a little something that will make her smile. What do you say to that?"

"Okay," the boy agreed easily. "What?"

Neil laughed, then quickly converted his chuckle to the requisite "Ho, ho, ho." "I'm a little weak in the Mom Department. I was hoping you could think of something."

"I dunno," Nicky said, biting his lip. "Can't you ask Mrs. Claus? She ought to know."

Neil ho, ho, hoed until his stomach hurt. He glanced at Maddie. Her cheeks were a bright pink and her eyes were shining with unshed tears. She looked so vulnerable, and Neil's chest tightened with longing. How he wanted to protect her, to shield her from any more hurt than she'd already experienced.

"I've got an idea," he said, nodding his head toward Maddie. "Mrs. Claus is all the way back at the North Pole. I *could* ask her for advice, but you know what? Your mom is standing right here. Why don't we ask *her* what she wants for Christmas?"

"Good idea," Nicky agreed, looking clearly relieved to have been taken off the hook. "Hey, Mom," he called out. "Come here. Santa needs to talk to you."

Neil let out another genuinely amused "Ho, ho, ho!" and glanced up at Maddie. "Why don't we have Mom come crouch next to us for a picture?" he suggested.

Her soft, moonlight scent wafted toward him as she approached to put her arm around Nicky. Neil smiled and inhaled deeply.

"And what do you want for Christmas, young lady?" he teased, slipping his arm around Maddie and her son.

He knew what *he* wanted for Christmas. A family. He was tired of being alone. He wanted a family to share his dreams with, to laugh and cry with.

And not just any family. He wanted Maddie and her son. To love and take care of and protect. For a lifetime and beyond.

Her smile was syrupy and her big brown eyes blazed as she leaned in toward him. Her breath warmed his ear, and he tightened his grip around her waist in response.

"You've got one coming, you rat!" she whispered from between clenched teeth. "I'm going to get you good for this one. Count on it."

"Oh, I will. I will," he murmured, smiling. Why did the thought of being *got* by Maddie not seem like something he wished to avoid?

To Nicky he winked and nodded. "I think we can handle your mom's request," he said confidently, then finished with a hearty "Ho, ho, ho!"

Nicky beamed so brightly that even Maddie smiled— a moment the photographer-elf caught deftly with a click of her camera.

As quickly as Nicky's smile appeared, it vanished. "If you get something for Mom… I mean, can I still have a model airplane?"

Neil glanced at Maddie, who nodded imperceptibly. "Yes, son, I think I can safely promise you an airplane under the tree on Christmas morning. And if I'm not mistaken, there may be one or two surprises under the tree for you, as well." And one of those surprises would be from him. He hoped Maddie would allow this small gesture, for the boy was coming to mean the world to him.

Maybe he could bring Nicky a puppy. Neil had wanted a dog when he was Nicky's age—a little golden Lab with big feet, floppy ears and a waggly tail. His father had been adamantly opposed to the idea, and, to this day, Neil had never had a pet.

If he were Nicky's father, he'd do things right, showering the boy with all the love and affection he deserved. He made a mental note to ask Maddie about a dog.

Nicky began to crawl off Neil's lap when Neil stilled him with his hand.

"One more thing I think would make a merry Christmas all around," he said, his adrenaline pumping. The idea hit him with such fervor that it made him want to bounce with joy the way Nicky was doing.

He averted his eyes from Maddie for fear she'd read his intention. It was now or never. He wasn't the type to pass by a golden opportunity, especially one so readily presented.

"What?" Nicky and Maddie asked in unison.

"Just this." Without giving her time to think or react, Old Saint Nicholas planted a warm, wet kiss on Maddie's lips.

The elf clicked the camera, capturing the moment for a lifetime of memories.

Chapter Fourteen

"Go long," Celia whispered as Maddie huddled head-to-head with her. "We're gonna finish them boys off completely this time!"

"Break!" mother and daughter shouted in unison.

"Look out, fellas!" Maddie warned as she approached the invisible line of scrimmage. "Gramma's on the rampage. And you both know what that means!"

"Means it's high time we men showed you ladies how to play football," Davis retorted. "Ain't that right, Nicky?"

It was boys against the girls. Nicky and Davis against Maddie and Celia. And the girls were outscoring the boys by a good three touchdowns.

Maddie crinkled her mud-smeared nose at her stepdad and crouched before the football. "We're gonna wipe you from the face of the earth and you know it!" she taunted playfully.

Nicky set himself to rush, while Davis held back and waggled his eyebrows at Maddie. "Don't count on it, sweetheart. We were just letting you play for a while before we show you what we're really made of."

"Yeah, Mom!" Nicky agreed, his breath coming out in

a puff of mist. It was a crisp day, and they were playing
in two inches of snow and enough mud to fill a pigsty,
but the Colorado sun was brightly shining, its warmth
cutting through the chilly air.

They'd all bundled in long johns, followed by jeans
and sweatshirts, then snow pants and parkas. It was a
wonder any of them could waddle, never mind run with
the football, but Maddie was genuinely enjoying herself, and she knew Nicky was enjoying the time with
his grandparents.

She was grateful to Davis for suggesting this im-
promptu game and picnic, though she suspected their picnic would consist of hot chocolate before a roaring fire.

One last down and they'd go back to the house, she decided, gripping the football between her mittened hands.
Providing, of course, that she scored a touchdown on
this play.

"Are we gonna talk or play?" Celia demanded, glaring cheerfully at the boys. When they growled back at
her, she hunched behind Maddie. "Hup! Hup! Hike!"

Maddie tossed the pigskin to her mother and dashed
past Nicky and down the length of the park. She continued at a dead run, turning and waving to signal her
readiness to receive the touchdown pass.

Davis was hard on her heels, his cheeks red and his
breath coming in short, tight gasps. "Gonna get you,
sweetheart!"

Maddie ignored him, concentrating on her mother.
She played like she meant to live—giving it all she had
and enjoying every second.

Just as Celia lofted the ball, Davis sprinted toward
her, screaming like a banshee. One eye on the ball and
the other on her attacker, Maddie didn't see the half-foot
snowbank until it was too late.

She lost her balance and her feet slid out from underneath her. Davis was barreling down on her, looking for all the world like a star linebacker, and going far too fast to stop without colliding into Maddie and sending them both into a rolling pile of arms and legs.

She hoped Davis remembered they were playing *touch* football. The competitive gleam in his eye made her doubt it. She was going to be sore tonight.

Just as she regained her footing, she began to fall backward. The football was high and wide, but within her reach if she dived for it. She had a split-second choice: try to save herself from the crash landing of a lifetime, or go for the ball and take a digger.

Either way, the result would no doubt be a body full of bumps and bruises. Besides, she was playing for keeps.

With a determined shout, she floundered for the ball, reaching for it with the tips of her fingers, willing her arms to extend a little higher. Stretching until she felt her shoulders were nearly popping from their sockets, she clenched the ball between her hands, squeezing it with all her might to keep it from popping out of her grasp. She panted for air and tucked the football hard to her chest so that it wouldn't bounce out when she hit the ground. Which, unless a miracle occurred, she was going to do momentarily.

"I got— Umph!" she shouted as she slammed into something rock-solid, knocking the breath from her with a *whoosh.*

At first she thought the ground was coming up to meet her, that she was falling faster than she anticipated. But the strong arms encircling her waist and the deep chuckle coming from the rock-solid something put that theory to a quick and painless death.

Her pulse elevated even more than the exercise had

lifted it. There was only one man whose voice could elicit electric shivers from within her, warming her despite the cold. Rory March.

"Not bad playing for a girl," he whispered. Maddie thrust her elbow into his ribs, but she quickly realized the gesture bruised her elbow far more than it dented his chest.

He shifted, drawing her closer. She froze in his arms. Her emotions were dodging back and forth. She didn't know whether she wanted to kiss him for catching her or punch him in the gut for interfering with her touchdown attempt.

"Thank you, sir," Davis said between huffs of breath. He stopped by Maddie's side and wiped his sleeve across the sweat lining his forehead. "You not only kept my stepdaughter here from taking a nasty fall, but you kept my grandson and me from losing our game to the girls. It's a fine thing you came along when you did. Mighty fine."

Maddie narrowed her eyes and turned on her semi-unwelcome intruder. "I would have scored a touchdown if you hadn't been in my way, you big, meddlesome hunk of muscle. I protest, or call foul play, or whatever it is the referee does when someone cheats!" She tossed Rory a good-natured glare over her shoulder. "Too many *men* on the field."

"It's the Fireman!" Nicky exclaimed, rushing to Rory's side.

"Hello, sport!" Rory greeted, ruffling the boy's hooded head affectionately. "See your mom's been teaching you to play football."

"Yeah, and she's awesome!"

"You've got that one right," Maddie said, trying to wiggle from Rory's embrace. She gripped both hands around his forearm and pushed with all her might, hoping to dislodge his laced fingers and find her freedom.

"Gramma and Gramps are helping me, too," Nicky explained. "You should see my gramma pass a football!"

"I did," Rory said, snaking his left arm completely around Maddie's waist and extending his other hand to Celia. "You have a wonderful throwing arm. I'll bet the Broncos are after you to play for them."

Celia primped her hair and giggled like a schoolgirl. With a delighted smile, she placed her hand in Rory's. "Naturally. But I have to turn them down, you know. *Someone* has to stick around and take care of this decrepit old man," she quipped, gesturing toward Davis. "I'm Celia Winthrow, by the way. And this handsome gentleman is my husband, Davis."

It warmed Maddie's heart to see the fond glance that passed between her parents. Her heart gave a sentimental tug, which was quickly squelched when Rory, his arm slung around her shoulder, nuzzled his face into her hair. "You're covered with snow," he whispered against her neck.

And despite her best intentions, she *felt* like snow melting into his embrace even as her mind commanded her to bail out and run for cover. It was bad enough that Rory was openly embracing her, in front of her parents, no less! But that she was reacting to his nearness absolutely mortified her.

She'd run if she could, but his grip was as strong, and she knew that it was pointless to try to escape.

Celia winked at Maddie, sending her a silent message that she was missing nothing of what was occurring between her daughter and the stranger.

"And this," Celia continued, her voice rising with mirth, "is my grandson, Nicky Carlton. The pretty young woman you're holding in your arms is my daughter, Madelaine Carlton."

Heat flared to Maddie's cheeks, and she stamped her heel down hard on Rory's foot. He didn't even budge, except to bring his mouth down closer to her ear.

"Madelaine." Rory whispered her name with his deep, rich baritone. "It suits you. Strong, but sweet."

Maddie was certain that the red in her cheeks would put a stoplight to shame. Any chill she'd been feeling earlier was long gone, replaced by a dismaying warmth.

"Mom," Maddie said through clenched teeth, "this is Rory March."

"Rory?" Celia repeated, her eyes lighting up with recognition. "Well! How *do* you do?"

Maddie threw her mother a don't-you-even-think-about-it glare and finally wrested herself from Rory's grasp. Or rather, he let her go.

"He was just leaving," Maddie continued without stopping to catch her breath. "I'm sure he's got things to do, places to go, people to see. He owns March's Department Store, you know."

Celia hesitated, catching her daughter's eye with a concerned glance. The inevitable question—the very question Maddie had been trying desperately to avoid since the moment she'd discovered Rory was really Neil March—was thrust silently at her through her mother's gaze.

"Actually, I don't have a single thing to do today," Rory objected happily. "I'd love to join your game. I'm a decent quarterback, too," he added with a grin.

Nicky raced up to Rory, holding out the football. "Can you show me how to catch a long pass, Rory?" he asked hopefully.

"Sure, sport. Go long," he said, pointing to the far end of the park.

"They never grow up, do they?" Celia commented with a chuckle of her own as the men began their scrimmage.

Maddie tossed a look backward, relieved that Rory didn't seem to be following her. She turned her mother toward the end of the park and increased her pace. They walked in silence until she was certain that they were well out of earshot of the men.

"Is Rory related to Neil March?" Celia queried, patting Maddie's hand in a reassuring gesture.

"No," she replied, choking on the word. "Rory *is* Neil March."

"But I thought—"

"I know." She blew out a frustrated breath. "But if you remember correctly, last time we talked, I didn't know Rory's last name. You can imagine how I felt when I found out the truth. I would never have…" She let the sentence trail into silence as they reached a playground.

Maddie seated herself on a swing and began rocking gently. Celia leaned her shoulder against a pole, her white eyebrows furrowed. "Why does he call himself 'Rory'?"

"It's his middle name." Maddie hesitated to offer more, to open herself up to the deluge of questions to which she herself hardly knew the answers.

"You're dating Neil March." Celia was clearly astonished, and Maddie cringed.

How could her mother not be surprised by the revelation? Maddie barely understood it herself. "I'm not *dating* him," she protested weakly.

"But you have feelings for him." It wasn't a question, and Maddie dropped her gaze from her mother's scrutiny.

"I don't know what I feel."

"He clearly knows what *he* feels," she observed with a chuckle.

"What's that supposed to mean?" The question was out of Maddie's mouth before she had time to think, to stop herself from asking.

She braced herself for an answer that she wasn't certain she wished to hear. Whatever inklings her heart held, putting a voice to her suspicions would make them all too real. And far too dangerous.

"It's as clear as the nose on your face," Celia said, looking back at the men, who were sauntering in their direction, passing the football back and forth to Nicky. "You may not be ready to hear it, but that man is in love with you."

Maddie closed her eyes against the waves of emotion washing through her. Rory March was in love with her? But what did she feel for him? How would she ever make sense of the swirling mass of emotions coursing through her?

She'd been considering a relationship with him before she discovered his true identity. When she found out, of course, she thought that she despised him. But that lasted all of two seconds. Until she gazed into those dark eyes of his and got all confused again.

She still couldn't reconcile the fact that her Rory was Neil March, but whatever his name was, she couldn't deny her attraction for him.

And there was no doubt that her mother could see it in her eyes. Celia had always been good at reading her daughter, and Maddie had no reason to believe today would be any different.

She sighed deeply and shrugged in defeat. "I suppose I do have feelings for him. I certainly can't deny I'm attracted to him."

"Physical attraction isn't enough to build a relationship on," Celia commented.

"I know, Mom," Maddie interrupted. "But cut me some slack here. It's not his looks I'm attracted to."

Celia tittered and clapped a hand over her mouth. Her eyes bubbled with merriment.

"Well, okay, so maybe I've noticed he's the best-looking man on the planet. But really, it's so much more than that." She tilted her head back and watched the clouds forming over the mountains. "Rory is the most gentle, compassionate man I've ever known. He's wonderful with Nicky. And he makes me laugh."

"Sounds serious."

"I'm not going to marry the man," Maddie blurted, her eyes snapping. "Not yet, at any rate. I've still got a lot of baggage clinging to me, some unresolved issues I have to deal with, before I can make any decisions about my future." She dug her boots into the mud under her feet.

"I'm the last person in the world to push you, dear," Celia agreed at once. "I remember just how it feels. Take your time, and enjoy every second of Rory's company. You've caught yourself one good-lookin' fella."

The last sentence was a boisterous exclamation that Maddie knew could travel the short distance to reach the approaching men. "Shh! He'll hear you!" she hissed, appalled.

"Don't care if he does," Celia insisted. "I'm young enough to appreciate a handsome man, and old enough not to care if he knows it."

"*Please* don't embarrass me," Maddie pleaded, not knowing whether to laugh or cry.

Rory approached Maddie from behind and gave her a push, swinging her high into the air. He continued to gently push her as Celia greeted Davis with a kiss.

"I was just telling Maddie that we ought to go back to her house for our picnic. It's getting too cold to be out in this weather much longer. Especially with Nicky. He might catch a chill."

Maddie ignored the fact that Celia had said no such thing. Her mother was quietly protecting her privacy, and Maddie gave her a grateful nod.

As Rory pushed her higher, she threw her head back, letting the wind whip through her hair. The crisp air brushing her face was invigorating, as was the feeling of weightlessness as she rocked back and forth. It had been ages since she'd been swinging. She felt light and free. Laughter bubbled up in her chest.

Rory chuckled. "I doubt anyone's going to come down with a cold, but I must admit the thought of a warm drink appeals to me."

Maddie opened her mouth to protest, but her mother beat her to it.

"It's settled, then." Celia wrapped an arm around Davis's waist and gave him an affectionate hug. "Now get that girl off the swing and let's go have a picnic."

Neil relaxed into the comfort of a well-used armchair. Closing his eyes, he leaned back, enjoying the sounds of home around him.

Home. That's what Maddie's house felt like. It put his own starkly furnished, utilitarian penthouse apartment to shame.

A steaming cup of marshmallow-laden cocoa warmed against his palm. The aroma of fresh, yeasty bread permeated the air—never mind that it was pizza from the local takeout. Even Max, Maddie's slobbery-jowled bulldog, added to his pleasure, despite the fact that the animal decided to use Neil's foot as a pillow only moments after he sat down, and was at this moment making repulsive snorting noises as he slept.

Neil chuckled and concentrated on more gratifying sounds, such as the fire crackling in the hearth, serving as a background to the cacophony of cheerful voices.

Nicky made loud siren sounds as he pushed his toy trucks across the living-room floor. Celia and Davis stood in the alcove, arguing about the pizza they'd ordered. Celia thought they should have ordered vegetarian for Davis, who was, she reminded him in low, biting tones, on a low-fat diet. Davis, who had eagerly ordered the triple-meat variety, insisted that they were celebrating. And what use was celebrating if he couldn't even cheat on his diet?

Maddie sang lightly in the kitchen. She really did have a lovely soprano. It made him feel warm, content. He counted himself fortunate to be a part of this family gathering.

Maddie had completely ignored his presence since she'd begrudgingly welcomed him, but Celia and Davis were going overboard to make him feel comfortable. He wished Maddie would accept him with the same enthusiasm, but for now it was enough just to be here with her—even if she wasn't speaking a word to him.

He opened his eyes when she entered the living room and warmed herself by the fire. Rising quietly, he joined her at the mantel. "Thanks for inviting me."

"I didn't invite you. My mother did."

His throat tightened. "Well, thanks for putting up with my presence, then."

"It's the least I could do," she bit out, her voice laced with a sarcasm that stabbed into Neil's gut.

He stuffed his hands into the pockets of his jeans. "Say the word, Maddie, and I'll leave."

He felt her rib cage rise and fall as she sighed deeply. She turned toward him, putting a tentative hand on his chest. "I'm sorry, Rory," she whispered, her voice cracking with emotion. "I don't mean to be so snippy. I don't know what's wrong with me tonight."

He pulled a hand from his jeans and laid his palm against her cheek. "Then let's pretend there *isn't* anything wrong. Just for tonight, Maddie. Can you relax and enjoy the evening? With me?"

Maddie lifted her gaze to him, her wide, brown eyes making his insides shout for joy. Without conscious thought, his other hand moved up to frame her face, to stroke her silky smooth skin with the pads of his thumbs. She was so soft, so vulnerable.

He couldn't help himself. He had to kiss her. Even if she kicked him out the moment he was finished.

He bent his head slowly, waiting for protest, but none came. Maddie closed her eyes and swayed into him, lifting her face toward his.

He brushed his lips across hers, savoring the feel and taste of her. It was all he meant to do. A soft, light kiss, something gentle and benign.

But when she wrapped her arms around his neck and pulled his face closer, he found himself no longer in control of his actions. Moonlight wrapped around him as he deepened the kiss. His heart pounded wildly in his head as she kissed him back.

"Mommy's kissing the Fireman," Nicky calmly informed his grandparents as they entered the room.

"Yes," Davis said, followed by a booming laugh. "We can see that."

"I asked Santa to give him to my mom for Christmas, but Santa said he couldn't do that," Nicky continued in a loud whisper.

"Seems to me maybe they don't need Santa's help," Celia said, patting Nicky on the head. "But I'll be sure to thank him if I happen to see him."

Neil dropped his hands as Maddie jumped away from him, her face flushed. It could be from their proximity to the fire, he supposed, but he hoped *he* was the one causing such an enchanting effect.

Her soft, cinnamon hair was tangled around her cheeks, and her eyes were wide and luminous. It was all he could do not to step forward and wrap her in his arms again.

And if he did, he'd never let go again. He raked his fingers through his hair near the back of his neck, willing himself to back off before he did something irrational. Like drop to one knee and propose.

She wasn't ready for the kind of commitment he desperately needed to give to her. He wanted to marry her, to spend his life trying to make her happy.

But if he proposed, she'd turn him down flat, regardless of how she'd responded to what he'd meant to be a light brush of their lips. He knew without a doubt that her mind was not yet ready to accept what her heart already knew.

She thrust and parried like a professional fencer, withdrawing just when Neil thought she would be advancing on him, and throwing him off every time.

He knew he'd overstepped the boundaries when he'd kissed her, but he also knew she'd wanted that momentary closeness as much as he had. Her response had been genuine, before her mind could override her heart's desire.

But if that were true, maybe his life wasn't doomed to solitary confinement. Maybe he *could* step beyond his past and embrace his future—a future that included

Maddie and her son. If he could make her see him as
"Rory," the man she believed him to be when they first
met… If he could convince her that her response to him
wasn't to be feared or thrust away, but embraced and
cherished.

If he could convince her that he loved her…every-
thing might turn out right.

"Are you two going to stand there smooching all day,
or are we going to eat?" Celia wrapped a hand around
Neil's arm and pulled him toward the couch. "Sit here,
where you can be with Maddie."

Maddie reluctantly joined him on the sofa and busied
herself fixing a plate of pizza for Nicky. Neil watched
her for over a minute, but she refused to meet his gaze.

He shifted his glance to Celia and returned her
friendly wink with a smile. He knew Maddie felt differently, but he would never be embarrassed by his affection for her, no matter who was watching.

"This evening has turned out far better than I ever
expected," Davis said pointedly.

"Thank You, Lord!" Celia exclaimed.

"Amen to that," Neil agreed heartily. He couldn't remember a time when his heart felt so much at peace—
not even before the accident. He rested a hand lightly
on Maddie's back, but dropped it when she stiffened.

"I know we can't talk here," he whispered into her
hair. "But will you meet me tomorrow night?"

She turned to him, her eyes full of questions. But
he didn't want questions. He wanted answers—one in
particular.

"Maddie, please. Let's settle this between us. Just
give me an hour. Say you'll meet me tomorrow night.
At eight. At that French restaurant off 16th Street. I'll

buy you dinner and we can talk…." His voice dropped off at the end of the sentence.

He was babbling like a teenager asking his dream girl to the prom. Here he was, a man of the world, a man others looked up to and emulated, reduced to feeling awkward and gangly and all thumbs.

Not that it surprised him. Maddie *was* his dream girl; and he could be everything she needed in a husband. All he wanted was a chance to prove it.

She dropped her gaze to her plate. "Excuse me," she said, then bolted from the room.

Neil clenched his jaw. He wanted to follow her, to make her admit she loved him, too.

Maddie tossed her plate on the counter in the kitchen and sat down at the table, swiping a frustrated hand down her face. Her mind raced in circles.

Celia entered with a tentative knock on the door frame. "Is it okay if I join you?" she asked, pulling up a chair without waiting for an answer. "You aren't crying, are you?"

"No, I'm *not* crying," Maddie ground out, slamming her palm down on the table. "But if I were, they would be tears of anger. That man makes me so…"

"So…?" Celia prompted.

"So… I don't know! He makes me feel so many things. Angry. Frustrated. Happy. Loved. Intrigued. Suspicious. Excited."

"And?"

"Loved."

Maddie saw Celia's lips quirk into a smile when Maddie repeated herself, making her feel five years old again, blurting out the truth when she meant to tell a lie. What did love have to do with what she felt for Rory?

"Not a single one of these emotions make any sense

to me. They all swirl around together in my brain until I think I'm going to go crazy trying to sort them all out."

"You're not going crazy, dear heart," her mother said, gently, reaching out a hand to squeeze her arm. "It's called falling in love. If we stopped to think about it, not a single one of us would ever do it, because it sure doesn't make a whit of sense."

"It wasn't this way with Peter," Maddie protested. "I didn't feel all giddy and confused."

"You and Peter were both children, dear. You were too young to experience the kind of feelings Rory stirs in you."

"But I did love Peter."

"Of course you did, dear. And a part of you always will. But that doesn't mean you can't embrace what Rory is offering you." Celia paused and took both her daughter's hands.

With a direct, piercing stare, she continued. "I don't know whether you're looking for advice or not, and I know sometimes meddling does more harm than good in affairs of the heart. But, Maddie, that boy is the genuine article. Rory March is one-hundred percent for real."

Maddie was suddenly very conscious of her own breathing. Her mother had the uncanny knack of reading people, and she was almost never wrong. Even considering that they'd only just met. But *could* Rory be "for real"? Could she really hope for a future with him?

And what would she do if she were wrong?

"Give it time, dear. Things always seem to work out when we wait on God."

Maddie nodded, her mother's words calming her.

Celia cleared her throat. "When Davis and I first married, he worked as a carpenter."

"I remember."

"I bought him a wedding ring—an *expensive* ring with diamonds in it. It was probably more than I could afford at the time, and I definitely think I was more than a little obsessed about him wearing it."

She chuckled, and Maddie laughed with her.

Celia's pale gaze clouded as she reached into her past. "Davis refused to wear the ring to work. After your father left, it wasn't easy for me, and I was terrified the same thing would happen with Davis. My fear made me furious, and I lashed out at him."

"What happened?" Maddie asked, squeezing her mother's hand.

"I got over it. Davis was right—that time, anyway."

Maddie chuckled.

"I thought he just wanted to be footloose and fancy-free when he wasn't home. At best, that he didn't want to lose those fancy diamonds. Turned out he was just being plain ol' practical Davis. The man stood to lose a finger doing carpentry with a ring. Could get caught up on the wood or something."

Maddie made a face, and Celia nodded.

"And here I was thinking that he was being vain. Even so, it was hard. Out there in the world among all them pretty women with not so much as a wedding ring for protection. Didn't sound like I had much of a chance to compete."

"But Davis loves you."

"Yes, he does. And that was the very thing I finally had to get through my thick, stubborn head. A man wearing a wedding ring out the door of his house don't mean diddly. Your father wore one. But wedding rings are notoriously easy to slip off and into a pant pocket."

Maddie's throat tightened. The message was coming through loud and clear.

"Davis isn't your father. And if he's gonna cheat on me, he's gonna do it whether he's wearing a ring or not. But I'm going to make myself miserable if I worry about it."

Celia rose and flashed a smile at her own wedding ring. "I can't control Davis. But I can trust him. The choice is mine. It was my decision then, and it's carried me through to this day."

Celia brushed a hand across Maddie's hair and placed a gentle kiss on her cheek. "That's all I wanted to tell you," she said, and left the kitchen.

Maddie gripped the edge of the table as the hope that had sparked within her fanned to life in her chest, soothing her with its warmth.

She was afraid, as much of herself as of Rory. But fear got her nowhere. Hadn't she learned that from the year she'd hidden from the world?

I can't control Davis. But I can trust him.

Did she have the courage to trust Rory the way her mother trusted Davis?

She wasn't sure. But she was tired of hiding, tired of second-guessing. It was time to move forward, to take the ball and run for the touchdown.

Maddie smiled to herself. Scoring touchdowns was her specialty.

Chapter Fifteen

For the third time, Neil looked at his watch.

She wasn't coming.

He wanted—no, *needed* to tell her what was in his heart. It was time she learned the whole story behind her husband's death. Why the display went up in flames. Where *he* was when it happened.

He prayed for the strength to tell her everything. If she hated him for it, well, he could hardly blame her. For the longest time he'd hated himself. Only now was he beginning to be able to distance himself from it, realize it had been out of his control.

If it came down to it, he would walk away and leave Maddie Carlton in peace, even though it would cost him his heart to do so.

The dynamics between them had changed on the day he found her in the park playing football. They'd shared something special that night, whether Maddie would accept it or not.

Why wasn't she here? he wondered anxiously.

Because she told him that she wasn't coming. It wasn't as if she'd given him any reason to hope otherwise.

And yet he *had* hoped. She'd been so soft and hesitant when she'd turned him down, as if she weren't sure herself whether it was the right thing to do.

He'd come anyway, an hour early, just in case.

And now she was an hour late.

No, he amended. She wasn't late. She wasn't coming at all. It didn't take a genius to figure that out.

Neil paid his check and walked out into the night air, the darkness closing around him like a cloud. The chill in the air matched the chill in his heart. Downtown Denver would always remind him of Maddie.

He had to let her go. Finally admit she was never really his to begin with, however much he wanted circumstances to be different. He couldn't change who he was: Neil March, her sworn enemy. A few stolen kisses weren't going to change that stone-carved fact.

He paused at the entrance to the Brown Palace Hotel and smiled grimly, pulling his leather jacket more tightly around his chest. He would always remember Maddie as he'd first seen her. Cinderella. Sweet and simple, and all dressed up for the ball.

How her eyes had lit up during the carriage ride, as she exclaimed over the horse and carriage and clapped with joy at the sparkling Christmas lights. How he'd enjoyed her laughter, the brief kiss they'd shared.

Had they met only a few weeks ago? It seemed to Neil like a lifetime. And then some.

In two days it would be Christmas Eve. The mark of the coming of the tiny Baby in the manger who meant life instead of death.

Life.

He needed to face the fact that Maddie Carlton might never capitulate, might never see past Neil March and find Rory inside.

Life without Maddie loomed like a gigantic cavern, empty and echoing. He couldn't do it alone.

But he knew where to go for help.

In the light of the setting sun, Maddie pulled her small car off the road and into a secluded gravel cul-de-sac. She parked between two eastward-facing cars and turned off the engine. Hers was only one of many cars already parked in what Maddie thought of as "Lovers' Lane."

From the top of the ridge, she watched airplanes take off and land, listening with a heavy heart to the roar of the engines as they passed overhead.

It was a bittersweet reminder, a reunion of sorts. With no money for a *real* date, she and Peter had often sat here watching the airplanes. They'd talked quietly about their hopes and dreams, their future plans, as they watched jets shooting off into the great unknown.

In hushed tones, they had speculated about the people on the plane, and imagined all the exotic places the two of them would someday fly.

They had known even then that there would be clouds, but with the eternal optimism of youth, they never imagined how black and stormy those clouds would be. How the hovering clouds would descend on them, strangling their relationship. And eventually taking Peter away.

It was here, in this car and in this place, that he had proposed to Maddie. If she closed her eyes and put all her effort into it, she could see him still. The way his white-blond hair fell across his forehead and into laughing azure eyes. His contagious, dimpled grin.

He'd been so sure of himself, so confident of her. Of them. She hadn't hesitated a moment in accepting his proposal, believing it to be the most romantic of circumstances despite his not spending a dime on extravagances.

She hesitated now. She'd come here for a purpose, but it wasn't easy to consider, much less perform.

It was time to say goodbye.

She knew that it needed to be said. Aloud. And his grave didn't seem like the right place for such a momentous occasion. The cemetery was a reminder of death. *Peter's* death.

Maddie wanted to remember his life. His laughter. His love.

Peter's spirit was with God. She believed that with her whole heart.

"I believe," Maddie said aloud, "that you loved me. Not only when you proposed, but right down to that last minute, when you walked away from me because you were too angry to talk.

"And I loved you, too. Even when you made me so furious I'd cry. Even when the doubts crept in, making me feel frightened and alone." She paused as a low jet roared over her car. "I loved you with all my heart. I finally recognize that I still love you. I always will. I can accept that now."

She folded her arms over the steering wheel and peered up at the darkening sky. "I don't know what happened to us those last few months. We lost focus…got sidetracked from what was really important.

"But I saw the faith in your eyes the day we made our sacred vows before God and our families. I remember the prayer you said on the eve of our honeymoon, how you asked the Lord to bless and keep us."

She paused to take a deep breath. "I don't know how to work out all of the feelings caught up inside me. We never got to talk. You left too soon. I never knew the truth."

She slammed her palm against the dashboard. "I still don't know. And that's what's eating me up inside. That's what I have to let go of. Not my love for you. Not my past. My *fear*.

"Problem is, I don't know how to do that. If only you hadn't walked away. If only you had told me if—"

She gripped the steering wheel with her fists. "But you never did tell me. We never did talk about it. You went into that stupid display and never came out again."

Leaning her head on her hands, she began to weep. "You abandoned me. You were my husband. You were s-supposed to protect me, take care of me. But instead you left me all alone.

"How am I supposed to raise Nicky? He needs a man around. A father."

She cried until there were no tears left, then rummaged through her purse for a tissue.

"I didn't come here to cry," she said, smiling through her tears. "I came here to tell you that I love you. I love you in spite of your leaving, in spite of whatever differences we had between us. I'm angry. And hurt. But my pain can't bring you back. It can't answer the unanswered questions, and I have to live with that. I have to trust you now like I didn't trust you then. And I have to trust that God knew what He was doing when He left me all alone."

She watched another airplane leave the ground, its methodical, blinking lights reminding her of a heartbeat. "God must have had His reasons for taking you when He did. I can accept that now. And I know—" her voice broke and her heart welled with love and sorrow "—I know you wouldn't want me to go on like I have been. I forgot how to trust. I lost my faith in God and in humankind. And I especially lost my faith in myself."

She smiled through her tears. "I'm ready to move on. I've met someone I want to share the rest of my life with, if he'll have me.

"He won't—he *can't* replace you, Peter. You were my first love. But I think you'd approve of Rory. I truly believe Rory and I are meant to be together, just as you and I were once meant to be together."

Her gentle laughter filled the car. "It feels funny talking to you about this. About another man. I don't even know if you can hear me. But I know God's listening, and I trust Him to relay the message.

"Do you understand?" She allowed the car to fill with peaceful silence. After a moment, she nodded, her chest brimming with love for Peter and Nicky. And for Rory. She had a lot to live for, and without the burden of unanswered questions on her shoulders, the future was bright. "Yes," she whispered into the still air. "I believe you do understand.

"And I think I'm beginning to understand, too." Comprehension suddenly engulfed her. "I thought it was *you* holding me back, and the agony of not knowing the truth."

Peace filled her heart until she thought she might burst from joy. "But it was me all along. It was *my* choice to hate. It was *my* choice to cling to the past.

"It was me all along," she repeated, amazed. "And here I was blaming everyone I could think of except myself—God, you, Neil March. Never accepting the fact that the choice to live—or to waste away hiding inside my shell—is mine."

She watched one last plane ascend to the heights, a smile in her heart. "I've made my choice. I'm going to give life everything I've got. And no matter what, I'm going to be happy."

She took a breath and repeated the affirming statement. "I'm going to be happy, Peter. And I wanted you to know."

Chapter Sixteen

W here was Rory?

Maddie sauntered down the open-air 16th Street mall, glancing behind her every time she detected a movement or a shadow. She was moving beyond irritated into just plain angry.

Two days ago the man had been around every corner, behind every bush. He'd even been Santa Claus, for pity's sake.

But now that Maddie was looking for him, it was as if he had fallen off the face of the planet.

She made a point of being visible, waiting with eager anticipation to see the familiar shadow of her Phantom following her. She ached to tell him the news.

She'd made it right with God. She'd made it right with Peter. And now she was ready to make it right with her dear, gentle Rory.

Except that she couldn't find the man.

Where *had* he run off to? She'd been grocery shopping, to the dry cleaner's, to the movies, to the mall. All places he'd tailed her in the past two weeks.

She was running out of places to look, and running out of patience.

With a frustrated sigh, she decided to return home. It was Christmas Eve, and the malls would be closing soon, anyway. Walking the mall had been her last-ditch effort to find Rory before Christmas. She had so wanted him to spend the holiday with her and Nicky.

Letting herself in the front door with her key, she inhaled the tangy scent of fresh pine. Silence greeted her. Nicky was at a neighbor's playing, leaving the house unnaturally quiet.

But it wouldn't take much to get in the Christmas spirit. A flip of a switch would get a roaring fire burning in the gas fireplace, and it would take only a few seconds more to tip three tall glasses of eggnog. All she needed to make the cozy scene complete was for her son to return home. And for Rory to materialize out of thin air.

Closing her eyes, she imagined his deep, rich voice as they sang familiar carols together. Or as he told the celebrated story of the first Christmas in hushed, reverent tones while they gathered around the ceramic Nativity scene.

Nicky needed to hear the story of Jesus come to earth to bring peace and goodwill to mankind. Christmas held so many unhappy memories for the boy. It was up to her to bring back the magic.

She needed to remind Nicky of God's constant and enduring love. In her own pain and doubt, she'd let regular church attendance slip into the cracks.

Come to think of it, she could use a little Christmas joy herself. Especially with her spirits so low at not being able to find Rory.

Her house was now fully decorated, with holly and garland strung in every conceivable location. Mistletoe had been added in high-traffic areas, a last-minute touch Maddie was especially pleased with.

If only Rory were here. Mistletoe didn't amount to a hill of beans if there was no one special to share it with.

She peeked out the curtain, hoping to see his tall, broad-shouldered form leaning on the lamppost across the street. But it was empty.

She could call his office. Or even more daring, she could phone him at home, if he was listed. He'd be home on Christmas Eve. Unless he was with family.

He certainly wasn't with her.

Perhaps he had nieces and nephews to visit. Or maybe he spent Christmas with his parents. She didn't know anything of his family. And suddenly her lack of knowledge seemed like a cavern in her mind, waiting to be filled.

She wanted to know everything about Rory. She'd gathered bits and pieces. How he put hot-pepper sauce on everything he ate. And how children made him smile.

But she ached to know more. Much more.

The sound of the doorbell startled her from her thoughts.

Rory!

She dashed down the stairs and tore open the door, her heart pounding and a gigantic grin creasing her face.

The smile faded when she caught sight of the pale-faced, over-rouged blonde on the other side of the door.

The woman patted her curls, which looked to Maddie as though they'd been pasted on with superglue. Or at least a decent-size can of hair spray. She had long, acrylic nails and a tall, lithe body that matched her four-inch spiked heels. And she was dressed in so much fur that she looked like a bear with her winter coat on. Not exactly the outfit Maddie would have chosen for appealing for money.

Max waddled to the front door and started woofing,

a sound guaranteed to make the most steadfast of mail-men run for their lives. The woman, however, gave Max one quelling glance and stepped a foot backward, not so much from fear of being eaten alive, Maddie thought, as from repulsion over Max's drool.

Maddie sighed. The woman was no doubt represent-ing one charity or another, though they usually weren't so bold as to knock on her front door, never mind face off her dog. Maddie was learning to give from what God—and Rory—had given her, but it was difficult. There were so many good causes. All the money in the world could not end suffering. Only God could do that.

Maddie felt inadequate, especially being face-to-face with the stranger. It was difficult enough to say no to fer-vent pleas when they were made by telephone or letter.

"I'm Victoria Hamilton," the blonde said, extending her hand.

Maddie shook her hand and attempted to make eye contact, thinking perhaps the obviously nervous woman might be reassured by a friendly smile.

But the woman looked away and clutched her hand-bag. She shifted from foot to foot, and Maddie had the curious notion she was ready to bolt down the stairs, across the grass and back to the safety of her long, pink luxury sedan. Which would be an interesting feat con-sidering the shoes the woman was wearing. Maddie tried to restrain a smile at the thought.

"Can I help you?" Maddie asked gently, finding her-self intrigued by the woman who refused to leave and had yet to say anything more than her name.

"Yes," the woman replied shortly. "No."

Maddie raised her eyebrows.

The woman blew out a breath. "Peter…your hus-band…" She stopped and wet her glossed lips with the

tip of her tongue. "Before he died, the two of us were...
meeting together."

Maddie's heart dropped like lead into the pit of her
stomach as all the fear and insecurity she thought she
had prayed away came rushing back upon her.

She gripped the doorknob, fighting for control. "You'd
better come in," she said grimly, her voice catching.

Mentally, Maddie calmed herself, all the while praying silently for the strength and courage to bear whatever
the next few minutes would bring—to face the woman
with poise and calm. She didn't have the heart to meet
this obstacle head-on, but she *wasn't* alone. And God
was strong enough.

Maddie seated the woman in her best Queen Anne
armchair, then perched on the edge of the sofa. "May I
get you something to drink, Ms. Hamilton? Coffee, perhaps?" She was surprised at how calm she sounded, that
her voice didn't waver.

"No, thank you, Mrs. Carlton. And please, call me
Victoria."

Victoria. Somehow, putting a familiar name to her
made the woman all the more real. And all the more
daunting.

"And you can call me Maddie," she croaked from a
dry throat.

"Maddie." For the first time, the woman met Maddie's gaze. She had lustrous, almond-shaped emerald
eyes. She was a beautiful woman.

Maddie folded her hands on her lap and leaned back,
welcoming the firm security of the sofa across her shoulders. She waited silently for the woman to continue. She
could see the interplay of emotions crossing Victoria's
face, not the least of which were fear and doubt.

The fur-clad woman was in a bizarre and stressful

situation, and she had come of her own volition. Perhaps to clear her conscience.

Maddie fought her rebellious anger, mentally replacing it with compassion. And forgiveness. Only in forgiving Peter could she move on with her own life. She could do no less for this woman.

"Maddie, I should have come here a year ago. But I didn't, and I regret that now. I've tried to put it aside, but my conscience will simply not let me be."

Maddie's chest tightened. She had been right. Peter *had* had something going on along the sidelines. She felt a surge of anger, but she ignored it.

She didn't feel right about the events that were unfolding. But she would *do* what was right. For herself. For Nicky. For Peter. For Rory.

And most of all, for God.

"Go on," she said, her voice coarse with emotion.

"I have a story to tell, a story I hope will not distress you too much." She looked Maddie in the eye. "Your husband had a secret."

At least she had the grace to look surprised when Maddie nodded calmly. "Yes. I know."

"You do?"

"Yes. But I'd like to hear it from you. You must have been through a lot to have come to my front door this afternoon."

"Me?" She sounded genuinely surprised. "Well, I guess so. But it's nothing compared to what you've been through. I'm terribly sorry about your loss."

"Thank you," Maddie said in the monotone that was her way of reigning in her emotions.

"It all began about a year before Peter passed away," Victoria started, then stopped and patted her well-starched coiffure.

Maddie could see that the woman was shaking. She should be shaking, coming here like this, she thought.

No. Maddie wouldn't let herself sulk, no matter how badly she hurt inside. Lightly clenching her jaw and hoping Victoria wouldn't notice, Maddie reached for the woman's hands and gave them a reassuring squeeze. "It's okay. You can tell me."

"This is a lot harder than I thought it would be. You can imagine how I agonized over coming here. But you want the story." She dragged in a breath. "You must have noticed how often your husband worked late."

Maddie nodded.

"He didn't want you to know."

Obviously, Maddie thought. Mentally she braced herself for Victoria's next words.

"He wasn't working late, Maddie. At least, not at the accounting firm."

"No?" No, of course not. He felt trapped there, like he had a noose around his neck that tightened with every passing day.

"No." Victoria's gaze pierced her. "He was bundling newspapers."

"He was *what?*" Maddie tried desperately to remain calm, but her outburst still sounded like a shriek.

"Bundling newspapers. Trying to make extra money so he could take you on that cruise you've always wanted."

"Oh!" Maddie felt a tidal wave of relief wash through her, but it was mixed with a healthy dose of guilt for her lack of trust in him. She burst into tears.

Her dear, beloved Peter, secretly working an extra job in order to give *her* the desire of her heart.

Why hadn't he told her? So many arguments could have been instantly stilled, so many doubts quieted.

But he'd wanted it to be a surprise. It was just like Peter. Working so diligently without a word to her. Doing grunge work without a single complaint. Placing an extra burden on his already weighted shoulders. Going above and beyond the call of love. Sacrificing his own pleasure, his own rest, all for her.

If only she had known. If only...

Maddie glanced through tear-blurred eyes at the woman seated across from her, and sobered instantly. Victoria was crying, too, distress apparent on her face.

"I shouldn't have come. I knew there was a risk that I... I've hurt you. I'm so, so sorry for opening old wounds. How you must be feeling!"

"You've *healed* my wounds, Victoria," Maddie said, happiness making her voice bubble. "My tears are tears of joy. You've reminded me of all the good and special things about my husband. I had no idea he would go to such great lengths for me."

"But I thought you said—"

"I was mistaken. I didn't know. You've—" she choked on the words "—given me a lovely Christmas present. And I have no way to thank you except to express my gratitude from the bottom of my heart."

Victoria rifled through her handbag for a couple of tissues. Handing one to Maddie, she then loudly blew her nose with the other. "There's more," she said hesitantly.

Maddie's heart billowed.

"The cruise. I am—was—Peter's travel agent. He paid for that cruise, but he never set a date." Again, she searched through her handbag, this time retrieving a travel itinerary and some colorful brochures.

"What—?"

"For you. I should have brought them to you a long time ago. But frankly, I was afraid to face a woman who'd just lost her husband to a tragic accident. Especially to hand her two tickets to the honeymoon suite on a cruise line."

"The *honeymoon* suite?" Maddie repeated, astounded.

Victoria nodded. "Peter said the two of you never had a honeymoon."

"That's right."

"He wanted you to have one now. I think it always weighed heavily on his mind that he'd never given you the honeymoon you deserved. He wanted to make it up to you with this cruise."

Maddie stared down at the itinerary in her lap. "And these are…?"

"Some suggestions for your cruise. I thought now that some time had passed, well, that you might be ready to take a cruise." She paused and cleared her throat. "The Caribbean was your dream, didn't Peter say?"

Maddie nodded, her eyes again welling with tears.

"Cruises really are a lot of fun. You can meet new friends. Do lots of sunbathing. Take in all the sights."

Maddie felt her head spinning. It was too much information, too much emotion, too fast. She put up her hands to call a halt to Victoria's rapid chatter. "I don't know about this."

"Of course, it's no problem switching your accommodations. You don't need to worry about having to stay in the honeymoon suite if you don't want to. I mean…" The color on Victoria's powdered cheeks heightened as she dropped the end of her sentence.

Maddie scrubbed a hand down her face and blew out a breath. She felt more than a little overwhelmed by the barrage of information. She needed time to sort through her emotions. Relief. Joy. Sorrow. Regret.

"I…can't make a decision right now," she said at last.

"Oh, there's no hurry," Victoria rushed to assure her. "I haven't booked a date or anything." She handed Maddie her business card. "You take all the time you want. When you're ready, I'll book you on the cruise of a lifetime."

Victoria stood and made her way down the stairs to the front door, then paused and turned back. "If you decide you'd rather pass, I understand. I can refund you the money. It's no problem."

"I'll think on it," Maddie promised as she waved Victoria off. She had *lots* of thinking to do.

But not now. Just as Victoria exited, Nicky dashed in from playing at a neighbor's house, and the phone rang.

Maddie quickly tucked the travel brochures into the pocket of her skirt. "Son?" she called as she raced for the phone.

Nicky stopped halfway up the stairs.

"Why don't you go get changed into your church clothes. Since it's Christmas Eve, I thought it might be nice to go to the service at St. John's."

The telephone rang a third time and Maddie blurted the rest of her words in a rush. "I think they're planning to have real sheep and donkeys there—maybe even a camel!" she coaxed.

"Sure, Mom," Nicky agreed with his usual enthusiasm. "A camel? Cool!"

She smiled and waved him off, her heart filled with love and gratitude, as she picked up the phone.

"Merry Christmas!" Maddie announced cheerfully into the receiver.

"It's Christmas Eve," Celia declared without pretense.

"So I've noticed," Maddie replied wryly.

"I called to ask you, Nicky and Rory to drive up to Benton and attend church with us tonight."

"Thanks, Mom, but we're already going to church here." She paused. "Nicky and I are, anyway."

"Rory out of town?"

Maddie sighed. "I wouldn't know. I haven't seen him since that day we played football."

"That's bad."

"No kidding."

"What are you going to do about it?"

Maddie rolled her eyes. Like she hadn't done everything in her power to find the elusive Rory March. "It's getting late, Mom. I've got to go get Nicky ready for church."

Celia mumbled something under her breath. "Okay, then. Have a good night. And, Maddie?"

"Yeah?"

"I'm glad you're going to church anyway."

"Yeah. Me, too."

Maddie gently replaced the receiver in the cradle. Nothing like a concerned mother to make her feel like a child again. But she wasn't a child. She was a stubborn, determined woman who was going to find Rory March if she had to comb every street in downtown Denver for a week.

In the meantime, she wanted to go to church. She needed to say "thank you" for everything she'd learned today, for answers to the questions she'd set aside as unanswerable.

And the Christmas Eve service at St. John's was the perfect place to do it.

Chapter Seventeen

Sheep, goats, a cow, a donkey, several chickens and even a sagging camel gathered round the makeshift crèche. A wide-eyed little girl about Nicky's age clutched her baby doll close to her chest. She was, Neil surmised, supposed to be the Virgin Mary.

Young Joseph—a boy Neil guessed to be a couple of years older than Mary—was clearly and vocally not pleased with the situation. Shifting the cloth tied to his head with a piece of coarse rope, he glared down at the girl, then attempted to snatch the doll from her grasp.

Little Mary wailed, attracting the attention of surrounding adults. Joseph howled and yanked on the doll's hair. "The Baby Jesus is *supposed* to be in the *manger,* stupid!"

"Son!" a young father sternly scolded. "Stupid isn't a nice thing to call someone. Apologize this instant."

"Well, she is," the boy insisted, before crossing his arms and mumbling "sorry" in the general direction of the little girl.

The moment the boy's father turned his back, the boy grabbed the doll's leg and yanked with all his might. The doll's head came loose from its body, and young Joseph waved it in the air, hooting his delight, while Mary burst into fresh tears.

It was a good thing that baby wasn't real, Neil thought with a smile. He patted Joseph on the head, earning him a scowl as the boy wriggled away from him.

The camel, disturbed from his rest, apparently decided he'd had enough of this standing around. One spindly leg at a time, the old dromedary drooped to the floor, heedless of the pair of sheep he nearly squashed in the process.

When the sheep protested, the camel silenced them with a severe hiss, to the delight of the children participating in the crèche.

A man brought two squirming pigs as his offering to the Nativity scene. Children of all ages crowded around, petting the goats, sheep and pigs, crowing in merriment as the animals squawked, bleated and grunted.

Neil wished Nicky were here. With his enthusiasm for animals, the boy would love the display, especially as some of the tamer species were made available for supervised children to pet.

He could just imagine Nicky's eyes shining, his face flushed with delight. Neil felt a lump form in his throat.

He missed Nicky. And he missed Maddie.

A thousand times he had wanted to go back on the promise he made to himself to give her some breathing room, and a thousand times he had forced himself to stay away from anywhere he might meet up with her. He knew beyond a doubt that if he saw her, he'd break his vow.

But he couldn't keep himself from thinking about her, not for one second of one hour. Even when he slept at night, which wasn't very often or very well, Maddie filled his dreams. When he heard a woman laughing, his mind translated it to Maddie's sweet laugh. When he saw a woman with short, cinnamon-brown hair, his pulse would quicken, even when he knew it wasn't her.

He could no more stop himself from loving Maddie than he could stop the sun from shining. Her heartwarming smile and adorable pout had gotten under his skin. On his mind. And in his heart.

He had every intention of finishing what the two of them started the night they met.

He reached out a hand to pet a brown-and-white goat that was nibbling on his pant leg. A new suit, too, Neil mused. Not that it mattered. He could always buy another one.

What he couldn't buy was Maddie's love. Her trust.

His happiness.

When the time was right, he would try to approach her again, though how he would know enough time had passed was a question he couldn't answer. It was ripping him apart inside not to be with her. Touching her. Loving her.

Ironically, it was his love for her that was keeping them apart. She needed space, more time to come to grips with her husband's death. Time to realize that Neil March, the man she hated, and Rory, the man who loved her, were one and the same.

And he loved her enough to give her the room she needed, hoping beyond hope that when all was reconciled, she would want him by her side and in her life. If she didn't, he didn't know what he'd do.

He moved away from the crowded crèche and into the church. Many people were already seating themselves in the pews, but Neil had somewhere else he wanted to go first.

To the chapel to pray.

* * *

Maddie balked when Nicky went straight for the camel, but the boy stopped short when the dromedary hissed and spat at him. A church parking lot, in Maddie's opinion, was not the place for a camel. Especially an ill-tempered one.

"He's sure a grouchy old fellow tonight!" she exclaimed, laying a restraining hand on her son's shoulder. "What do you say we check out the goats?"

Maddie stuffed her hands into the pockets of her parka, wishing she'd brought mittens. It was chilly, and the weather forecasters were predicting snow for Christmas.

Nicky moved from goat to sheep and back, exclaiming his delight when a goat licked his hand. Maddie kept a sharp eye on the ground. She came from the country and knew what these animals were capable of.

She experienced a moment's regret that Nicky hadn't had the advantage of country living. He certainly enjoyed animals, and the fresh country air would do him good. Maybe she should consider moving....

She shook her head. She couldn't consider anything until she'd spoken with Rory.

"Hey, Mom, look! A pig!" Nicky exclaimed, pushing a black-and-white potbellied pig by its haunches toward her.

A *pig?* Who put a pig in the Nativity scene? Granted, it made a great addition to the petting zoo, but she couldn't remember ever having heard of pigs being present at the holy birth. Then again, maybe they were. In any case, Nicky was having a blast.

She glanced at her watch. "Only a couple more minutes, son, then we'll have to head inside." She looked to see if Nicky had heard, but his attention had been drawn elsewhere.

His blue eyes, so like Peter's, were huge and brilliantly aglow in the setting sun. And they were locked on the manger underneath the awning where a young Mary and Joseph were kneeling.

"Look, Mom. It's Baby Jesus." He started to walk toward the scene, then stumbled and stopped. He looked back at Maddie, his gaze uncertain. "Is it okay if I…"

"I'm sure it is, son. I'm right behind you."

Reassured by his mother's answer, Nicky approached the awning, his eyes and smile widening as he looked down into the manger. His mouth formed a perfect O as he stared in wonder.

Maddie gaped, too, as she approached the crèche. Of all the incredible notions! Someone had placed a serene, plump-faced sleeping baby boy in the cradle of hay. A very *real* baby boy.

The way Mary and Joseph were carrying on, arguing over whose turn it was to kneel before the child, it was a wonder the poor baby could sleep. The older children's parents soon shushed them as the sun finally dropped underneath the outline of the mountain peaks majestically rising in the distance.

With more people arriving as the time for the service drew near, the area around the Nativity became crowded. Maddie waved her arms at Nicky, hoping to pull him away so they could find a decent pew.

But Nicky didn't notice his mother's gestures. His eyes were locked on the sleeping baby.

Maddie held her breath as the boy reached out a tentative hand to stroke the baby's pink cheek. When he glanced back at Maddie, his eyes were misty with unshed tears.

"Can I…give him something?"

Maddie gulped down her initial reaction, an immediate refusal, when she saw the earnestness in his eyes. He had to know that the baby sleeping in the manger wasn't the real Baby Jesus. She'd discussed it with him before they came. What he would see. What they would do.

She was certain he hadn't misunderstood. She'd been clear that these events had happened many years ago. She'd answered the dozens of questions he pelted her with as best she could. Who, after all, really knew why God had chosen to come to earth as a tiny infant with nowhere to sleep but a manger? And had He really slept on hay?

Maddie didn't even know if pigs had been present.

Unable to speak, she nodded her assent.

With a double-dimple smile, Nicky turned back to the baby. Slowly, reverently, he removed his favorite superhero watch from his wrist. He looked at it long and hard, his fist tightening around the band. Then he took a deep breath and gently laid the watch beside the sleeping infant.

When he turned back, his cheeks were flushed with pleasure and his eyes were filled with love.

"Unless you change and become like little children, you will never enter the kingdom of heaven."

In that moment, Maddie understood. Nicky gave a gift to the representative Baby Jesus for the same reason adults kept up the facade of Santa Claus long after they finally realized that reindeer didn't fly.

Because underneath it all, deep down in the heart of every person, was a still, small voice declaring that love is real.

Maddie walked beside her silent son as they entered the sanctuary and found seats at the end of a row near the middle of the church. Not so far back that they would be unable to see and hear well, but with easy access to the aisle should Nicky need to use the bathroom.

She put her hand into her skirt pocket, smiling to herself when her fingers closed around the travel brochures. It was a lovely gift, even if it would never be used. Maddie knew she wouldn't be able to use those cruise tickets—not without Peter.

Somehow, though, love transcended all that. It beamed through the murky waters of life like a spotlight. She could enjoy her love for Peter, her thankfulness for their time together, and still move forward with her life. She had love overflowing, plenty to go around. For Peter, Nicky, and even Rory, if he wanted her.

Love was, is and ever shall be. That was the way God made it. And love was the reason she could embrace the past, enjoy the present and hope for the future.

As the organ began filling the cathedral with the rich tones of "Joy to the World," Maddie slipped an arm around her son and opened her hymnal.

Her heart swelled with love. She felt like singing.

Chapter Eighteen

Neil paused after praying to light a candle in remembrance of Peter. He ran a hand down the side of his face, his fingers finding the soft, puckered skin of the scar that marred his temple.

For the first time since that Christmas display had turned into a deathly inferno, Neil felt no guilt, and only a mild sense of regret. His soul was clean. God had long ago forgiven him for his part in the accident. But only now had he finally learned to forgive himself.

He still felt restless, but he couldn't place it. Some unnamed anxiety fluttered in the back of his mind, and he resolved to put it aside, at least until the service was over.

He could hear the strains of "Joy to the World" through the thick chapel door, and wondered if it would cause a commotion for him to slip out into the main sanctuary.

Of course, the chapel *had* to be located in the middle of the right wall, rather than at the back of the church, where he would have been able to make a quiet exit.

He chuckled. He was making a mountain out of a molehill. Besides, he was missing his favorite hymn. All he had to do was slip through the door and into the nearest pew. Such a trivial action would hardly hold up the service.

He gripped the handle and slowly pulled the door back, praying it wouldn't squeak. He breathed a sigh of relief as the door closed behind him, but it was short-lived.

"Look, Mom! It's the Fireman!"

At the familiar sound of Nicky's voice, Neil froze. His peaceful smile faded as his restlessness turned into full-fledged churning.

His gaze met that of the woman he wanted most in the world to see, and had tried hardest to avoid.

His heart hammered in his chest during the long seconds he stood motionless, his brain whirling with the options available to him. He couldn't possibly walk past Maddie without a word. She and Nicky had both seen him.

More to the point, he didn't want to walk away. He wanted to sit down in the pew between them and put his arms around them both.

He shrugged off a sense of foreboding and threw caution to the wind. He'd break his vow and spend time in their company. Just a minute or two. Such a minor concession couldn't hurt. They were in church, after all. And he *hadn't* followed her here.

He nodded his head in greeting, expecting Maddie's eyes to flare with anger and mistrust, emotions that would help Neil keep his distance, make it easier for him to excuse himself and break away.

Instead, he found her huge brown eyes warm, inviting. He even thought he saw a flicker of something more.

He was imagining things. He must be. But when she extended her hand toward him, he covered it with his own.

"Rory. I mean, *Neil.* It's nice to see you."

Whatever he'd expected to hear from her mouth, that wasn't it. A few days ago she'd gone to great lengths to get rid of him. She hadn't shown up when he'd invited her to dinner. And now she was welcoming him like an old friend, though he hoped all her friends' hearts didn't lurch like his was doing. He swallowed hard.

"You don't have to...call me Neil," he said hoarsely, feeling as if he were strangling. "I've always...thought of myself as Rory with you."

Maddie nodded. "Rory." Her tongue rolled over the syllables, savoring them like a chocolate truffle. Her eyes affirmed his words. He was "Rory" to her.

There was no condemnation, no distrust.

This is it, his mind confirmed, and his heart soared. Here, in church, was the opportunity he had prayed for. He could make everything right again.

It was time to tell all, and take the consequences, come what may. He loved this woman with the boy. He needed with all his heart to claim his place by her side.

"Mind if I share your hymnal?" he whispered, ruffling Nicky's hair.

Surprise crossed Maddie's features, but only for a moment. She bent down and whispered to Nicky, who scampered to the other side of her, leaving a spot free for Neil.

He stepped in next to her, inhaling her sweet, moonlight scent. Her hand felt warm where their fingers met holding the hymnal.

She was trembling. And he wanted to hold her and comfort her. Desperately.

And if it weren't for the hundreds of people lining the cathedral pews, he would.

"What are you smiling about?" Maddie whispered, seeing the corner of his lips quirk. She elbowed him lightly in the ribs when his shoulders began to shake.

"Tell you later," he whispered back. "That's a promise."

Later.

With amazing swiftness, Maddie's holiday spirit when from glum to exhilarated. Could it be that she would not be spending Christmas alone? Or was she reading too much into a single smile?

Eggnog, a blazing fire, mistletoe—and Rory. It was a scene that warmed her heart.

She closed her eyes to listen as Rory began to sing. The congregation had moved on to "Angels We Have Heard on High," a song that suited his rich baritone to perfection.

She could stand here all night singing Christmas carols, blending her soft soprano with his deep tones, inhaling his spicy male scent. And when he covered her hand with his own and their fingers entwined, it felt like the most natural thing in the world.

Reality intruded like an alarm clock on an early morning when Nicky shifted on his feet and yanked at her sleeve. "I don't know this one, Mom!"

Maddie put a finger to her lips, silently reminding her son not to talk in the middle of a church service.

Rory leaned around Maddie and gestured to Nicky. "Why don't you come stand next to me, sport? That way you can holler if I sing off-key."

Nicky beamed and launched himself at Rory, who, caught off guard, nearly tossed the hymnal in favor of the boy. Both of them broke into muffled laughter, which Maddie chilled with a warning look.

Rory pulled a face and shrugged.

And she thought six-year-olds were trouble!

Smiling at the gentle lapping of peace washing through her, she attempted to shift her thoughts to the service. Her heart stood amazed at how easily Rory fit into their lives. As if he belonged here. As if it were meant to be.

She was intensely aware of how the three of them sat, Nicky sandwiched snugly between the two adults, Rory with his arm casually slung around the back of the pew, his fingers lightly dusting her shoulder. They looked for all the world like a family.

And Maddie felt safe. Warm. Wonderful.

Loved.

Chapter Nineteen

Even Nicky forgot to squirm as the revered tale of the first Christmas was told, and when the lights were dimmed for the final Christmas hymn.

Only the cross at the front of the sanctuary remained illuminated as the acolytes passed their vibrant flame from row to row, candle to candle, down the aisles.

"Hold the candle steady," Maddie whispered in Nicky's ear. "Don't touch the flame."

She was more than a little anxious about allowing her young son to have a candle of his own, but his eyes had been so bright when he'd asked. She couldn't refuse him.

But as Rory bent to light Nicky's candle with his, she saw the boy's expression turn from delight to sheer terror. Too late, she realized the threat the fire represented: the nightmare her son would never be able to forget.

To Nicky, fire was the ultimate enemy. It was bad. It had torn his daddy away from him. It had left scars, both internal and external. It was something to be feared.

It's okay, Nicky. You don't have to light your candle if you don't want to. The words were on the tip of her tongue, clamoring from the depths of her soul.

But Rory was already kneeling by the boy, laying a strong, comforting hand on the boy's shoulder.

"It's okay," Rory soothed, and Maddie felt the tension drain from her shoulders. Rory was here. He would say the words.

But he didn't. He just looked deep into Nicky's eyes, slowed the child's breathing by matching it with his own.

"Look at the flame, Nicky," Rory urged, slowly moving his candle between them. "Do you trust me?"

Nicky's eyes widened, but after a moment's hesitation he nodded.

"This fire won't hurt you." Rory's voice was deep and even, his gaze steadily locked with the boy's.

Maddie held her breath, wanting to stop Rory from pushing Nicky too fast. Her brain felt frozen, her tongue unable to form the words.

"You see, Nicky? You can hold this fire. Do you want to hold it?"

No! Maddie's mind screamed, but her mouth remained rebelliously quiet. Why was Rory pushing Nicky so hard? He was just a boy!

Nicky reached out a tentative hand. Rory wrapped it around the candle, keeping his own hand on top of the boy's until he stopped shaking.

As Nicky stood staring at the flame in his hands, Rory stood and lit Maddie's candle.

Maddie didn't know whether to laugh or cry. But when she met Rory's eyes she read there understanding, not only of her fear, but of the boy's.

She glanced back down at Nicky, who was still quietly staring at his candle. Holding the fire, containing it, controlling it, was exactly what he needed to do.

And Rory had known.

Nicky's eyes were still wide with fear as he held the tiny flame aloft, but his fear was mixed with pride.

The sanctuary glowed with the luminescence of hundreds of candles as the congregation began singing "Silent Night" a cappella.

It was the one hymn to which Nicky knew all four verses. Still carefully holding the candle in two fists, he sang the carol with all the joy and reverence of childhood. If he sang a little off-key, no one noticed. The choir of voices echoing through the cathedral sounded almost heavenly.

Rory moved to her side and put a gentle arm around her shoulders. She looked up into his face and saw in his eyes the reflection of the flame.

He smiled.

She returned the smile and leaned into the strength of his muscular frame. Together, they finished the hymn, Rory's magnificent baritone blending with Maddie's hesitant soprano. And Nicky, with his high, squeaky little-boy voice, made the trio complete.

When the hymn was over, the lights remained low. People blew out their candles and spoke in hushed voices as they bundled up in their winter wear and made their way toward the back of the sanctuary.

Maddie's heart began beating in her throat. Everything had been fine as long as the service had been going, and when she and Rory could be together without tension, without the pressure of making conversation.

He had said they'd talk later. But he really had no reason to stay, other than to tell her what he'd been smiling at earlier. It didn't seem like much. And she *had* to make him stay.

Her mind scrambled for something to say, something

benign that would keep Rory by her side while she figured out what to do.

He was clearly lingering, leaning his hip against
the edge of the pew, arms folded across his chest as he
watched her flutter around, digging through her purse,
helping Nicky into his jacket.

She didn't know what to do with her hands. And she
didn't want to look at Rory. She had been so anxious
to see him, to tell him of her love, proclaim it from the
highest mountaintops. It had appeared incredibly easy,
in her mind.

But now that he was here, she found herself tongue-
tied and visibly shaking. The butterflies in her stomach
were doing loop-de-loops. Some had even escaped to
whirl around in her head.

What in the world should she say? And what would
she do if he turned around and left before she said anything?

Stop! Wait! You can't go yet. I love you!

"Yeah, right, Maddie. Classy," she mumbled to herself.

"Mom?" Nicky asked, pulling on her elbow.

She glanced down to find her son had been joined
by several of his Sunday-school friends. She smiled and
nodded at each boy.

"They're serving cookies and hot cocoa in the fellowship hall," Nicky explained, his gaze brimming with excitement. "Can I go down with my friends?"

Maddie smiled. Nicky never had been one to resist a
cookie. "Sure, son. But don't you boys make a ruckus,"
she warned.

"We won't," the boys said in chorus, racing for the
back of the sanctuary.

Chuckling at their laughter, she met his gentle gaze.

He brushed his hand through the hair near her cheek, then stroked her chin with the back of his fingers. "Well," he said after a full minute of simply staring into her eyes, "guess we've got a few minutes to ourselves. And we *do* need to talk."

Maddie nodded. "Yes. We do." It was difficult to pull herself from the magnetism of Rory's gaze. She could easily lose herself in those dark, flaming eyes. She mentally fortified her bulwarks, knowing that the time had come to put things right.

And there was no guarantee as to what that would mean to her future. She shivered in apprehension.

Facing one another, they sat down together in the nearest pew. Rory gently touched her shoulder, then his hand dropped away.

"It's time that we—" she began.

"You need to know—" he said at the same time.

He chuckled. His low, rich voice sent shivers tingling down Maddie's spine. How she loved this man! And how afraid she was to admit it.

"Ladies first." He nodded for her to continue.

"No, you first," Maddie insisted, her heart in her throat. She had to blurt out the truth before she lost the ability to speak completely.

"I love you," they said in unison.

Maddie broke into nervous laughter, which was echoed by Rory's deep chuckle.

"You do?" she asked, tears of relief and joy pooling in her eyes.

Rory cupped her chin in his palm and met her eyes. She could see the truth there, the warmth of love radiating from those obsidian depths. "You bet I do, lady. I think you stole my heart the night you appeared in my life as Cinderella."

"And you, my mysterious Phantom." She placed her hand over his. "I've got so many things I want to tell you."

His eyes clouded and his smile washed away as if it had never been. Maddie questioned this sudden withdrawal with her gaze, but he looked away.

"What is it?" she whispered, her voice rough with emotion. She couldn't imagine what had brought about the sudden change, but a definite chill had filled her heart as the gap widened between them.

"Maddie, I…"

She turned his hand over and laced her fingers through his. His hand felt so warm and strong, enveloping hers. "There is nothing you can say that will change my love for you, Rory March."

"No?" His eyes blazed. "What about the fire that took Peter's life? I'm responsible for that, and you know it."

"I do know," Maddie agreed quietly. "I know that, in my helplessness—and grief—I turned my anger on a name. Neil March. A faceless man I could make any sort of despicable creature my mind cared to create."

With her free hand, she stroked a finger down his strong jawbone, then turned his head so she could meet his eyes. "Neil March gave me an outlet for my rage, a way for me to feel in control. A place to lay the blame."

"Yes, but I *am* Neil March," Rory protested, his voice lowering an octave.

She felt his grip tighten on her fingers. "No, Rory. You're not the man I imagined. The Neil March I created doesn't exist. You…" She shook her head, smiling gently. Her heart felt ready to burst, she was so happy. The man she loved returned her affection!

Yet she could see the self-condemnation, the loathing in his eyes. All the times she'd reamed Neil March, not knowing she was talking to the man himself, rose to haunt her, and she wished them away. Her mind searched for something to say, something to bring him into her arms, not only now, but forever.

"You feel responsible. I understand that. It was your store. But it was an *accident,* Rory. The police investigated and cleared your store of any blame."

A sound came from Rory's chest that was a cross between a groan and a snort. "Of course they did. Money talks, Maddie. And walks. And clears the guilty in the public eye. But I was there."

Maddie's throat tightened. "What do you mean?" she asked, her mouth dry. Her stomach spun as madly as her thoughts. She was on a precipice, and Rory's next words would either sweep her off her feet and into his arms or over the edge and into the darkness.

Rory's gaze pierced hers. "I mean, I was *there* that day. The day of the fire." He ran his hand over the scar.

"I never… I mean I…" Maddie tried to speak, but words left her as the scene of the fire flashed into her mind. Peter and Nicky entering the workshop display. The cottony snow bursting into a fiery inferno. A man carrying Nicky out of the flames.

Look, Mom! It's the Fireman!

Understanding hit Maddie as the details came together. The mad whirling in her chest was an almost physical sensation.

Rory was the man who saved Nicky's life.

"It was you." She leaned forward, touched the soft, puckered scar with her fingertips. "Nicky knew. He's known all along it was you."

Rory nodded and swallowed twice in rapid succession. "I wanted to save Peter, Maddie. I tried." He clenched his hands into fists as his face contorted with pain and frustration.

"I know." And she did. It was clear as the dawn of a new day. The man she'd blamed as the culprit was actually the hero. She'd spent months hating the man who had rescued her son.

Rory's tortured eyes met hers. "When I jumped through the flames into the workshop, Peter was struggling with Nicky. He thrust the boy into my arms, begged me to save him. I—" he drew a ragged breath "—I promised Peter I'd be back. I *promised*."

"What happened?" She could see each moment of the excruciatingly painful scene in her mind. Only this time, the soot-covered face of Nicky's rescuer was Rory's.

A shirtless, soot-covered man stumbled from the inferno, a small, drooping form in his arms.

"Nicky!" Maddie choked out the name.

Paramedics swept the boy from the man's arms just as Maddie rushed forward.

Oh, God, no! Her soul cried out to heaven as she approached the still, charcoal-dusted form of her son.

They were wrapping him in sterile bandages, gently coaxing an oxygen mask over his nose and mouth.

"Is he...?" Maddie stammered, touching the shoulder of a waiting paramedic. "I'm his mother."

"He's alive," the man said crisply.

Maddie's shoulders slumped in relief.

"But we're taking him to Children's Hospital. You can ride with him if you like." The man turned a grave face toward her. "He's been burned pretty badly, ma'am."

Maddie's breath caught in her throat. "Will he...?" she began again.

The paramedic's eyes clouded with compassion as

he shook his head. *"You'll have to wait until we get to the hospital."*

"Of course," Maddie agreed dully, her voice nothing more than a squeak.

But what about Peter? He was still inside the blaze. How could she go with Nicky when Peter had yet to be rescued?

Her mind pulled for an answer while her heart pumped furiously.

Just as suddenly, she was enveloped with calm, and she reached for it, embraced it. She knew what to do.

Peter would want her to go with their son.

She turned toward the ambulance.

"Let me go!" The man's voice was low and threatening.

The sudden commotion momentarily distracted Maddie. She glanced over to see the soot-covered man who had rescued her son struggling between two uniformed firemen, who were holding him by his arms.

"Let me go!" the man demanded again, his voice coarse from smoke. He wrenched this way and that, clearly trying to wrestle from their grasp.

All Maddie could make out of the man was his broad shoulders and coal-black hair. Or was that soot?

But when he turned his face toward her, she gasped in shock. One whole side of his face had been burned.

"I've got to go back in there!" the man insisted, seemingly unaware of his injury.

"You've been burned," one of the firemen reasoned, keeping his voice at a low, even timbre. *"We're taking you to the hospital."*

"No!" the man yelled, loud enough—despite the crowd—for the sound to echo off the walls. *"I must go back! There's still a man in there!"*

The firemen continued to restrain him.

As the ceiling of the workshop collapsed, there was a rushing sound and a billow of flame.

"No-o-o-o!" the soot-covered rescuer screamed, echoing the agony of her own heart.

"Peter!" Maddie cried simultaneously, reaching her arms out in a powerless gesture.

"P-e-e-e-t-e-r-r-r!"

"Maddie?" Rory took her by the shoulders, his voice low and gentle.

"They wouldn't let you go back for him." It was barely more than a choked whisper.

Rory's shoulders slumped as he recalled the event that haunted him with such ferocity. He'd given his *word*. But the firemen were too strong for him. He'd tried. God knew he'd tried. But they forced him into the ambulance, literally manhandling him despite his adamant protests.

And then it was too late. The workshop made a nightmarish *whooshing* sound as flames engulfed it. A man was dead, and Neil was helpless to stop it.

"When I found out Peter died in that fire, I lost faith. I had been so sure of myself, so ready to conquer the world single-handedly. Even when the fire broke out, I still thought I was in control. But I wasn't."

He paused and swiped a hand down his face. "It's taken me a while to realize I never *have* been in control. I'm not even supposed to be. It was God all along. I placed my faith in the wrong person."

Maddie reached for his hand and gave it a reassuring squeeze.

"I should have learned my lesson. Trusted God. But I couldn't. My father let me down, and then I let myself down. I thought God would do the same."

"God isn't like that," Maddie said, "though I'm a fine one to talk about great faith and trusting God."

"You're wonderful." He hugged her to his chest, filling the empty ache inside with Maddie's love. "I thought God was punishing me when I met you."

"Gee, thanks."

Neil chuckled. "That came out wrong, didn't it? What I meant to say is that I felt it was divine retribution of some sort to fall in love with the one woman who could never love me back. And all because Peter died in my store, and ultimately, I was responsible."

"I love you, Rory March." She squeezed his ribs, making him feel like a giant teddy bear.

He liked it.

"Peter is with God. And you're here with me. Let it go. God forgave you. I forgive you. All that's left is for you to forgive yourself."

He chuckled again, and this time the laughter reached his heart. The restlessness he'd earlier experienced was replaced by a warm glow that felt to Neil like a crackling hearth on a cold winter's night.

"I was so blind." He pulled back, framing her face with his hands, laughter and love welling in his chest. "He wasn't punishing me when He put you in my life. He was giving me the greatest gifts I could ever imagine. He sent his Son." He nodded to the ceramic Nativity scene at the front of the church, shadowed by the cross above it. "And then he sent *you,* Maddie. You and Nicky."

Maddie launched herself into his arms. He spun her around with a whoop, then planted her firmly on her feet again, his voice echoing in the empty sanctuary.

"Your love is all I've ever wanted, more than I ever hoped for. I love you. And I want to spend every day of the rest of my life proving that to you. Will you marry me, Maddie?"

She nodded, tears pooling in her big brown eyes. Smiling, Neil dabbed at the wetness on her cheek with the pad of his thumb.

"I'll ask Nicky, too. Man to man. I want this to be as easy on him as I can make it. I love him too much to hurt him."

"He *did* ask God to make me fall in love with you, remember?"

"So he did." Neil hesitated, then broached a tender subject. "Um, speaking of Nicky…?"

Maddie raised an expectant eyebrow.

"I hoped, I mean I thought that if we spent Christmas together…"

"Yes?"

"I bought Nicky a gift."

"Rory, that's so sweet!"

"I'm not so sure you'll say that when you hear what I got him."

Maddie laughed. "Surprise me."

"Can't do that. This is the kind of gift a mother needs to be prepared for."

"Please don't tell me you bought him a car. He's only six, Rory."

Neil laughed. "No car. I, um…bought him a puppy."

"A *what?*"

"A dog." Neil held up his hands to suspend her protest. "He's a yellow Lab, top-of-the-line champion."

"We have a dog. Max, remember?"

"How could I not? He drooled on my feet." He chuckled. "I wanted to get Nicky a dog of his own, something of the non-drool variety."

"Oh, Rory, that's so sweet!" she exclaimed, bussing him on the cheek.

"It is?" he asked, expecting further argument.

"Nicky's been asking for a dog of his own for ages. He'll be so thrilled!" She wrapped both arms around him and squeezed until his ribs hurt.

"All right, already. Enough gratitude. Now, weren't we talking about a wedding? I want a big one, but I want it soon."

"Then we need to enlist Mom's aid. She's a wonder at pulling big productions together fast."

"Then we'll get ahold of Mom first thing Monday morning," he agreed easily, his business acumen momentarily clicking into gear. "And I'm sure Davis will want to help, too. But first—" he wrapped his arms around Maddie's waist and leaned down until their foreheads were touching "—we have one other small item of business to take care of."

"We do?"

"We do. I promised to tell you what I was chuckling about earlier. I was…" He brought his face closer to hers. He could feel the warmth of her sweet breath against his lips, and his pulse doubled. "…going to kiss you."

"In church?" Maddie whispered with a shaky smile.

"Can you think of a better place to seal our love?"

"I must say I'm relieved that you at least waited till the sanctuary cleared."

"It was difficult, believe me."

"I can't believe you were thinking about such things in the middle of the church service! You were supposed to be paying attention to the service and—"

"Maddie," Neil murmured over her lips.

"Mmm?"

"Shut up and kiss me."

Maddie willingly complied.

Epilogue

Maddie gripped her cream-colored satin wedding dress in one fist and the sleeve of Davis's tuxedo in the other. At the far end of the church, Rory was waiting, but there was a lot of space and a sea of faces on her way to his side.

"Nervous?" Davis asked with a low chuckle.

"No," Maddie growled through clenched teeth. "Mom put a stupid penny in my shoe for good luck, and it's killing me."

"Can you walk with the weight on your heels?"

"Not a chance, with these spikes. What possessed me to have a big church wedding, anyway?"

"You didn't have one the first time around, since you and Peter eloped. Besides, you're a fancy society lady now. Both the major newspapers are covering this event."

Maddie rolled her eyes as her stomach fluttered. "Don't remind me." She *was* nervous, despite what she told Davis. She didn't have a single qualm about tying her life to Rory's, but she definitely feared making a spectacle of herself in front of three hundred people and the five-o'clock evening news.

The wedding march started and Davis patted her hand. "Time to go. You ready?"

"Yeah. Just don't walk too fast or I'll roll down the aisle instead of floating gracefully like I'm supposed to do."

"Don't worry," Davis assured her. "I'm not going to mess up my only chance to walk my daughter down the aisle."

Maddie tightened her grip on his arm and they began their slow march toward the front of the cathedral. Happy faces rose before her. Aunts and uncles she hadn't seen in years. Good friends from the local university, where she'd just begun taking classes in occupational speech therapy. And her mother in the front row, dabbing at her tears with her tissue.

Maddie's eyes widened as she realized Celia was holding Nicky's squirming yellow Lab puppy in her other hand. Who had let a dog in church?

Panic seized her. Something was going to go wrong. *Everything* was going to go wrong. And then there would be no honeymoon at the Brown Palace Hotel.

Then she looked forward, meeting Rory's loving gaze with her own. Nicky stood proudly beside Rory, her "little man" the best man for the day.

Her eyes shifted back to Rory, who held out his hand to her. Love shone from his face, calming the turmoil inside her. The crowded cathedral vanished as she stepped forward, and Rory's warm hand enveloped hers.

He smiled down at her, mouthing "You're beautiful" before turning her toward the minister. Her heart melted as he repeated the vows in his rich, deep voice—vows she echoed loudly, clearly, for the world to hear.

She was facing her future, her love, her life, and she wanted everyone to know. Finally, the minister declared the groom could kiss the bride, but Rory was a tad too slow.

The bride kissed the groom.

* * * * *

AN ANGEL FOR DRY CREEK

Janet Tronstad

This book is dedicated with love to my parents, Richard and Fern Tronstad. First they gave me roots and then they gave me wings. Who could ask for more?

Be not forgetful to entertain strangers: for thereby
some have entertained angels unawares.
—*Hebrews* 13:2

Chapter One

Glory Beckett peered out her car window. She'd driven all day and now, with the coming of dusk, snowflakes were beginning to swirl around her Jeep. The highway beneath her was only a faint gray line pointing northeast across the flatlands of Montana. Other than the hills and a few isolated ranches, there had been little to see in miles. Even oncoming traffic was sparse. For the first time in three days she questioned her hasty decision to leave Seattle and drive across country.

She must be a sight. For ease, she'd given up on curls and simply pushed her flaming auburn hair under a beige wool cap her mother had knitted one Christmas long ago. Her lips were shiny with lip balm and she'd forgotten most of her makeup in Seattle. She considered herself lucky to have remembered her toothbrush. She hadn't had time even to pray about the trip before the decision was made and she was on the road. She'd let the captain scare her for nothing. He'd been a cop too long. Just because a stray bullet had whizzed by her last Wednesday, it was no reason to panic and leave town.

Ever since he'd married her mother last month his worrying had grown worse. She'd reminded him she'd picked up a lot of street savvy in the six years she'd been a sketch artist for his department, but it didn't help.

And maybe he was right. She could still feel the stress that hummed inside her, not letting up even when she prayed. The bullet was only part of it. It was the shooting she'd witnessed that was the worst of it. Even though she'd seen this crime with her own eyes instead of the eyes of others, it still rocked her more than it should. Crimes happened. She knew that. Sometimes she spent a long time in prayer, asking God why something happened. God had always given her peace before.

But prayer hadn't been able to calm her this time. Her nerves still shivered. She didn't feel God was distant. No, that wasn't it. He comforted her, but He didn't remove the unease. Not this time. Since Idaho she'd been thinking maybe stress wasn't all there was to it. Her nerves didn't just shudder, they itched. Something was pushing at her consciousness. Something that she should remember, but couldn't. Something to do with what she'd seen that afternoon at Benson's Market when the butcher, Mr. Kraeman, had been killed. *Dear God, what am I overlooking?* The kid who had shot Mr. Kraeman had been arrested and taken to the county jail. The investigation was closed, awaiting nothing more than the trial. The killer had been caught at the scene. She should relax.

Maybe this cross-country trip would help. She'd always wanted to just take off and drive across the top of the United States. Idaho. Montana. North Dakota. Minnesota. Right to the Great Lakes. And now that her mother had married the captain, there was nothing holding her back. It was odd, this feeling of rootlessness.

In a small town farther east on Interstate 94, the bare branch of an oak tree rested lightly against an upstairs window. Standing inside and looking out through the window, a man could see the soft glow from the security light reflected on the snow in the crevices of the old tree. The snow sparkled like silver dust on an angel's wing.

The midnight view out this second-story window was appreciated by his young sons, but Matthew Curtis didn't get past the glass. All he saw was a window without curtains and his own guilt. If Susie were still alive, she'd have curtains on all the windows. If only Susie were alive, the Bible verses the twins memorized for Sunday school would have some meaning in his life. If only Susie were still alive, everything would be different. If only… Matthew stopped himself. He couldn't keep living in the past.

"Is so angels," Josh was saying as Matthew helped him put his arm into the correct pajama opening. Tucking his five-year-old twin sons into bed was the best part of the day for Matthew. "Miz Hargrove said so. An' they got a big light all round 'em." Josh was fascinated with lights.

Mrs. Hargrove, the twins' Sunday school teacher, was the closest thing to a mother the two had these days. She was one of the reasons Matthew had put aside his own bitterness and rented the old parsonage next to the church when they'd moved to Dry Creek, Montana, six months ago. He wanted the twins to be able to go to church even if he didn't. In Matthew's opinion, a man who wasn't talking to God during the week had no business pretending to shake His hand on Sunday morning just to keep the neighbors quiet.

"I'm sure Mrs. Hargrove is thinking of the angel Gabriel," Matthew said as he smoothed down Josh's hair. Josh, the restless one, was in Power Rangers pajamas. Joey, the more thoughtful twin, was in Mickey Mouse pajamas even though he didn't really like them that much. Joey wasn't enthused about anything, and Matthew worried about him. "And that angel definitely exists."

"See," Josh said to no one in particular. "And my angel can have ten wings if I want and a Power Ranger gun to zap people."

"Angels don't carry guns," Matthew said as he scooped the twins into bed and tucked the quilt securely around them. The weatherman on the news had predicted a mid-December blizzard. "They bring peace."

"Peace," Josh said. "What's peace?"

"Quiet," Matthew said as he turned down the lamp between the twins' beds. "Peace and quiet." And a reminder. "No guns. Angels don't like guns."

Matthew kissed both twins and turned to leave.

"I want to see my angel," Joey whispered. The longing in his voice stopped Matthew. "When can I see her?"

Matthew turned around and sat down on the edge of one of the beds again. "Angels are in heaven. That's a long way away. Most of the time it's too far—they can't come down and see people. They just stay in heaven."

"Like Mommy," Joey said.

"Something like that, I guess." Matthew swallowed.

"Miz Hargrove said that when God took our mommy, He gave us a guardian angel to watch over us," Josh explained.

"I'm here to watch over you." Matthew pulled the covers off his sons and gathered them both to him in a hug. He blinked away the tears in his eyes so his sons would not see them. "You've got me—you don't need an angel."

"We got one anyway," Josh said matter-of-factly, his voice muffled against Matthew's shoulder. "Miz Hargrove says."

* * *

The night road was sprinkled with square green exit signs marking rural communities. Glory had pulled off at a rest stop close to Rosebud and slept for a few solitary hours, curled up in the backseat of her Jeep. Finally, around four in the morning, she decided to keep driving. It was quiet at that time of night even when she came into Miles City, where over 8,000 souls lived. Once she left Miles City behind, the only lights Glory saw were her own, reflected in the light snow on the ground. If all of this darkness didn't cure her stress, nothing would.

Glory needed this time to think. The shooting at the grocery store, and the long minutes afterward when she waited for the paramedics to arrive, reminded her of the accident that had changed her own life six years ago. Gradually, sitting there in the grocery store, all of the old feelings had surfaced. The terror, the paralyzing grief and the long-lasting guilt. Her dreams had stopped the night of the car accident that took her father's life. That night Glory stopped being a carefree college graduate and became a tired adult. She'd awakened in the hospital bed knowing her life was forever changed. Her father was dead. Her mother was shattered. And the words inside Glory's head kept repeating the accusation that it was all her fault. She'd had the wheel. She should have seen the driver coming. It didn't matter that the other driver was drunk and had run a red light. She, Glory, should have known. Somehow she should have known.

There was nothing to do. Nothing to bring her father back.

She tried to put her own pain aside and comfort her mother. Her mother had always seemed like the fragile one in the family. Glory vowed she would take care of her mother. She would do it even if it meant giving up her own dream.

Glory didn't hesitate. Her dream of being a real artist wasn't as important as her mother's happiness. She took the job as a police sketch artist and packed away her oils. Right out of art school, Glory had wanted to see if she could make it in the art world, but the accident had changed all of that. Dreams didn't pay the bills. She'd be willing to live on sandwiches while she painted, but she couldn't ask her mother to do that with her.

But now, seeing her mother happy again, Glory could start to breathe. She no longer felt so responsible. The captain would take care of her mother. Maybe, Glory thought, she could even dream again. She'd always wanted to paint faces. All she needed to do was give her notice to the police department and take out her easel full-time. She had enough in savings to last awhile. When she put it that way, it sounded so simple.

The more miles that sped beneath the wheels of Glory's Jeep, the lighter her heart felt. Maybe God was calling her to paint the faces of His people. Faces of faith. Faces of despair. All of the faces that showed man's struggle to know God. She needed to rekindle her dream. For years she'd been—

"Dry…" Glory murmured out loud as she peered into the snow at the small sign along the interstate. Even with the powerful lights of her Jeep she could barely read it. "Dry as in 'Dry Creek, Montana. Population 276. Five Miles to Food and Gas.'"

Glory turned her Jeep to the left. A throbbing headache was starting between her eyes, and her thermos of coffee had run out an hour ago. It was five-thirty in the morning and she wasn't going to count on there being another town along this highway anytime soon. There was bound to be a little café that served the ranchers in the area. She didn't have much cash left, but her MasterCard had given her a healthy advance back in Spokane and it would no doubt be welcomed here, too. She'd learned that roadside coffee was usually black and strong—just the way she liked it.

Matthew woke with the dawn and went to check on the twins. Ever since Susie had died, he'd been aware of how easy it was for someone to simply stop living. He couldn't bear to lose one of his sons. So he stood in his slippers and just looked at them sleeping in their beds. The security light from the outside of the old frame house shone through the half-frosted window and gave a muted glow to the upstairs bedroom. He pulled the blankets back up on Joey. The electric heater he'd put in the twins' bedroom kept the winter chill away. But the rest of the house was heated with a big woodstove, and he needed to light it so the kitchen would be warm when the twins came down for breakfast.

There were no windows in the hall and the dawn's light didn't come into the stairway that led down to the living room. He took one sleepy step down the stairway. Then another. He needed to add a light for the stairway. Just one more thing in the old house that needed fixing. Like the— Matthew stepped on the loose stair at the same time as he remembered it. The board's edge cracked and his foot slipped. All he could think of as he tumbled down the stairs was that the twins would have no one to fix their breakfast.

Matthew clenched his teeth and fought back the wave of black that threatened to engulf him. Thank God he was alive. "Josh, Joey," Matthew called in a loud whisper. The pain the words cost him suggested he'd broken a rib. That and maybe his leg. "Boys—"

He didn't need to call. They must have heard his fall, because almost immediately two blond heads were staring at him. "Go next door." Matthew said the words deliberately, although his tongue felt swollen. Pain continued to swim around his head. "Get help."

Glory left her Jeep lights on so she could see to make her way to the door of the house next to the church. She had stopped at the café long enough to see that the Closed sign had fly specks on it. It didn't look as if a meal had been served there in months. By then she needed some aspirin for her headache almost more than she needed her morning coffee. When she saw the lights on inside the house that must be the parsonage, she was relieved.

Matthew relaxed when he heard the knock at the door. The twins must have already gone for help. Maybe he'd blacked out. That must be it. Someone had turned the lights on.

Glory heard a rustling behind the door and then she saw it open slowly. She had to look down to see the small blond head, covered by the hood of a snowsuit, peek around the edge of the door. The boy must be going out to play before breakfast. "Is your father here?" she asked as she pulled off her cap. "Or your mother?"

"Who are you?" Another blond head joined the first one. This one had a scarf tied around his neck, even though his Mickey Mouse pajamas didn't look warm enough for outdoor playing.

"My name's Glory. But you don't know me." And then remembering all the warnings children received about strangers, she added, "Don't worry, though. And don't be afraid."

"Don't be afraid." The boy in the snowsuit echoed her words slowly. Glory watched his eyes grow big. "Where are you from?"

Glory decided they didn't get much company around here. They'd probably never heard of Seattle. She pointed west. "A long way away—over those mountains."

"Do you like guns?" the boy in the pajamas demanded.

"Guns? No, I don't approve of guns. Not at all."

"And she's got a big light behind her," the other boy said. "Just like Miz Hargrove said. A glory light."

"Those are my Jeep headlights. Special high beam," Glory explained. "They'll turn off in a minute. If I could just see your father. All I want is an aspirin and maybe a little peace and quiet…and then—"

"Peace and quiet." The twins breathed the words out together as their faces started to beam. "She came."

"Boys," Matthew called weakly. Who were they talking to? He couldn't make out the words, but surely it didn't take that long for someone to figure out he needed help.

"We need you," the twins said as they opened the door wide and each reached out a hand. Glory noticed they were both in slippers. "Our daddy's hurt."

Matthew decided he'd blacked out again, because a woman's face was staring at him. She had hair the color of copper, and it fanned out around her face like a halo. He'd never seen her before. Maybe he was hallucinating, especially because of that sprinkling of freckles that danced across her nose. No one could have freckles like that. So pretty. He tried to concentrate, but felt the darkness closing in on him. He wondered what the perfume was that she wore. It smelled like cinnamon. Cinnamon and something else. That reminded him he hadn't fixed breakfast for the twins. And his job at the hardware store—old Henry would be fretting mad if he called in from his vacation in Florida and no one answered the phone at the hardware store.

Glory looked down at the man in dismay. She could see he'd fallen down the stairs and his leg was at an awkward angle.

"Where's your phone? We've got to call 911," she said as she turned around to the twins. "We'll need an ambulance right away."

The boys just looked at her expectantly. The one had already taken off his scarf and the other was halfway out of his snowsuit. "Can't you just make Daddy all better?" one of them finally asked.

"I'm not a doctor," she said quickly as her eyes scanned the living room. Old sofa, wooden rocker, plaid recliner, Christmas tree with lights but no ornaments—ah, there, on the coffee table, next to a magazine, was a phone. She dialed the numbers: 911. Nothing. Glory shook the phone. She must have dialed wrong. She tried again: 911. Still nothing. What was the matter? There was a dial tone. Surely—then it dawned on her. There was no 911 here. Probably no ambulance, either.

"Who's your nearest neighbor?" Glory put down the phone and turned to the boys. She could already feel her hair flying loose as a result of the static from taking off her cap earlier.

"Mr. Gossett," the boy in the Power Rangers pajamas finally said, but then he leaned closer and confided, "But you won't like him. He drinks bottles and bottles of whiskey. I seen them. Miz Hargrove says he's gonna go to hell someday."

"Well, just as long as he isn't planning to go today,"

Glory said as she pulled her knit cap over her head and walked toward the door.

The next time Matthew woke up he was in the clinic in Miles City. He'd recognize the antiseptic smell of a clinic anywhere. And the gruff voice of Dr. Norris in the background.

"My boys." Matthew croaked out the words. His mouth felt as if it was filled with dry sand.

"Don't worry, your boys are fine," Dr. Norris said as he turned around. "At least for the moment."

"What?"

"Your angel is unloading the vending machine downstairs on their behalf," the doctor said with a smile as he leaned over Matthew. He picked up a small light. "Open wide. We need to check for concussions." The doctor peered into Matthew's eyes.

"What angel?" Matthew asked, and then brightened. "Oh, you mean Mrs. Hargrove. I was hoping someone would think to call her."

"That's not Mrs. Hargrove," the doctor said as he frowned slightly. "At least, not the Mrs. Hargrove I know. I assumed Angel was a family nickname."

"For who?" Matthew asked, bewildered.

"I meant I assumed you called the woman Angel and that's why your sons…" The doctor's voice trailed off and then he added suspiciously, "It's not like a five-year-old to call a woman Angel."

"What are you suggesting?" Matthew started to rise. The room tilted, but he bit his lip and kept going. "And why you would let my boys just go off with a stranger—"

"Don't worry." The doctor put his arm around him and forced him to lie down again. "I'll have the nurse go bring them here. I'm sure it's just some simple misunderstanding. The woman certainly looked harmless enough."

Harmless isn't how Matthew would have described her a few minutes later. She was too pretty to be harmless. Her copper hair was still fanning around her face. This time he saw her gray eyes more clearly. They looked like a stormy afternoon in summer when the blues and grays swirled together without quite mixing. And his sons were looking at her as if they were starstruck. "What are you doing with my boys?"

"What am I doing?" Glory said, dumbfounded. Whatever happened to thank you? Thank you for getting that grumpy Mr. Gossett up in the early-morning hours so he could get help from Mr. Daniel, who ran the volunteer fire department's medical transportation unit. Thank you for writing a fifty-dollar check so the volunteer department would respond to your request, since you were new in town and not on the "paid" list. Thank you for following along in the Jeep the forty miles into Miles City just so the twins could be with you.

"What am I doing?" she repeated, trying to keep her voice calm. "You mean when I'm not emptying my last quarters into the machine out there so that Josh can get a package with only yellow M&M'S in it?"

"They don't make them with only yellows," Matthew said. She reminded him of fire. The way her hair shone in the fluorescent light.

"I know," the woman said wearily.

"You asked me what I wanted," Josh said simply. "I thought it'd be easy for you, since you're—"

Glory held up her hand to stop him.

Matthew watched as Josh closed his mouth. The woman had more powers than he did, Matthew thought to himself ruefully. He could never get Josh to close his mouth when he wanted to speak.

"That might be the wrong way to say it," Matthew said, easing back to the bed. He needed to clear his mind. "I'm grateful for all you've done, of course."

"You're welcome," Glory said politely. She needed to remember the man was disoriented. Disoriented and not nearly so naked now that the doctor had wrapped a wide white bandage around his rib cage. She wondered if he remembered that she'd been the one to gently run her fingertips over his chest to check for broken ribs before she put a blanket over him and they waited for the fire department to come. His chest was the kind that would inspire her if she were a sculptor.

"It's just—" Matthew bit his lips. "I don't know who you are. And with all the strange people around lately…"

"She's not strange people," Josh protested. "She's—"

"I'm Glory." Glory interrupted the boy and gave him a stern look. "Glory Beckett."

"She's an angel," Joey said, his eyes sparkling with excitement.

"And she's got a glory light," Josh added. The boy literally glowed with pleasure.

Glory bowed her head. She'd been through this explanation already. Four times. And that was before the requested M&M'S miracle. "I've got special beams on my Jeep. That's all it is. No angel magic." She turned to look at the man in the bed. Now he'd really be worried. "I'm sorry, this isn't my idea."

"I know." Matthew smiled, and then he started to chuckle until he felt the pain in his ribs. "But you haven't tried to argue with the logic of our Mrs.—"

"Your Mrs.?" Glory interrupted stiffly. She should have known there would be a Mrs. somewhere in this picture. "If I'd known you were married, I'd have tried to locate your wife. But the twins didn't mention—"

"Married? Me? No, I meant our Mrs. Hargrove," Matthew echoed, his smile curling around inside himself. He liked the way her lips tightened up when she talked about him being married. "Mrs. Hargrove isn't married. I mean—" he fumbled "—of course, Mrs. Hargrove *is* married, but not to me. I'm not, that is. Married."

"I see," Glory said, and drew in her breath. "Well, that explains the boys. A single father and all."

"Oh," Matthew said ruefully. The woman hadn't been thinking of his being married at all. At least, not in those terms. "Is there something wrong with the boys?"

"Of course not," Glory protested. "They're wonderful boys." She'd already grown to like them. "They're bright—and warmhearted." She stopped. Sometimes, looking at children, she'd feel the pain again from the accident that had robbed her of the chance to be a mother. She was determined to fight that pain. She refused to be one of those sentimental women who either wept or gushed over every child they saw. She cooled her enthusiasm. "And they have good bone structure."

Glory patted the twins on the head. She was safe with bone structure.

Josh scowled a minute, before Joey poked him with his elbow.

"Is that something angels have?" Joey asked hopefully. "That good bone stuff?"

"No, I'm afraid not," Glory said as she knelt so that she was at eye level with the boys. "Angels aren't worried about bone structure. I don't even know if God created them with bones. Although I suppose with those big wings and all they'd have to have something like bones…."

"See, I told you," Josh began. "She knows—"

Glory held up her hand. "The only thing I know about angels is what I've read in the Bible. I wouldn't know an angel if I met one on the street."

"You wouldn't?" Joey asked sadly.

"Not a chance," Glory assured him. She started to reach out to ruffle his hair again, but then pulled back. Maybe little boys didn't like that any more than she'd liked it as a little girl. "But you don't need an angel. You've got a father—" She eyed Matthew a little skeptically and then continued determinedly, "A good father—and you've got Mrs. Hargrove, and each other."

"We don't have a dog," Josh said plaintively.

"Well, maybe someday you can get a dog," Glory said. She was handling this pretty well, she thought. "Wouldn't you rather have a puppy than an angel?"

Glory didn't look at Matthew. She knew she had no right to even suggest he get the boys a puppy. But it seemed like a small thing. And they really were very nice little boys. Josh was already starting to beam.

"Can it be a yellow dog?" Josh asked, looking at Glory as if she had a dozen in her purse. "I'd like a yellow dog."

"Well, I don't know if today is the day," Glory stalled.

"I don't want a puppy." Joey shook his head and looked at Josh. "A puppy hasn't been in heaven. He can't tell us what our mommy looks like."

Joey looked expectantly at his father. "Mommy used to sing to us and make us cookies."

"Oatmeal with extra raisins," Matthew assured him. The trust in his son's eyes made him forget all about his cracked rib and his sprained knee. If he had been wearing more than this flimsy hospital robe, he would have walked over to them and hugged them no matter how his ribs felt. "And she loved you both very much."

"I don't even care about the cookies," Joey said bravely. "I just want to know what she looked like."

"Well, surely you have pictures." Glory turned to look at Matthew.

"There was a fire," Matthew said. The fire had burned down the first house they'd lived in after they moved away from Havre. At the time, it felt as if the fire was just finishing the job fate had already begun. He hadn't known the twins would miss a few pictures this much.

"Well, your father can tell you what she looked like," Glory offered softly. For the first time, she wished she was an angel. She'd give those little boys a puppy and a cookie-baking mother, too.

"But I can't *see* her," Joey said. "Telling isn't seeing."

"I can help you," Glory said without thinking.

"What?" Matthew and Dr. Norris both asked at the same time and in the same disapproving tone.

"I can help them see their mother," Glory said, turning to Matthew. She would do it, she thought excitedly.

"Look, I guess it's fair play after all they've put you through," Matthew said indignantly. "But I won't have you making fun of their make-believe."

"I wouldn't do that," Glory protested. How could such a distrustful man raise two such trusting sons? "And I can help. I've drawn hundreds of pictures from descriptions I've been given."

"You could?" Matthew asked, and then blinked suspiciously fast. "You really could draw a picture of the boys' mother—of Susie?"

"Yes," Glory said. Why was it that the same dreamy quality in the boys' eyes irritated her when it was mirrored in the eyes of their father, the man who had been married to the woman she was going to paint? She squared her shoulders. She didn't have time to worry about a man. She was an artist now. She was going to paint a masterpiece. The face of one of God's creations. "It'll be my pleasure."

"Hallelujah," Dr. Norris said as he bent down and swabbed Matthew's arm. Then, as he stuck a needle in Matthew's arm, he added, "Sounds like maybe she's an angel after all."

Matthew grunted.

Glory swallowed her protest. She was the only one who saw the self-satisfied nod the twins exchanged.

The Bullet kept his eyes averted. He wore his cap pulled low over his forehead even though the musty darkness shadowed his face. The inside of the parked limo was damp and the rain slid silently over the windshield. A streetlight overhead cast a feeble glow inside the car, outlining the man next to him.

"You're sure she's a new hit?"

"Not technically," the man finally admitted. His words were low and clipped. "But she's as good as…the other try was nothing…a gang shooting—slid by easy."

"I charge extra for repeats," the Bullet said, his lips drawing together. He didn't like it when clients tried to get gang kids to do their dirty work. "Extra for cops, too."

"She's no cop," the man said impatiently. "Draws pictures. That's all."

"Still, they look out for their own," the Bullet pressed further. "She got any cop training? Guns, anything?"

"Naw. She's easy."

The Bullet grimaced. "I'll settle for fifteen," the Bullet said. "Half up front."

The client nodded and held out a paper bag full of cash. "Here's seventy-five hundred, Mr. Forrest Brown."

The Bullet froze. Nobody knew him by name. He was the Bullet to all of Seattle. *If he knows who I am, he knows where I live. My God, he knows about my Millie!*

Chapter Two

"You best behave yourself," Mrs. Hargrove whispered to Matthew as she leaned on the counter of the hardware store. Matthew was sitting on a folding chair behind the counter with his leg propped up on a trash can. He wasn't feeling too well, and Mrs. Hargrove's powdered violet perfume didn't help.

"I assure you…" Matthew started, but he didn't have a full head of steam going and it was almost impossible to stop the older woman without one. Besides, truth to tell, he didn't really mind her scolding him. Listening to her gave him time to watch Glory set up an easel with the twins' help in the front of the store.

"Humph," Mrs. Hargrove said, turning to follow the aim of his eyes before continuing, "You may be a man of the cloth—"

"What?" Matthew jerked himself back to the conversation. That was his secret. No one here was supposed to know. "What do you mean?"

Sweat broke out on Matthew's forehead. He had hoped no one here would ever find out. How could he explain that his faith was tied in knots? He used to love the ministry, knowing he was helping people find God's mercy.

He'd known he needed to leave the ministry when he no longer believed in that mercy, when he couldn't even pray in public anymore. That last morning, he'd just stood in the pulpit, unable to speak. Finally the choir director figured out something was wrong and had the choir start a hymn. But the hymn didn't help. He was still mute. All he could remember were the words of the prayers he'd prayed for Susie and the confidence he'd had. The words of those prayers rose like bile in his throat. His prayers had turned to dust when she died. How could a man with no faith be a minister? "I'm not a minister. Not anymore…"

"But a man's a man in my book," Mrs. Hargrove continued, and pointed her finger at him. "And that woman over there is a sight more tempting than a real angel would ever be. And don't think other people haven't noticed."

"What other people?" Matthew looked around. The only two other people in the store were Elmer and Jacob, two semi-retired ranchers who stopped by the hardware store every morning for their cup of coffee. They were arguing across the checkerboard Henry kept by the woodstove. When Matthew looked at them, Elmer lifted his bearded face, gave him a slow knowing wink, stood up and then started walking toward the counter.

When Elmer reached the front of the counter, he looked squarely at Matthew. "Heard you got yourself an angel."

"She's not an angel," Matthew protested automatically.

Elmer nodded solemnly. "Looks like an angel to me. You lucky dog. Got an inside track with her, since she's staying at your place."

"Staying at my place—" Matthew echoed in panic. He

hadn't given any thought to where Glory would stay. The only hotel around was back in Miles City. That would be too far. But where would she stay at his place? He supposed she'd have to stay in his room. The old house had only two bedrooms, and the sofa was too lumpy for a guest. No, he'd have to take the sofa. Which was fine, but he worried about her up in his room. He couldn't remember if he'd put his socks away last night or not. Last night, nothing—try the past week. Socks everywhere.

"She can't stay at my place. I'm single," Matthew said, relieved to remember the fact. Glory would never see his dirty socks. Or the calendar on his wall that was stuck back in September even though it was December 19. "It wouldn't be proper, would it, Mrs. Hargrove?"

Matthew smiled confidently. Being single did have certain advantages.

"I would ask her to stay with me. She seems like a very nice lady," Mrs. Hargrove said earnestly, and then shrugged her shoulders. "But I can't."

The smile that was forming on Matthew's lips faded. "Why not?"

"The twins love the Christmas story," Mrs. Hargrove explained. "They'd be very disappointed if they couldn't keep the angel in their house. Besides, the doctor says there's no way you can get up those stairs, so it's perfectly proper."

As though that settled the matter, Mrs. Hargrove ran her finger over the plastic jug of wrenches standing on the counter. "Doesn't that Henry ever dust anything in here? Decent folks wouldn't shop here even if they had any extra money."

"Henry doesn't notice the dust," Matthew said. He wondered if Glory had noticed how dusty it was in the hardware store. Of course she'd noticed, he thought.

He could see her frowning at the window beside her. It could use a good washing. He'd started to clean up Henry's store now that the man was gone to his daughter's in Florida for a long winter vacation, but Matthew had started in the back, in the stockroom.

"Excuse me, Mrs. Hargrove," Matthew said as he reached for his crutches. "I think I best get my bottle of window cleaner and——" Matthew nodded in the general direction of Glory.

But before Matthew could stand, Glory came over to the counter.

"I'd like to buy a brush," Glory said. The hardware store looked as if it could use some business, and she assumed they had a fine-tip brush that could serve her uses. "Make that a dozen and a can of turpentine."

"Brushes are over there," Matthew said, and started to rise. "Most of them are for real painting—I mean, not for artists, but there might be one or two small enough."

"You just sit back down," Mrs. Hargrove said as Matthew fitted the crutches under his arms. "You aren't in any shape to be fetching brushes." Mrs. Hargrove walked toward the shelf and returned with a dozen paintbrushes. Glory put her platinum plastic card on the counter. "I assume you take credit cards."

"Some days that's all we take," Matthew said as he pulled out the credit card duplicator and picked up the phone for verification.

Matthew punched in the numbers of Glory's credit card. He didn't want to admit it, but hers was the first platinum card he'd ever processed. Most people in Dry Creek thought they were rich if they qualified for the gold card. "Is there something different about a platinum card?"

"Different?"

"Your numbers aren't taking," Matthew said as he punched another number to speak to an operator. "Maybe I'm doing something wrong."

"Oh." Matthew's frown had grown deeper as the operator on the other end spoke.

Matthew hung up the phone. "Your card's been canceled."

"Canceled? How could it be canceled?"

"It seems you're, ah, dead."

"Dead! But that's ridiculous. I mean—how?"

"They didn't say how it happened," Matthew offered. He didn't want to think of the implications of Glory trying to run a fraudulent card through his system.

"There's no 'how' to it," Glory snapped. "It hasn't happened. I'm perfectly healthy, as anyone can see."

"Perfectly," Matthew agreed. She did look healthy, especially with the indignant flush on her cheeks. Maybe she'd simply missed a payment or two and that was the reason they were canceling her card.

"Can I use your phone?" Glory finally said. She'd call the captain. He'd said he'd take in her mail while she was gone. He could solve the mystery. "Collect, of course."

Matthew handed her the phone, and Glory turned her back slightly to make the call.

"Thank God you called," the captain said when he heard her voice. "I was worried."

"I just called two days ago," Glory protested. "I'm fine, except for my credit card."

"Ah, yes. I canceled your card. Not as easy as you'd think. I had to claim official business and tell them you'd died."

"You *what?*" Glory protested and then, remembering her audience, turned to give a reassuring smile to Matthew and Mrs. Hargrove. She didn't want them to think she was broke, let alone dead. She turned her back to them.

"Someone jimmied your mailbox yesterday," the captain said. "Took your credit card bill."

"The bill—they can have it."

"With the bill, someone can trace you," the captain pointed out patiently. "Find out what hotels you're staying at. Where you're buying gas. It's not that hard. Someone real sophisticated will find a way to get your charges the same day you make them. By now, they probably know what state you're in. Remember that shot. First the shooting at the grocery store and then that shot coming the next day so close to you. I don't like it. Not with someone taking your credit card bill."

"Surely you don't think—" Glory sputtered. "Thank goodness I haven't used the card since Spokane. But I can't believe— It was probably just some kids breaking in."

"They didn't break in to the other mailboxes in your building."

"Maybe they got tired. Thought of something better to do."

The captain was silent. "Maybe. Then I keep wondering if something wasn't fishy about that shooting at Benson's. Could be more was happening than you've remembered."

"Just the butcher standing by the meat counter. Had a package of steaks in one hand and the time card of one of his assistants in the other."

"We checked the name on the time card. The clerk didn't have a dispute."

"Least, not one they're talking about," Glory added.

"No extra keys on him, either," the captain continued. "If it was a robbery, there was no reason to shoot the man. He wasn't holding anything back."

"But if it was a robbery, why wait to make the hit when the armored transport had just made the pickup to go to the bank?"

"Ignorance?"

"Yeah, and anyone that ignorant wouldn't think to trace a credit card." Glory pushed back the prickles that were teasing the base of her spine. The captain was paranoid. He had to be. She hadn't been the only one at Benson's. She'd already told the police everything she knew. Besides, the bullet that had gone whizzing by a day later was gang related. The department was sure of that.

"Yeah, you're probably right. I'll go ahead and call the credit card company."

"Good." Glory took a deep breath. "When can I use the card?"

"Ten days. Takes them that long to verify," the captain said hesitantly. "I'll wire you some money. Your mom and I are heading off for that trip we told you about, but we'll drop it on our way. Tell me where you are."

"Dry Creek, Montana," Glory said. She looked over her shoulder. Matthew and Mrs. Hargrove were trying to look inconspicuous, a sure sign they'd overheard everything.

"Trouble?" Matthew said sympathetically as Glory hung up the phone and turned around. He could see she was embarrassed. "Don't worry about the brushes. Henry runs tabs for people all the time. You can pay when you can."

"No problem. I'm expecting a money order to come here to the post office, maybe even tomorrow," she said brightly.

Matthew looked at Mrs. Hargrove. Mrs. Hargrove looked at Matthew.

"We don't have a post office," the older woman finally said.

"No post office?" Glory said as her stomach started to sink. "Can I borrow the phone again?"

The captain's phone rang seven times before the secretary came on the line to say he'd just walked out the door to leave for his vacation.

"Can you leave a message just in case he calls before he leaves?" Glory asked. She wished she'd brought the captain's new unlisted home phone number with her. She hadn't bothered, because her mother and the captain were going to be on their trip.

After she left the message, Glory turned around. She was stuck. Stuck in Dry Creek. Unless. "I'd be happy to work in exchange for the brushes. The store looks like it could use some more help."

Matthew hesitated.

"I'm willing to work for minimum wage."

"I wish I could," Matthew said apologetically. "But we've already got a dozen job applications in the drawer. There aren't many jobs in Dry Creek this time of year. There'd be an uprising if I gave a job to an outsider when so many people here want one," Matthew finished lamely. Maybe he should chance the anger of the townspeople.

"I didn't know it was that bad." Glory said.

"We get by." Mrs. Hargrove lifted her chin. "In fact, there's talk of starting a dude ranch over on the Big Sheep Mountain place."

"That's just talk," Elmer said sharply. "The Big Sheep's been a cattle ranch for more than a hundred years. Started out as the XIT Ranch and then became

the Big Sheep. We've got history. Pride. We don't need
a bunch of city folks messing things up with their Jeeps
and fancy boots. You know as good as me, they won't
stay inside the fences. They'll scare the elk away. Not to
mention the eagles. Before you know it, the Big Sheep
Mountains will be empty—no animals at all, not even
the cows."

"Better that than empty of people," Mrs. Hargrove
replied as she tightened her lips. "It's old fools like you
that can't make way for progress."

"Old fool? Me?" Elmer protested. "Why, I rode in the
Jaycee Bucking Horse Sale last May. On Black Demon.
Nothing old about me." He sighed. "Ah, what's the use.
You're just worried about your son's family."

Mrs. Hargrove nodded slowly. "He said they'd have
to move come spring if something doesn't open up. He's
worked for the Big Sheep Mountain Cattle Company for
ten years, but this rustling has them in a bind. They're
losing too many cattle and they're going to start laying
off hands." Mrs. Hargrove refocused on Glory as though
just remembering she was there. The older woman settled
her face into a polite smile. "I don't mean to go on about
our troubles. We get by just fine. God is good to us."

"Of course," Glory said carefully. She knew a wall of
pride when she bumped into it, and Mrs. Hargrove had
it in abundance. Matthew did, too. She hadn't given any
thought to how Matthew managed on his salary, but now
she remembered the frayed collars on the twins' shirts
and the mended pocket on Joey's jacket. She'd have to
send him some money when she got home. In fact—

"How about a check? I can pay for the brushes with
a check," Glory offered in relief. She wasn't totally
stranded, after all.

"A check is fine," Matthew said heartily. He'd remember to pull it out and replace it with cash from his own pocket before he took the checks to the bank. He had no doubt her check would bounce as high as her credit card had and he didn't want to embarrass her further. "It's 12.64 for the brushes and turpentine."

"Good." Glory started to write the check. "And I'll add a little extra for you—"

"You don't need to tip someone who works in a hardware store," Matthew said stiffly. A red flush settled around his neck. "The service is free."

"Of course," Glory said quickly. There she'd gone and offended him. She finished the check. "Twelve sixty-four exactly."

Glory counted the checks in her checkbook. She had ten left. That was enough to pay for meals and a hotel for a few nights.

"Where's the hotel from here?" she asked. She couldn't remember seeing one, but there must be one. Every town had a hotel.

"There's no hotel here," Mrs. Hargrove said as she nudged Matthew.

"Oh. Maybe a bed-and-breakfast place?"

There was a long pause as Mrs. Hargrove nudged Matthew again.

Matthew finally said, "I'm sure there's someone in town with an extra room who would let you—"

"Well, aren't you in luck, then," Mrs. Hargrove said with a determined enthusiasm. "Since Matthew hurt his knee, his room will be empty. The doctor says he can't climb the stairs with his sprain, so I'm sure no one will think anything of it. Besides, the twins are good chaperones."

Matthew felt trapped and then guilty. The least he

could do was provide her lodging. "We'd be honored to have you stay with us for a few days."

"There's no one who does this more like a business?" Glory asked. The thought of staying in this man's room made her feel uneasy. She'd smell his aftershave on the pillows and see his shirts in the closet. "I can pay." Surely one of those families that wanted a job would take in a boarder for a few nights. "I'll even throw in a turkey for Christmas dinner."

"I'm afraid there's only Matthew and his boys," Mrs. Hargrove said.

Glory bent her head to start writing her check. "How does one hundred dollars a night sound?"

"One hundred!" Matthew protested. No wonder she had financial troubles. "We're not the Hilton. Besides, you'd be our guest."

Glory had finished the check by the time he finished. No wonder he had financial troubles. "I can be your guest and still pay a fair price."

"No, there's no need," Matthew said.

"I insist," Glory said as she ripped off the check and presented it to him.

Matthew raised his eyebrows at the amount of the check. He supposed it didn't matter what amount she wrote the check for when it was going to bounce anyway, but three hundred dollars was a lot to pay for several nights' food and lodging.

"Consider it a Christmas present," Glory said grandly. "For the twins."

"They'll appreciate it," Matthew said dryly.

Glory flipped her wallet to the plastic section. "You'll want to see my driver's license."

"Henry doesn't bother. He knows the folks here who write checks," Matthew said as he took a sidelong look at the driver's license anyway. He was pleased to see she was Glory Beckett. She might be a bad risk from the credit company's viewpoint, but she wasn't a thief. That is, unless she was so polished she had gotten a fake driver's license to go with her story.

"He doesn't know me," Glory said as she moved her driver's license so it came into Matthew's full view. "You'll want to write down the number."

"All right," Matthew said as he noted her driver's license number.

"Good," Glory said as she put her checkbook back in her purse and turned to walk back to her easel.

"You're not going to cash those checks, Matthew Curtis," Mrs. Hargrove demanded in a hushed whisper as they watched Glory sit down to her easel across the store in front of the display window.

"Of course not," Matthew agreed as he slipped the checks out of the drawer.

Carl Wall, the deputy sheriff, was running for re-election and his campaign slogan was No Crime's Too Small To Do Some Time. He'd happily jail an out-of-towner for writing a bad check and brag about it to voters later.

Ten minutes later, Glory repositioned the easel. Then she arranged her brushes twice and turned her stool to get more light. She was stalling and she knew it. She suddenly realized she'd never painted a portrait as agonizingly important as this one. The sketches she'd done of criminals, while very important, were meant only for identification and not as a symbol of love.

"Do you want your mother to be sitting or standing?" Glory asked the twins. The two identical heads were studying the bottom of a large display window. They each had a cleaning rag and were making circles in the lower portion of the window while Matthew reached for the high corners, standing awkwardly with one crutch.

"I don't know." Josh stopped rubbing the window and gave it a squirt of window cleaner. "Maybe she could be riding a dragon. I've always wanted a picture of a dragon."

"Mommies don't ride dragons," Joey scolded his brother. "They ride brooms."

Matthew winced. Susie had been adamantly opposed to celebrating Halloween and, consequently, the twins had only a sketchy idea of the spooks that inspired other children's nightmares.

"No, sweetie, it's witches who ride brooms." Mrs. Hargrove corrected the boy with a smile as she picked up a cleaning rag and joined Matthew on the high corners. "Maybe you could have a picture painted of your mother praying."

"No," Matthew said a little more loudly than he intended. His memories of Susie praying tormented him. He knew she would be heartbroken that her death had brought a wedge between him and God, but his feelings were there anyway. If he lived to be a hundred, he'd never understand how God could have answered his prayers for so long on the small things like good crops and passing tests but when it came to the one big thing—Susie's recovery—God had let him down flat. No sense of comfort. No nothing. He'd expected his faith to carry them through always.

Matthew didn't feel like explaining himself. His arms were sore from the crutches and he hobbled over to a stool that was beside Glory. "I want the twins to remember their mother laughing. She was a happy woman."

"Well, that'd make a good picture, too," Mrs. Hargrove said, and then looked at the twins. The twins had stopped wiping their circles and were listening thought-fully. "You'd like that, wouldn't you?"

The twins nodded.

"Okay, smiling it is," Glory said. This Susie woman sounded like a saint, always smiling and praying and baking cookies, and Glory had no reason to resent her. None whatsoever, she thought to herself. "I assume she had all her teeth."

"What?" Matthew seemed a little startled with the question.

"Her teeth," Glory repeated. "If I'm going to paint her smiling, I need to know about her teeth. Were there any missing?"

"Of course not."

"Were any of them crooked?" Glory continued. "Or chipped? Did she have a space between the front ones?"

"They were just teeth," Matthew said defensively. Why did he suddenly feel guilty because he couldn't remember what kind of teeth Susie had? He knew her image was burned onto his heart. He just couldn't pull up the details. "Her eyes were blue—a blue so deep they'd turn to black in the shadows."

"Eyes. Blue. Deep," Glory said as she wrote a note on the butcher paper she'd stretched over her easel. "And her nose, was it like this? Or like this?" Glory sketched a couple of common nose styles. "Or more like this?"

"It was sort of like that, but more scrunched at the be-ginning," Matthew said, pointing to one of the noses and feeling suddenly helpless. He hadn't realized until now that the picture Glory was going to paint was the picture that was inside his head. He'd spent a lot of time trying to get Susie's face out of his mind so he could keep himself going forward. What if he'd done too good a job? What if he couldn't remember her face as well as he should?

"Pugged nose," Glory muttered as she added the words to the list on the side of the paper. "Any marks? Moles? Freckles? Warts?"

"Of course not. She was a classic beauty," Matthew protested.

"I see," Glory said. She tried to remind herself that she was doing a job and shouldn't take Matthew's words personally. "I have freckles."

Glory winced. She hadn't meant to say that.

"I noticed them right off." Matthew nodded. "That's how I knew you couldn't be an angel."

"I see," Glory said icily. Couldn't be an angel, indeed. Just because Susie didn't have freckles. She'd show him who couldn't be an angel. "Any other identifying facial marks?"

"I liked the way your hair curled," Matthew offered thoughtfully as he remembered lying on his back after his fall and looking up at Glory. "It just spread all out like a sunflower—except it was brass instead of gold." He had a sudden piercing thought of what it would be like to kiss a woman with hair like that. Her hair would fall around him with the softness of the sun.

"I meant Susie. Did she have any other identifying facial marks?" Glory repeated.

"Oh," Matthew said, closing his eyes in concentration. Could Susie have had freckles after all? Even a few? No, she'd made this big production about never going out in the sun because her skin was so fair—like an English maiden, she used to say. What else did Susie always say? Oh, yes. "Peaches and cream. Her skin was a peaches-and-cream complexion."

"Well, that's a nice poetic notion," Glory said as she added the words to her list.

"What do you mean by that?" Matthew opened his

eyes indignantly. Glory had gone all bristly on him, and he was trying his best to remember all the details just as she wanted.

"It's just that peaches have fuzz—and cream eventually clots. The whole phrase is a cliché. It doesn't describe anything. No one's skin looks like that. Not really."

"Well, no," Matthew admitted. "It's just hard to remember everything."

"True enough." Glory softened. She had gotten descriptions from hundreds of people in her career. She should know not to push someone. Often a victim would have a hard time recalling the features of their assailant. She imagined the same thing might be true when grief rather than fear was the problem. "Don't worry about it. We'll do it one step at a time. We'll be done by Friday."

"But Friday's not the pageant. You've got to stay until the pageant," Josh said solemnly. "They've never had a real angel before in the pageant."

"I'm not an—" Glory protested automatically as she turned to the twins. They both looked so wistful. "I'm sorry, but I can't stay. Even though I'd love to see my two favorite shepherds in their bathrobes."

"How'd you know we're wearing bathrobes?" Josh demanded.

"She's an angel, that's how," Joey said proudly. "She's just an undercover angel, so she can't tell anyone. Like a spy."

"Do you know everyone's secrets?" Josh asked in awe.

"I don't know anyone's secrets," Glory said, and then smiled teasingly. "Unless, of course, you do something naughty."

"Wow, just like Santa Claus," Josh breathed excitedly. "Can you get me a *Star Trek* laser light gun for Christmas?"

"I thought we talked about that, Josh," Matthew interjected. "You know Santa is just a story."

"I know," Josh said in a rush. His eyes were bright with confidence. "But she's an angel and she can tell God. That's even better than Santa Claus. God must have lots of toys."

"We'll talk about this later," Matthew said. He'd have to sit down with Josh and explain how the universe worked. Whether he asked God or Santa Claus for a present, it didn't matter. Neither one of them could buy Josh a gift unless it could be found in Miles City for twenty dollars or less.

"Can you tell God?" Josh ignored his father and whispered to Glory. "I've been a good boy, except for—well, you know—the bug thing."

Glory didn't think she wanted to know about the bug thing. "I'm sure you have been a good boy," she said as she knelt to look squarely at the boy. "I'll tell you what, why don't you draw a picture of this laser gun and color it. That way, if you want to send God a picture, He'll know what it looks like."

"Me, too," Joey asked. "Can I make a picture, too?"

"Why not?" Glory said, and included him in her smile. Even if her credit card wouldn't live again by Christmas she could send a check to one of her girlfriends. Her friend Sylvia ran a neighborhood youth center and would be visiting that huge toy store in Seattle anyway. Even though most of the kids Sylvia worked with were more likely to own a real pistol than a water pistol, Sylvia insisted on treating them as though they were ordinary children at the holidays. The kids loved her for it.

"But…" Matthew tried to catch Glory's eye.

"Daddy needs one, too," Joey said. The twins both looked at her with solemn eyes. It had taken her several hours to figure out how to tell them apart. Joey's eyes were always quieter. "But Daddy's old."

"No one's too old for Christmas wishes," Glory said.

"Really?" Joey smiled.

It was dusk by the time Glory finished her sketch of Susie and they all went home for dinner. Glory offered to cook, but Matthew declared she had already done her work for the day. Glory was too tired to resist. Sketching Susie had been difficult. Matthew had never wanted to look at the full face of the sketch, and so she'd pieced it together an eyebrow at a time. Even when she'd finished, he'd pleaded fatigue and asked to look at the sketch on the next day.

Matthew went to the kitchen to cook dinner, leaving Glory on the sofa with a *Good Housekeeping* magazine.

"I've learned to be a good cook," Matthew said a little bleakly as he sat down a little later and leaned his crutches against the dining-room wall. The smell of burned potatoes still hung in the air even though all the windows were now open. "Dinner doesn't usually float in milk."

"Cereal is all right," Glory assured him. She'd realized when the smoke drifted into the living room that dinner would be delayed.

"I like the pink ones," Joey said as he poured his bowl full of Froot Loops.

"I always keep cornflakes for me," Matthew said as he handed the box to Glory. "I'm afraid we don't have a wide selection."

"Cornflakes are fine," Glory said. "I often eat light."

Matthew chided himself. He should have realized. She lived on the road, likely by her wits. Of course she ate light. He should have made sure she had a decent meal.

"We'll eat better tomorrow, I promise. Something with meat in it. And if you need anything, just ask."

"I will," Glory assured him, and smiled.

Her smile kicked Matthew in the stomach. The sun shone about her when she smiled. No wonder his sons thought she was an angel.

"Daddy?" Joey was looking at Matthew.

Matthew pulled himself together. It was time for grace.

"Hands," Matthew said and offered his hand to Joey on the one side. He didn't realize until his hand was already extended that Glory was on his other side.

"I'll say grace," Josh offered as he put one hand out to Joey and the other to Glory. He looked shyly at Glory. "I washed. I'm not jammy."

"I know." Glory smiled softly as she reached easily for his hand. His small hand snuggled trustingly in her palm. She held her other hand out to Matthew. His hand didn't snuggle. Instead, it enveloped her. She swore her pulse moved from her wrist to the center of her palm. She wondered if he could feel the quickening beat in her. What was wrong with her? He'd think she'd never held a man's hand before. Not that she was holding his hand now. It was prayer hand-holding. That's all. Just because his thumb happened to caress the inside of her finger.

"Okay, Daddy?" Josh asked again, looking at his father. "It's my turn to say grace."

Matthew nodded his permission. What was wrong with him? Even Josh was looking at him funny. Matthew was beginning to think he'd never held a woman's hand before. Glory's skin was softer than fine leather. She must use some kind of lotions on her hands because of her work in paints. That must be it. Just lotions. He cleared his throat. "Sure. Go ahead."

Josh bowed his head and carefully screwed his eyes closed. "Thank you, God, for this day and for this food and for our comp—" Josh stumbled "—company. Amen."

"Thank you, Josh," Glory said when he looked up again. "I'm honored to be your company."

"If there's anything you need..." Matthew offered again.

The only thing she needed, she thought later that evening, was some more paint. The twins had been put to bed and she was sitting on the sofa reading her magazine and talking with Matthew as he sewed a button on Josh's winter coat. The light from the two lamps made round circles on the ceiling and bathed Matthew in a yellow glow. She hated to tell the twins, but it was their father who looked like the angel. His chestnut hair waved and curled all over his head and down to his collar. Forceful cheekbones sloped down to a square chin. He was the most manly-looking man she'd seen in a long time. Not that, of course, she assured herself, there was anything personal in her admiration.

"I best get the fire banked for the night," Matthew said.

"Let me do it," Glory said as she set aside the magazine. "Rest your leg. Just tell me how and it won't take a minute."

Matthew pulled himself up by holding on to the bookshelf and then put one crutch under his arm. "No need, I can do it."

"But I'd like to help," Glory protested as she rose. "You're in no condition to be banking a fire."

"I'm fine," Matthew said. "It takes more than a sprained knee to stop me."

Glory looked at him. A thin sheen of sweat was showing on his forehead and it was definitely not hot in the room. "You've got more pride than sense."

"Pride?" Matthew said as he hobbled over to the woodstove. "It's not pride. It's learning to take care of yourself. I've learned not to rely on others. I can do whatever I need to do to take care of me and my boys."

"Without help from anyone," Glory said dryly. Relying on others was the key to trust. Trust in others. Trust in God.

"We don't need any help," Matthew said as he lifted the grate on the stove. "It's best not to count on anyone else. I can do what needs doing."

"Can you?" Glory said softly as she watched Matthew reach down and pick up several pieces of wood. The fire wrapped golden shadows around his face. His frown burrowed itself farther into his forehead. She had no doubt Matthew could do everything that needed to be done in raising his sons—everything, that is, except teach them how to have faith. For how can you have faith in God if you can't trust anyone, not even Him? No wonder the boys clung to the belief she was an angel. It would take an angel to bring healing to their little family.

The Bullet folded his socks and put them in an old duffel bag that was carefully nondescript. No logos. No fancy stripes. Just brown.

"My uncle..." the Bullet said as he added a sweater. "He's sick. Spokane."

Millie nodded. She'd just come back from her job at Ruby's Coffee Shop and sat on the edge of the bed with her back straight and her eyes carefully not looking at the socks. She always looked so fragile with her wispy blond hair and slender body.

"I—ah—I'll be back soon," the Bullet continued. *She*

knows where I'm going. Oh, not the location. But she knows the why. "A week or so is all."

Millie nodded again and stood up. "Better take another sweater. It's cold in Spokane." She walked to the closet.

"No, let me." The Bullet intercepted her. He didn't want Millie to be part of any of this, not even the packing.

"Don't go. You don't have to go." Millie turned to him and spoke fiercely.

"I already told my uncle I was coming," the Bullet said slowly. It was too late to change his mind.

Chapter Three

Matthew stared at the glass coffeepot in his hand. He'd come to the hardware store at eight o'clock just like any other regular working day. But never before had the coffeepot been so sparkling clean and never before had a can of gourmet hazelnut coffee stood beside it. Old Henry was fussy about his coffee, and he always made it plain and strong. "Nothing fancy," he'd often say. "My customers are ranchers, not ballet dancers."

Glory and Matthew had shared a ride to the store after dropping the twins off at the church's nursery. "I think your customers might like some of these coffee flavors," Glory said.

"Coffee flavors?" Matthew hadn't slept well last night and he wanted his coffee thick and black with no frills. It wasn't the sofa that had kept him awake or even the pain in his knee. No matter how many times he turned over on the old sofa, his mind kept wandering back to dreams of Glory. Now he needed a good kick of coffee to keep him awake.

"You know, orange, raspberry, chocolate," Glory replied as she pulled the three bottles out of her purse. She hadn't slept well last night. She assured herself it was the creaking of the old house that had kept her awake and not the picture that stayed in her mind of Matthew adding more wood to the fire last night. She had gotten up this morning determined to make good progress on her painting today. That meant coffee.

"That's nice," Matthew said as he tried to hide as much of the white doily under the sugar bowl as he could. He'd have to tell Elmer and Jacob that the doily was a Christmas decoration. He expected they'd tolerate the concept of a few holiday decorations more kindly than the idea that their domain was being citified. Citified wasn't popular here. As it was, the two old men spent half their time here arguing about the dude ranch over on the Big Sheep Mountain Ranch. Anything that smacked of change and city people was suspect. And coffee flavors. The next thing you knew she'd want a...

"Cappuccino machine—that's what we need," Elmer said a half hour later. He was sipping his orange-flavored coffee most politely and beaming at Glory as she set up her easel. "I've always had a hankering to have one of those coffees."

"I don't even know if they have a cappuccino machine in Miles City. We'd have to send to Billings to buy one," Matthew protested.

What was wrong with Elmer? Once he'd complained because Henry put a different kind of toilet paper in the bathroom. And yet, here he was, wearing a new white shirt, the kind he only wore to funerals. "And no one's complained before. You've always liked the usual."

"But sometimes it's good to have a change," Glory said from her place by the window.

"Yeah, don't be such an old stick-in-the mud," Jacob said as he peered into his coffee cup suspiciously. Apparently Jacob didn't find anything too alarming in his cup, because he took a hot, scalding gulp. "Ahh, none of us are too old to try something new."

"I thought I'd set Susie's sketch up in the display window, too," Glory said. It had occurred to her last night that most gas stations wouldn't take checks. She could use some cash. "I might get another order for a portrait."

Matthew swallowed. He'd prefer to rearrange these receipts and dust the merchandise all morning. Anything to put off looking at the picture of Susie.

"I've got the sketch ready," Glory said. She'd placed the drawing of Susie on her easel. She'd drawn Susie smiling and holding a plate of oatmeal cookies almost level with her chin.

"I see that," Matthew said as he stood and hobbled over to the sketch. He took a deep breath. He felt the rubber band squeeze his heart. He'd been unable to cry at Susie's funeral. He'd just sat there with that rubber band squeezing the life out of him. This time he'd take a quick look and be done with it. He felt as if he'd been called upon to identify someone in the morgue. It wasn't a duty he wanted to prolong.

"That's her," Matthew said in surprise. He'd expected an identification picture of Susie, something that looked like a passport photo where you see the resemblance but not the person. But Glory was good. It was Susie's eyes that smiled at him from the paper.

"I wasn't sure about the cheekbones," Glory fretted. She didn't like the stillness that surrounded Matthew. "I think they might be a little too high."

"No, it's perfect. That's Susie."

Matthew braced himself for the inevitable second wave of pain. Susie had trusted him to save her life, trusted his faith to make her well. He'd never forgiven himself for letting her down. Somehow he hadn't prayed hard enough or loud enough to make any difference.

"Did she have a pink dress?" Glory interrupted his thoughts. Matthew's face had gone white and she didn't know what else to offer but chatter. "I thought I'd paint her in a pink dress with a little lace collar of white."

"Pink is good," Matthew said as he turned to walk away on his crutches. The sweat cooled on his brow. He'd made it past the hard part. He'd seen Susie again. Seen the look of trust on her face. He'd promised he'd take care of her and he had failed. He had told her God would come through for them. But he'd been wrong. In the end, Matthew had bargained bitterly with God to let him die. But God had not granted him even that small mercy. Matthew kept his face turned away from everyone. He'd fight his own demons alone.

"You like pink, do you?" Elmer said as he walked over to Glory.

"Who, me? No, I'm more of a beige-and-gray type of person," Glory said. She didn't like the closed look on Matthew's face or the ramrod straightness of his back when he'd turned around. But he'd made it clear he didn't want to talk.

"Beige—gray—that's good," Elmer murmured as he leaned closer to Glory.

Matthew hobbled stiffly back to the counter and sat back down on his chair. The air cooled the remaining sweat off his face as he watched Elmer make his moves. The old fox. Matthew took a deep breath. Today he'd rather watch the nonsense with Elmer than hold on to his own pain. He wanted to live in today and not yesterday. It made him feel better to know he wasn't the only one being charmed by Glory. No wonder the old man drank his orange coffee as if he enjoyed it. "No checker game this morning, Elmer?"

"Checkers—ah, n-no." Elmer stammered a little. "I thought I'd sit and talk a bit with the ang—with Miss Glory." Elmer gave a curt nod in Glory's direction. "Get acquainted, so to speak."

"That's very friendly of you," Glory said. She'd watched Matthew make his way to the counter and had relaxed when he turned to face them. When he started watching them, she turned her attention to Elmer. The old man was safer. She didn't mind company while she painted and almost welcomed it while she set out her brushes as she did now. Since Matthew had approved the sketch, she'd move on to the first stages of the oil painting.

"My pleasure," Elmer said, and then took another dainty sip of his orange coffee. "It isn't often we have a young woman visiting—at least, not one your age."

"Hmm," Glory murmured pleasantly. She'd need to mix some blue with that mauve to get the eye color right.

"Your age," Elmer repeated. "And what might that be?"

"Twenty-eight."

"Ah," Elmer said.

Matthew watched as the older man marked down a figure in a little notepad he pulled out of his pocket.

"And your birthday?"

"March 15."

"Good month," Elmer said as he nodded and marked another figure in his notepad. "That means you were born in oh three, fifteen, ah, 19…ah…?"

"Say, what are you doing?" Matthew demanded in surprise as he hobbled over to Elmer and stared at the older man.

"What?" Elmer bristled as he slid the notepad into his jacket pocket. "Just making conversation."

"You're planning to buy a lottery ticket from your daughter in L.A., aren't you?" Matthew said in amazement. "And you're getting some lucky numbers."

"It's all right." Glory looked up at the two of them and smiled. "At least that way, he'll have to call her."

"Yeah," Elmer said smugly as he patted the notebook in his pocket. "It'll be our family time. Nothing better than talking to your family."

Matthew grunted. "You've got better things to talk about than numbers and lottery tickets. Besides, her numbers aren't magic. She's not an angel."

"And how do you know that?" Elmer lifted his chin. "She could be. The Bible says we sometimes entertain angels unaware. Right in Hebrews 13:2. I looked it up."

"But the angels aren't unaware." Glory didn't like the direction this discussion was going. She was as earthbound as anyone. "And an angel? I assure you, I'm not one." She was just finishing up the right eyebrow on Susie's picture. Eyebrows were important character pieces. They could make a face look innocent, bewildered, sad. Glory had settled on innocent for Susie.

"You could be," Elmer stubbornly insisted. "You just might not want us to know."

Matthew snorted. "An angel wouldn't lie." He didn't know why he cared, but it gave him a funny feeling to have people talk about Glory as though she was an angel.

Not that the people of Dry Creek didn't need an angel. Fact is, they needed a whole troupe of angels and a basket of miracles, too. He didn't begrudge them their hope. It's just that he, of all people, knew the disappointment that came when expected miracles didn't happen.

The bell over the door rang as the door swung open

and a half dozen little children in snowsuits walked in. A huge gust of wind and Mrs. Hargrove came in behind them.

"Josh! Joey!" Matthew recognized his sons, or, at least, he recognized their snowsuits. There was much flapping about before the hoods were down and the young faces looked around the hardware store.

"There she is!" Josh shouted to his friends, and pointed at Glory.

Matthew tensed.

"Hi, there." Glory looked up at the children and smiled. Their bright snowsuits made a lovely study in color. Blue. Red. Pink. Even a purple one. "I should paint you all sometime. Just like this."

"I see you do have everything set up," Mrs. Hargrove said in satisfaction as she stepped out in front of her charges. "I was hoping you did. The children have never seen a real artist at work. If you don't mind them watching. I thought it'd be educational."

Matthew relaxed. That's why they were here.

"And she's an angel, too," Joey boasted quietly.

Matthew bit back his tongue. If Josh had done the boasting, he'd have corrected him in an instant. But it had been so long since he'd seen Joey care enough to speak up about anything, he didn't have the heart to correct him.

"Well, maybe not quite an angel," Matthew did offer softly. "Sometimes a good person can seem like an angel to others without really being one."

"Josh said she'd take our pictures to God," said another little boy, Greg, glancing sideways at Glory. "For Christmas."

Glory put down her brushes and turned to face the

expectant faces looking at her. She noticed that most of the pockets had a piece of paper peeking out of them.

"I'd be happy to take your pictures," Glory said as she stepped forward. It had been a long time since she'd done this much Christmas shopping, but it'd be fun. Sylvia, she knew, would enjoy being her go-between and Glory had enough in her checking account to cover it. "Just be sure you put your full names on the pictures—first and last."

"Last, too?" one of the boys asked, his forehead puckering in a quick frown. "I can't write my last."

"Maybe Mrs. Hargrove can help you," Glory said. "But I do need first name and last name so the right present gets to the right child."

"I thought God knew our names," a little girl in a pink snowsuit said suspiciously as she stepped out of the leg of her suit. "If you're his angel you should know, too."

"I'm not an angel," Glory said.

"Then why do you want our pictures?" the little girl demanded.

"She'll give your pictures to your parents." Mrs. Hargrove stepped in front of the children. "It's your parents that—" She stumbled. Glory could see why. Those shining little faces looked up with such trust.

"My parents already said I won't get no Betsy Tall doll," the girl said. "They said it's too ex...cen...sive."

"Expensive, dear." Mrs. Hargrove corrected the pronunciation automatically. "Too expensive. And I'm sure there are other dolls."

The hope was beginning to fade on the young faces.

"I'd be happy to take your pictures," Glory said again softly. She held out her hands and the children quickly stuffed their pictures into them.

"Mrs. Hargrove will help me figure out who's who," Glory assured the children.

Glory was watching the children and didn't hear Matthew coming up next to her.

"I'll help with the pictures," Matthew whispered in her ear.

Glory jumped. Matthew startled her. He was so…well, just so close. He unnerved her. She pulled away slightly. "I don't need help. I'm fine. I can take care of it."

"How? You're not an angel."

"Just because I'm not an angel doesn't mean I can't buy a few gifts."

"For children you don't even know?"

"I know them now." Glory shrugged. What was it with this man? Didn't he believe anyone could do something for someone else just because?

The bell over the door rang again, and this time a teenage girl slipped inside. She had a tiny gold ring in her nose and a streak of red dye going through her hair. Fashion, it appeared, hadn't neglected southeastern Montana.

"Linda." Matthew greeted the girl carefully. "What can we help you with?"

"What do you think, big guy?" Linda cooed softly. The girl lifted her eyes to Matthew. She was holding a five-dollar bill in her hand and she waved it around.

Glory winced. The girl was playing at something she obviously didn't even understand. And she was looking at Matthew as if she was starving and he was a super-sized hamburger. Which was ridiculous, Glory thought. Sure, he was good-looking in a rugged kind of a way. And sure he smelled like the outdoors and sure he had biceps that would get second looks at the beach and— Glory stopped herself. Okay, so the girl wasn't so far wrong. He was worth staring at. But that didn't mean the girl had any right to do it.

"Hey, Linda," called the little boy, Greg. "Come meet the angel. She's gonna get us presents."

Linda flicked an annoyed glance down that then softened at the enthusiasm on Greg's face. "That's nice. But I need to talk to the angel myself."

"I'm not—" Glory began.

"I need some advice," Linda interrupted impatiently. The teenager looked assessingly at Glory and held out the five-dollar bill. "Some love advice."

"From me?" Glory squeaked.

"I need to know if I should marry the Jazz Man."

"The Jazz Man?" Matthew asked as he leaned his crutches against a wall and sat down on a chair. "You don't mean Arnold's boy, Duane?"

"Yeah." Linda looked at him and snapped her gum. "He's forming a band. Calling himself the Jazz Man." She stood a little straighter. "Wants me to be his lead singer."

"And he's proposed?" Glory asked in studied surprise. She might not know a lot about love, but she did know about business.

"Yeah, why?" Linda looked at her cautiously.

"Mixing business and pleasure." Glory shook her head in what she hoped was a convincingly somber fashion. "He won't have to pay you if he marries you."

"Yeah, I never thought of that," Linda said slowly, and put the five dollars on Glory's easel. "Thanks."

"What's the money for—" Glory began, but was interrupted by the bell ringing over the door again.

This time the ringing was incessant and loud. A stocky man in a tan sheriff's uniform stepped into the store and looked around quickly. His eyes fastened on Glory.

"There you are," he said as he walked toward Glory and put his hand on the end of the gun that stuck out of his holster. "You're under arrest for impersonating an angel. You have the right to—"

"You can't arrest her." The protest erupted from all across the store.

"Oh, yes, I can," the deputy said as he clicked the handcuffs from behind his back and picked up the five dollars Linda had left on her easel. "I won't have no con woman plucking my pigeons. Not in my town she won't."

Plucking his pigeons, Glory thought in dismay. *Dear Lord, what have I done now?*

The Bullet leaned against the cold glass of the phone booth. The credit card company records showed the woman had stopped at a gas station in Spokane and then at a bank for a cash advance. He'd followed the usual procedure to find her. He knew loners in a new town found a bar.

"You'll never find her that way," the voice on the other end of the phone snorted.

"Why not? She's a cop."

"A Christian cop," the voice clarified. "Religious as they come. Doesn't drink. Try looking in the churches."

The Bullet swallowed hard. "Churches? Me?"

Chapter Four

"Easy now," Deputy Sheriff Carl Wall warned Glory when she stood up. He'd forbidden the others to follow them when he escorted her up the church steps and into a small office off the church's kitchen. She'd been sitting on the edge of the desk for ten minutes now while he argued on the phone. The cuffs he'd put on her hands hung open at her wrists. The key to unlock them was in his patrol car and so he did not lock them shut. They were more for show than because he thought the woman would bolt.

"Well, there's got to be a law against it, Bert," Carl was saying for the second time into the phone. He twisted the cord around his chubby ginger. "We just can't have folks going around claiming to be angels and things."

"I never claimed to be an angel," Glory said, even though she doubted he heard her. He hadn't paid any attention to her the past two times she'd said it. It wasn't because he hadn't heard her, she figured; it was because he wasn't listening. In her experience, hearing and listening were two different things.

"But an angel's different from Santa Claus," Carl argued into the phone's mouthpiece, ignoring Glory. He'd already twisted part of the cord around his finger, so now he looped another section around his hand. "Everyone knows Santa Claus isn't real, but folks and angels, well, that's a different story. She's more like a fortune-teller. Gotta be laws against that."

Glory looked around at the office. There was a boxy window at the end of the room. Everything else was long and skinny. The whole thing wasn't much wider than the desk. She guessed the room had been a pantry at one time, running as it did side by side the whole width of the kitchen. A bookcase lined one long wall and a chair stood to the side of the desk. A filing cabinet was tucked behind the door.

"Of course she hasn't got wings on," Carl sputtered in exasperation as he eyed Glory suspiciously. He untwisted the cord around his hand and rubbed the red mark he'd created. Glory pulled a book off the shelf and tried to ignore him. "But a person doesn't need a costume to con people. Crooks don't wear signs, for Pete's sake."

Glory opened the book she held. She loved the smell of old books. They were like old friends. Just holding the book steadied her. If she had to, she could call the police station in Seattle and have them vouch for her honesty. She doubted there were any laws against claiming to be an angel anyway, not even if she sprouted wings and flew off the Empire State Building.

"Well, I can't just let her go," Carl Wall whined into the phone. Then he looked at Glory again and turned his back to her as though that would muffle his voice. "I've already taken her in. I'll look bad saying there's no law against it now. I'm going to write her up for impersonating even if the judge says no later."

A movement through the window caught her eye. Something was happening in the street. Glory looked at the deputy sheriff's back and slid closer to the window. She saw Matthew, standing in the middle of the dirt street and waving a crutch around. The people from the hardware store were gathered around him and Matthew wasn't the only one waving something. Mrs. Hargrove had a broom. Elmer had a yardstick. It looked as if Matthew was giving a speech, but she couldn't hear it through the closed window. She braced her fingers against the frame of the windowpanes and pushed up. A puff of cold air came inside, a puff of dirty cold air, Glory decided as the dust beneath the window blew onto her coat. But she could finally hear the voices outside.

"He'll listen to voters. That's all he wants," Matthew was saying. A trail of white breath rose from Matthew's mouth. It was cold. Matthew wore a wool jacket over his shirt. It wasn't nearly enough to keep him warm, in Glory's opinion. "There's no need to threaten him with any more than that."

"But he's got our angel," Elmer protested.

"We don't know she's an angel," Matthew said. Glory noticed he had only a slipper on his injured foot. He needed to be inside. She was pretty sure the doctor had told him to stay inside.

"But we don't know she's not, either," Elmer persisted as he dipped his yardstick for emphasis. "The Bible talks about angels. It could be. We don't know. And who wants to take a chance! Do you?" Elmer took a breath. "Do you want to be responsible for turning an angel out of Dry Creek?"

The question hung in the air like brittle frost.

Glory pushed the window higher. This was getting interesting.

"Shut that window," Carl yelled. He was putting down the telephone and had finally noticed where she was.

"You aren't going to get far, jumping out that window and evading arrest."

"I wasn't going to jump," Glory said in astonishment. "I was just listening to the people in the street out front. I think they're campaigning against you."

Carl Wall scowled at her. "Mighty lippy for an angel, aren't you?"

Glory grinned. "I'm not an angel."

"Oh, I know that, but do they know it?" Carl pointed out the window to the people on the street. Glory looked at them. They were gesturing as they talked, and periodically someone would wave a broom. They looked like a mob of janitors. Carl cleared his throat and continued. "These people are my responsibility. As I said, I won't have anyone plucking my flock—not while I'm on duty."

"I've not asked for a dime from anyone," Glory protested indignantly. "Linda put that five-dollar bill on my easel. I didn't ask for it. I would have given it back if you hadn't stepped in. I don't want anyone's money."

"Maybe not yet. But you'll want it sooner or later, won't you?" Carl said as a sly smile slid over his face. "What else can you do? You don't have a job—"

"I have a job," Glory interrupted firmly. "Not here, of course, but I do have a job with the Seattle Police Department."

Carl snorted. "Expect me to believe that. You—a police officer. Where's your badge?"

"Well, I don't have a badge…."

"I didn't think so," Carl said with satisfaction.

"I work for them as a sketch artist. You know, drawing pictures of criminals from the descriptions given by the witnesses."

"Hmph." The deputy appeared to consider her words and then shook his head. "Naw, I don't think so. What

I think is you're a slick customer trying to make a buck off the poor folks of Dry Creek. Taking advantage of their good holiday spirits. And I aim to catch you at it. The minute you ask for a dime, you're mine."

"It looks like I'm yours anyway," Glory said dryly. She wondered why she wasn't fighting harder to leave this little town. But she felt as if she'd begun a story, and she wanted to stay around a couple of days to see what the characters did next. "Sounds like you're all set to make a false arrest."

Carl scowled. "Don't be telling me how to do my job."

Glory didn't answer, because there was a loud knock at the door. Well, it wasn't so much of a knock as it was a pounding. A very loud pounding. The sort of sound a crutch would make in the swinging arm of an impatient man.

"Open up!" The command came with the crutch pounding.

Carl Wall walked back to the door and swung it open.

There he stood. Her avenging angel. Glory swallowed. It must be a trick of light. Maybe the reflection of the snow outside. She'd read in her Bible about angels last night and her imagination was being overactive. But Matthew sure looked like Daniel's vision, even down to the halo of golden light surrounding his head. She mouthed the words silently. *"There stood a certain man—his face like the appearance of lightning, his eyes like torches of fire."*

Glory swallowed again. Definitely torches of fire.

"Your game's over," Matthew said, and stepped inside the room.

Glory started to breathe again. The halo of light didn't follow Matthew. It stayed just where it was and, when her eyes followed the beam downward, she saw the flashlight in Josh's mittened hands. The boy loved lights even in the day. She smiled. She wasn't crazy. It was artificial light. That's all. She was perfectly able to tell the difference between an angel of God and an ordinary man.

"You can't arrest her," Matthew said as he looked squarely at Carl Well. "She hasn't done anything illegal."

"Loitering," the deputy said smoothly. "There's always loitering."

"She wasn't loitering." Matthew took a deep breath.

"Then what was she doing in the hardware store?" the deputy pressed.

"Painting." Matthew paused.

"For pay?"

"No, not for pay, but—"

"Then it's loitering," the deputy said in satisfaction. "Next thing to panhandling. Street artists. If she's got no job, she's loitering."

"Well, if she needs a job, she's got a job," Matthew said in exasperation. "She's working for me."

Carl looked from Matthew to Glory and then back to Matthew. The satisfied look on the deputy's face grew. "Told me she worked for the Seattle Police Department."

"Well, she doesn't. She's working for me," Matthew said forcefully, as though he could convince the deputy of his statement by the sheer pressure of his words. "As of today."

"But I—" Glory started to protest. Why was it these people were so willing to believe she was an angel and so reluctant to believe she worked for a police department? Which was more likely? Then she saw the look on Matthew's face. Pain was drawing his skin tight. He shouldn't be on his feet. She looked back at the deputy. "What difference does it make where I work—if you're going to arrest me, do it. If not, let me go."

"Arrest you? He can't arrest you!" Mrs. Hargrove pushed her way into the room and stood there looking solid and indignant.

"Don't be telling me how to do my job."

"I'm a voter and I can jolly well tell you how to do your job!" Mrs. Hargrove jabbed her finger in the deputy's face. "Besides, I've known you since you were in diapers. That ought to count for something."

Glory watched the muscles slowly coil in the deputy's face.

"Hmph!" Mrs. Hargrove crossed her arms and said smugly, "Can't lock her up anyway. We don't even have a jail."

"Well, I won't have to lock her up. I'll settle for a ticket if I can find an upstanding citizen to take responsibility for watching her—maybe see she does some community service." The deputy looked pleased with himself. "Yes, an upstanding citizen is just what I need. Maybe someone like a minister."

"But we don't have a minister, Carl Wall, and you know it," Mrs. Hargrove said indignantly.

"We would have if you'd given the nod to my cousin Fred," the deputy said smoothly.

"Your Fred isn't trained to be a pastor." Mrs. Hargrove put her hands on her hips. "Besides, he isn't even a believer."

"Well, he needs a job. He sent in his résumé. You didn't have any other applicants. In my book, that makes the job his."

"Being a pastor isn't just a job. It's a calling. Besides, it's a good thing for you we don't have a minister around." She drew in her breath sharply and looked at Matthew.

"If there's no minister, that leaves jail. I can always send her to the jail in Miles City."

"But that's an awful place," Mrs. Hargrove protested. "They're talking about closing it down. It's not even heated, just a big old cement block. You can't put someone in there in winter!"

"Well, it's not my first choice. But since you're too good to have the likes of Fred as a minister, I guess I don't have any other options now, do I?"

"The voters won't like this."

The deputy shrugged. "I tried to be reasonable. I'm sure Fred mentioned he was willing to read the Bible and get an idea of what the thing was all about. On-the-job training, so to speak. But no, you need to have someone who believes the whole thing. It's not too late. Fred's probably at home right now. We can call him and make the deal," he added smugly. "Remember, no minister means the angel goes to jail."

"But…" Mrs. Hargrove struggled to speak. "This is outrageous!"

"No minister means the angel goes to jail," the deputy repeated stubbornly.

"I'm a minister," Matthew said softly. It was freezing outside and still a thin sheen of sweat covered his forehead. "At least, according to the state. Marrying, burying—I can do all those. I expect I can keep my eye on an angel."

"You're a what?" The deputy looked skeptical.

"A minister." Matthew had a sinking feeling. He shouldn't have said anything. But he couldn't stand the thought of Glory spending time in that jail.

"You had a church?"

"Yes, in Havre."

"Well, why aren't you preaching here? We could use

a minister at the church," the deputy persisted. "Even Fred would give way to a real preacher."

"I don't preach anymore," Matthew said evenly. His breath was shallow, but he was plowing his way through. He couldn't let his annoyance flare. Not if he wanted the deputy to cooperate.

"What? You retired from it?"

"In a way."

"Mighty young to be retired."

"Most people change jobs over a lifetime."

"But ministers?" the deputy asked, puzzled. "I've never known a minister to just quit his job before."

"Well, now you do," Matthew snapped. "Just let me know what I need to do to supervise the ang—I mean, Glory, and I'll do it."

"See, we do have a minister," Mrs. Hargrove said triumphantly. "God provides."

"Well, God isn't providing much," the deputy said as he nodded toward Matthew. "But I suppose it'll be all right." The deputy admitted defeat grudgingly. "I'll just write that ticket and you can set her up with some worthwhile community service. She works off the fine. If she messes up, she pays the fine. Simple. I'll check in later this week."

"Community service?" Matthew asked in surprise. "Doing what? All our roads are snowpacked. We don't have a jail. Or a library. Not even a post office. We don't need anything done."

"Except," Mrs. Hargrove interrupted hesitantly, "we do need an angel for the Christmas pageant."

"Ah, yes, the pageant." Matthew sighed. Odd how this pageant had grown so big in the minds of everyone this year. Several of the churches in Miles City had decided to send a few visitors to Dry Creek for the annual

Christmas Eve pageant. It all sounded very friendly. But Matthew knew enough about churches to know what was happening. A few do-gooders in Miles City had asked a handful of single people, likely mostly widows, to visit Dry Creek on Christmas Eve and they'd accepted, feeling righteous. No doubt it was a gracious way for the churches to deliver food baskets to some of the poorer families in Dry Creek. But even after they hosted their pageant, Matthew doubted the people of Dry Creek would accept charity. The people of Dry Creek were proud and they'd get by on their own or not at all. Food baskets from outsiders would not be welcome.

"We've got the costume—wings, robe, everything," Mrs. Hargrove continued, "All we need is the angel."

"That's settled, then," the deputy said as he pulled out his ticket book.

It wasn't settled at all in Glory's mind, but she decided to take the hastily scrawled ticket so the deputy would leave. There'd be no fine. She knew any judge would dismiss the charges when he saw the ticket. She'd save her objections for later.

The only reason Glory let Mrs. Hargrove talk her into looking at the costumes was so Matthew would sit down. He was being gallant and standing with his shoulder leaning on his crutch. At least if they moved to the costumes, he'd take a seat.

The costumes were stored in a small room on the other side of the church kitchen. Mrs. Hargrove pointed it out and then left with the children. The room had one small square window, high on the wall, and a single light bulb hanging from the ceiling. Glory stood on a small stool to pull down the angel wings. Matthew sat on a hard-backed chair in the corner of the room.

"Watch the dust," Matthew warned as Glory pulled

the wings off the high shelf. Waves of dust floated down over her.

Glory sneezed. "Too late."

Yes, it is too late, Matthew thought to himself glumly. He'd vowed to keep his secret, and now it would be all over Dry Creek in minutes. And the irony was it wasn't true anymore. He was no more a minister than Glory was an angel. Less, in fact, because when she stood with her head in front of that single bulb, she at least looked like an angel. Flying copper hair with flecks of gold. Milky skin. A voice that melted over him like warm honey. He found himself wishing he were still a minister, that his life had been uncomplicated by searing grief and confused pain. He already knew Glory well enough to know she'd never settle for less than a godly man. A man of faith. A man he, Matthew, couldn't be anymore.

"I expect the halo's up there, too," Matthew added as Glory dusted off the white cardboard wings. He could see the strand of gold Christmas garland hanging over the top shelf.

"You know, I'd be happy to do something else for community service," Glory said as she pulled the old garland off the shelf. It had lost most of its glitter and all of its fluff. "I could give painting lessons or something."

Matthew didn't voice his protest. He'd developed a longing almost as intense as his sons to see Glory dressed up in an angel costume. "I think Henry has some gold garland at the store. You could use that if you want."

"I don't know." Glory sat down on the stool. A faint cloud of dust still fell down around her. "I just don't feel like an angel this year."

"Oh." Matthew didn't want to press. He hoped the one word was enough.

"Well, look at me," Glory said. "Here I am—broke,

in a strange town, almost arrested, uncertain what to do next with my life."

"Yeah, I suppose angels never wonder what to do," Matthew agreed. For a minute he thought Glory was reading his mind and heart. Then he saw the confusion on her face. He shifted on his chair so he could see her better. "They just get their marching orders and they march. Piece of cake. But none of the excitement of being human."

"I guess the grass is always greener. We look at them. They look at us," Glory agreed quietly and then asked, "Do you believe angels are really jealous of us?"

"I'm not a minister anymore." Matthew began his standard disclaimer. He was no longer qualified to give spiritual advice. "I mean, I'm licensed still. But that's all. Just for the state."

"I figured that out," Glory said. When she'd heard Matthew admit to being a minister, she'd felt the pieces click in her heart. Matthew as a minister made sense. "But that's not why I'm asking. I just want to know what you think."

Matthew leaned back. He tried to separate what he believed from what he'd trained himself to believe. When he was a minister, he'd chased away any question, any doubt. He believed in confidence. Now he was just Matthew.

"Yes," Matthew finally said. "Yes, I think they must envy us. We can have babies."

Glory smiled. "I never thought of that."

Matthew caught his breath. He was grateful for the shadows that hid him in the small room. She was beautiful when she smiled. Like a Botticelli goddess.

"What's it like?" Glory asked quietly, and startled Matthew. For a second he thought she was reading his mind; then he realized she was talking about babies. "When you had the twins," she continued. "What was it like?"

"Like winning the World Series."

"I thought it might be something like that," she said. "I envy you."

"Someday you'll know what I mean," Matthew said. The picture of Glory with a baby glowed warm inside of him. He bet the little thing would have milk-white skin and red hair. "It's like no other feeling. I can't even describe it. You'll just have to wait and see for yourself."

"I guess so," Glory agreed. She didn't want to tell him that there was no point in waiting—she knew she'd never have a baby. The accident had snatched that dream away from her. It wasn't that she didn't think he'd understand. He'd obviously known pain in his life. Maybe he'd understand too well. She just didn't want to see pity fill his eyes when he looked at her. And what else could he feel but pity? That's one of the reasons she'd avoided becoming close to men. She didn't want to see that look in the eyes of someone she loved.

"Will you have more babies?" Glory asked, and then hurried on at the surprised look on Matthew face. "I mean, if you remarried, would you want to have more children?"

"Children are the trump card in life. I'd have as many as I could."

Glory nodded. That was good. It was as it should be. He was a good father. His sons were good. It was all very good. It just didn't include anyone like her. "I'd like to go look for that garland now."

Matthew watched the light leave Glory's face. She put the cardboard wings under her arm and headed for the door. He had no choice but to follow.

The cold air hit Glory in the face and pinched the color out of her cheeks. It was only a hundred feet between the door to the hardware store and the door to the church, but it felt as if the few steps iced her to the soul. She needed to stop thinking about babies that would never be born. Her guilt was over. Her mother had forgiven her. God had forgiven her. Some days she'd even managed to forgive herself. It was over. She needed to stop grieving.

The smell of coffee greeted her when she stepped back into the warmth of the hardware store. Elmer and Jacob were still arguing.

"Heard them federal boys are going to close in on the rustlers now that they figured it isn't just happening here," Jacob insisted.

Elmer waved the words away. "They aren't even close. They don't know how. Why or when. What've they got? Nothing."

"They'll find them at the inspection plants, now that they're requiring papers before they grade the meat," Jacob said almost fiercely. "They'll find them. They've got to."

Elmer opened his mouth and then saw Glory. His mouth hung open for a full minute before it formed into an excited oval. He turned to Jacob and gummed his mouth several times before he got the words out. "Blazes, why didn't we think of it before?"

"Huh?"

"Look at her." Elmer pointed to Glory.

Glory's heard sank. She had a feeling she was falling deeper.

"She's a government agent," Elmer said triumphantly. "I heard rumors they were hiring a civilian to look into the cattle problem. She's a spy."

Glory shook her head. First angels and then spies. "You boys need to get out more."

"Don't worry, we understand," Elmer said with a wink. "You don't want to blow your cover."

"I don't have a cover," Glory said patiently as she heard the door open behind her. A gust of wind blew against her back and then stopped as the door closed.

"Why would you need a cover?" Matthew said as he used his crutch to hobble over to the counter. The dreams of Glory in his bed had stayed with him all day. "Didn't the twins get you an extra blanket last night?"

Glory blushed. "It's not that kind of cover." Glory pulled herself together. Maybe she'd sleep on the floor tonight. It didn't seem quite right to sleep in Matthew's bed. "They mean cover like spy cover. They think I'm a spy for the government. Looking into some cattle business."

Matthew leaned his crutch against the counter. So that was it. Maybe it was business that brought a woman like her to a small town on the backside of Montana.

"You never did say why you were driving through," he said, keeping his voice light and casual. She'd be a good spy. That innocent look of hers hid a quick mind. He wondered if she worked for the FBI or the Department of Agriculture. "Or where you were headed."

"I wasn't headed anywhere. I was just driving," Glory said.

"It's winter. Most folks don't go driving through Montana for pleasure this time of year," Matthew countered. The passes were slippery over the Rockies and even the flatlands had their share of ice and snow. No, Montana wasn't a pleasant drive in the winter.

Glory shrugged. "I'm not most folks."

She had him there, Matthew thought. There was nothing ordinary or plain about her. She was the exotic orchid of the flower kingdom. The red-hot pepper of the spice family. The flaming gold of the color spectrum. He had a fleeting desire to tell her so. But then a thought came from left field and slugged him in the stomach. If she was undercover, she was someone else in another life. She could be someone's mother. She could be someone's daughter. Worse yet, she could be someone's wife.

"I could talk to the deputy if you've got somewhere else to be on Christmas," Matthew said. His stomach muscles tensed. She'd want to be with her husband on Christmas if she had one. "He can't hold you here."

"I'd thought about spending Christmas with my mother."

Matthew's stomach knotted. The mother could be a husband as easily as he stood here. "In Seattle?"

Glory nodded.

"You won't have a white Christmas there," Matthew offered. It was none of his business if she had another life that had nothing to do with Dry Creek, but he couldn't stop himself. "The twins would love to have you stay."

Glory stopped her head from nodding. She'd love to spend Christmas with the twins as much as they wanted her to spend it with them. But she had more wisdom than the twins. She knew that sometimes a day's happiness came with a price tag attached. If she stayed for Christmas, she'd regret it later when she had to leave. And leave she would. Because as much as she might dream about a life with someone like Matthew, she wasn't the woman for him.

No one could accuse the churches in Spokane of being quiet. It was prayer meeting night, and the Bullet sat first on the outside steps of one church and then another. He heard it all. John 3:16. "Amazing Grace." The Lord's Prayer. He'd felt a little self-conscious just sitting outside, but he did anyway. He wasn't fit to go inside, and he knew it. Besides, he needed to be at the door before anyone came out so he could be sure to see the woman if she left.

His plan earned him a few curious looks, but he congratulated himself on doing fine until he reached a church on the east side.

"Give me a hand," the old man asked as he started to climb the stairs.

The Bullet looked around, but everyone else was already inside the church. There was no one to help the man but him.

Chapter Five

Matthew was true to his word, Glory thought. Dinner her second night not only didn't float in milk, it didn't come from a cardboard box, either. He made a salmon loaf, baked potatoes and green beans. There were fresh chives for the baked potatoes and mushrooms in the green beans. Betty Crocker couldn't have done better.

"I could help," Glory said for the tenth time since Matthew had shooed her out of the kitchen. She listened to pans rattle as she sat on the sofa and Matthew did dishes. Glory tried to remember if she'd ever had a man make her dinner before—and then insist on doing the dishes even though he was on crutches. Not that Matthew had made the dinner especially for her, she reminded herself. The twins had needed dinner, too.

"Please, let me help. I'm not used to being waited on." She started to get up from the sofa.

Matthew grunted from the kitchen. "Stay put. Do you good to take it easy."

Two pairs of twin arms reached up to pull her back to the sofa.

"Don't angels have daddies to cook for them?" Joey asked quietly as she settled back down. He pressed so close to her she could feel his worry. "I told my daddy he needed to make angel food cake. Maybe then you'd stay."

Glory smoothed back the hair on Joey's forehead. "You don't need to feed me angel cake."

"We had to give our fish some fish food. That's all they ate," Josh added solemnly as though she hadn't spoken. He was on her other side. "They ate and ate, but they died anyway."

"Do fish go to heaven when they die?" Joey looked up at her quizzically.

"No, silly," Josh answered for her. "There's no water in heaven. Only clouds. Isn't that right?" He looked to Glory for reinforcement and then added scornfully, "Besides, fish can't be angels. They can't fly."

"You know, we should learn about angels," Glory said decisively. She remembered her father always took this tactic when she was a child. Everything led to a lesson. Once the twins learned about real angels, maybe they'd let her be human. The truth did set people free, even if those people were only five years old. "Let me go get a Bible."

"We got one." Josh ran to a shelf and pulled down an old black Bible. The gold lettering on the front said "Family Bible," and the back of the leather cover looked as if it had been scorched. Josh carried the Bible to her as if it was a basket of precious jewels. Glory put her fingers to the burned mark around the edge just to be sure. So, she thought, smiling, something had been snatched from that fire after all. There was hope for Matthew yet.

"Are you going to tell us about an angel?" Joey asked, his voice low and excited.

Glory flipped through the Bible. She knew just the angel for the boys. "Not only an angel, but some big cats, too."

Glory saw their eyes grow big.

"The king made a rule…" Glory said, beginning to paraphrase chapter six of Daniel. She knew the story well. She didn't need to read it from the Bible that lay on her lap.

The twins listened to the king's dilemma and the story of his evil advisors.

"Finally the king had no choice. He'd been tricked. He needed to put Daniel in a den with big cats called lions."

"Mrs. Hargrove told us about the lions," Joey whispered as he moved closer to Glory. "They eat people."

Josh shivered and snuggled closer to her other side. "I want a dog. No cats."

"These are special cats." Glory put an arm around each boy. They both shifted closer. "Not like the cats you know. Much, much bigger than the cats around here."

"A trillion times bigger?" Josh asked. He was clearly relishing the story.

"Almost. And there's no need to be afraid. There aren't any lions around here."

The twins looked momentarily disappointed and then Josh said. "But there's cats. Mr. Gossett next door has cats. They'll get you."

"Cats might scratch you, but they won't eat you."

"But they're *Mr. Gossett's* cats," Josh said as though that explained everything. "He doesn't eat. He drinks his meals. Mrs. Hargrove says."

"Maybe his cats don't eat, either." Joey took up the thought excitedly. "Maybe they lick you instead. Like an ice cream cone. Maybe that's how they eat. Lick, lick, lick—then you're gone. I've seen them lick people." He shivered. "I don't want them to lick me."

"You can't get licked away." Glory had forgotten how much young boys liked to flirt with danger. "Or get drunk away. Or bitten away. You're completely safe with cats."

Glory showed the twins the picture in the Bible. The reds and blues of the scene had faded, but the lions looked scary. And the angel still looked majestic with his flowing white robes and golden hair.

"That's an angel," Joey said in awe as he traced the picture. "With real wings."

Glory felt a pair of little hands reach up and lightly touch her shoulder blades as though checking.

"No wings," she assured them.

Matthew turned the light off in the kitchen and leaned against the doorway leading to the living room. He'd built a fire earlier, and the light made Glory and his sons look golden. Their heads were bent together over a book, two little blond heads with a bronze one in the middle. He had heard the excited whispers as he washed the dishes in the kitchen. He felt a swell of contentment fill him. He'd do more than wash a few dishes to give his sons time with a woman like Glory.

Then the shadows shifted, and Matthew saw what the three were reading. He tensed. The Bible. He'd bought that Bible when the twins were born. Susie had used it to record the twins' births—their weight, height and first gestures. They'd planned to be a family around that Bible. He and Susie had read from it for family devotions when the twins were in their strollers. They'd planned to record their anniversaries in the book and the births of more babies.

"It's time for bed," Matthew said abruptly. He supposed he shouldn't be surprised the twins had found the Bible. It wasn't hidden. He just hadn't expected to deal with their claim on it so soon.

"Aah," Josh groaned. "We were just at the good part."

"We can finish it tomorrow night," Glory said as she hugged each of the boys and then took her arm away so they could scoot off the sofa.

"Can we get a den?" Josh turned to Matthew. "Ricky's family has a den."

"Different kind of den." Glory tried to pluck the thought from him before he got going in that direction. "This kind of den is a cave. It's made from rock. All dark inside."

"Oh." Josh seemed to be thinking.

Matthew smiled. He didn't tell Glory, but he already knew a den would be made from blankets tomorrow. Josh loved acting. "Get washed up and I'll tuck you in." The boys ran out of the room.

"You can't!" Alarms went off in Glory's stomach. All thoughts of cats and dens vanished. *Tuck them in! Tucking in meant Matthew upstairs in the twins' room!* Matthew wasn't supposed to be able to climb stairs. She wasn't sure she wanted him to see the cocoon she'd built in his bed last night. She'd wrapped blankets around herself snugly, but she'd lined up one of his pillows to lie beside her in the night. She'd told the twins the pillow was her teddy bear, but a grown man would…well, he might see it differently.

"Figure of speech," Matthew said as he watched Glory's face. The gold from the fire and the blush fanning out over her face made her look like rare porcelain. "I meant I'd give them a kiss good-night. Down here, of course."

"Of course." Glory smoothed down her skirt. "I should go up, too."

"It's only seven-thirty," Matthew protested as he lowered himself onto the sofa and propped his crutches against the wall. His shoulders ached and the palms of his hands burned where he leaned on the crossbar of the crutch. He should be thinking of sleep himself, but he was wide-awake. It occurred to him that his twins weren't the only ones who missed having some quiet time with a woman. "Sit with me for a while and talk."

Glory hesitated. The sofa that had seemed so large when she and the twins were sitting on it seemed to have shrunk now that Matthew was on the other end. She didn't want to be skittish and scoot over to the edge of the sofa, but she wasn't sure it felt safe to be within reaching distance of Matthew. Not that she expected him to reach for her, she told herself. *Be reasonable. He only wants some light conversation after a day's work.*

Matthew watched the reluctance streak across her face, and he remembered Elmer's words about her being an undercover agent. He wondered if she was remembering a husband or boyfriend who laid claim to her real life. He sure wished he knew if she was undercover.

"We don't usually have salmon, not even canned—not this close to the Big Sheep Mountains," he began. His mouth was dry. He wasn't used to entrapping a federal agent. "These mountains are cattle country through and through. Folks here pride themselves on beefsteaks, even now with all the…" He deliberately let his voice trail off to see if she'd pick up the scent like a federal agent would.

"Yes, the rustling." Glory latched on to the topic with relief. Nothing could be more impersonal than beefsteaks, she thought to herself with satisfaction. "How long has that been going on? Tell me everything you know."

Matthew's heart sank. She'd taken the bait with gusto. Maybe she was an agent, after all. Why else would a woman from out of town care about the rustling? "Cattle have been missing for the past year, I suppose. Probably started last winter. They free range most of the cattle around here in the winter, and so they don't do a complete count until the snow thaws and it comes close to calving time."

"Surely they don't leave those cows out all winter?" Glory asked in alarm.

Matthew smiled. That narrowed the field some. Unless she was a very good actress, she didn't work for the Department of Agriculture. "They have windbreaks set up, sometimes sheds, and the cows grow a thick coat. If it's real cold they can always wander down to the fences and someone will let them into the barn area. And they drop bales of hay to them, by pickup mostly. In bad winters they've dropped hay from small planes or helicopters."

"Well, maybe there's no rustling at all," Glory offered. She was having a hard time concentrating now that Matthew had started rubbing his shoulder. The crutches must be giving him trouble. His hands were what were giving her trouble. They were large and muscled, lightly haired and lightly tanned. "Maybe the cows are still out there."

"That's why it's so hard to know for sure when it all started," Matthew admitted. His hands found the knot in his shoulder and he sighed as he rubbed it. "A few cows here and there—who knows? Maybe they're holed up in a gully somewhere. But the Big Sheep Mountain Ranch has had their hands riding all over the range—covered it with a fine-tooth comb and didn't find the cattle or any carcasses. There needs to be one or the other. Even the buzzards can't carry off a whole cow."

"Sounds just like the Old West," Glory said. She'd never given too much thought to the life of a cow. Or a buzzard. Or a cowboy. "Is it the Big Sheep Mountain Ranch that's thinking of becoming a dude ranch?"

Matthew winced. His fingers had hit a nerve on his shoulder. "They don't call it dude ranch around here. I think the politically correct term is guest ranch. Doesn't offend the 'guests' as much. And, yes, it is the Big Sheep. If they follow through. They've had some tourism consultant down from Helena. It appears the scenery around the Big Sheep Mountains is as valuable as the cows. Maybe more so when you throw in the fact that we've got the Tongue River and the Yellowstone River close by and we're not far from Medicine Rock State Park. Some say we're the not-so-bad part of the Badlands, too."

"Well, at least the town will survive, then." Glory bit her lip. She shouldn't say anything, but Matthew was going to be even more sore after he finished trying to massage his one shoulder. His angle was all wrong.

"There's survival and there's survival. Some folks think the dudes will change the town so much we might as well lie down and die in the first place. Go with dignity. Elmer keeps going on about how he doesn't want to have to look the part of a rancher when he's face-to-face with some fancy lawyer who's only coming here for two weeks to pretend he does something real with his life. Says the old ghosts of all those cowhands who used to ride for the XIT Ranch in its glory will rise up and protest if we sell out like that."

"What do the women think?" Glory shifted on the sofa. Now Matthew was both massaging at the wrong angle and twisting his shoulder the wrong way, too. He'd throw his back out if he wasn't careful.

Matthew chuckled. "Mrs. Hargrove is all set to evangelize the dudes."

Glory couldn't stand it any longer. "Here. Let me massage that for you. You're going to end up back in the clinic."

Glory stood behind the sofa and put her hands on Matthew's shoulder. She'd kneaded the shoulders of a fair number of tired cops in her day down at the station. This shouldn't be any different. It shouldn't matter that firelight instead of fluorescent light streamed into the room or that her heart beat a little too fast when she touched one particular man's shoulders.

Matthew sighed. Maybe Glory was an angel, after all. Her touch certainly put him in mind of heaven.

"Well, Mrs. Hargrove might do some good that way." Glory refocused on the conversation. She needed to concentrate. "With her evangelistic zeal."

"I don't know about that. You know as well as I do they'll only see her as 'local scenery.' A person has a right to be taken more seriously than that. I'd rather folks openly disagreed with her rather than see her as scenery."

"What was it Paul said? 'I am all things to all men whereby I might win some.'" Glory located the knot on Matthew's neck and rubbed it gently.

"He didn't mention anything about being scenery."

Glory felt the knot on Matthew's neck tighten beneath her fingers. He was even more tense now than when she'd started.

Glory had a flash of insight. "Was that what it was like for you?"

"Huh?" Matthew looked up at her too quickly.

"Being a minister," Glory said softly, and stopped massaging him. "Was that what it seemed like when you were a minister?"

Matthew took a deep breath and exhaled. How did she know? "Only at the end."

"After Susie died?"

Matthew nodded. "I was standing up there in front of the congregation and I felt so empty inside. Like I was only the picture of a minister standing in a pulpit. Like none of it was real."

"Grief will do that to you."

Matthew shook his head. He'd thought about this every day since he'd made the decision to walk away from that pulpit. "A real minister would have been able to cope. Oh, maybe not easily, but somehow. If I'm not able to be a minister in the bad times, what kind of a minister am I in the good times?"

"A human minister," Glory reassured him emphatically. She saw the defeat on his face. And the sorrow.

The sound of little feet padding swiftly down the steps distracted them both.

"I'm first," claimed Josh as he flung himself into his father's arms.

There goes one good massage wasted, Glory thought wryly. Pain didn't stop Matthew. He opened his arms wide enough to gather both boys to him. No matter what Matthew thought about his role as a minister, it was clear that his role as a father came naturally to him. Love between Matthew and his sons was a given. It was the bedrock of the twins' lives.

"Kiss?" Josh had left his father's arms and now stood before Glory.

Glory smiled. "Of course." She leaned down and hugged Josh. Then she gave him an exaggerated kiss, the kind she'd loved as a child. She "smacked" Josh so hard on the cheek that he started to giggle. Then she offered her own cheek. "Now me."

Josh puckered up and put his lips on her cheek for a big smack.

"Now Joey." Glory saw Joey was hanging back shyly.

When she opened her arms to him he smiled and ran up to her. She repeated the ritual with him.

Then both twins went to the edge of the sofa and knelt down as if it was the expected thing to do. This was obviously their habit.

"God bless…" Josh ran down his list first and then Joey followed. They both blessed classmates, Mrs. Hargrove, their father, the angel and even Mr. Gossett's cats.

Glory had to admit she was surprised. The night before she'd been upstairs putting clean sheets on her bed when the twins had made their trip down for a kiss. She'd had no idea Matthew prayed with them. Correction, she thought to herself, Matthew didn't pray with them, he watched over them while they prayed. Rather fiercely at that, as though challenging God to refuse their simple requests.

"Susie would have my hide if I didn't raise them to pray," Matthew said when the twins had gone upstairs.

"But don't they wonder why you don't pray?"

"We haven't really come to that bridge yet." Matthew picked up the family Bible, intending to stand up and put it back on the shelf. But then he realized he couldn't stand, not holding the crutches and the Bible. So he set the Bible back down on the coffee table. "So far they just assume I pray beside my bed when it's my bedtime. Since I have a later bedtime, they don't see me."

"Before too long, they're going to realize—"

"I know. I'm a coward. I keep hoping that maybe by the time they're old enough to ask the question they'll be old enough to understand." Matthew shifted his shoulder. He wished Glory would massage his neck again.

"I hope you're right." Glory watched fatigue and pain sketch lines on Matthew's face as he sat there. "Your shoulder still hurt?"

"Yes."

Glory stood up and walked behind the sofa. She reached down and began to knead Matthew's neck muscles again. This time she felt him relax. He leaned his head back and closed his eyes. The light from the fireplace gave a golden cast to his face. She had a swift urge to lift her hands from his neck and trace the line of his jaw. The suddenness and the strength of the feeling surprised her. Abruptly she pulled her hands away from him. "You need your sleep. I should be going upstairs."

Matthew's eyes opened. "You're really good at giving neck massages."

"Experienced, anyway," Glory said. She was glad she was standing behind him and he couldn't see that her face was flushed. "I give them all the time to the men in the department."

"The police department?" Matthew asked warily. He remembered that's where she said she worked. He supposed it was possible. The FBI might borrow someone like her to do a little preliminary research on cattle rustling. She would find out things a regular agent wouldn't. Just look how the folks in Dry Creek had already taken to her. She inspired confidences. He certainly found it easy to talk to her. Too easy.

Glory nodded. "The captain taught me. He used to give them, too. Said it was one thing a policeman always needed." Glory was chattering and she knew it. But it helped her collect her composure. She'd never had these feelings while giving a neck massage to anyone else. "From all the time in the patrol cars. And then the stress."

Matthew listened. Okay, so the police department angle was true. He didn't think Glory would lie. Not even if she was undercover.

Glory didn't stop. "Some of the worst stress. The captain used to say being on patrol was like being squeezed into a little box for hours and then stepping out for a few seconds to get shot at."

Shot at! Matthew stiffened. "You don't work where you get shot at, do you?" The thought of anyone shooting anywhere near Glory made him want to lock her in the house and never let her out. He hadn't thought about the undercover job in that regard. Surely no one would shoot at Glory.

"Well, not often—"

"*Not often!* What's not often?"

"Well…usually not really," Glory said, stumbling.

Matthew relaxed. "That's good. But just for my peace of mind, tell me, when was the last time someone shot at you?"

"Last Wednesday."

"Last Wednesday!" Matthew turned around and looked at her. She was already making her way to the stairs. "That's not often? *Last Wednesday!*"

"But it was nothing. Just some gang kids."

"Nothing! I don't care if it was kids, their bullets are just as real!"

Matthew stood up. He forgot he needed the crutch. He didn't even feel the pain in his knee. He knew he didn't have the right to order Glory to quit her job. But last Wednesday! She made it sound as if getting shot at was an everyday thing.

"Well, their bullets are not as straight as some," Glory said softly. She had one foot on the first stair and she smiled. She could tell Matthew that last Wednesday was the only time a bullet had come anywhere near her, that her job was as safe as being a plumber—but she found she liked the fierce look of protection that covered his face. In the firelight, with his chestnut hair mussed from the massage, he looked like a Highland warrior.

Matthew stopped himself from demanding that she quit her job. It was not his place. He knew that. But surely someone should stop her. "What does your mother think about that?"

"My mother thinks I'm a grown woman," Glory said. It was true. Her mother had been shocked that a bullet had hit the building close to where Glory was standing. But she hadn't worried about Glory's ability to take care of herself. Only the captain ever worried about her.

"Well, there's no doubt about you being grown." Matthew ran his hand over his hair. He was beginning to feel the pain in his knee, and he sank back down to the sofa. "It's just, well, bullets. That's not good."

"I'll be fine," Glory said softly. She was touched he would worry about her. "I really don't get shot at often."

Matthew snorted and shook his head. "Not often. Last Wednesday."

"Not often," Glory repeated firmly as her feet climbed the second stair. She felt a smile curling around inside her. He cared about her. Matthew cared. Well, she thought as she tried to rein in her happiness, he cared that someone didn't shoot at her. It might not be so much after all. Even a stranger might care that she not be shot and killed. Or run over by a truck. Or fall off a building.

"Say, who fixed the step?" Thinking of tragic accidents reminded her of the loose board that had tripped Matthew the day before. Only it wasn't loose any longer. She saw the bright heads of the new nails that held the board firmly in place.

"I did."

"But you can't get up these stairs?" Glory measured the distance. The loose board had been near the top of the stairs. She looked down at Matthew sitting on the sofa in the firelight.

"I can if I do a kind of backward crawl—push, sit, push." Matthew looked up at her and grinned. "Mrs. Hargrove didn't think about crawling."

"No, I guess she didn't."

Mrs. Hargrove might not have thought about it, but Glory couldn't think of anything else. She thought about it when she brushed her teeth and slipped on her pajamas. She thought about it when she turned down the sheets on Matthew's bed. She even thought about it as she lay slipping into dreamland. And every time she thought about it she smiled. Matthew's virtue, not his knee, kept him downstairs. That was as it should be. She didn't want to start getting attached to a man she couldn't trust— What? The thought pulled her away from sleep and made her sit up straight in bed. Attached? Was she getting attached to Matthew? She knew she was a little attracted to him. Okay, a lot attracted to him. But attached and attracted were two different things. She couldn't afford to be attached. They had no future together. No future at all. And she'd best remember that. She couldn't afford to get attached. No, there must be no attachment. Absolutely none.

The Bullet carefully cut into his piece of lemon meringue pie.

His plans hadn't worked out. He hadn't counted on the floor inside the church being wet from all the rain. But when they reached the doorway, the Bullet saw the slickness. The old man didn't walk very well and the Bullet worried he might slip. *I can see him to his pew. Then I'll leave. Just a quick dive in and then I'll be gone.*

But the hymn started before he got the old man set-tled, and a woman pressed a hymnal into his hands.

After the service the old man, Douglas was his name, insisted on buying him a piece of pie. The Bullet gave up. What would it hurt to sit with the man a bit and have a piece of pie?

Chapter Six

The hoofbeats in Glory's dream turned to pounding. She woke uncertain if the pounding was real or in her head. It took a minute to remember where she was, but in the half-light of morning the room was beginning to look familiar. Matthew's room. She was safe in Matthew's room. But something had startled her, she decided. There, she heard it again. A pounding from downstairs.

Matthew was in the kitchen starting the fire when he heard the first pound on the door. He hadn't brought his crutches with him, but had hobbled from sofa to wall to doorway to chair so that he wouldn't need to prop them up when he lit the stove. It was a good plan, but it didn't get him to the front door any too soon.

"What's wrong?" Matthew yelled when he finally pulled the door open.

There stood Duane Edison, a slender teenager with dark hair that needed cutting and a scowl on his lean face that needed tending. The boy paused for a moment before demanding. "I need to talk to the angel."

Matthew didn't open the door any farther. "Can't it wait for morning?"

"It is morning," Duane said in surprise. "It's past six. The sun's even coming up."

"Not everyone lives on Montana farm time. She doesn't get up at five."

"I'm up." Glory could hear them as she walked down the stairs. She'd thrown a woolly robe on over her pajamas and put a pair of heavy socks on her feet. Her hair wasn't combed and her teeth weren't brushed, but she was up. "What's wrong?"

"You the angel?" Duane asked as he peered past Matthew's shoulder.

"Around here I guess I am." Glory sat down on the sofa. She was too tired to debate the fact before she'd even had any coffee. "What do you need?"

"You the one that got Linda all funny on me?" Duane entered the house.

"Aah, you're the Music man," Glory remembered.

"Jazz Man," Duane said, tight-lipped. The cold had pinched his face and left it colorless. He wore a black leather jacket and had his hands jammed far down into his pockets. "I'm the Jazz Man."

"Of course, I remember." Glory pulled her robe closer. It was cold in the house. "You're her boyfriend."

"Was her boyfriend," he corrected her sourly as he joined her on the other end of the sofa. He took his hands out of his pockets and rubbed them together. He looked up at Matthew. "Want me to start a fire for you?"

"Just got one started. It takes a few minutes to warm up. But thanks for the offer."

"Heard about your leg," Duane mumbled. "Need any help, let me know."

"Thanks. I appreciate that."

"It's not like I have lots to do now, anyway." The boy

looked sideways at Glory. "Not since Linda gave me her ultimatum."

"Well, it's not like it needs to be forever. You kids are awfully young to get married." Glory stuck by her decision. Neither one of them looked a day over sixteen. It might not even be legal for them to marry without parental consent. "Way too young."

"Oh, we're still getting married." Duane looked up at her in determination. "It's just that now she wants a prenuptial agreement, says she won't even—" He stopped himself and looked at Matthew. "Well, you know, she won't—unless I sign an agreement." He looked at Matthew again, measuring him. "Is it true you're a preacher?"

"Was a preacher." Matthew nodded. Dry Creek didn't need a newspaper to get the news around. "Not anymore."

"Still, you probably don't..." Duane hesitated and then he hurried on. "I mean, you don't know what it's like."

Matthew squelched his chuckle. "I was a minister. I wasn't a eunuch. I know about sex and the trouble it can cause."

"It can get you into trouble, all right," Duane agreed with a sigh.

Glory decided the room was definitely getting warmer, even without the fire. "What kind of trouble are you and Linda in?"

"Oh, not that kind." Duane blushed. "We're careful."

"You wouldn't need to be careful if you didn't—" Glory stopped herself. If she knew anything about teenagers it was that one didn't inspire confidences by scolding them for the obvious. "What trouble is it, then?"

"It's money."

"Money?" Glory was surprised.

"Yeah, we need money if we're going to get married. Five thousand dollars."

"Why five thousand?"

"If we had five thousand we could put a down payment on the old Morgan place, not John's place, but his father's old place. It's not much, but it's good dry land and it's got a small house. Needs a new roof, but I could fix that. Already talked to the bank in Billings. They said we'd need five thousand at least. But neither of our folks have that to spare—couldn't ask them, anyway. So that's why I thought of music. I play a fair guitar and Linda sings real good. My friend Bob is good on the drums. Thought maybe we'd pick up some money at small county fairs and rodeos. Nothing big." Duane's face glowed proudly while he talked about their dream. "We'd have done it, too, except, well, you talked to Linda and…"

Glory's heart sank. "I didn't mean she should never marry you. Why, you both must still be in high school."

"Graduated last fall. Both of us."

"That'd make you how old?" Glory wasn't feeling any better. Giving love advice wasn't her calling in life. She should have sent the girl back to her mother.

"I'm nineteen. Linda's eighteen. We hadn't planned on going to college, so I've been helping my folks and Linda's working at a doughnut place in Miles City. We've both been saving our money, but so far all we have is twelve hundred dollars. That's why I thought of forming the band. Thought we'd maybe even get some Christmas gigs."

"I know some retirement homes up near Havre that might be willing to pay for a music program," Matthew said. His minister friends would be so happy to hear from him they'd probably pay the kids twice the usual rate. "That's if you know any church music."

"We grew up in Sunday school," Duane said indignantly. "We know them all from 'The Old Rugged Cross' to 'This Little Light of Mine.'"

"Well, that sounds like a good plan," Glory said. "Tell Linda to invite me to the wedding."

"Oh, she'll have to be the one inviting, all right," Duane said with a bitter edge to his voice. "After the prenuptial agreement, she'll make all the decisions."

"What?"

"The prenuptial," he repeated as though she must know. "She said you told her not to let me take advantage of her talent, so the prenup puts her in charge of everything. She's the lead singer. The money person. First on the deed to the Morgan place when we sign the paper. First in everything." Duane slumped down on the sofa. "She's even the one calling the shots about, well, you know…. Even kissing," he wailed indignantly. "Everything. She's in charge."

"Oh, dear," Glory murmured as her eyes met Matthew's over the slumped figure of Duane. Matthew's eyes had a sympathetic twinkle in them.

Matthew leaned over and whispered to Glory, "Not as easy as a person would think to be an angel. Lot like being a preacher. Everyone expects you to always know everything and always be right."

"Well, they picked the wrong person for always being right."

"No one's ever always right."

"How do I fix things now?"

Matthew straightened. "Duane, why don't you bring Linda here for supper tonight? Glory and I will talk to her."

"I hope you'll set her straight," Duane muttered as he stood. "A man can't have his wife wearing the pants in the family."

"There's nothing wrong with a woman making decisions," Glory began indignantly. "Most women have good heads on their shoulders."

"She going to be talking to Linda?" Duane looked at Matthew skeptically and cocked his thumb at Glory.

"You don't have a clue, do you, son?" Matthew put his arm around Duane's slender shoulders. "Being married isn't about one person making all the decisions. Being married is about teamwork. And a good team takes the best from both parties."

"Yes, sir," Duane agreed glumly as he walked toward the door.

"See you and Linda tonight at five-thirty," Matthew said as he opened the door for the young man. "And remember, think teamwork."

"Yes, sir."

Matthew waited for the door to completely close before he grinned and announced, "How about we start out with you talking to Duane? Then we switch."

"Sort of like good cop, bad cop?"

"Just giving them two perspectives."

"I don't think Duane wants two perspectives."

"That's why he needs them," Matthew said as he hobbled back to the kitchen door, whistling all the way.

Glory studied his face. It wasn't just the whistling. He was excited. "You like this, don't you? This people stuff. Giving advice. Solving problems. Helping out."

Matthew turned around as he reached the kitchen. "Yeah, I guess I do."

Glory fretted about Linda and Duane until she turned the key in the hardware-store door. Matthew was late taking the twins to school, so he'd asked her to open up for him so that Elmer and Jacob could get their coffee.

"Brrr." Glory watched her breath turn white. The hardware store was as cold inside as it was outside. "It'll take more than coffee to take the edge off this morning."

"It's a cold snap, all right," Elmer agreed. "Almost didn't get the pickup started to come down."

Yesterday Glory had set up her easel close to the front window of the hardware store. The night cold had frosted over the edges of the large window, but the middle was clear. She could look out and see the whole main street of Dry Creek.

Coffee could wait a minute, she decided. The view from this window was postcard perfect.

The Big Sheep Mountains stood solid and round in the distance, their low peaks wearing blankets of fresh velvety snow. About halfway down, the thick snow changed to thin gray patches mingled with muddy-green shrubs. On the frozen ground right outside in Dry Creek, old snow lined the asphalt street and bunched up against the buildings.

"How long has this town been here?" Glory asked as she turned to Elmer and Jacob. The two men were putting wood in the fire.

"Since the days of the Enlarged Homestead Act of 1909," Elmer said as he put a match to the kindling. "Folks—a lot of them from Scandinavia—came here. Trainloads of them—a body could lay claim to 320 acres of Montana and all they had to do was live on it for three years. Sounded like a dream come true."

Elmer paused to put his hands out to the warming fire. "Course, they couldn't predict the drought. And the hard times. Wasn't long before people all over these parts were leaving. They couldn't scrape together enough to plant crops, to eat, to live. But old man Gossett—father to the Gossett who lives next to the parsonage—owned the land here and he told folks we'd make it if we worked together. That's when they founded the town—called it Dry Creek after a little creek that used to flow into the Yellowstone. Folks thought the creek would come back after the drought ended and we could change the name of the town. The creek didn't return, but we kept the name. Kinda liked it after a while. Reminded us things have been worse. Gave us hope. We've always scraped by in Dry Creek before and we'll do it again."

"Hmph," Jacob added as he shut the door to the old woodstove.

Glory didn't know if he was agreeing or disagreeing "What do the young people do?" She was still thinking of Duane and Linda. "Do they stay or move away?"

"Most leave," Elmer said with a touch of scorn as he reached behind him for the electric coffeemaker. "There's not much work here and what work there is is hard work. Kids nowadays want it easy."

"Can't blame the kids for wanting to eat." Jacob defended them as he measured coffee into the filter.

"Maybe you need to start some kind of business here," Glory offered as she walked closer to the fire and rubbed her hands "I've read about Midwestern towns that brought in businesses so there'd be jobs for people. Maybe you could try that."

Elmer gave a bitter chuckle. "You see the window there. Look out it. Do you see anything that would make a big corporation move here?"

"I didn't say it needed to be a big corporation," Glory persisted as she spread her hands out to catch the heat that was already coming from the small cast-iron stove. "All you need is a few small businesses. Maybe an outfit that makes something."

"The women at the church made up a batch of jams

one year that were good—I always thought they could sell them," Jacob said thoughtfully as he put his wooden chair in front of the fire.

"Well, that would be a start," Glory said as the bell over the door rang. A gust of cold air followed Matthew into the store. "Maybe they could hook up with a catalog. Do special orders. It'd definitely be a start."

The crutches kept Matthew from swiveling to close the door quickly, so another gust of cold came in before he got the door shut. "Sorry." Matthew wiped some fresh snowflakes off his wool coat. "Start of what?"

"Glory was thinking of new business ideas for Dry Creek," Elmer informed him as the coffee started to perk.

"What kind of businesses?" Matthew asked as he took off his jacket and hung it on a nail behind the counter.

Glory tried not to look, but the snowflakes made Matthew's hair shine. He had flakes on his eyelashes and eyebrows. The cold drew the skin tight against his cheeks and forehead. Lean a pair of skis against his shoulder and he could be an advertisement for sweaters or skis or some resort. He could be a model.

"Any kind of business." Glory shrugged. "Jams. Woodworking. Modeling."

"Modeling? You mean sitting for a painting?" Matthew asked thoughtfully. "Would anyone pay for that?"

"I've heard they do if you're nude." Jacob poured himself a cup of coffee.

"I wasn't thinking of nude modeling." Glory blushed.

"Kind of artistic for the folks around here," Elmer said as he joined Jacob at the coffeepot. "But I suppose folks would do it to make a buck." He looked at Glory. His face was suspiciously deadpan. "What do you art people pay for nude modeling, anyway?"

"I've never paid anything," Glory protested.

"Well, you can't expect someone to do it for free," Jacob chided her, and then paused. "Well, maybe they would for you. What do you think, Reverend, would you model for free for the little angel here?"

Matthew choked on his laughter. He didn't know if it was possible for Glory's face to turn pinker. He kind of liked it that way. "Maybe if she did one of those abstract paintings so no one would recognize me. I wouldn't want to embarrass the boys."

"I don't paint nude pictures. I wasn't even thinking of nude pictures. I meant modeling for catalogs and things."

Elmer nodded wisely. "Ah, underwear."

"No, not underwear." Glory forced her voice to stay calm. "I meant sweaters. Jackets. Clothes. That kind of thing. But that's only one idea. The jam idea is better. Why doesn't one of you mention that to the women?"

"Guess we could," Jacob conceded.

"There could be a big market for it if the dude ranch—I mean, the guest ranch goes into operation."

"Don't remind me," Elmer said.

But reminding him was exactly what Glory intended to do. It allowed her to sit back while the two older men lamented what the dudes would do to Dry Creek. She felt like fanning her face, but she knew the men would notice her behavior and remark on it, since it was still chilly inside the store. So she resolutely began to mix some oils on her palate. Blue and green. She'd use blue and green for something. She never should have thought about modeling—any kind of modeling. Even sweaters made her think of broad shoulders. And hats made her think of masculine chin lines. And belts of trim waists. No, she should wipe out any thoughts of modeling from her mind. She'd focus on the blue and green. She had the colors mixed before she realized she'd mixed the exact color of Matthew's eyes.

Matthew watched Glory bristle and pretend to ignore the older men. He wondered if he should remind her that she'd neglected to put on the smock that she'd worn yesterday when she was working with oils. It'd be a shame if she got paint on the sweater she was wearing, a light pink that emphasized the color in her cheeks. He rather liked that pink sweater—it made her look cuddly. Maybe instead of saying something he should just take her smock over to her.

It was hard to be gallant on crutches, Matthew thought, grimacing as he held out the smock to Glory. His hand had pressed wrinkles in it where he'd clutched it close to the bar of his crutch handle.

"Thank you."

The day passed slowly for Matthew. Glory spelled him at the counter so he could go home and bake the cupcakes he'd forgotten to make. The church day-care staff was having a bake sale to help pay for the set design for the Christmas pageant.

"They need any bales of hay?" Elmer asked when Matthew got back. "Tell them I can donate all they need."

"And if the manger needs fixing, I can see to it," Jacob offered.

"I don't know if hay and a manger is going to be enough this year," Matthew said as he hobbled behind the counter and sat down on his stool. "Everyone's got it in their head that this year the pageant needs to be special."

"I could spray-paint the manger gold," Jacob suggested. "Maybe put some bells on it or something. Tack on some holly, even."

"I'll pass the word along to Mrs. Hargrove." Matthew chuckled. "Don't know how else to jazz things up."

"Jazz," Glory muttered as her brush slipped. She'd been so engrossed in painting she'd completely forgotten about the Jazz Man and Linda.

"Saltshaker's on the stove." Matthew called directions to Glory from his place by the sink. Tonight he was letting everyone help with the dinner. The twins were in the living room making sure the magazines were set straight. Glory had an apron on and was boiling water for pasta. They were having chicken parmigiana.

"So you're going to go with the 'just a team' theme?" Glory asked as she bent down to locate a strainer to drain the pasta once it cooked. "Horses in harness, that sort of thing?"

"Well, I suppose."

"So what do you want me to say?"

"Whatever you want," Matthew said as he grinned over at her. "You're half of the team. You decide."

"Well, this half of the team isn't so good at giving advice." Glory found the strainer. "Look at what my advice has already done."

"Now, that wasn't your fault." Matthew defended her staunchly. "Linda came to you and asked for your opinion. Besides, all couples have this discussion—best to do it before the wedding."

"Let's just hope there'll still be a wedding after I'm through with them."

Matthew laughed.

"More garlic bread?" Glory offered the plate to Duane. He was wearing a suit and tie and Linda was wearing a long gray dress. The couple were obviously nervous and on their best behavior. Even the twins were sitting at the table politely eating.

Duane nodded and took a piece.

"You'll have to give me your recipe," Linda said, smiling slightly at Glory.

"Not my recipe. Matthew made the garlic bread."

"Oh, really?" Linda appeared interested and gave Duane a meaningful look. "So Matthew helped with the meal."

Glory choked on the sip of water she'd taken. "No, *I* helped. Matthew cooked the dinner—garlic bread to chicken parmigiana. I helped by boiling water for the pasta."

"He did it all!" Linda's face lost its politeness. She was delighted. She nudged Duane. "He cooked the dinner!"

Duane groaned and looked at Matthew in disgust. "Now see what you've done."

Matthew nodded. "I'd guess the guys tell you cooking is women's work?"

Duane nodded.

"Ever think how helpless that makes you?" Matthew helped himself to another piece of garlic bread.

"Helpless?" Duane growled. "What do you mean?"

"Well, look at me," Matthew said. "I've had to learn how to cook the hard way. Every man needs to know how to cook and clean. The chores should be split."

"But I thought you said being married was teamwork," Duane protested. "I do half, she does half. Nothing that says my half needs to be meals. Besides, getting married better be about more than who's going to do the cooking!"

Matthew laughed. "It is. But I've got to warn you. Being married has its surprises!"

"Like what?"

Matthew sobered. He didn't want his failures to dampen the enthusiasm of the young couple before him. "I never knew what it would feel like to be so responsible for someone. I'd sworn to take care of that other person with all of my heart and all of my might. To do anything to keep her safe."

Matthew stopped himself. When the dull pain of loss at Susie's death had begun to ease, the guilt had started. He hadn't kept Susie safe. His faith had not been enough. But that was his failure. It was between him and God. No one else needed to suffer it with him. He should have sidestepped that question.

"Anyway, back to cooking." Matthew forced himself to smile. "The twins have paid the price of my learning to cook."

Duane cleared his throat. "Guess I could learn to cook some things. Maybe breakfast. Or spaghetti. Or something."

"My daddy can even cook angel cake," Josh boasted.

Glory groaned. "I'm not an angel."

"Not even a little?" Linda asked hesitantly.

Glory shook her head. Something was going on here. She didn't like the guilty look on the girl's face.

"Well, Debra Guthert asked me about you. I think she's writing you up as an angel for the paper in Billings."

Matthew had a sinking sensation. Debra Guthert lived in Miles City and wrote the "Southeastern" column for the *Billings Gazette*. Her column covered the ranches and small towns along the Yellowstone River, northeast of Billings past Terry and Glendive to the North Dakota border and the area south of Interstate 94 from Hardin to the Chalk Buttes. Except for a few colorful announcements from the Crow Indian Reservation, it was usually mundane things like family reunions and rattlesnake sightings. "Why didn't someone stop her?"

Matthew didn't need an answer to the question. An angel would make the Dry Creek Christmas pageant the social event of the winter. Which would mean—suddenly Matthew felt much better.

"You have to stay now." Matthew turned to Glory. Even Glory couldn't refuse the power of the press. "It's in print."

Glory looked around her. Five pairs of hopeful eyes. She groaned. How could she leave Dry Creek now?

Matthew stared into the embers of the fire. He'd wrapped so many blankets around himself he felt like a mummy. He was warm enough. The sofa was soft enough. The house was quiet enough. But he couldn't sleep. The frozen pain he'd lived in for the past four years was shifting. He could hear the cracking inside him as surely as he could hear the cracking of the Yellowstone River when the spring thaw came. And that cracking scared him. If his pain left him, he knew he'd want to love again. And how could he love again? He couldn't take another chance on love. He'd failed one woman. He didn't need to fail another one, especially not Glory.

"Go ahead and call her," Douglas urged the Bullet. The sadness in the old man's eyes was steady. "You don't know what I'd give for one last phone call with my Emily."

Douglas was standing in the guest bedroom of his house with the receiver of a black phone stretched out to the Bullet.

What have I gotten myself into? The Bullet didn't know what to do. He was sailing in uncharted water. He knew how to act around other hit men. He knew how to act around clients. But a friend? A new friend? He didn't know the rules.

Chapter Seven

Glory wished she had a pair of sunglasses to hide behind. Two people had already stopped by the hardware store to ask her to sign their copy of the "Southeastern" column in this morning's *Billings Gazette*. Linda had not exaggerated. The column talked in glowing terms of the two little boys who believed an angel had come to Dry Creek for Christmas.

Mrs. Hargrove predicted that attendance at the Christmas pageant would soar now that everyone from Billings knew about the angel. In fact, it appeared that attendance might be too high. No one knew what to do with all the people they were expecting.

"We could open the windows to the church and people could stand outside and watch the pageant through them," Jacob said. Earlier he'd noted that the "Southeastern" column might have spread farther than Billings. "They might not hear the shepherds singing, but they could at least see them come down the aisle."

Jacob, Elmer and Mrs. Hargrove were gathered around the potbellied stove, drinking coffee and planning the Christmas pageant. Mrs. Hargrove had called a substitute to take over for her in the day-care program so that she could devote herself to planning for the pageant now that it looked as if it would be such a big affair. It was already December 22. They didn't have much time to plan for all the extra people coming. Glory decided that if you didn't listen too closely to the words, you would almost think the three were planning a war. Or at least a Southern ball.

"We'll need a place for coats." Mrs. Hargrove had a clipboard on her lap and a pencil in her hand.

"It'll be too cold. People won't give up their coats," Matthew said from his stool behind the counter.

Matthew was, Glory would almost swear to it, sorting nuts and bolts. What else could he be doing? He had a long piece of twine and he kept attaching first one nut and then a bolt to it. She was the only one who was sane this morning, she assured herself as she added the Madonna look to her sketch. She'd found out that Lori, the little girl who wanted the Betsy Tall doll, was going to be Mary in the pageant. Glory had decided to do a rough ink sketch of the girl from memory. It might come in useful for a program for the pageant. Now that she'd decided to stay for the event, she found herself getting excited.

"There's not going to be enough room." Mrs. Hargrove repeated her worry as she wrote a number on her notepad. "The church won't hold more than a hundred people. And that's if we put folding chairs in the aisles, open the doors to the kitchen and move the tract rack into the office."

"The young'uns are smaller, they'll squeeze in, sit on a parent's lap—maybe even on the floor," Elmer suggested. He rested his elbows on the table that usually held a checkerboard. Today the game board was missing and a pot of coffee stood in its place.

"Maybe we could get in a hundred and fifty." Mrs.

Hargrove frowned as she added some numbers on her notepad.

"Wonder if we should charge?" Jacob asked from the sidelines. He'd stood up to get a new mug and was walking back toward the stove.

"Charge!" Mrs. Hargrove puffed up indignantly. "Why, we can't charge! It's a holy moment. Christ coming to earth. Shouldn't be any money changing hands."

"I just thought it'd make things easier for Christmas." Jacob spread his hands and sat back down on a straight-backed chair. "Raise a little money for the children and all."

"Well." The puff went out of Mrs. Hargrove, and she glanced sideways at Glory. "It would help. Don't suppose God would mind if it was for the children. Maybe we could just ask for a donation. We could get some of the things they wished for. Awful hard to see children go without at Christmas."

Glory stopped her sketching. She'd spent some time last night sorting the pictures she'd received from the children of Dry Creek. "I'm going to place the order. I've already called my friend Sylvia. She's going to help me. I'm just waiting to find out if there are other children who want to bring me a Christmas wish. Josh and Joey said they'd spread the word."

Matthew looked up from the ornament he was making, but kept silent. Josh had told him Glory had asked them to invite all of the children of Dry Creek to bring her a drawing. He knew Glory couldn't possibly be buying presents for all of the children in Dry Creek. Why, there must be forty children under twelve in the area. And there'd be another fifteen or so who hoped they were young enough for an angel present. And if all the children were like his two, that'd mean the presents were at least twenty dollars apiece. It'd add up to a thousand dollars minimum.

Matthew knew he should speak out. But he couldn't. If it was anyone but Glory making such ridiculous claims, he'd have no trouble. But this was Glory. He wanted to believe in her as much as the children of Dry Creek did.

"Well, we need to have faith this Christmas," Mrs. Hargrove said. "We might not have all of the money in the world. Fact is, we may not have much of it. But money isn't everything with God. The Lord fed the five thousand with a few loaves and fishes." Mrs. Hargrove had a determined look on her face that said if He could do it, they could do it. "We should be able to get the children something. Christmas isn't about big gifts, anyway."

Glory gave up. It was clear the adults in Dry Creek did not believe her. But she knew the children did, and that's what counted. "If you want, you could give out sacks of peanuts and candy."

"Jacob and I could make popcorn balls," Elmer said, his eyes lighting up in anticipation.

"And the angel could give out sacks of candy," Jacob suggested.

"The children would love that." Mrs. Hargrove spoke authoritatively as though that settled the matter. "And it would make a good picture for the *Gazette* if they send a photographer."

Glory looked around the hardware store. The shelves had been recently dusted, but it was obvious the merchandise took a long time to sell. There were some hammers. An assortment of screwdrivers. A row of small household goods like toasters and irons. Even a row of doorknobs and plumbing fixtures. The people inside the store were so convinced she was penniless that she didn't know how to convince them otherwise. All they knew of her was what they'd seen in this store and Matthew's house. She had money in neither of those places. Therefore, in the eyes of the adults of Dry Creek, her resources were limited. They liked reading in the newspaper that she might be an angel, but they didn't believe she had the power to buy even a few gifts.

Matthew watched the thoughts chase themselves through Glory's mind. He wondered if she knew how expressive her face was. When she was happy, she glowed. When she was mad, she steamed. When she was embarrassed, she blushed. Right now she was feeling frustrated. Her face was a clear road map. He liked that.

"If we're going to do candy for the children, I can also get the Ladies' Fellowship to make cookies and coffee for the adults," Mrs. Hargrove offered. "Doris June can make her lemon bars."

"You might even set up a table and sell some of that jam I hear about," Glory suggested. She wondered what was making Matthew frown like that. She'd been watching him out of the corner of her eye all morning.

"The ladies would love that." Mrs. Hargrove beamed. "We could raise money for the church. Maybe we'll raise enough to get a substitute pastor for a few services next year. I do so miss having a preacher on Sunday mornings."

Matthew kept his eyes on his ornament. He was stepping close to quicksand. First Susie and now this. "Sounds like you do pretty good, though. I hear hymn singing every Sunday morning."

"We take turns reading from the Bible, too," Mrs. Hargrove agreed, and then sighed. "But it's not the same. And I've been thinking for the pageant it'd be nice to have a real preacher to at least give a small devotional. Especially with all the people coming. They'll expect—"

The bell above the door rang, announcing the entrance of Tavis, the son of the Big Sheep Mountain Ranch owner.

Matthew breathed more easily. He was saved by the bell. He didn't like the direction Mrs. Hargrove's thoughts were taking. He would rather wear angel wings than preach.

The cowboy was a distraction. In his early twenties, Tavis was lean and wiry. Since it was December, he wore his winter Stetson, the one with wool flaps that could be pulled down over his ears if needed.

"Hi." Tavis nodded to Matthew and then to the group around the stove. His gaze slid over to Glory, and he tipped his hat. "Ma'am."

Glory looked up from her sketch. She supposed the man in the hat was another autograph seeker. He certainly was walking toward her as if he had a mission in mind. He didn't get more than two strides toward her before Matthew spoke up.

"Can I help you?" It didn't take Matthew more than a minute to remember that Tavis was single and the reputed ladies' man of the Big Sheep Mountain Ranch. Matthew had not dated anyone in Dry Creek, so he assumed the few other single men in the area didn't even count him as competition when someone like Glory landed in town. He supposed word of the angel had gotten to the bunkhouse at the Big Sheep just as soon as this morning's *Gazette* was delivered, and Tavis had come to investigate.

"Ah, just picking up some nails." Tavis turned to Matthew with a wink.

Matthew grunted. It was the angel, all right. The Big Sheep Mountain Ranch bought their nails by the double case a couple of times a year. Henry had the boxes shipped directly to the ranch from his supplier in Chicago. They'd just processed an order last month. "Ran out, did you?"

"Ah, no—just wanted a handful of those little ones." Tavis twisted his hat. He stood in the middle of the floor, not moving closer to Glory, but obviously not retreating, either. "Thought I'd, you know, hang a few pictures in the bunkhouse."

"Oh." Elmer busied himself with his coffee cup. "Since when do you hang pictures in the bunkhouse?"

"Aunt Francis has been trying to get us cultured, and now that the *Gazette* said there's an artist in town—well, we thought we should get a picture for the wall."

Glory measured the cowboy with her eyes. He'd gained a few points with her by calling her an artist instead of an angel, but she hadn't worked with the guys in the police department for nothing. She knew a man on the prowl when she saw one. And this one was not just on the prowl. He was out to prove a point. She'd wager Tavis was duded up for her benefit. His Stetson was midnight black with no smudges or unplanned dents. His jeans were so new they still had the package crease down the leg. His face was freshly shaven and his hair neatly trimmed. She wondered if he'd be nearly as interested in her artwork if she hadn't been written up in the newspaper or recommended by his aunt.

"I could paint you a scene around the Big Sheep Mountains," Glory offered. The snowcapped mountains took her breath away each morning. The sky was pale blue today and the sun shone off the snow as if it was freshly polished silver. "But I won't have time until the pageant is all taken care of."

"The Christmas pageant? I haven't been to that for years."

"It's going to be special this year," Mrs. Hargrove said, determination giving an edge to the words. "Tell everyone at the Big Sheep—this year will be special."

"If you need any help, let us know. The boys and I are always glad to help." Tavis managed to face Mrs. Hargrove and smile at Glory at the same time. "Lifting things—that kind of thing."

Tavis held up his arm and flexed his muscle. "Comes from lifting hay bales."

"We might need to have you hoist some of the visitors up on your shoulder," Matthew suggested from the counter. He supposed Tavis was harmless. Glory didn't seem to be taking the bait. The cowboy kept flashing his smiles in Glory's direction, but she didn't beam back at him. She was polite, but that was it. "Trying to figure out how to get everyone inside the church to see it. Now that it's been mentioned in the *Gazette,* more people will be coming."

"Well, who says you need to have it in the church?"

Matthew almost chuckled at the look of horror that spread across Mrs. Hargrove's face as she spoke. "Not have it in the church? Where else would we have it? We can't have it here. The café's closed, the school's too small and we can't have it in the street!"

Tavis twirled his black hat around in his hands. He'd gone full circle. "You could use our storage barn."

"Your barn!"

Matthew was the first to see the possibilities. "Why not? The Big Sheep barn is huge. We could build some bleachers. There's lots of space for parking. It's right on the edge of town. Everyone knows where it is."

"But a barn?" Mrs. Hargrove wailed.

"Jesus was born in a stable," Glory reminded them

all. She liked the idea. "That's about as close to a barn as you can get."

"But a barn? I think you still have cows there. What'll you do with them?"

"We can move them out," Tavis said.

"Or not," Matthew said. "A few cows around might add atmosphere."

"Cows in the pageant!" Mrs. Hargrove was horrified. "What will people think of us?"

"They'll think we're high society," Elmer said as he leaned over and put another piece of wood in the stove.

"And the carol does say 'The cattle are lowing,'" Glory offered.

"That's true." Mrs. Hargrove perked up. "It just might work. Think your dad will go for it? He hasn't been in church for years."

Tavis grimaced. "I know. But he'll do it for the town. Work is slow this time of year and the boys and I could do most of the setup."

"It just might work," Mrs. Hargrove repeated as she ripped off her old page in the notebook and started a fresh page. "We'll need ten, no, fifteen bleachers and…"

Glory half listened throughout the afternoon to the plans for the pageant. Her attention was primarily on the front window of the hardware store, however, or rather, what was happening outside the window. The children did not care about the article in the *Gazette*. They had other thoughts on their minds. Every few minutes she would see a timid wave from a child, and Glory would go to the door. First a pink mitten. Then a blue mitten. Then a gray mitten. All of the children wore warm coats, but she noticed that some of the coat sleeves were too short, as though the coats were several years old and too small. Still, each mittened hand held the same thing: a painstakingly drawn picture of a toy.

Glory made sure each child told her what the toy was called and his or her full name. She was careful to write both on the slip of paper before she went back into the store. She wanted to be sure that each child had their individual present. She knew that any present would be appreciated, but she also knew that the feeling of having a present given especially to you was one that helped children develop self-esteem and the ability to trust.

Matthew knew what Glory was doing. She was making too many quick trips outside for him not to notice. Especially because each time she came back in her cheeks and nose were rosy from the cold. He couldn't decide which he liked better—Glory with the cream-colored skin and freckles or Glory with the roses. She would make a beautiful angel. He was glad she'd been coaxed into staying. He and the twins hadn't had a really happy Christmas since Susie died. He'd barely had the energy to put a tree up this year, and it still wasn't fully decorated. But now this Christmas promised to be one they would never forget. He'd have to get the rest of the Christmas bulbs down from the upstairs closet so the tree could sparkle the way it should.

"You're welcome to listen," Glory said after she'd asked Matthew for the use of his phone again that evening. Her phone card guaranteed she could call from his phone with no charge to him, but she wanted him to know she was making arrangements for the presents. She accepted the fact that Mrs. Hargrove and the two older men didn't believe she could bring the children the presents they wanted, but she had hoped Matthew would believe her. He'd become important to her, and she wanted to know he trusted her.

"I have to set the things out for the twins' lunch tomorrow," Matthew said as he pulled himself up from the sofa. He had no reason to keep sitting there, anyway. Glory had read the twins another Bible story, and they had had their good-night prayers. This time he'd listened from the doorway with a dish towel on his shoulder. He'd been tempted to give up all pretense of not listening and just go in and sit down with his sons. But he hadn't. Glory's voice reading from the Bible lulled him into thinking everything was all right with his soul, and he knew it wasn't. He didn't want a Band-Aid slapped on his relationship with God. He wanted to feel the pain of it until it healed from the inside out.

"Joey said he wants peanut butter," Glory reminded him as she reached for the phone sitting on the coffee table.

"Joey always wants peanut butter," Matthew said as he slipped the crutches under his arms and began to hobble toward the kitchen. "He likes the way it sticks to his mouth."

Matthew limped into the kitchen and then turned and closed the door between the kitchen and the living room. He wanted to give Glory privacy in his home. He particularly did not want to make her feel as if she had to lie to make him think she was really ordering presents. A gift, after all, came from the heart, and Glory's heart had opened wide to his sons. That was a more important gift than a laser light gun and a Lego machine set.

Glory dialed the number and said hello.

"Glory?" Sylvia's voice came through sounding breathless. "I'm so glad you called."

"Why?" Prickles were running down Glory's spine again. Her friend's voice didn't sound relaxed.

"I've heard some disturbing news." Sylvia paused. "I don't know if it's true—you know how kids are. I wasn't sure if I should say anything yet. I told the police, but I don't know for sure."

"What is it, Sylvia?"

"Two of my kids—they're good kids, but they hang with a bad crowd."

Glory started to breathe more easily. There were always kids in trouble at the youth center where Sylvia worked in Tacoma. Most of the teens were part of tough criminal gangs. "You'll help them go straight—remember the judge will work with you."

"Oh, they didn't do anything—at least, it didn't turn out the way they planned." Sylvia took a deep breath. "They told me there's a hit out on you. Two of the older boys in the gang had been contracted to do it. But then, last night, something happened. My two boys got scared and ended up at the mission. Even went forward for an altar call. I had mentioned your name with the presents you were buying and this morning they came back and told me. Said the hit hadn't gone through, that the guy doing the shooting had missed you and hadn't found you again. No one seems to know who the contact was or if the hit's still on. My boys feel so bad about it they want to go find you and stand in front of you so no bullets can get through."

A sliver of fear raced down Glory's back.

"Thank God you're in Montana," Sylvia continued in a rush.

"Yes, I should be safe here," Glory repeated in a daze. She slowly twisted the phone card around her finger. "These boys don't know where I am, do they?"

"No. Thank God I didn't mention where you were when I talked about the presents."

"Good."

Sylvia paused. "They did seem genuinely worried. I think they'd protect you if they could."

"Yeah, well, if I stay out of sight I won't need any protection."

Glory kept calm. She went over the list of presents with Sylvia. Glory was used to stress. She knew about shootings and crime. She would be fine. She kept repeating that phrase to herself. But when she hung up the phone she started to shake.

Matthew waited for the lull of voices to stop before he came back into the living room. He knew something was wrong. Glory's face was ashen. Even in the firelight, all warmth had left her face. No smile remained. Her hair still picked up the fire flecks and reflected them back, but all else about her was still.

"It's all right." Matthew hobbled over and sat down on the edge of the sofa. He wanted to reach over and put his arm around her, but she looked too fragile. As though even that movement would snap her control. "No one really expects them."

Glory looked up at him. "What do you mean?"

"The presents," Matthew continued patiently. "No one really expected you to be able to deliver on the presents. It's enough that you wanted to."

Glory started to laugh, even though she knew nothing was funny. Hysteria started this way. She knew that. But she couldn't stop. Matthew thought she couldn't deliver the presents. But the presents were all settled. Her problem was worse than that. She didn't know if she'd ever be able to walk the streets of Seattle again. Someone had been shooting at her. It wasn't a stray bullet. It was meant to hit her. She was the target. *Dear Lord, she was the target!*

Matthew watched Glory's teeth start to chatter, and her laughter calm down to hiccups. Suddenly he didn't care if she pulled away from him. He moved closer and put his arm around her shoulder. She whimpered. He wrapped his arm more fully around her and gathered her to his shoulder. He stroked her head and hummed a lullaby in her ear. He hoped to calm her. But it didn't work. She started to cry in earnest.

"What's wrong?" Matthew had to know. He felt a vise squeezing his heart. Something was wrong.

"They're shooting at me," Glory wailed.

"Who?"

"I don't know."

It was the bullet. Matthew knew the bullet on Wednesday had been too close. "You'll stay in your room. You're not leaving this house unless I'm along. No, you're not leaving even then. You'll just stay here. I can bring you what you need."

The determination in Matthew's voice quieted her. "Forever?"

"If necessary." Matthew nodded grimly. "I'll lock you in."

Glory smiled. She felt much better. "But that's kidnapping."

"Whatever it takes to keep you safe."

Strangely enough, Glory decided, she did feel safe. She'd just learned that there might be a contract out on her life, and yet, she felt safe here in this house. She'd like to pretend that had nothing to do with the man sitting beside her on the sofa worrying about her. But it wasn't true. His fierce protection made her feel as if nothing could harm her, not while he still drew breath.

* * *

The Bullet set down his coffee cup.

He shouldn't have stayed, but his phone call last night with Millie had unnerved him. She'd heard Douglas's voice in the background and assumed Douglas was the uncle he visited.

"Yes, I'll invite him to visit," the Bullet had told Millie last night after she kept insisting. "But he doesn't travel much. He won't come. No, not even for Christmas."

If the Bullet had known Millie was making Christmas plans, he would have stalled her. He'd never thought about Christmas coming. Santa stockings and roasting chestnuts were not for a man like him. He usually celebrated Christmas at an all-night bar with a bottle of tequila. That's where a man like him spent Christmas.

Chapter Eight

"You're going to call?" Matthew was making pancakes for breakfast. He had been up early worrying and had decided to stir up some batter. Glory was in trouble and he needed to find a way to keep her safe. "They must know more at the precinct than they've told you. And they have the photos. They might offer a clue."

"It's not even morning there," Glory said. The small Franklin stove had a fire going in it, but the air inside the house was still cold enough to make foggy breath. She rubbed her hands together. She had pulled on her jeans and a heavy sweater when she heard Matthew moving around the kitchen. They had spent time last night talking about the shooting she'd seen inside Benson's Market. "I don't know for sure if they'll send me copies of the photos—it's not exactly regulation."

"Forget regulation," Matthew demanded as he poured more batter on the griddle and automatically made the batter into a snowman. "Someone's out to get you."

"Only in Seattle."

"That's bad enough." Matthew reached up into the cupboard and found a small canister of raisins. He put eye, nose and button raisins on the snowman.

Glory nodded. Matthew wasn't even aware of what he was doing—making cute pancakes while talking about violence. He did everything a mother would do for his sons. "I'll ask them to send copies of the photos—but I don't know what good they'll do."

"Henry's got a fax at the store. Fax copies of them there," Matthew said as he poured another pancake snowman. He didn't know what good the photos would do, either. He just knew he needed to do something. "And don't talk to anyone but that guy Frank you say you can trust."

"Nobody on the force would sell me out," Glory said, and then thought a minute. She took some silverware from the drawer. The metal was cold to her touch. Maybe Matthew was right. How did she know for sure none of them would tell a hit man where she was if the price was right?

"And you'll work on those drawings? You must have seen something," Matthew said.

Glory had agreed to draw the crime scene again. The captain and she had been over this already. But Matthew sounded a lot like the captain. Both men believed she must be a target because of her trained eyes.

"Someone's worried you're going to remember something." Matthew repeated what he had said last night. "Our job is to find out what that is."

"I've been over it hundreds of times in my mind."

"Have you drawn out the sketches of everything?"

"Just the face of the guy doing the shooting." Glory had thought about that, too. Surely there wouldn't be something in the grocery store itself. Who would leave evidence of a crime in plain sight for dozens of shoppers to see?

"And he's in jail?"

Glory nodded. "And nothing to gain by killing me at this point. I did sketches, but it wasn't necessary. He was arrested at the scene. And there were ten witnesses."

"Now, why would a guy shoot someone in front of ten witnesses?"

"Poor planning," Glory joked as she gathered four cups from the cupboard.

"Or something was happening that required immediate action," Matthew said as he flipped the first snowman pancake. "Something important enough to risk jail time."

"But that's just it—nothing was happening. The butcher was just walking out of the meat department with a package of steak in his hands."

"What kind of steaks?"

Glory looked at Matthew as if he was crazy. "What kind of steaks?"

"Yeah, T-bone, porterhouse, cube…"

"What difference does that make?"

Matthew flipped the other snowman pancake. "Who knows? My guess is it's that kind of little detail that we're looking for, something all of the other ten people have long forgotten. But with your eye, it's still in your head. If you draw it out, who knows? That's what someone is worried about."

"Makes sense." Glory walked toward the kitchen table and set down the cups. Matthew did make sense. If someone was out gunning for her, it was time to empty her mind of all the crime details and put them out front on paper. Maybe then they'd know who—or what—they were up against.

Matthew looked up. He heard the sound of the twins coming down the stairs before Glory did. "Juice in the refrigerator. Apricot syrup, too. Maybe some maple, as well."

Glory nodded and went back to the cupboard to collect plates.

"And butter," Matthew said. "Joey won't eat pancakes without butter."

Once the plates were on the table, Glory went to the refrigerator.

Glory turned when she heard the twins enter the kitchen. They were in slippers and pajamas with sweatshirts pulled over them. Their hair was mussed and their eyes were still sleepy. Joey, in particular, looked as if he was still dreaming.

"Hi, sport," Glory said softly as she put the juice on the table and walked over to Joey, lifting him up. He looked as if he needed a little bit more time to wake up.

Joey snuggled into her shoulder with a sigh.

"Mommy." Joey whispered the word so softly Glory wasn't sure she'd heard it right. But she knew by the look of pain on Matthew's face that he had.

"He's still dreaming," she whispered to Matthew. "He doesn't know what he's saying."

"I know," Matthew said quietly. Some days he could convince himself he could give his sons everything they needed. Today, apparently, was not going to be one of those days.

"It's Glory, honey," she whispered in Joey's ear.

His eyes opened, and he smiled contentedly. "You're still here. You didn't go back to heaven. I dreamed you were still here."

"I wouldn't go anywhere without saying goodbye."

Joey nodded. "Not even to heaven?"

Glory shook her head. "Not even there."

Joey put his head back on her shoulder and put his thin arms around her neck in a tight hug.

Glory wondered how she was ever going to say goodbye to the twins.

* * *

It was midmorning before Glory relaxed her fingers. She was holding her sketch pencil too tight, as though she could force some memory out through her fingers. At first her fingers had been too cold to sketch, but Matthew had taken a pair of women's knit gloves off the shelf and cut the fingers out of them. That kept her hands warm while letting her fingers be free.

"You remember the clock?" Elmer had walked over to where she sat with her sketch pad.

"I remember everything," Glory said as she set her fifth sketch aside. Matthew had fixed up a table for her to work at. By now it was covered with sketches.

"Not quite everything," Elmer said as he looked closely at the sketch she had made of the manager lying on the floor, a bullet through his stomach and the things in his hands scattered. The time card was halfway out of the dead man's pocket. The package of steaks was near his left shoulder.

"What do you mean?"

"That." Elmer pointed at the sketch. "On that package of steaks. That isn't packed right. A T-bone and a cube together. Who'd do that?"

Glory looked at the sketch. She must have made a mistake. Odd, though.

A harsh scraping sound from the storeroom distracted them.

"Matthew." Glory had told Matthew she would help him move any stock he needed to relocate. Elmer had told him the same thing. Even Jacob had appeared eager to pitch in and help. "Stubborn man."

"Found the garland," Matthew announced triumphantly as he hobbled into the main part of the store. A trail of gold-and-white garland followed him and he had a cape of garland wrapped around his shoulders.

"You risked falling to get some garland?"

Matthew grinned. "I didn't know you cared if I fell."

"Of course I care if you fall," Glory said softly. The fool man. "I'm the one that has to pick you up and get you to the clinic."

Matthew's grin disappeared. "Did I ever thank you for that?"

The bell over the door rang. Glory looked up in time to see the deputy sheriff, Carl Wall, walk into the store.

Glory bit back her groan.

"Expected everyone to be out working on the pageant," the deputy said. He looked slowly around the store and his eyes rested on Glory's worktable. He walked over and picked up one of her sketches of the victim after the shooting. "Hmm, not exactly scenery." He looked at Glory.

Glory was leaning against the counter. "I told you I worked for the police."

The deputy grunted. "Maybe you do, at that."

"Want some coffee?" Matthew offered. "You public officials never seem to take time for breaks."

"Some folks say all we do is sit around drinking coffee and eating doughnuts."

"Well, I'm not one of them," Matthew said staunchly. "You have a lot to do making sure there are no undesirables coming into town."

Carl Wall looked puzzled. "I thought you were on the side of the angel."

"The angel—no, no, I don't mean her. I mean any undesirables asking about her."

"Who'd be asking about her?"

"I don't know. Just keep an eye out, all right?"

The deputy shrugged. "Most folks have accepted her. They kind of like someone who might be an angel. Makes them think the Man upstairs cares."

"God can care about Dry Creek without sending an angel," Glory said as she walked back toward her work-table. "Maybe God sent you to Dry Creek instead."

The deputy grunted and rolled his eyes. "Now don't go getting funny on me. I wasn't thinking of me. But at least I'd remember the Price boy."

"Billy Price?" Elmer looked up from the checker game.

"Yeah, I got to thinking. No one would remember him, and he'd like a visit from the angel—maybe a sack of the candy I hear is coming."

"Well, I'll add him to the list."

Glory could hear the silence in Matthew's house. A clock ticked in the kitchen and the water heater gurgled in the distance. She was making her Christmas list and checking it twice. She'd decided to order six extra bas-ketballs and ten extra painting sets plus a couple of ad-ditional teddy bears. She wanted to be sure there were enough presents to go around.

With her list in hand, Glory called Sylvia.

The phone rang five times before Sylvia's breathless voice came over the line. "Tacoma-Seattle Youth Cen-ter, Sylvia Bannister speaking."

Glory could hear muffled laughter and cheers in the background. "Sounds like someone's happy there."

"We should be. We just got a grant to set up that sum-mer camp you've heard me talk about for two years now. The money's not much, but it's a big start."

"Congratulations! I wish I could be there!"

"The volunteers are going wild. Pat Dawson is even dancing a jig on the table."

"I'm surprised you're not up there with him."

"I had to get down to answer the phone. Besides, I'm too old for that sort of thing."

"Forty! That's not old!"

"Well, I do feel younger since I got the news." Sylvia laughed. "If we can get some of these kids away from the gangs for a summer, I believe we can turn their lives around. Take them someplace where they don't need to worry about being jumped or shot."

"Even with the gangs, you make a difference," Glory reminded her. She herself had volunteered many weekends at the youth center, tutoring or just talking with teenage girls. "I've seen you change the most unlikely ones."

"Ah, the power of prayer. It surprises me at times, too. I always remind myself that I never know what heart God is going to open up next."

"If you have a few extra prayers, you could send them this way." Glory knew of no heart that needed softening more than Matthew's.

"I've been worried about that, too."

"What?" Glory was startled. How had Sylvia known about Matthew?

"I don't want you to worry about that contract, though," Sylvia continued. "The two boys who told me about it are being very responsible today. I think they have made a sincere decision to follow Christ."

"Oh, of course." Glory relaxed. Sylvia was talking about the shooting.

Silence.

"Is there something else bothering you?" Sylvia asked. "Something else I should pray about?"

How did Sylvia always know? Glory wondered. It must be her years of talking with teenagers.

"Just a stubborn man who hasn't forgiven himself and holds it against God."

"Ah, this would be the man you mentioned, the one you're staying with." Sylvia's voice was rich with unspoken speculation. "The minister."

"I'm not staying with him," Glory clarified. "I'm really staying with his five-year-old sons. That's all."

"If you say so."

"I know so."

Sylvia let the subject be changed to the gifts for the children of Dry Creek. Sylvia assured her there were thirty days to pay on the account, and Glory told her she would mail a check tomorrow to cover the presents and the overnight shipping. The total came to twelve hundred dollars.

"I called the shipping place and they said they can only guarantee next-day service to Miles City. They're short-staffed, since it's Christmas, and aren't taking next-day service to places like Dry Creek."

"If they can deliver it to the clinic in Miles City that'll be fine," Glory said. "I thought this might happen, and I called one of the nurses I met there. She said I can pick the boxes up anytime before five." She wanted to go to Miles City, anyway. She had some Christmas shopping to do that she didn't want to do in the toy store.

"You'll need a pickup truck." Tavis from the Big Sheep Mountain Ranch smiled at Glory. He, unlike Jacob and Elmer, was not sitting in a chair. Instead he crouched, cowboy-style, in front of the stove. "I'd be happy to drive you in. I've got a half-ton pickup, a three-quarter ton or a cattle truck. Your choice."

"I can take her." Matthew bristled. He was sitting on his stool by the counter.

"Your old car won't hold a load," Tavis challenged.

"I can take her anyway." Matthew didn't want to spell out the obvious. By now he figured Glory was honest about placing the order. But he knew her credit was no good. He figured she believed the order was coming. He wanted to be the one with her when she found out it wasn't there. She'd need a friend and not a fancy cowboy at her side to help her with her disappointment. Besides, he had some money set aside for a rainy day. He figured they could buy enough little presents in Miles City to make the children of Dry Creek happy.

Glory looked from one man to the other. "I might be able to fit everything in my Jeep."

"Matthew will take you," Mrs. Hargrove calmly announced with a silencing glance at Tavis. "I need Tavis's help with the bleachers."

It was only a trip to town, Glory chided herself that evening as she looked through her suitcase. So far she'd pulled out her gray sweatshirt with Seattle Seahawks written on the back and an ivory turtleneck with a tan vest. Neither one was exactly right. She couldn't remember the last time she'd given this much thought to the question of what to wear. Jeans were an obvious choice because of the cold weather, but she suddenly wished for a sweater with bright colors to go with them. Of course, she had the pink sweater. It was paler than she'd like, but maybe it would do.

She sat on the edge of Matthew's bed, with her suitcase and clothes scattered all around, and shook her head at herself. She was acting as if this was a date. Worse yet, she wanted it to be a date. And that was a fantasy that would be short-lived. She could sit and count the reasons she shouldn't become involved with Matthew. He was a good father; he would want more children. Children she couldn't give him. Even more important, Matthew wasn't following God at this point in his life. She believed he was still a Christian in his heart, but he wasn't willing to let go of his grief and admit it. And then there was his grief. Glory felt her breath catch in her throat at this one. What if Matthew had loved Susie so much he could never love anyone else? Would every other woman seem pale in comparison?

Maybe, she thought as she shook her head again at her clothes, that's why she wanted something bright to wear. She wanted to get Matthew's attention tomorrow. But she'd need more than a bright sweater to do that.

The Bullet watched the inside glass of the telephone booth fog up as he breathed. He was outside a drugstore in Spokane, calling his contact to tell him the search was off. He hadn't picked up the scent of the hit and he was ready to go home.

"You're looking in the wrong place." The clipped voice came through the phone lines. "She's in Montana. Wonders of modern technology. Do a word search on the AP wire—a name search—and there it is. Glory Beckett in Dry Creek, Montana."

Chapter Nine

Snow, turned grayish-brown by the exhaust of passing cars, lined the isolated highway as Matthew drove down the road. After breakfast he had quickly washed his car, almost freezing his hands in the process. He was a fool to wash anything outside when he was on crutches and the weather gauge read ten below. But he wanted Glory's first impression of his car to be good even if the cleanliness she'd see would be fleeting. Cars might mean something to her. He stole a glance over at her as she sat in the passenger seat.

"The radio doesn't work, but I fixed the CD player." Matthew fumbled in the storage compartment next to the driver's seat. He couldn't remember what was in there, but he thought he had a Mozart CD. He pulled out three CDs. All three were made by Disney. "I'm afraid I have mostly sing-along music for the twins. But I'll keep looking. I've got one classical and I've been meaning to get some instrumentals, too—maybe a flute CD."

"That's okay. I like the silence."

What does she mean by that, Matthew thought in desperation. Should he be talking more? Should he be talking less? Ever since this morning when he'd decided this trip to town was the closest thing he'd had to a date in years, he'd been tongue-tied. Worse than when he had been a teenager and had been dating. At least back then he'd known when he was on a date and when he wasn't.

"That's one thing we have in Montana. Silence—it goes with the snow."

Montana was known for her open spaces and big blue skies. Both could be seen through the car's windshield. Matthew felt as if they were driving along in a warm cocoon. The car's heater kept the air cozy, and the hum of the engine was soothing.

"In Seattle we have noise and rain."

"You like it there?" Matthew tried to keep the question light, tried to pretend he hadn't wondered if there was any chance she'd move to a small town in Montana if asked.

"I've got my family there."

Matthew held his breath.

"My mother and the captain."

Matthew took a deep breath. So far so good, but he had to know. "Any—you know—boyfriends?"

A butterfly took flight in Glory's stomach. "Not really."

Matthew frowned. What did that mean?

"Well, of course, you date…." Matthew stumbled along.

"Of course." Glory's hands went up to finger her dangling silver earrings. Maybe the jewelry had been a mistake. The zipper of her black ski jacket was open to show her pale pink sweater. Even with denim jeans the silver jewelry might be too dressy for a shopping trip. But it was the only thing in her suitcase that seemed the least bit festive. When she had looked in the mirror this morning, she'd looked colorless, so she'd put on what little makeup she had. Usually red hair clashed with pink, but the pink in her sweater was more pearl than pink. She wore a natural lipstick and barely-pink blush. She'd brushed her hair until it settled around her face in waves. She'd even put a tortoise clip in her hair. She wanted to look good, but now she wondered if she had overdone it. She didn't want to make Matthew feel uncomfortable, as if she had expectations for this trip. Date expectations. Maybe that was why he was asking about boyfriends. Maybe he wanted to be sure she had one and wasn't expecting anything from him. Maybe she should have worn the Seattle Seahawks sweatshirt, after all. There was no mistaking the nondate look of that.

"But is there someone you date regularly?" Matthew persisted with the question. "Someone you are involved with?" Even if she was undercover, she would answer this honestly to tell him there was no chance. Even a government agent would give him that courtesy.

Glory glanced at him. He had his eyes straight ahead, his chin straight forward, his hands squarely on the steering wheel. He was a study in browns. Deep brown leather jacket, open all the way down to show a pressed white shirt. Chestnut-brown hair with blond highlights. Tanned face. Fierce dark eyebrows. It was the small nervous twitch at the edge of his mouth that gave her courage.

"No," Glory said softly. "There's no one special."

"Good." Matthew breathed again. "Good."

The morning suddenly looked brighter to Matthew. The slush at the side of the road didn't look just gray anymore; it looked more like pure silver with the sun shining on it the way it was. And his car might be old, but the seat cushions were made of leather. And the trim looked like wood. He was cruising.

"I was wondering if I could buy you lunch when we're

in town." Matthew tapped the steering wheel lightly and turned to smile at Glory. He came from the era when a date meant someone did the inviting, even if it was only for lunch. "There's a steakhouse if you want to play it safe. Or we can go to Billy's—never know what you'll get, but it's good."

"I'd like that—Billy's sounds good." Glory tilted her head so her earrings could sparkle. And she lifted the collar of her sweater and flipped her silver chain outside. The more jewelry the better. She, Glory Beckett, was on a date. Granted, it was a date with the wrong man, but for today she didn't care. She was going to forget he was a grieving widower who'd had a perfect wife. She was going to forget he was not following God because of that wife. She was going to forget she couldn't give him children as that wife had. She was even going to forget that wife had ever existed. She would let her jewelry sparkle like laughter. Just for today she'd forget about his past and their lack of a future. They were definitely on a date.

"We'll have lots of time to shop." Matthew slowed down some. There were likely to be patches of white ice along this strip of road, and he couldn't count on his leg with the sprained knee. Besides, they had plenty of time. "There's a department store—and Buffy's Drug. Buffy's usually carries some toys this time of year, just in case your order doesn't get here in time."

"The boxes should be at Dr. Norris's office already."

"Well, just in case they're held up," Matthew persisted. He didn't want anything to ruin their day. "We can pick up what we need at Buffy's."

"Buffy's won't have a Betsy Tall doll," Glory protested. She'd gone over the children's wish pictures. No small store in Miles City could carry all of the different things the children wanted.

"Maybe not, but they'll have another doll."

"But that's the problem." Glory had seen the hope on the children's faces. "They each have a special request for a present. Something they especially want. Not expensive things, either, just particular things. This Christmas I want them each to have the exact thing they asked for."

"Sometimes we don't get the exact thing we want in life."

"I know, but—" Glory stopped. How could she explain the need children have to be unique in the eyes of God? To be known individually? "They're expecting their angel to make arrangements to see that they get their special gift. It won't be the same if it's just any old gift. It has to be the one."

"They'll be fine." Matthew's face settled into grim lines. "They'll make do."

"Will they?" Glory watched the shutters go down over Matthew's face. She knew they weren't talking about the children. They were talking about Matthew. "Or will they be like you and decide God doesn't care about them?"

A muscle flexed across Matthew's cheek, but he didn't answer.

Miles City was dressed up for Christmas. Matthew told her the town had grown up around Fort Keogh, an outpost built in 1877 to force the Crow to stay on the nearby reservation.

"We have always been half-decent and half not around here," he continued. "Starting out it was divided—brothels and beer halls to the south, banks and pawnshops to the north."

Glory imagined she could still see the old town in its heyday. The sidewalks were scraped clean of snow and many of the store windows had been decorated with winter scenes and outlined with tiny white lights. Most of the buildings along the main street were solid old buildings, which fit in well with her fantasy. The place, Glory decided, had charm. Some of the stores had Christmas carols playing, and the sounds carried out into the street. Even the other shoppers looked festive in their snow boots and knit scarves.

Matthew drove down the main street and then turned around. "I'm checking the cars."

Glory looked at him.

"Making sure they're all locals," he said.

"Surely you don't think a hit man would be looking for me in Miles City?"

"No, but I'm not taking any chances." Matthew finally pulled into a parking space. "Let's try Buffy's first. I want to get something for the boys."

"Me, too."

Glory wanted to get a gift for the boys that was from her and not from the angel. Some little thing they could have to remember her visit.

The door into Buffy's opened with the ringing of a bell. Buffy's smelled of the perfume and scented soaps she could see in front of the long mirror at the end of the store. Racks of merchandise ran sideways down the length of the store and a checkout counter was located near the front door.

"Can I help you find anything?" An older woman wearing a lilac-flowered dress spoke from behind the counter. The woman smelled of dusting powder. "We've got a special on gloves this week. Men's. Women's. Children's. The lot."

"You must be Buffy?" Glory said, even though she knew the woman couldn't be.

"No, she's my daughter." The woman smiled indulgently and patted the braided bun loosely knotted at the back of her neck. "She's home baking cookies for her two boys for Christmas. Boys need cookies at Christmas."

Cookies and Christmas! Glory had forgotten. She'd decided earlier to buy some chocolate chips before they left Miles City. She wouldn't compete with their mother's oatmeal raisin cookies, but she was sure the twins would love the Beckett family chocolate chip cookies.

"Do you have any children's books?" Glory asked. Buffy must stock good books if she had children of her own. Both Josh and Joey loved having a book read to them. She'd already seen their favorites—*Curious George, The Runaway Rabbit* and a couple of Dr. Seuss books. She knew they loved adventure, and she might even find a book with lions and tigers in it.

The saleswoman nodded to the right. "Over there, behind the lunch boxes."

Matthew watched Glory out of the corner of his eye. He also kept his eye on the door to the store. He'd already studied the three other customers inside Buffy's and decided they were harmless. But he wasn't going to be careless. Not about Glory's safety.

He watched as she looked over the book rack. He knew she was buying presents for his sons, and he'd had a whispered conference with them before he came this morning. Josh had pressed a few nickels into his hand, asking him to buy Glory a golden crown that would light up like the one he'd seen on a Christmas card at school. Matthew suggested a shiny necklace instead. Joey, with his pennies, wanted him to buy her a mirror because he'd seen her use one when she brushed her hair at night. They both advised him that he should buy her a present, too. Matthew knew his sons were worried.

They didn't want Glory to leave. He was worried, too. He hadn't known his sons would get so attached to her in just a few days. But then, why shouldn't they? He'd gotten attached himself.

"The other store is just next door." Matthew walked over to Glory. "I don't want to rush you. Why don't I go over there now, and you can come when you're done?" The department store would take longer to check out and he didn't want Glory to know what he was doing.

Glory nodded. She had been wondering how to get Matthew out of the store so she could buy his present. She'd seen a selection of CDs near the counter and she'd decided to get him one. It was a gift with the right balance. It showed she didn't expect him to get her anything. It was just a friendly gift.

She waited for Matthew to walk out of the store before she headed for the CD display. She put two books on the counter. Josh's was about a red dragon. Joey's was about a lost kitten that found his way home. "I'll take these, and do you have any James Galway music?"

"I don't think so." The salesclerk scanned the titles.

"Any instrumentalists?"

"Let me see, we've got *Piano Selections for...*" The salesclerk started to read the title as she pulled the CD from the display. Black and white piano keys ran the length of the cover and there was a red rose lying across them. It looked slow moving, if nothing else.

"I'll take it," Glory said quickly. She thought she saw Matthew's outline in the window. He was doubling back. "Just put it in the bag quick. Christmas present."

The older woman smiled and slipped it into the bag under the two larger books.

"I thought you might want that twenty dollars I owe

you," Matthew said quietly as he came inside and held out a twenty-dollar bill.

"What twenty?" Glory looked up from her purse. She opened her wallet. There was her own twenty dollars. "It's not mine."

"Take it anyway," Matthew said, his voice even. "I'm sure I owe it to you for something."

"But—"

"Go ahead and take it, sweetheart," the clerk advised with a shrug of her shoulders. "It isn't every day your husband gives you an extra twenty for Christmas shopping."

"He's not my husband." Glory felt the blush creep up her neck.

Matthew smiled.

"Even more reason to take it, then." The clerk straightened herself and glared at Matthew. "It's the least he can do if he isn't willing to make an honest woman out of you."

"I'm an honest woman already." Glory lifted her chin indignantly.

"Already married?" The older woman smoothed down the skirt of her flowered dress and shook her head. "In my day—well, you don't want to hear that. It's none of my business whose bed you're sleeping in."

"She's got you there," Matthew whispered. "You *are* sleeping in my bed."

"Well, you're right in there with me." Glory spit out the words and then stumbled when she realized what she'd said. "And if either one of us should care about their reputation it's you—you live here. Besides, you've got the boys."

"My boys couldn't care less about my reputation. They'd love it if I slept with an angel." Matthew chuckled. The one thing he didn't miss about the ministry was worrying about what people thought about him.

"Well." The salesclerk softened as she looked at Matthew. "If he thinks you're an angel..."

"The whole town of Dry Creek thinks I'm an angel."

"Oh, you're the angel at Dry Creek!" The older woman brightened. "Wait'll I tell Buffy. We were reading about you in the 'Southeastern' column."

"I'm not. Look. I've got no wings. No miracles. No divine message."

"Yeah, but you're sweet," the woman said, measuring her with friendly eyes. "And sweetness never hurt anyone. Right?" The clerk looked at Matthew.

Matthew nodded. The clerk was absolutely right. That's why people were drawn to Glory. She was a kind, sweet woman. She didn't need to be an angel.

"Let's eat lunch and then we'll hit the department store." Matthew put his hand under Glory's elbow. They were on the sidewalk outside Buffy's. He looked both ways for suspicious-looking cars and didn't see any. Mostly there were farm pickups parked on the street, since it was winter. "Slippery out here."

"Let's stop by Dr. Norris's first. The clinic might close early, since it's so close to Christmas."

"Okay." Matthew felt helpless. His worry shifted. He could protect Glory from suspicious-looking cars, but he didn't know how to protect her from disappointment. "You're sure you don't want to eat first?"

"Come on. Let's get the boxes."

Forty-five. Forty-six. Glory was sitting across the restaurant table from Matthew and counting to one hundred. She'd taken her ski jacket off and draped it over the back of her chair.

Glory barely noticed the knotty pine paneling in the room or the ferns that hung from the ceiling. Everything was clean, but old. The air smelled of cooking meat and she faintly heard the rattle of silverware coming from the kitchen as well as the murmured talk of the other customers sitting at nearby tables.

Glory hadn't realized it until now—Matthew didn't believe her. He fussed all over her in his worry about a hit man, but when it came to believing in her integrity, he didn't. She knew he hadn't believed her at first. But she'd thought that somewhere during the past days he would have decided she wasn't crazy. The boxes were coming. Sylvia had called to tell her the order had been processed. Just because the nurse at the clinic said the boxes hadn't come with the shipment today didn't mean they wouldn't come tomorrow. The nurse had promised she'd bring them with her when she came out to see the pageant tomorrow. The nurse—a stranger, really—seemed to believe her. Matthew didn't.

"We can go back to Buffy's." Matthew wasn't looking her in the eyes. Instead, his gaze kept focused on the wall behind her. "I can buy some things. You know, backup presents. Some puzzles. Some books. Maybe some coloring books."

Glory shook her head. "These kids have asked for specific things. The boxes will be here." The right presents simply needed to come. She'd call Sylvia when she got home.

Glory was at a loss. She didn't know how to manufacture faith or trust in Matthew. He didn't believe her, and there wasn't anything she could do about it. No one ever forced another one to have faith. Faith and trust came from the heart. Maybe that's why it was so upsetting to her that Matthew did not trust her. She had thought they were friends. And friends should stand beside each other.

"So what is it—crazy or lying?" Glory finally asked.

Matthew was startled. He stopped staring over her shoulder and looked her in the eye. "What?"

"Me and the boxes. Do you figure I am crazy or lying?"

"Well, n-neither…" Matthew stammered.

Glory noticed with satisfaction that he looked uncomfortable. "It's got to be one or the other. Which is it? Am I lying about the boxes coming or am I crazy to say they are coming?"

Silence. "I know you *want* the boxes to come." His blue-green eyes looked bone weary and his shoulders slumped

Glory nodded sadly. So that was as far as he could get. "Overly optimistic, huh?"

Matthew nodded. His eyes moved to a spot on the table. Glory wondered what was so fascinating about a red-checked plastic tablecloth with silverware wrapped in a paper napkin.

"Hi, folks." A bearded man set down two menus in front of them. "Welcome to Billy's, home of the best food west of the Dakotas."

Matthew looked up at the waiter in pure relief. "What've you got?"

"The special today is meat loaf with mushroom sauce and garlic mashed potatoes." The man smiled fondly. He wore blue jeans, a red-checked logger's shirt, work boots and—over it all and spotless—a white BBQ apron. "Wife's in the kitchen today and she likes to make things fancy. When I'm cooking, it's plain meat loaf and plain potatoes. No chives. No parsley. No garlic."

"Which is better?" Glory liked the way the man's eyes lit up when he talked about his wife. He couldn't be over forty, but he looked as if he'd worked long and hard in this life. The only softness on his face was the love that showed when he talked about his wife.

"Hers are," the man leaned down and whispered. "But don't tell her I said so. I like to keep the rivalry going. Keeps the marriage interesting."

"In that case, I'll have the meat loaf." She'd have to remember this man and his wife for her next talk with Linda. Apparently even meat loaf recipes could be part of what kept a couple happy. "See how your wife makes it."

"You know, my wife is really something." The man had a scar on his cheek and a faint trace of whiskers on his face, but he looked like an old-fashioned knight. "When I started this place, no one believed I could stick with it. I'd been a drifter—cattle hand mostly—until I met her three years ago. But when they said I couldn't do it, she stood by me. We weren't even married then, so she didn't have to take my side. She believed in me when no one else did. I'll never forget that."

"Good for her," Glory said softly. She envied the couple their devotion. "She must be special."

"She is." The man cleared his throat. His neck grew flushed and he had a suspicious moistness in his eyes. "Didn't mean to go on like that."

"I'm glad you did." Glory handed back her menu. "It'll make the meat loaf more memorable."

"You want extra mushroom sauce with that? Her sauce is sure good."

"I'd like that."

"And you? What'll you have?" The man looked at Matthew.

"I don't suppose you have any crow on the menu, do you?" Matthew asked sheepishly.

"Well, no…" The man looked momentarily puzzled and then he grinned. "Too close to home, huh?"

Matthew nodded.

Glory watched the shadows lift from Matthew's face. His weariness shifted, and it was as if a load was lifted off him. He looked directly at Glory. "I know I should trust you. Please forgive me."

"Should?"

"I want to do better. I just don't trust easy."

Glory nodded. She saw the sincerity in his eyes. "I guess wanting to trust someone is a step in the right direction."

"And the answer is neither crazy or lying," Matthew said firmly as he handed his menu back to the man.

Glory grinned.

"And I'll have the meat loaf, too." Matthew looked up at the man. "With extra sauce."

"I'll be back in a jiffy," the man said, then carried their menus to the back counter and took their order slip into the kitchen.

It was one o'clock, and they had just eaten the last bite of meat loaf. Matthew had to admit he'd been loitering. He checked the door for suspicious-looking people periodically, but the people who came into Billy's were humble. Besides, Mrs. Hargrove was watching the twins, and he wanted this date to last as long as it could. He loved to watch Glory's eyes when she laughed. He'd told her some of the twins' favorite jokes just to get her started. Josh had a whole series of chicken-crossing-the-road jokes that were pure corn. Her blue-gray eyes crinkled with gold when she laughed. Her bronze hair sparkled in the sunlight coming in the side window. She threw her head back and the delicate curve of her neck made him think of a swan.

"You're beautiful." The words came out before Matthew thought about whether he should say them.

Glory stopped laughing and blushed.

He cleared his throat and added, "Very beautiful." He'd never seen anything prettier than Glory blushing. She didn't blush red like some people—she just pinked. She was a pearl. He smiled. "You truly do look like an angel."

"Oh—" Glory looked flustered. Then she glanced down at her watch. "Speaking of angels, I better get back and make sure the costume fits."

Matthew nodded. All dates did come to an end. Then he brightened up. The date didn't end until he pulled in to the driveway. They still had the drive home left.

The afternoon sun reflected off the snow as Matthew drove his car back to Dry Creek. The backseat was filled with groceries and lumpy bags. The heater made the inside of the car a little stuffy.

"Mind if I turn it down?"

Glory nodded. She'd been thinking about Matthew's reluctance to trust her or anyone else, up to and including God. He couldn't have been born that distrustful. Her experience with young children was that trust came easily. "Did you grow up around here?"

"Here and a million other places."

"Father in the service?"

"Maybe." Glory noticed Matthew's fingers tighten on the wheel of the car until his knuckles were white.

"Maybe?"

"My father left us when I was six. We never heard

from him regularly. But shortly after he left one of his old friends called one day—drunk—asking for Sergeant Curtis. Mom thought maybe Dad had enlisted. He'd always wanted to be in the military. Least, according to her."

"I'm sorry." Glory wanted to reach over and put her hand over Matthew's fingers, but she wasn't sure he'd welcome her touch. He looked brittle.

"Don't be." Matthew took his eyes off the road briefly to look over at her. "He wasn't much of a father when he was around."

"Your poor mother. Where is she now?"

"Died when I was eighteen. I'd just barely graduated from high school. It was like she was waiting to finish her job with me so she could leave."

"Oh, dear, no wonder you have a hard time trusting God."

Matthew grimaced and looked back at her. His eyes were deep with pain. "What makes you think it's God I don't trust?"

"Why, who else?"

"It's myself I don't trust." Matthew spit the words out. He tried to stop them, but they seemed to come of their own power. "It's me I don't trust. It's me that messes up. It's me that can't get it right."

"And was it you that let Susie die?" Glory felt as if they were lancing a boil. Was this the poison that Matthew kept inside his heart?

"Yes," Matthew whispered. "It was me that let her die. Me that let my mother die. Me that let my father leave. It was all me."

"No, oh, no." Glory reached over to touch Matthew's hand. "It wasn't you at all."

Matthew grimaced and then turned coldly polite. "Then who was it? God?"

"No. No." Glory was at a loss. How could she convince Matthew he did not carry the fate of the whole world on his shoulders? That the choice was not just between him and God. Life threw curves. She'd had her own battles with guilt over her father's accident, but it was nothing like the burden Matthew carried.

Dear Lord, help Matthew. Help me help Matthew. Show me how to help him.

Glory wished Socrates were sitting in this car next to Matthew instead of her. Or Solomon. Even Dear Abby would do. Glory felt so inadequate. She'd tried to talk to Matthew about his feelings three times already as they drove back to Dry Creek, but each time he'd put her off with a joke or a shrug. The snow-covered tops of the Big Sheep Mountains in the distance were more likely to thaw out and talk to her than Matthew was.

"If you don't want to talk to me about it, that's fine." Glory gathered her ski jacket closer to her. It was still only midafternoon, but the outside cold seemed more of a threat than it had earlier. "Not talking isn't good. It's not healthy. But it's fine."

"I just don't want to talk about it now," Matthew said patiently. Some charming date he'd turned out to be. She probably thought he was a basket case. In his mind they were supposed to be talking about amusing things, light things—date things. At least, that was the way it was back when he was dating. Things couldn't have changed that much. "You never have told me about your artwork. What your favorite medium is, who your favorite artist is, your favorite art museum…"

"Refusing to talk about these things won't make them go away," Glory persisted. They'd turned the heater off to let the car cool down somewhat and Glory's ears were beginning to be chilly. She rubbed her left ear.

"Talking about them won't make them go away, either." Matthew shrugged as he slowed down so that a car behind him could pass. He switched the heater back on. "And I thought you were going to let me know when you felt chilly. I have this leather jacket on—I'd be warm in a snowdrift. But you've only got that light ski jacket."

"My jacket's warm enough. Nothing wrong with it."

Matthew sighed. He couldn't seem to say anything right. "Of course there's nothing wrong with it. You look beautiful in it. Black's a good color for you. And that shade of pink of your sweater is good, too."

Out of the corner of his eye, Matthew could see Glory smile. Now, this was the way a date was supposed to be. "I noticed you've done your hair different, too. Sort of softlike. It's good. And your earrings. I've watched them all day. They put me in mind of dolphins, with the graceful shape they have to them."

"Okay, you win," Glory said. "We won't talk about your issues now, but we will later."

Matthew nodded. He hoped he and Glory would have lots of laters to talk about all of their issues. If he was lucky, he could keep her talking to him all winter. Maybe by then she'd be charmed by eastern Montana and decide to stay. He chided himself. He shouldn't think long-term with Glory. He knew he wasn't good enough for her. He wasn't the Christian man she deserved to marry. But even if they didn't marry, he'd like to have her in his life somewhere. *Who am I fooling? Could I bear to have her in my life and not have her belong to me as my wife?*

"Mail it for me, will you?" The Bullet was back at Douglas's. He pulled two twenties from his pocket and handed them to Douglas along with an addressed box that he'd had wrapped at the store. "Overnight it. It's Millie's Christmas present and I can't wait for the post office to open."

"You're not going to be there for Christmas? Not with Millie?"

"No."

Chapter Ten

The afternoon sun was starting its slide down by the time Matthew pulled the car into Dry Creek. He'd primed Glory with a question or two, and she'd spent the rest of the drive back telling him about her desire to paint faces. He told her about the Custer County Art Center back in Miles City. He knew Glory loved art, and he wanted her to know art had a place around Dry Creek. They were, in fact, close to Charles M. Russell country, and they had his museum in Great Falls. Not that far to drive if she stayed awhile.

Matthew loved to watch Glory. Her whole face lit up when she talked about art. She was a woman who noticed color and shadow and— Matthew looked down the street of Dry Creek. Over half of the houses needed painting. The whole town definitely needed tending. He hadn't noticed that it was run-down when he moved here. But now, driving up with Glory in his car, he wondered if a city woman, an artistic city woman, could ever live in a place like this. And it wasn't just the lack of a coat of paint. He could get a brush out himself and do most of the houses if needed. There were so many other things. Dry Creek wasn't Seattle. Why, there wouldn't be movies in town if it wasn't for the rack of family videos they carried for rent at the hardware store. And there wasn't a hair salon, unless you counted the back room at Marcy Enger's. She'd never had any formal training, but the people around agreed she had a knack for cutting hair. An art center and an art museum wouldn't make up for all that. Not to a woman who liked flavored coffee.

"Look at that!" Glory said as she pointed to the old café.

Matthew groaned. And the old café—it was an eyesore. He didn't need that called to his attention. "Sorry about that. Businesses don't always make it in Dry Creek."

"Well, this one just might," Glory said as she pointed again. "Look at that sign."

Matthew looked again. He was so used to seeing the old café, he hadn't really looked before. He'd missed the banner. And the clean windows. And the open door.

"Christmas Jazz and Italian Pasta—5.00." Matthew read the words of the foot-high banner that had been strung across the door. "What in the world is that?"

The trim around the big window had been painted a bright red, and someone was pasting a frosted star inside the window's left corner. The person's head was bent, but Glory thought the hair and angle of the neck looked familiar. She was right. Matthew hadn't even parked his car before the woman in the window looked up and waved.

Linda called to them before they even got the car parked. "Come and see."

The first thing Glory noticed when she stepped into the old café was that Linda's black lipstick was gone. The young woman's face was bare of any makeup—which was a good thing, since that left room for the traces of dust that trailed over her cheek. But, while there was dirt on Linda, there didn't look as if there was a speck of dirt hiding anywhere else in the large room. Wooden tables had been righted and scrubbed. The floor had been freshly mopped. The pine smell of disinfectant came from the kitchen.

"Jazz, honey," Linda called into the kitchen. "The rev and the angel are here."

Matthew winced. Glory laughed.

Duane came out of the kitchen. He didn't look like the Jazz Man now. Instead of a black leather jacket he wore an old flannel shirt that had holes in the sleeves and grease spots on the front. He was even more thoroughly dirty than Linda. He waved his arm in the direction of the back room. "Been getting the heater set up back there. Can't open up without heat."

"Open up? You're going to open up?"

"Just for Christmas Eve, at least so far," Linda said. Her eyes shone with excitement. "And word is spreading. We have a ton of cousins that are helping. The Alfsons and the Bymasters had to go home for supper, but they'll be back. So will the Lucas kids. It was Jazz's idea, really." Linda stopped to look at her boyfriend adoringly. "He got to thinking that all those people coming to the pageant might like to have a spaghetti dinner."

"Actually, Mrs. Hargrove gave me the nudge. Told me God answered prayers. It's just that sometimes He answered with our hard work. Then she gave me the keys and suggested Linda and I take a step of faith, as she called it. I wasn't so sure at first, but then I figured if the reverend can cook so can I. And then Linda said that music makes any meal better." Duane pointed to a raised area at the side of the room. "The band'll set up there."

"What a great idea!" Glory said, and turned to Matthew. "We could help them get ready, can't we?"

"I don't see why not. At least, until I have to get the twins."

Matthew disappeared into the back to help the Jazz Man with the furnace and Glory rolled up her sleeves to help Linda explore the cabinets under the counter next to the kitchen. Glory could smell that the cabinets had been cleaned. Everything that could be done in a short period of time had been done.

Linda pulled on one of the cabinet doors. She had to tug to open it. "Those two ladies who used to own this place had good taste, all right—and they didn't mind spending some money. This café was some kind of a hobby with them. I think they were planning to bring tea and civilization to the wild West."

"They seem to have left it soon enough."

"Dry Creek didn't match their dreams." Linda held out a large apron for Glory. "Here, wrap this around you. You don't want to get dirty like I did."

"Not match their dreams? Why not?" Glory said indignantly as she slipped the apron over her neck and tied the strings around her. "Everything I've seen is charming, quaint, full of real people and their lives."

Linda laughed as she opened a bottom cupboard door. "Not everyone wants real."

Glory leaned down with Linda to look into the cupboard. Inside the cupboard were stacks of old-fashioned restaurant dinner plates, the white plates with a thin green band around the rim. "Well, well, look at this. There must be a hundred plates there." Glory quickly counted the stacks of plates. She'd estimate there might be 120.

"This'll be great!" Linda lifted out a small stack of

the plates. "We thought we'd have to spring for paper plates—but this, this has more style."

Glory pulled open a drawer and found it full of stainless steel spoons.

"And forks!" Linda pulled open another drawer.

"They must not have even packed when they left," Glory said as she reached up and opened a top cupboard. There in thick plastic bags were linen tablecloths and napkins.

Dust filtered down as Glory and Linda pulled the bags off the shelf. Neither one of them saw the glass pitcher leaning against the bags. When Glory pulled out the last bag, the glass pitcher rolled off the shelf, fell to the floor and shattered.

Surprised, both Linda and Glory screamed.

"No!" Matthew's roar could be heard before he burst from the kitchen and into the dining area. He didn't stop in the doorway of the room to look around. Instead, wielding a piece of pipe, he simply threw himself in front of Glory and gently but quickly pushed her to the floor. He stood, half-crouched, over her.

Only then did he look around. "Where is he?"

Matthew's face had gone pale, and he looked fierce. He had a streak of black soot on his cheek and his hair had a film of white ash covering it. His eyes were pink from some irritant in the kitchen. He even wore a dish towel slung around his hips like a holster. He looked more like a back-alley bum than a hero. But all Glory saw was a warrior ready to do battle to defend his friend.

Glory was humbled. She'd never had anyone leap to her defense. She lay on the linoleum catching her breath. "It was a pitcher."

"A water pitcher?" Matthew was puzzled until Glory gestured to her left. His face went even whiter when he saw the pieces of glass. "Well—why—thank God I didn't push you in that direction. I could have hurt you myself."

"But you didn't," Glory quickly offered. She felt nothing but smooth linoleum beneath her arms and legs. "You thought it was a bullet, and you rushed to my defense."

Glory had forgotten she and Matthew were not alone.

"A bullet?" Linda whispered. Her voice cracked. "A real bullet? Here?"

Glory pushed herself up until she was sitting. The Jazz Man was standing in the doorway from the kitchen, and Linda was still standing beside the counter with the bag of table linens in her hand.

"There's no need to worry." Glory stood and brushed her jeans off even though she knew there was no dirt left on the floor. "It's nothing."

"But why would you think there'd be a bullet?" Linda persisted. Her eyes had grown round, and she looked even younger than the first day Glory had met her.

"You some kind of crook or something?" the Jazz Man questioned Glory. He measured her and still appeared unconvinced. "The police after you?"

"No, the crooks are after her." Matthew laid his piece of pipe down on the counter and took two steps over to Glory.

Matthew willed his panic to still itself. His pulse was pounding. His hands had been too scared to sweat until now. He knew he wasn't the man for Glory. Not really. But none of that mattered to him when he thought the bullets were flying. He felt a primitive need to protect her, as an animal needs to protect his mate. It was unthinking and unquestioned. If Glory needed protection, he needed to protect her.

And that wasn't all. Matthew stepped closer to Glory and tucked her into his arms. He could smell her spice perfume and feel stray strands of her hair as they brushed his chin. But for all that, he held her loosely. It was her, not him, that he was most aware of. He didn't kiss her. Didn't dream of doing more than hold her. For now, holding her within the circle of his arms was enough. Just to simply stand together with his arms wrapped around her. Matthew slowed his breathing until his pace matched hers, and they breathed as one.

The Jazz Man cleared his throat, but neither Matthew nor Glory responded. They just stood together. Finally Linda tugged at the Jazz Man's sleeve, and they both walked into the kitchen.

Glory didn't even notice they had gone. She was wrapped in a safe, safe cocoon. She felt as if she was underwater. As if everything that was noisy or demanding was distant. Nothing could reach her. Nothing could touch her. She had never felt as safe as she did now.

"We need to check back with the department," Matthew finally said. He uncurled himself from around her. "They might know more about this hit."

"Yeah," Glory agreed as she fought her sense of loss. Reality was intruding, demanding her attention. She missed the sense of being detached with Matthew. If all that ever happened with a scare like this was that Matthew hugged her because he was worried about her, she wouldn't mind a bullet drill every half hour.

"I see," Glory said fifteen minutes later as she stood beside the counter in the hardware store and talked to her friend Frank back at the department. The fire from the potbellied stove warmed the inside of the hardware store. The air smelled faintly of this morning's coffee and fresh popcorn. The hardware store was much too homey to be a backdrop for the hesitant words she heard over the telephone from Frank's mouth.

"What'd he say?" Matthew asked, tight-lipped, when she hung up the phone.

"Sylvia called him." Glory kept her voice even. She wondered if this was how a person in shock felt. The sense that she was not inside her own body. "Those two boys she told me about—the ones that said there was a hit out on me—didn't show at the center today. Not even for basketball. Another kid said they had flown out on business last night. Frank checked the airport. They bought tickets for Billings, Montana."

Matthew felt the breath leave his body. It just whooshed away. *Dear God, we are in trouble. Help us.* He didn't even notice he had uttered his first prayer in two years.

"Can they ID them? Has the flight landed in Billings yet? Maybe we could contact the authorities there."

Glory smiled. Matthew thought like a cop. "Yes, Sylvia gave pictures to the Seattle police. Frank will fax them to us with the ones of the crime scene, said he'd fax them all right away. And yes, they contacted the Billings authorities. And yes, the boys were on the plane. But they were too late. The plane had landed, and they'd picked up their luggage forty minutes before Sylvia knew they were gone. They'd already left the airport terminal."

"So they're here."

Glory nodded. She felt like a guppy in a fishbowl. No matter which way she turned she was too visible. Where would she be safe now?

"Car rental agencies? Did they check with car rental agencies?"

"The Billings police have the whole airport under surveillance. But Sylvia didn't think they would rent a car.

They don't have a credit card, don't even have legitimate driver's licenses." Sylvia had added that they probably had fake licenses, since they'd gotten on the airplane, but Matthew didn't need to know that.

Matthew raised an eyebrow. "How old are these kids?"

"One's fourteen. The other's fifteen. They probably look older."

"Great. We're doing battle with babies," Matthew muttered as he ran his hand through his hair.

"These babies have been in a gang for the past five or six years." Glory bit her lip. She needed to think. "They can probably kill someone with a knife quicker than they can cut up an apple—and with less mess."

Matthew smiled wearily and started to pace. Even on his crutches, he seemed to need to move. "I know. I'm just not used to how tough children are these days. Makes me worry about the twins."

"The twins have you. They'll be okay."

Matthew nodded, then suddenly turned. "Kids like that—how'd they get the money for airplane tickets?"

"I don't know." Glory hadn't wanted to tell him this. The tickets were a problem.

"Did they pay cash?"

Glory nodded. She bit her lip again. She desperately needed to think.

Matthew stopped pacing and sat down in a straight-backed chair beside the counter. "Somebody gave them the money, then?"

Glory nodded. She didn't need to say what was obvious. The boys were on a job. How else could they afford to fly to Montana?

Matthew ran his hands through his hair again. He stood up as though he couldn't bear to sit and, once he was up, sat down again as though he couldn't bear to stand, either.

"Where are those drawings you've made?" Matthew demanded. "If we can figure out why someone wants to shoot you, they won't have just one target. They'll have to kill us both."

"What! That'd be crazy!"

"We could let Frank in on the theory, too," Matthew continued. "Once the authorities know why you're a target, you won't be a target."

Glory nodded. It made sense. Besides, work sounded good. If nothing else, it would stop the slow scream she felt working its way up from her belly. She'd never been hunted before. And to have the hunters be two of Sylvia's kids… Something was wrong with the world.

The drawings she'd made yesterday were still on the table near the front window of the store. She'd drawn the murdered butcher from several different angles and at several different times, ranging from when he'd just been shot to a final picture of the chalk outline just after the police came and were ready to take the body away.

"You have a photographic memory?" Matthew asked as he looked at the set of drawings for the fifth time.

Glory nodded. "For pictures, when I see something I remember it."

"Do you think it through or just close your eyes and remember?"

"Mostly, close my eyes and remember. Why?"

"Then maybe somebody switched that package of meat on you," Matthew suggested. He pointed at the only two drawings that included the fallen package of meat. Each drawing had the meat in the corner where it had flown out of the butcher's hand when he was shot. At first glance, the packages looked alike. But then Glory

saw the differences. The sticker was on the right for one
package and on the left for the other. There were three
small steaks in one package and two medium-size ones
in the other.

"I must have remembered it wrong."

"Have you ever remembered something wrong before—a picture you were drawing?"

Glory thought of the hundreds of photos she'd drawn
as a student and as a sketch artist. She'd gone from bowls
of fruit to crowd scenes. In school she'd learned to be
quick with details and at the police station she'd learned
to be accurate. Even now she could close her eyes and
see the scenes from the murder scene. "No, I've never
gotten it wrong before. At least, not that I know of, and
I would have known."

Matthew nodded as though that's what he'd expected.
"Then we have our first clue."

"But why in the world would anyone switch the packages of meat?"

"And who would do it?"

"And when," Glory added. Matthew was right. They
just might have their first clue. "They had to do it while
we were sitting there waiting for the police to arrive."

"Was the gunman still loose?"

"No, he was tied up with some guy's belt. A customer tied him to the end of a display case. The gunman didn't even try to escape. He just lay there on the
floor and waited."

"So whoever changed the meat was just hanging
around, then."

"I suppose, but there was hardly anyone near us. The
store manager had some of that 'Caution—Wet Surface'
tape on his counter and he taped us in."

"Us?"

"Myself, the gunman and two other customers. But the other customers were holding the gunman down. Even when he was tied up, they didn't leave his side."

"Was the meat package close enough to the tape that a customer outside the taped area could switch it?"

"Not unless he had arms the size of King Kong's."

"Then that leaves the manager."

"The manager?"

Matthew nodded. "Wasn't it Sherlock Holmes who said once you've eliminated the impossible, whatever remains, however improbable, is the truth?"

"I suppose the manager could have done it. He was walking around swinging that tape here and there. He had big pockets in his butcher's apron, too."

"Now all we need to do is figure out why."

"That's the hard one."

"We don't have time for hard." Matthew picked up the telephone. "What did you say was the name of that market?"

"You're going to call Benson's Market?"

"How else am I going to talk to this manager?"

It took Matthew five minutes to be connected to the manager at Benson's Market. It took him only two minutes and four questions to have the man swearing at him and threatening to turn state's evidence and tell the feds.

"Who'd he think you were?"

Matthew shrugged. "I told him I was Matthew. He must have heard there was a Matthew somewhere."

"Or he's so eager to squeal, he doesn't care who knows what."

Matthew nodded. "He told me there wasn't supposed to be any hassle. That the meat deal was supposed to be low risk. The money isn't that much, not when there's the murder, and he swears he didn't know about the murder.

And then someone's calling asking pointed questions sounding like they know something..."

"Not that you know anything."

Matthew grinned. "He didn't know that."

"We'll have Frank call him and lean on him, too."

Matthew nodded. "I'm beginning to think the road between here and Seattle is probably sprinkled with stolen meat."

"The rustling!" Glory put the two together.

"What better way to make a profit on stolen cattle than to have them butchered and sold in independent stores?"

"But why change the package of meat?"

"Something about the codes. The manager was actually pocketing a good sum of money by buying the stolen meat. When the butcher started talking about the computer red-flagging super sales based on the price the meat was logged into the system, the manager panicked. The manager was shadowing the real prices behind the invented prices to keep track of his windfall and something was going wrong."

Pieces of the puzzle clicked together in Glory's mind. "And the butcher figured this out. That's why they killed him." They'd solved the mystery. That's what had been itching at her mind. The fact that her visual pictures were different when she recalled the scene. Someone must have found out about her memory. She was noted in the police department for never forgetting a crime picture.

"I'm safe. Now that the pictures are out, there's no reason to kill me."

"All we need to do is find those boys and convince them of that."

Glory nodded. That was the problem, all right. Finding those boys before they found her.

Matthew spent the afternoon making and waiting for phone calls to Seattle. He talked to Frank. He tried to talk to Sylvia, but he finally found out that she had left shortly after warning Glory about the boys and was flying into Montana herself.

"Billings airport is going to be busy."

"Billings can't possibly be busier than this place," Glory grumbled. Mrs. Hargrove came into the store carrying a bent shepherd's staff.

"What's this I hear about bullets flying and hit men coming to town?" Mrs. Hargrove demanded as she walked toward the counter. She was wearing a black wool coat over a green gingham dress.

"I know now's not a good time, with the pageant and all," Glory said. "I didn't plan this."

"Well, of course you didn't, dear. And don't worry about the pageant. A few bullets won't stop us."

"Speaking of the pageant, I might not be able to be your angel."

"Well, surely you don't think they'd try anything at the pageant." Mrs. Hargrove was shocked. "That's a holy moment!"

"That didn't stop Herod in the original pageant." Matthew was worried. With everyone in costume, two teenagers could sneak up before he could pick them out. A bathrobe and a loose turban was all the disguise they'd need. He wasn't sure he'd be able to pick them out fast enough to protect Glory.

"Well, if need be I'll fly from those rafters myself," Mrs. Hargrove said starchily. "I won't fit into the costume, but I can wear a big white apron and some of my husband's winter long johns."

Glory blinked. Had she heard right? Long johns and… *"Fly from the rafters?"*

Mrs. Hargrove gulped. "I guess we haven't told you yet. Tavis had this great idea." Her face beamed. "A flying angel. Now, won't that make the pageant special?"

Glory blinked again. "A flying angel? Me?"

"Well, it won't all be flying. First you'll start out standing on the rafters, singing a carol."

"Singing? Me? I haven't even practiced." Glory didn't know what was more alarming, the singing or the flying.

"Don't worry about it, dear. I'm sure whatever you sing will be just fine."

By nine o'clock that night Glory had practiced "Silent Night" exactly three times. Each time Matthew and the twins sang it beautifully. She wasn't so sure herself.

"Hang this one on that low branch," Glory directed from her place on the chair. She, Matthew and the twins were finishing decorating the five-foot pine tree at Matthew's house. She held out a golden ornament to Matthew.

"And don't bunch all the red ones together."

"Are you really going to fly?" Joey asked for the fourth time that evening.

"It's more like a swing." Glory had gotten very specific descriptions from Mrs. Hargrove and Tavis. The ropes were heavy and the rafters strong enough to hoist machinery. The angel's long robe would hide the seat of the swing, and the ropes, Tavis had assured her, would be scarcely visible in the darkened barn.

"Nobody's going to fly or swing anywhere unless we find those two boys," Matthew said sternly. After closing the hardware store, he'd looked both ways down the street before he'd rushed Glory to the car. They'd stopped at the café so Matthew could show the faxed photos to Duane and Linda and ask them to keep an eye out for the boys.

"Don't stop them," Matthew had directed the two. "You've got the number. Call the police. Those two are armed and dangerous."

"I'll show them dangerous." Duane scowled and pushed up the sleeves on the flannel shirt he was wearing.

"No heroics," Matthew ordered. "We just need an ID. I've already put Carl Wall on alert. We just call him—he'll come running. Let the other kids know."

Duane nodded. "I'll pass the word around. If they come, we'll pick them out."

"Thanks."

When Matthew had got Glory and the twins inside the house, he'd rummaged through a kitchen drawer until he'd found the keys to his house. For the first time since he'd moved to Dry Creek, he'd locked both doors. The windows were all frosted shut, but he'd checked the latches on them anyway. Then he'd pulled the shades down. Halfway through locking up, he'd started to pray—actually, it wasn't praying exactly. It was more like cursing at God for allowing Glory to be in danger. But as the words spent themselves, his anger had dried up and left him feeling empty. Glory would not appreciate him cursing at God on her behalf. Still, his anger was there anyway, ready to defend her against anyone, even God himself.

The Bullet was in the airport in Billings, Montana. He wasn't two feet inside the place before he started spotting the cops. A dozen of them, at least. He never checked his luggage, so he went to the first car rental booth he found.

The clerk seemed nervous and excited, but not about the Bullet.

The Bullet smiled. "Busy day?"

"The police have been here for hours looking for two boys," the clerk leaned over and whispered confidentially.

"Runaways?" the Bullet asked, careful to keep his voice only mildly interested.

The clerk pulled his credit card toward her and shook her head. "Much worse than runaways. The woman at the snack counter dates one of those officers, and he told her these kids are contract killers. Think of that! Hit men! In Billings!"

The Bullet clucked sympathetically. His blood went cold but he didn't let it show. There couldn't be two contracts so close to Christmas in this part of Montana. No, these kids were trouble. His trouble. They needed to be taken out of the game.

Chapter Eleven

December 24. Glory repeated the date to herself while she lay in bed the next morning, feeling lazy. It had snowed last night, and a thick layer of frost covered the window to her room. She hadn't had a white Christmas for years. It made her feel as if she was wrapped inside a Norman Rockwell sketch. Surely, contracts and hit men had no place in her life. Especially not on the day of the pageant. Not the day before the birth of Christ was celebrated.

Glory turned over and looked at the luminous hands on the alarm clock sitting on the bedside table. Almost six. Matthew would be up. She could hear him stirring around already, his crutch making an irregular thump on the floor in the kitchen. She breathed deeply. And she could smell the coffee. A gourmet orange flavor if she wasn't mistaken.

The floor was cold enough to make her dance from foot to foot when she stepped out of bed and looked in her suitcase for a pair of socks. There she found some gray woollies. Perfect. Glory sat back on the bed and pulled the socks over her tingling toes. She had a busy day today. She needed to check with the nurse in Miles

City to make sure her boxes had arrived. She'd spoken last night with Mrs. Hargrove about the bags of candy the angel was to distribute. She decided she'd count on the twins to spread the word that the children's Christmas gifts would be given out after the pageant was over and the children had all taken off their costumes.

Glory pulled out a hunter-green turtleneck to wear with her jeans. Ideally, she should have red, but she hadn't packed anything with Christmas in mind. Green would have to do. Maybe she could snag a sprig of holly somewhere to pin on her collar. Lacking that, she might tie a string of Christmas ribbon around her neck. Matthew had assured her he had wrapping paper for Christmas. He must have ribbon, too. She glanced over at the presents she'd purchased yesterday. They were still in the bag; she'd need to wrap them this afternoon. Maybe while she made cookies.

Glory had promised the twins they would sit together and read the Christmas story before they got ready for the pageant. She wanted both boys to have a cookie in their hands while she read to them. Christmas, after all, was the birth of hope. Every child deserved to have Christmas memories of abundance.

Once Glory was dressed and ready to go downstairs, she picked up her Bible. She always had her morning devotions before breakfast. She'd read a psalm and then pray. Since she'd been in Dry Creek, she'd had these devotions alone in Matthew's bedroom. But today was the day before Christmas. A miracle could happen. She was going to march downstairs and ask Matthew to have devotions with her.

Miracles didn't always happen on Christmas Eve day, Glory thought. Matthew had made a blueberry coffee cake and gourmet coffee for her, but he wouldn't have devotions with her.

"It wouldn't be right," he mumbled vaguely as he opened a can of frozen orange juice.

Wouldn't be right, Glory fumed. "And why not?"

"Sometimes devotions are just a habit. That would be all it would be for me. Just words."

"Well, sometimes lack of faith is just a habit, too." Glory didn't add that bullheaded stubbornness could be a habit, too. And refusing to take another risk once you've been burned could be a habit, too.

"I suppose," Matthew said mildly as he gave her the plate of coffee cake to put on the table. "But I have other things to worry about today instead of habits."

Glory wasn't finished with him. "Well, then I guess I'll just go off by myself and have a few minutes of Bible reading and prayer…" She paused to be sure she had his attention. "Maybe on the front porch."

Matthew almost dropped the pot of coffee. "You can't sit on the front porch! There are hit men out there."

Glory shrugged and started to walk away. "I've got other things to worry about today besides hit men."

Matthew growled and set the pot of coffee back on its stand. "This is blackmail, you know." He walked over to the table and sat down.

"I know." Glory grinned and sat down at the table, too.

Matthew decided it wasn't so bad. He loved watching Glory's lips move while she read, and it was cozy here in the kitchen. The sun was beginning to flirt with the idea of rising, making the light outside soft. He never got over the morning light in Montana. It was as if the day just snapped into focus.

Matthew smiled. Glory had given him a reprieve so

he could bring them both a cup of steaming coffee, and he sipped his now. He could get accustomed to flavored coffee. He even half listened to the words Glory was reading—Psalm 61. A psalm full of faith from its "Hear my cry" to its "vows day after day." He'd preached a sermon on that psalm once—a rather compelling one. He'd used the old-fashioned illustration of a tapestry that was beautiful on the top even though a person looking at the back might not see the pattern. He hadn't realized at the time that a single snag could pull the whole tapestry apart. The threads were so connected. He'd never seen the backside of faith, the side he was on now. He wished he had the words to tell Glory about the confusion in his heart. Sometimes he thought the problem wasn't that he had too little faith now, but that he'd once had too much faith. If he had not expected so much of God, he wouldn't have fallen flat on his face when God let him down. But he hadn't thought it was too much to ask for Susie to live. Not from his God. He'd gripped God with all his might and refused to let go, never once thinking that God might let go of him.

"'Lead thou me to the rock that is higher than I.'" Glory reread the words aloud. "'For thou art my refuge, a strong tower against the enemy. Let me dwell in thy tent for ever! Oh, to be safe under the shelter of thy wings!'"

Nothing but the sound of the oven timer ticking could be heard when Glory finished. Glory stole a glance at Matthew. His face was stoic. Only the white knuckles on his hand gripping the coffee cup gave away his feelings.

Glory opened her mouth to speak, but Matthew stirred instead.

"Yeah, well," Matthew muttered as he drained the last of his coffee.

"Isn't it inspiring?" Glory ignored Matthew's indifference and continued. "It's one of my favorite psalms."

"I'm glad it means so much to you."

Glory held her breath. She usually didn't push. She knew no one was ever forced into faith. But she had to try. "It could mean as much to you."

Matthew grimaced. "It did once."

"It could again." Glory looked directly at Matthew. She thought she'd see annoyance in his eyes, but she saw only sadness. "Just ask Him to help you."

Matthew didn't answer for a long minute. Then he took a final gulp of coffee and rose from his chair. "I need to finish getting breakfast ready for the twins."

"With me it was guilt," Glory said, talking to Matthew's back as he reached into the cupboard for the cereal boxes.

"Hmm?"

"Guilt. That's what stopped me from accepting God's love. I didn't see how I could take in His love when I was alive and my father was dead. I was driving the car. I should have died. Not him. I didn't deserve God's love."

"Oh, no." Matthew turned around and balanced on his one crutch. "You must never think that. Accidents happen. It wasn't your fault. God wouldn't hold that against you."

"What does it matter to you? You don't accept His love, why should I?"

Matthew frowned. "You're not me, that's why."

"You're not the only one who can be a martyr."

"I'm not a martyr—"

The phone rang, interrupting Matthew.

"I can get it." Glory stood.

"Sit down," Matthew commanded as he began to hobble across the kitchen. "And watch the windows. No one's supposed to know you're here."

Glory snorted. "The whole town of Dry Creek knows I'm here."

"It's not the people of Dry Creek I'm worried about," Matthew said from the living room as he grabbed the telephone. "It's who else that might be snooping around."

"Hello." Matthew twisted the telephone cord as he sat down on the sofa.

Glory went to the door to the living room and listened. In Seattle, a 6:00 a.m. phone call was unusual and likely to be bad news, but here six o'clock was almost prime time.

"It's your friend Sylvia." Matthew held the phone out to her.

"From the airport?" Glory walked to the sofa and sat down next to Matthew.

The telephone connection was filled with static. "Sylvia?"

"Glory, thank God it's you. Are you all right?"

Glory gripped the phone. Sylvia sounded a million miles away. "I'm fine. Where are you? Can I come get you?"

"No." There was noise in the background. It sounded like the grinding of metal objects. Sylvia herself sounded breathless and shaken. "I can get a ride into Dry Creek."

"Where are you? You're not thinking of hitching a ride, are you? It's not safe."

"No, Mr. Elkton is going to give me a ride."

Glory strained to hear Sylvia's voice. Something was definitely not right. Usually cheer spilled out of Sylvia's lips. Even when she was worried, Sylvia always sounded confident. But her voice now reminded Glory of a little girl, a little orphaned girl with no friends.

"Are you all right?" Glory pressed. "Mr. Elkton, who's that?" Glory searched her mind. The name was familiar. Then she saw Matthew mouth some words. "You don't mean Tavis Elkton's father? The owner of the Big Sheep Mountain Ranch?"

"Yes," Sylvia said at the same time as Matthew nodded.

"But how did you meet him?"

"I took a wrong exit off the interstate. Someone moved the exit sign to Dry Creek. Instead of leading to Dry Creek the sign led to a dirt road on Mr. Elkton's property. I took the exit and ended up with my car in the ditch."

"You weren't hurt?"

"No, I'm fine," Sylvia said. "Mr. Elkton found me."

"Well, thank God for that. Who would do a fool thing like move the exit sign?"

"That's what Garth—I mean Mr. Elkton—would like to know."

Glory listened. She had heard Sylvia talk about pregnant teenagers, arrested teenagers, addicted teenagers, but she'd never heard this particular tone in her voice before. Then it dawned on her. Glory grinned. Sylvia was flustered. That's what she was hearing through the telephone lines.

"I haven't met Mr. Elkton," Glory said calmly. "About how old is he?"

"Old? I don't know. Maybe in his forties."

"Hmm, a man of forty is in his prime here in Montana. Lots of outdoor exercise. Sunshine. Nature. I suppose he's attractive."

Glory looked at Matthew sitting on the sofa. He was eyeing her as if she'd lost her senses.

"He probably thinks so," Sylvia fumed.

"It's awfully nice of him to drive you into Dry Creek."

"He said he needed to drive in anyway. Something about getting some nails from the hardware store."

"Nails from the hardware store," Glory repeated for Matthew's benefit. "Mr. Elkton needs nails." Glory smiled as Matthew raised his eyebrows. It was as she thought. "Well, then, I'll see you when you get here."

"You're not going outside, are you?" Sylvia asked, sounding worried. "They didn't pick up K.J. and John at the airport. They're around here somewhere. You should just stay put."

"There's no point in hiding. They could shoot me inside as well as outside. Besides, it's probably safer at the hardware store than here. It's inside, too, and I stay away from the windows."

"Well, be sure to have the police check the place out before you go in. And tell them to give you an escort across the street."

"That'll be the day," Glory muttered. She could just see Carl Wall escorting her anywhere

"I'll get to Dry Creek as soon as I can. If they're hiding, they might come out if they see me."

"It'll be good to see you. And to meet Mr. Elkton. Just have him bring you to the hardware store."

"I'll be there soon. See you then."

"Yeah, see you then." Glory hung up the telephone.

Glory couldn't stop smiling. It was definitely Christmas.

"You look like the cat that swallowed the cream," Matthew observed.

"I think Sylvia's got a boyfriend."

"Garth Elkton?" Matthew asked dubiously. "I doubt that. He's a confirmed bachelor these days if I've seen one. His last marriage soured him on women. Not that he might not have an affair. But marriage? No."

Glory shrugged. "Well, Sylvia isn't the kind of woman a man has an affair with, so maybe you're right."

"But he is coming in for nails," Matthew muttered as he shook his head. "The last thing the Big Sheep Ranch needs is more nails."

Matthew thought Sylvia's idea of an armed escort was a good one. "Carl Wall doesn't have anything better to do. Besides, he likes to stop at the store for coffee."

Glory was sitting on the sofa with the twins, looking at the Christmas tree. The boys sat huddled in quilts, one on each side of her. They were still drowsy with sleep. Glory smoothed back Josh's hair. "Call him if you want to, but let's not talk about it now."

"They know about it anyway," Matthew said quietly with a pointed look at the twins. "I'm sure the whole town knows. News like this doesn't keep quiet."

"But we still don't have to talk about it before breakfast."

"No." Matthew smiled. "We don't."

"We have enough to talk about, anyway," Glory said as she squeezed each twin. "This afternoon we make cookies and then we celebrate just a little before the pageant."

"I need a new scarf for my costume," Joey said. "To tie me in with. Judy Eslick got gum on my old one."

"Well, we'll see to that before cookies. Maybe we can get the gum out. And I'll want to hear your lines for the pageant."

"I say, 'Look yonder,'" Josh announced.

"And I point at the angel," Joey added. "That's you."

Matthew cleared his throat and sat down on the sofa

next to the twins. "I know how much you're looking forward to having Glory be the angel, but she might not be able to, not tonight."

The twins nodded. "That's what Mrs. Hargrove said."

"But I can watch you," Glory offered.

Matthew frowned. "I don't know if that's a good idea."

"Well, the whole town is going to be there," Glory said. "It's probably safer there than anywhere else."

Glory was surprised that Carl Wall agreed to escort her and Matthew over to the hardware store. She gathered from his comments that she was now one of his pigeons and, as such, would be defended from outsiders like every other citizen of Dry Creek.

"I've cleared the street," the deputy said as he stood on Matthew's porch. "We best move while everything's empty."

"But it's only seven-thirty," Glory protested. Mrs. Hargrove had stopped by to pick up the twins already. "Matthew doesn't open the hardware store until eight."

"I can open early," Matthew said as he balanced on one crutch so he could put on his leather jacket.

"That's right. You don't want to go by your usual schedules," the deputy warned them. "Do the unexpected. Change your routine. That way no one can set an ambush."

"Makes sense." Glory put her arms into an old army jacket the deputy had brought with him. It was his version of a disguise.

"And put your hair under this." The deputy held out a gray scarf and then a baseball cap. "Then put this on."

"Sorry for the trouble I caused you earlier," Glory said.

"Ah, that was just a little misunderstanding. No hard

feelings, I hope." The deputy had done an about-face with her. Glory suspected he might have run a check on her and found out that she did work for the Seattle Police Department.

Glory smiled. "No. No hard feelings."

"Matthew?" the deputy asked.

"All's forgotten and forgiven." Matthew held the door open for Glory, then, before she could go through it, put a hand out to delay her and went through the door himself instead. "Need to change the order. Keep it unexpected."

"But if—" Glory gulped. If someone was planning to shoot her while she was going through a door, she wouldn't want them to shoot Matthew instead. For the first time, the bullets seemed all too real. It wasn't just her life that was in danger; it was the lives of those she cared about, too.

The few steps to the deputy's patrol car were cold and slippery. A fine sheen of frost was still on the ground from the night's low temperatures. Glory almost slipped twice hurrying down the sidewalk to the patrol car. Matthew struggled to keep up with her on his crutches, but she deliberately kept ahead of him. If she was a target, she didn't want him near her.

"Keep low in the seat," Carl said when Glory slid into the backseat of the car. He already had the heater going and the ice scraped off all the windows. Except for the sound of the car's engine, the day was silent. No traffic. No children outside walking anywhere. Not even any dogs barking.

It was only three blocks to the hardware store, but the deputy kept his eyes darting about the whole time. He studied the porch of each house that lined the street, starting with Mr. Gossett's. Nothing was unusual.

The deputy pulled up as close to the hardware store

as possible, even though he had to park in a crust of old snow that had been shoveled up next to the store. Car exhaust had turned the top of the snow gray.

Glory had her hand on the door handle when Matthew reached over from the seat beside her to stop her.

"Not now," Matthew commanded, and jerked his head toward the store. "We got company inside."

"What?" The deputy rolled down his window and lifted his nose in the air as if he could smell something. "Smoke."

"There's a fire going in the stove."

Glory looked up. The sky was a washed-out morning blue, but she still saw the thin trail of vapor. It was so small it was almost invisible. "I don't suppose Elmer or Jacob would have gone inside and built a fire?"

Matthew shook his head.

The deputy reached for the radio in his car. "I'm calling for backup."

"Backup won't do us any good if they're inside watching us. It'll take the guys from Miles City twenty minutes to get here." Matthew ran his hands through his hair and looked over at Glory. "And stay down on the seat, for pity's sake."

"I won't stay down unless we all stay down."

"What?"

"I know about decoys," Glory said stubbornly. She refused to be the only one who wasn't a target. "Making them think they have a target just to draw a reaction."

Matthew grinned. "Now you're thinking."

Glory gasped. "I meant I don't want anyone to be a decoy. You're not to take any chances." Glory looked at the deputy, who was speaking into the radio. "Either of you!"

"But what about him?" Matthew pointed to his crutch

that was lying sideways on the floor of the backseat. "We could put the deputy's hat on my crutch and wave it in front of the window. Those windows are so frosted up all anyone will see is a shadow."

"It's worth a try." The deputy hung up the radio. "Especially since everyone's out on a call already. I'd guess it'll be forty-five minutes before anyone gets here to help us."

Matthew pulled a handkerchief out of his pocket and wrapped it around the handle of his crutch to make the shape of a face. The deputy took off his cap and handed it back to Matthew.

"I'll walk it along," the deputy said to Matthew. "You stay with Glory."

"No, you stay with her." Matthew touched the door handle.

"But…" the deputy started.

"You have the gun," Matthew answered simply. "Even if you left it with me, I'm not sure what my aim would be. If something happens, I want the gun with you."

"You can't do this," Glory protested. No one had ever risked their life before for her, and now Matthew seemed to be doing it all morning. "You could be hurt." *Or worse.*

The windows on the car were still iced, even though the heater in the patrol car was spitting out coughs of heat. Glory herself was shivering. But Matthew's forehead had a thin sheen of sweat covering it.

"Don't worry." Matthew tied his jacket around the crutch, too. His crutch now looked like a skinny scarecrow.

"Of course I'll worry," Glory fretted.

"Well, pray instead, then," Matthew offered mildly as he unlatched the door.

"Pray," Glory squeaked. She tried, but the words spun in her throat. Matthew stepped out of the car. His boots crunched on the snow. She wanted to close her eyes. But she couldn't. *Dear Lord*— the words finally came —*Oh, dear Lord. Help this man, this exasperating man, the one I don't want to see hurt, the one I care about....*

The car windows were beginning to fog over, so Glory saw Matthew as if he was in a grainy out-of-focus film. He crouched low, keeping his crutch held high. With every step he took Glory expected an explosion of gunfire. But the silence held. Finally Matthew was in front of the side window to the store. His jacket waved in front of the window. Whoever was inside wouldn't resist a target like that.

Glory felt she didn't breathe for the next two minutes. It seemed like hours, but she knew it was only two minutes because she watched the minutes change on the digital clock in the patrol car. One minute. Two minutes.

"I better go in the front door," the deputy finally said, pushing open his car door. "Maybe someone just forgot to put the fire out yesterday."

Glory began to breathe again. That must be it. So much had been happening yesterday that everyone's nerves were stretched. Matthew had just forgotten to see that the fire was completely out. Maybe Jacob or Mrs. Hargrove had put in a large chunk of wood at the day's end and it had lain smoldering all night. That must be it.

The car door handle was cool to Glory's touch. "I'll go tell Matthew."

Matthew had already turned toward them, and gave a relieved thumbs-up sign.

Glory pushed the store door open first. Matthew had twisted the key in the lock. The deputy took his hand off the butt of his gun to put his cap back on his own head.

All three of them were standing in the doorway unraveling Matthew's crutch decoy.

Glory looked into the dim store first. It was too early for the morning sun to come in through the display window, and the inside was poorly lit. Matthew had left three salt blocks and a small box of bolts close to the counter for Timothy Stemm to pick up this morning. Glory reached for the switch to the overhead lights.

The overhead lights came on.

"What the—?" Glory blinked. It looked as if there was a big bundle of blankets tied to the large center post. Gray blankets. Khaki blankets. Then she saw a foot.

Matthew slammed the door shut and looked at Glory. "Back into the car."

"But—"

"This time he's right," the deputy said as he drew his gun.

Glory stepped back to the side of the store. "That's as far away as I can go."

Matthew frowned, but the deputy was already slowly opening the door.

"Deputy Sheriff Wall here. Don't try anything. We're coming in."

"We ain't done nothing." The muffled wail came from inside the store.

When Glory got to the door, Matthew was holding two thin teenage boys by the scruff of their necks as if they were puppies. When she got closer, she saw that their hands were tied behind their backs and they were both anchored with another rope to the center post.

"You've got it all wrong," one of the boys protested. "We're the good guys. We was here to stop the hit man. He's the one that tied us up."

"Contract killers aren't known for using rope to do

their business," the deputy said wryly as he patted the blankets in a weapons search.

"Or building fires to keep their victims warm," Matthew added. He'd sat down on the floor next to the boys so he could keep them still while the deputy searched.

"But he did!" the boy with a Seahawks cap insisted. "We was trying to help. We tried to keep him away. Even moved the road sign off the interstate so he'd get lost."

"You know it's illegal to tamper with road signs?" Matthew scolded.

One of the boys shrugged. Glory figured they had done worse than move a road sign or two in their short lives.

"No wonder Sylvia got lost," Matthew half muttered.

"Sylvia?" The jaws of both boys dropped. They were clearly worried more about her than they were about the law. "*Sylvia's* here!"

"You'll have some explaining to do." Glory looked at her watch. "In about one hour, I'd say."

"What's Sylvia doing here?"

"She came to keep you out of trouble," Glory scolded.

"Ahh, man."

"No guns," the deputy reported after a thorough search of the blankets.

Glory watched the boys exchange worried looks. It was clear they didn't want to disappoint Sylvia. Glory wondered how long they had been gang members. They each had a small gold earring in each ear, but that was more fashion than rebellion these days. The one with a Seahawks cap had a recent haircut and a bruise on his chin. The other boy had a tattoo that ran the length of his arm. Both wore white T-shirts and jeans.

"Where are your coats?" Matthew asked.

Glory noticed for the first time that both boys had

goose bumps on their arms and the tips of their ears were red.

"Don't need none," one of the boys declared defiantly. "It's not cold."

Matthew looked at the two boys a moment and then nodded. "I'll see what we have in back. I think we have a jacket or two. That'll keep you until we rebuild the fire."

The deputy shook his head as he laid one of the wool blankets over each boy's shoulders. "You boys would have frozen out there last night without even a coat. This is Montana. You need to thank whoever brought you here."

The boy with the tattoo scowled. "Ain't going to thank no killer."

"Wonder who it was who put them here." The deputy looked up as Matthew hobbled back into the main room of the store. Matthew had his crutch under one arm and two worn jackets under the other.

Matthew tossed the jackets to the deputy. "I figure the whole county saw that picture I gave to Duane and Linda. Most likely one or two of the hands at the Big Sheep Mountain Ranch caught them asking questions. They wouldn't have wanted to wait for morning to come—chores awaiting—so they left them here for us to find this morning."

The deputy nodded. "Makes sense."

Glory was glad something made sense. She hadn't caught her breath all morning. Something was chewing its way into her consciousness, but she couldn't grasp it. Maybe it was because she was still reeling from the way Matthew had risked taking a bullet from these two boys and then noticed so quickly that they needed coats. If she hadn't already decided Matthew was a natural minister, she would have known it after this morning. Matthew was someone who was off course with his life. He'd given up his calling because his wife had died.

That must be it, Glory decided with relief. She was only worried about Matthew. Worried that he wasn't doing what he wanted with his life. Worried that he was so wrapped up in remembered love that he couldn't live.

That must be it, Glory tried to convince herself. She was only worried for Matthew. She let her breath escape—and that's when it hit her.

She remembered the moment. The stab of knowing. She'd sat in the backseat of the patrol car, watching Matthew wave his crutch around to tempt a bullet out of the boys inside the store, and fear had emptied her mind. And then her mind had filled in a flash with one thought and one thought only. She'd sat there motionless and realized that if a bullet hit Matthew it would hit her, too. Square in the middle of her heart. She'd seen the truth and then she'd pushed it away until now. Cautiously she let the thought come back. She worried over her revelation, afraid to even say the words to herself. But she couldn't stop them. It was true.

She was in love with Matthew.

Yes, she, Glory Beckett, was in love.

She knew it was foolish to love him. She knew he did not love her now and probably would not love her in the future. She knew they would never marry. They would probably not even see each other after Christmas. But she knew when she left Dry Creek she'd leave her heart behind. This wasn't at all how she'd planned to fall in love.

The Bullet pulled the brim on the Stetson down lower. He wondered if the farmer would notice that his hat and overalls had been stolen out of his pickup last night.

It had snowed last night—frigid, stingy flakes with

more wind than moisture—and the porch where the Bullet chose to hide was cold.

The sun had barely risen when the Bullet heard the patrol car drive up to the house where he knew Glory was staying. He didn't even raise his head to look over the porch railing at her. No, it was too soon in the game. A patient cat waited for the mice to weary themselves before he stretched out his claws.

Chapter Twelve

Glory watched Sylvia question the two boys. Sylvia was petite, only four-eleven in the short stacked heels she wore. But Sylvia didn't need height. She was second-generation Italian and waved her arms around fearlessly while she spoke. Her gold rings flashed and her long fingernails pointed. She towered over the teen-agers, who still huddled by the stove. Sylvia alternated between sympathy and scolding. The love she had for the teens was so obvious she had them talking in minutes. They told her everything.

"But what about the plane tickets?" Matthew was sitting on a stool behind the counter watching Sylvia's drama.

"I told you, man. I earned that money," insisted K.J., the teenager with the tattoo. "Busted my butt all last summer sweeping up in my uncle's restaurant."

"You told me before you worked for him for nothing," Sylvia challenged. Her blue eyes snapped and her lips drew together reprovingly.

K.J. grimaced. "Yeah, well…"

Sylvia looked at the two teenagers for a moment. Her face relaxed.

Glory saw that Sylvia was tired. Faint lines gathered

around her usually laughing eyes. Her black hair, shiny and full, was bunched up and tied back with a scarf. *A scarf?* Glory looked more closely. It wasn't a scarf. The material tying Sylvia's hair back was a red bandanna, the kind the ranchers here used. And unless Glory was mistaken, the thick knot holding the bandanna in place could only have been tied by the expert fingers of a rancher.

Glory slid her gaze over to the only rancher in the store. Garth Elkton. He didn't look any too fresh, either, now that she looked at him closely. He needed a shave and his scowl seemed to fasten on Sylvia with some regularity.

"What's your uncle's name?" Matthew asked K.J. "I'm sure the police can find out if you worked for him."

"Ah, don't call the police," K.J. whined. "My uncle'll freak. Besides, you shouldn't keep worrying about us when there's a killer out there."

"A killer?" The deputy paused. "Describe him."

"Well, he's sort of average looking."

"What color's his hair?"

"Brown. No, black." The boy looked miserable. "Just hair. No particular color."

"Can't you describe him any more than that?"

K.J. frowned. "He's hard to remember. The kind of guy that hangs out in the shadows at school. You'd hardly know he was around except for the gun."

"I thought so," the deputy said smugly. "You never saw anybody."

"Hey, I ain't lying. We're innocent. All we did was move the road sign."

"Son, you're lucky you're dealing with Sylvia and not me." Garth Elkton spoke for the first time. His voice was low and gravelly. "I'd turn you over my knee and show you the consequence of moving road signs. This is snow country. People could die if they take the wrong turn in a blizzard. Someone could have died last night because of you."

"Nobody did, did they?" K.J. asked in alarm.

"Hey, we didn't mean to kill nobody," protested John, the other boy. "We've been trying to do good to show—"

John bit back his words to a mumble.

"To show what?" Sylvia persisted.

"That we meant it." John looked down at the floor and whispered, "The other day in church, we meant it."

Glory looked at their faces. They looked honest. Besides, it was almost Christmas, and they were so young. She turned to Sylvia. "Maybe it has all been one of those misunderstandings."

"Maybe." Sylvia looked thoughtful.

"I guess no harm's been done," Glory offered.

"You don't want to press charges, then?" the deputy asked.

Glory looked at Matthew. He answered, "If they leave today with no funny business, we'll let it go."

"I already called the airport in Billings and got two tickets back to Seattle for this afternoon. If no one minds, I'll put them on the plane myself," the deputy said eagerly. He clearly wanted the boys out of there.

Sylvia nodded. "I'll go with them."

"Can't. I had to pressure the agents to get these two tickets. There's a waiting list a mile long. Seems everyone wants to go someplace the day before Christmas."

Sylvia bit her lip. "I see. Well, I guess I'll need to stay, then."

"Good." Garth Elkton rocked back on his boot heels. He'd already removed his Stetson and laid it on the store counter. His sheepskin coat was open, showing off a green flannel shirt. He looked down and smiled politely at Sylvia. "You can go to dinner with me, then."

Sylvia looked up at him as if he'd just grown two heads. "Us? Dinner?"

The polite smile ended. A muscle tensed in the rancher's cheek. "It's a custom."

"I—I can't," Sylvia stammered, frantically looking around until she latched on to Glory. "I have to—to help Glory with the pageant."

"We can eat before the pageant." The rancher's eyes grew flint hard.

Sylvia flushed, and she looked at the floor. "Before the pageant I, ah, I need to help Glory get dressed up in her angel costume."

The rancher looked around coldly. "Matthew here can help her. It's only wings and a halo."

"It might only be wings and a halo to you, but Glory here cares how she looks in that costume," Sylvia protested as she walked over and put her arm around Glory.

"I do?" Glory squeaked. Sylvia pinched her. Glory corrected herself. "I mean, yes, of course, I do care."

The rancher looked exasperated. "Look, we eat and talk or we just talk. Take your pick. We've got business to finish. And we might as well eat while we do it. If you want to stay in Dry Creek, we'll eat the spaghetti dinner those kids are fixing up. After all their hard work, they deserve some support."

"Kids?" Sylvia looked up.

Glory smiled. Whether the rancher knew it or not, he had hooked Sylvia. Nothing got to her like kids.

"They're going to have music," Glory offered mildly. "You have to eat anyway."

"I suppose we could eat a short meal together."

"We'll call it a snack." The rancher smiled.

Sylvia took her eyes off the rancher and returned them to the boys. "I'm going to call Pat Dawson and have him meet your plane. I'm also going to call the police. And don't even think of ditching this flight along the way. If I hear you're not in Seattle by tonight I'll have the police in fifty states looking for you."

"Yes, ma'am," both boys said.

"Well, we best get going into Billings," the deputy said. "I want to make it back and see this pageant myself. Especially now that the angel is going to be in it."

Matthew pondered. "I guess there's no reason why she can't be the angel now."

Glory grunted. She could think of a reason or two not to be the angel. But she doubted anyone would listen. "In that case, I better see about my halo."

The midday sun shone in the display window of the hardware store. Jacob and Elmer were sitting beside the wood-burning stove with their legs stretched out in front of them. Matthew was moving around in the back storage room. He'd already brought out the gold garland and cut off a length for a halo. He was back there now looking for glitter to sprinkle on the cardboard wings they'd brought over from the church.

Glory was putting the last of the oils on the portrait of the twins' mother. She added a smudge of light gray paint to the woman's cheek. Glory patted it to make it look like a dusting of flour. She was going to give the painting to the twins to be opened after the pageant. That reminded her she would need to go back to the house soon and make cookies for the twins.

The bell above the door rang, and Glory looked up to see Linda come in. The young woman was all dressed up for the holidays. She'd dyed one streak of hair Christmas red and another hunter green. A jingling bell earring dangled from each ear and she had a sprig of holly behind one ear. She wore red leotards and a white sweater.

"Figure I'll get more tips if I look Christmassy," Linda whispered as she came over to where Glory painted. "Least, that's what my friend Sara Enger said. She even took a picture of me with Gus in his Santa suit."

"Gus?"

Linda shrugged. "This old cowboy that's been helping us. Used to work for one of the ranchers up north that sold out. Jazz told him he could bunk down in the kitchen for a while if he helped us tonight by being Santa. He don't talk much, but he sure can look jolly."

"How's the sauce coming?" Glory asked. Matthew had already reported that there were several gallons of spaghetti sauce simmering away at the old café. Young people and apparently some older ones had been coming and going from the place all day. The smell of Italian herbs was settling over Dry Creek, and when a person walked down the street they could hear the faint sounds of a band practicing inside the café.

"We're almost ready for everyone. You and Matthew are coming, aren't you?"

"Wouldn't miss it," Glory assured her.

"Hey, you should wear your costume for dinner." Linda snapped her gum.

"This angel would need a bib as big as a sheet if I had to eat with my wings on."

"Yeah, I suppose it wouldn't work too well with the wings."

The door to the hardware store opened again, and Sylvia came in.

"Cold out there." Sylvia blew on her hands to warm them.

"It's not too bad, really." Glory felt like a Montana

native. "Not cold enough to crack the vinyl on car seats or to freeze your nose hairs or to—"

"I get the picture," Sylvia interrupted.

Glory grinned. "I thought maybe a certain rancher would keep you warm—give you his jacket, that kind of thing."

Sylvia snorted. "The only thing Garth Elkton is going to give me is high blood pressure. That man is impossible."

"If you say so," Glory assured her friend with another grin.

Just then Matthew hobbled out from the back storeroom. Glory's grin faded. It was all she could do to keep her mouth from dropping open. His chestnut hair was rumpled and shot through with gold. In fact, he was golden all over from his forehead to his big toe. His face was sprinkled with gold. His clothes were sprinkled with gold. It appeared Matthew had found the glitter.

"Speaking of keeping warm," Sylvia leaned over and muttered to Glory. "You never did tell me how you ended up catching a man like him."

"Catching? Matthew?" Glory's voice squeaked. She continued in a whisper. "I didn't catch anyone. Matthew is just a friend. He's not caught at all."

"If you say so." Sylvia righted herself and patted her hair. "I better get back to the barn. Mrs. Hargrove needs help with some pine cones she's arranging."

"She still at it?" Elmer groaned and stood up. He slapped Jacob on the knee. "Guess we better go give her a hand."

Matthew shook his head. Glitter spun off him. "Give me a minute to get this stuff off me and I'll go give everyone a hand, too. I'll just put a note on the door so anyone who wants to buy something knows where to find me."

* * *

They all stood in the door to the barn. It was high noon and the air was cold enough so that they all looked like smokers when they breathed. Each word brought a puff of gray-white air. The barn itself was rough-hewn. Unvarnished pine boards lined the walls and the thirty-foot-high ceiling. A hayloft hung down from the front of the barn and Glory could see the angel's swing that the ranch hands had built. Two thick ropes hung from a hoist and met at the swing's bottom with a wide plank to stand on. The swing looked like every child's fantasy. Glory was beginning to anticipate soaring over the heads of everyone as she swung from side to side in the barn.

"You'll have to wear some ruffled petticoats," Sylvia offered. "They'd swish and sway when you swing. It'll look very feminine. Southern belle-like."

"Petticoats?" Matthew frowned. Suddenly he wasn't so sure about Glory and this swing. There were too many single men out at the Big Sheep Mountain Ranch. They'd love to get a glimpse of Glory's petticoats. "Long johns," Matthew said decisively. "You'll wear a pair of my long johns. I won't have anyone ogling your legs."

"Long johns?" Glory frowned. "I don't think an angel would wear long johns."

"In Montana they do. We've got cold winters here," Matthew insisted.

"It is cold, isn't it?" Mrs. Hargrove said as she walked over to them. She rubbed her hands even though they were in knit mittens. "We've been trying to think of a way to warm up this barn for tonight."

"Henry has some secondhand camp stoves," Matthew suggested. "They'd at least take the edge off the cold."

"I'll buy them from you," Tavis offered.

"I'm sure Henry won't mind if we use them on loan. They're already used."

"I'd like to buy them anyway. I've been thinking we might use this barn for other things, too. Plays, maybe concerts."

"We could have rock concerts," Linda gushed. "Wait'll I tell the Jazz Man. We could set up right here!"

"Not a bad idea," Mrs. Hargrove agreed, and turned to Tavis. "But what will your dad say? I'm surprised he even agreed to the pageant."

"Me, too." Tavis grinned. "That's why I thought I'd ask about the rest—he's not himself lately. Aunt Francis has him rattled. She's cleaning everything in sight. Even threw away his favorite coffee mug because it was stained. He probably doesn't even know what he's agreeing to, but he's a man of his word. Once he's said yes, he won't back down. Besides, we've built all these bleachers and we don't need the barn anyway. Only use it for trucking, and that was before we built the good road to the main corrals."

Glory looked around her. The barn had been transformed. Six rows of sturdy bleachers lined both sides of the barn. The floor of the barn had been hosed down and polished until it shone. At the front of the barn, a fake building front stood with the words *Bethlehem Inn* painted across it. Nearby an open stable was fashioned with bales of hay strewn around. A metallic gold star hung down from the hayloft above the manger. As she looked more closely, she noticed that the gold star was on a pulley so that it could travel on a wire from one end of the barn to the other.

"Amazing," Glory complimented Tavis and Mrs. Hargrove.

The older woman beamed. "Tavis and the other ranch hands did most of it."

Tavis shrugged. "Just some sawing and hammering."

"It's perfect." Sylvia added her praise.

Mrs. Hargrove nodded proudly. "We've got it all set to go. The only thing we're missing is a minister to say a prayer before we begin." Mrs. Hargrove looked at Matthew. "It could be an already printed prayer. Maybe from a book or something."

"Then anybody can say it." Matthew leaned on his crutch.

"Not everybody has the voice," Mrs. Hargrove explained wistfully. "There's something about the voice of a minister. It would add the right touch." She added quickly, "Don't say no yet. Think about it. If you don't do it, Elmer will stand in."

"I'll think about it," Matthew agreed as he turned around to leave.

Glory watched Matthew walk slowly out of the barn. The floor was smooth and he had to place his crutches with care. She wished she knew what he was thinking.

"He won't do it." Glory spoke aloud.

"I'm thinking he will," Mrs. Hargrove contradicted confidently. "He's been walled in long enough. It's time for him to take back his faith."

"I'm not even sure he's planning to read the Christmas story to the twins," Glory said, worrying aloud. "If he won't do that, he surely won't pray."

"Wait and see," Mrs. Hargrove advised. "That man may surprise you."

The smell of chocolate chip cookies carried all through the house. Glory had added a few more ornaments to the tree so that it shone and sparkled from every angle. The nurse from Dr. Norris's clinic had called and told her the boxes had arrived and she would bring them with her to the pageant. Knowing that the children's presents were taken care of, Glory carefully wrapped her own gifts and placed them beneath the tree. The books for the twins were easy to tie up in red tissue paper. She had more trouble with Matthew's gift. She hadn't looked closely enough at the CD when she bought it. It was *Piano Selections for Lovers. Lovers!* Since she didn't have anything else for him, she'd put it in her purse. If he gave her a present, she'd give it to him.

The big present for the twins was still upstairs in Matthew's room—the picture she had painted of their mother. Glory imagined the look on the twins' faces when they saw their mother for the first time. She wondered if they would ever realize that half of the love that shone out at them from the picture belonged to her, Glory. In the last brush strokes of the painting, Glory had begun to cry herself. She felt the love of the twins' mother as surely as though the woman were standing in the room with her. And Glory felt her own love pour out of her heart onto the canvas.

"Are you all right?" Matthew pushed open the front door and hobbled into the house. Snowflakes covered his hair and the shoulders of his wool jacket. He wasn't using his crutches properly. He'd obviously been using his own feet and carrying the crutches.

"Yeah, why wouldn't I be?"

Matthew frowned. "I told you to keep the door locked."

"Oh, there's no need now," Glory said. "The boys are on a plane back to Seattle."

"Still, we can't be too careful." Matthew turned around and twisted the lock.

"Well, nobody around here is going to hurt me," Glory protested. "At least, not with a bullet. I'm more likely to fall off that angel swing than anything."

"We're going to tie you in. I've already thought of that and fixed it so you can't fall. And I thought of a way to tie your skirts down while we're at it."

"A straitlaced angel?"

"Angels are supposed to be straitlaced. Besides—" Matthew caught himself and stopped.

"Besides what?"

Matthew smiled slightly. "Besides, you're so beautiful nobody's going to care about sneaking a look at your legs. They'll just be looking at your face."

Glory blushed. "You're just saying that so I'll weaken and give you one of the cookies I made for the twins."

"I thought I smelled chocolate."

It was almost five o'clock, but it was already dark outside. The winter sky was sprinkled with stars. Matthew had added a large log to the fireplace in the living room and made spiced cider for everyone. Glory had plugged in the lights to the Christmas tree, and the twins had taken their baths early in honor of the evening.

The twins sat on the sofa with a cookie in each hand, waiting impatiently for Matthew to finish pouring the cups of cider.

"Before we open the presents we need to read the Christmas story." Glory twisted two new bulbs onto the strand of lights. All of the lights shone now.

"We could read it real fast," Josh suggested as he took another bite of cookie.

"Not too fast. You'll want to know about the presents they gave to the little baby Jesus before we open ours," Glory said, trying to make the story relevant to the boys.

"What'd He get? Lego?" Josh asked.

"Not exactly. He got gold, myrrh and frankincense."

"We know about frankin—whatever," Josh explained. "We got a book about him at preschool."

"Him?" Glory was bewildered.

"Yeah. Frankin—frankin—sense." Josh laid his cookies down and stood up from the sofa. "He walks like this." Josh held his arms out stiffly and clumped along.

"Oh, Frankenstein." Glory deciphered his meaning. "But that's not—"

"I'll bet he's a Terminator," Joey said excitedly. "And God sent him to be a bodyguard for the baby Jesus."

"That's a cool gift." Josh sat back down on the sofa. "And I bet this Frank guy has a laser gun that zaps people." Josh held out a pretend gun and took aim at the fireplace. "Rat-tat-tat-tat!"

"Nobody is zapping anyone around here," Matthew said firmly as he set down four mugs of cider on the coffee table. "And no guns."

"I was pointing at the fireplace," Josh explained. "That's okay. It's not people."

"Frankincense wasn't a person or a machine," Glory said as she moved one of Josh's cookies and sat down beside the twins.

"Oh." Josh picked up the cookie and thought a moment. "Was it a car?"

"They didn't have cars when Jesus was born."

"No cars!" Joey squirmed closer to Glory. "What was it, then?"

"It's a…well, a…perfume."

"Like in soap?" Josh asked skeptically.

Glory nodded. "Something like that."

"Who'd give a baby soap for Christmas?" Josh was getting indignant.

"Had Jesus been a bad boy?" Joey asked in awe.

"Well, no, not at all. Jesus was only a baby. A very good baby."

Josh snorted. "Good boys don't get soap in their stocking."

Glory looked at the two boys and then looked at Matthew. "It wasn't like that at all," she protested weakly.

"Maybe I better read the story from the Bible," Matthew said, and grinned at Glory. "We can't have them thinking Jesus was a bad boy or that He needed a Terminator to protect Him. Of course—" Matthew eyed his two sons thoughtfully "—He did have that trouble with the bad guys coming to get Him."

"Bad guys?"

Matthew hobbled over to the bookshelf and pulled the family Bible down. He held it in his hands briefly before he turned around and came back to the sofa. "It all started two thousand years ago halfway around the world in a town called Bethlehem."

"Is that farther away than Billings?" Joey asked.

"It's a lot farther away than Billings," Matthew assured his sons, and then looked at Glory. "Remind me to get a globe for these boys. They have no idea."

Glory smiled. She thought it was rather sweet for five-year-old boys to think the whole world was in their backyard.

Glory leaned back. She couldn't believe it. Matthew was reading the Bible to his sons as if he did it every day.

She watched his face in the firelight. She smiled as he made donkey noises to make his sons giggle when he told of Mary and Joseph's trip to Bethlehem. The two boys looked up at their father with rapt attention.

Glory felt the happiness squeeze into her heart. She'd never thought she'd love someone like Matthew. Someone strong and good and kind. Someone who took in a stranger like her just because his sons thought she was an angel. *How many ways do I love you, Matthew Curtis?* she asked herself. *How many ways?*

"No," she heard Matthew say to Josh. "The wise men couldn't just call the cops. Besides, they weren't lost. They were following the star."

The Bullet patted his very red stomach and hitched up his very black belt. He circulated through the little café and gave out candy canes to everyone. He even posed for pictures with some of the diners. He hoped all of the jolliness would pay off.

The Bullet had spent the day planning. The more he thought about when to shoot the woman, the closer he came to realizing he couldn't do it. He just wasn't up to pulling another trigger. He'd be a marked man, of course. But he was so tired of killing people.

He was going to march outside to the pay phone and call Millie. He'd spend Christmas with her and then head down to Mexico. She might even come with him.

The air was brittle, and the Bullet needed to take his gloves off to punch the numbers on the telephone. He'd expected Millie to pick up on the first ring. But the phone rang right through to the message.

He heard Millie's breathless voice. "Forrest, if that's you, your uncle stopped by. We're out to dinner." A giggle. "He said to tell you he's taking real good care of me."

The Bullet's mouth went dry. This client that knew Forrest's name would know he used an old uncle as a screen for his trips. Since the Bullet had no uncle, that left only one conclusion. The client had Millie. The Bullet let the knowledge slice through him.

Chapter Thirteen

The early-evening light filtered into the church. Glory could hear the women outside in the church kitchen as they put the coffee on to brew. Through the open door she saw the kitchen counter piled high with cookies. Lemon bars. Gingersnaps. Sugar cookies. Plus trays and trays of date bars. Glory wished she was out there chatting with the ranchers' wives she'd just met—Margaret Ann and Doris June. But instead she was the angel, so she was inside the costume room listening to Matthew's quiet breathing as he helped her adjust her wings. The bare overhead light was bright and, once Matthew had pushed some choir robes out of the way, she could see herself in the old full-length mirror.

Glory wrinkled her nose at her reflection as she circled her head with garland. She'd loosely pulled her hair up on top of her head to help keep the garland in place. Tiny flecks of gold fluttered down on her nose. Not that it mattered. She was already covered with specks of glitter from when Matthew had hooked her wings onto the harness she wore under her white angel gown. The wings had been recently dipped in glitter.

Glory blew a strand of hair off her forehead, knowing she had to be careful what she touched. Mrs. Hargrove had unearthed a pair of long white gloves so that Glory could point with a white finger when she said, "Behold…"

"Not many angels look like they're ready to swear," Matthew observed mildly as he bent the flap on Glory's left wing to attach it more firmly. "Well, I expect the Archangel did a time or two—all that wrath and destruction."

"They all would look that way if they had to fly around in wings like this." Glory cautiously flexed a shoulder. She had a tiny little itch under the harness.

Matthew chuckled. "I doubt they could even get off the ground with those wings."

"Now you tell me."

"They'll do fine in the swing, though." Matthew cleared his throat. He thought he was doing pretty well with the chitchat. No one would know his hands trembled from adjusting Glory's wings. She wasn't an angel; she was a goddess. Her flaming red hair, more copper than gold, was gathered on top of her head. But it was so fine, wisps of hair circled her head. She scarcely needed a halo. Her hair floating around her sparkled as much as the glitter. Matthew leaned just a little closer to her hair and breathed deeply.

"Peaches?"

"My shampoo," Glory answered. She had forgotten her lipstick and rouge, but she had remembered her favorite matching shampoo and lotion.

Matthew nodded. "I'd better pin your garland on better. Wouldn't want the halo to slip when you're out there."

Matthew stood behind Glory, positioning her halo and noticing once again the graceful line of her neck. Swanlike didn't begin to cover it. Glory looked so much like an angelic bride as she stood there that Matthew couldn't help himself. He leaned closer and pressed his lips very lightly to the back of her neck. His kiss was more of a breath than an act.

"My hair's falling down." Glory tried to reach her arm up to her neck. That's all she needed. "I just felt it fall."

"You're fine."

"Yeah, men always say that, even when we have broccoli in our teeth."

"You don't have broccoli in your teeth."

"I know. It's my hair."

Matthew decided he was a rat all the way. He put his hands up to Glory's hair and did what wasn't necessary. He pretended to smooth it back up. Her hair was silky soft. He smoothed it again. "There." His voice was little more than a whisper. "Your hair's fine."

"Thank you."

"It's time we got you to the barn." Matthew's voice was thick. He knew they still had a half hour before the performance started, but he also knew that he'd better get Glory over to the barn and away from this small room before he gave in to the urge to kiss more than her neck. Not even that growing stack of cookies on the counter would distract the church women if they happened to look over into the small room and see him kissing the Christmas angel the way he wanted to right now.

Glory stood in the door of the barn. Matthew had walked over with her, refusing to use his crutch so that he could hold a blanket around her shoulders even though it was almost impossible to do so with her wings jutting out behind them. The night was cold and starless. Fluffy snowflakes were beginning to fall. When they got to the door of the barn, Glory had had to enter sideways so that her wings would not be bent.

"I don't know what I'd do without you," Glory said to Matthew as he bent to unhook the hem of her white gown that had caught on a nail by the door.

"I'll get a hammer and come back and smooth that over," Matthew muttered as he stood. "Yours won't be the only hem it catches."

Matthew was right. Glory looked around. There was an abundance of long, flowing robes. She'd never seen such a colorful array of little boys in bathrobes, most of them dragging along the barn floor. Some had pastel-striped robes; some had white cotton robes; some had plain colored robes. All of them had a striped dish towel wrapped around their heads with a band of red material holding it in place. Several boys had a wooden staff in their hands. Two of the boys even had leashes. Leashes? Glory looked again. If there were leashes, there must be— Yes, there they were. The animals.

"Come see," Josh called excitedly to Matthew and Glory. "We've got sheep!"

"I'll believe this when I see it," Matthew whispered to Glory as they walked over to where a group of boys stood.

"Don't knock it. The sheep are as real as the angel."

Glory had never realized that a dog wrapped in a fluffy white towel could look so much like a sheep in the shadows.

"Hey, Glory," a woman called to her from the front of the bleachers.

Glory turned and recognized Debra Hanson, the nurse from Dr. Norris's office, who had promised to bring the boxes of toys Glory had ordered.

"I got them, honey," Debra said in a stage whisper as

Glory walked closer. Debra snapped her gum and spoke with a Southern accent. She wore a red scarf wrapped around her head like a turban and a long black coat. Christmas bell earrings shimmered as she spoke. "Where do you want me to put them?"

Glory looked around. She'd like to surprise the children. "Behind the stable."

"I'll tell the boys." Debra turned and smiled at a couple of the hands from the Big Sheep Mountain Ranch. She raised her hand to wave and used one of her red-tipped fingers to summon the men over to her. They came eagerly.

Glory decided her boxes were in good hands, so she could mingle. Since this was a barn, there was no backstage area. The six-foot-high, ten-foot-wide stable was the only structure. The actors were in plain sight doing last-minute errands. One little choir angel had a nosebleed, and one of the older shepherds took him outside to get some snow to put on his nose. One of the boys was teasing Mary about the makeup someone had put on her. Mrs. Hargrove was muttering to herself.

Glory decided Mrs. Hargrove was the one who needed rescuing the most. "Everything looks ready," Glory said reassuringly when she came near the older woman. Glory had noticed the musicians from the café setting up their small sound system at the side of the stable.

Mrs. Hargrove had abandoned her usual gingham dresses and wore a green wool suit with a hat. She was rubbing her hands so fiercely Glory feared for the woman's skin.

"It'll go all right," Glory added. "The pageant will be just fine."

"Well, not with *him* here," Mrs. Hargrove seethed. "It's practically blasphemy!"

"Who?"

"Him." Mrs. Hargrove jerked her head in the direction of the Santa Claus who had entertained diners at the café earlier.

"Oh, he's all right," Glory said. Linda had told her the man was an old cowboy who was down on his luck. He certainly looked down on his luck with his fake white beard and red stocking hat. His shoulders slumped as if he carried the weight of the world. Even at that, though, he was handing out candy canes. "He's just cheering folks up."

"Folks don't need cheering up! This is Christmas." Mrs. Hargrove pursed her lips.

Just then the girl who was playing Mary tugged on Mrs. Hargrove's arm.

"Yes, dear?" the older woman said as she leaned over.

Mrs. Hargrove's voice softened when she talked to the girl and Glory could see why. Lori was all pink and blue in her costume. She looked sugar sweet, except for her eyes.

"Johnny Ellis stole the dish towels!" The girl's eyes snapped with anger.

"Dish towels?" Mrs. Hargrove seemed disoriented.

"The swaddlin' clothes!" the girl wailed, and burst into tears. "For my baby!"

Mrs. Hargrove soothed the girl and then straightened herself for battle. "Just wait until I get my hands on Johnny Ellis."

The girl stopped crying and perked up significantly when Mrs. Hargrove left.

Matthew came over and stood slightly behind Glory. She would have known he was there by the smell of his aftershave even if she hadn't heard the quiet thumping of his crutches. She'd noticed the pleasing scent at dinner and wondered if he was meeting someone special at the pageant. Not that it was any of her business, she reminded herself.

"Boys can be so annoying, can't they, Lori?" Matthew said sympathetically.

Glory was inclined to agree, but she didn't expect the girl to nod her head so vigorously.

"Thinks he's so smart—ordering me around saying he's my husband," Lori said.

"Well, he won't be your husband for long," Glory consoled her. "After the pageant he goes back to being plain Johnny Ellis." Glory couldn't resist a little consciousness-raising. "Besides, just because he's your husband doesn't mean he gets to order you around."

"Yeah." The girl brightened. "I could order him, too."

"That's not what I meant," Glory said, but it was too late. Lori had gone off to find Johnny Ellis.

Glory looked at Matthew. He was a constant surprise to her. Just when she thought his head was filled with hammering loose nails she found out that he'd had time to watch over the little children.

She fought the impulse to adjust Matthew's tie. It didn't need adjusting, not really. But he wouldn't know that and it would give her a good cover as she leaned closer to smell his aftershave.

Fortunately, she was saved from her own foolishness by Mrs. Hargrove, who fluttered by gathering up children like a mother hen circling her chicks. "It'll be time to start soon. I'm having the children go to the back of the barn, by the far bleachers, so we can file in when we start the Scripture reading."

"I better get up in the hayloft, then." Glory picked up her long skirts.

"Let me go with you," Matthew said. "Make sure your skirt doesn't get caught on those narrow stairs."

"Oh, I asked Tavis to help her." Mrs. Hargrove looked down at a clipboard that she had picked up from somewhere. "Someone needs to go up with her and help her with the swing. You're on crutches."

"I'll help her," Matthew muttered as he positioned the crutches under his shoulders. A look of stubborn determination settled on his face. "I'm the one that knows how to add the extra train to the outfit so that people won't be looking at the angel's legs. Besides, I don't trust Tavis alone with the angel around all that hay."

"Well." Mrs. Hargrove studied Matthew with a bright, pleased look in her eyes. Then she took the pen off the clipboard and made a couple of check marks on her list.

There was a rail instead of a wall on the inside of the stairs leading to the overhead hayloft, and it was just as well. Glory could never have squeezed between two walls with her seven-foot wingspan.

"Ever wonder why angels just appear?" Glory muttered as she twisted her shoulders so her wings wouldn't be dented. "They can't get around in these things, so they have to—puff—appear out of nowhere. Puffing is a lot easier than flying."

Matthew looked down at her. He had half hobbled, half crawled to the top of the stairs and stood waiting for her. He leaned his crutches against the wall of the hayloft and reached down a hand to Glory. "Here, let me help you."

The smell of dry hay greeted Glory when she stood on the floor of the hayloft. The decorators for the pageant had not come up here. It was still ready for cattle. Several bales of hay were broken and strewn around. A pitchfork stood upright, embedded in one bale. Straw and wisps of hay lay all over the rough wood floor.

The hayloft was dim. The bright light from downstairs filtered through the end of the hayloft and gave everything a warm cast. Glory looked around. While she and Matthew could see the people down below, no one from down there could see the two of them. It was a perfect place for— Glory pushed the thought aside. She knew this ex-minister would never kiss an angel. Best not to even think about it.

Ten minutes later Glory was sitting on a bale of hay watching Matthew. Men! He had spent the entire past ten minutes going over every inch of the swing that she was going to use. "You're making me nervous. Besides, Tavis has already checked everything."

Matthew scowled up at her from where he was crouched by the ropes.

"It's even got a safety rope. See?" Glory pointed to her backup rope.

Glory sighed. Mention of the safety rope only gave Matthew another thing to check out.

People were filling up the bleachers down below them. Glory saw just the tops of everyone, but she could tell people had dressed up for the occasion. She saw black Stetson hats and gray Stetson hats. The men who didn't have Stetson hats wore hunter-green caps. And the women's hair—from gray to towheaded—was shiny and curled.

The only one who stood out was Santa in his bright red cap. He'd stopped giving out candy canes and sat at the end of one of the far bleachers. The old man must be tired. Glory could think of no other reason why he seemed to be staring up at the hayloft where she was.

Just then a crackle of static sounded through the barn.

"It's—" Elmer's voice came out over the loudspeaker "—time."

The rustle of the audience stilled. Elmer stood beside the manger. Someone turned off a few of the lights.

Elmer cleared his throat. "I want to thank all you friends and neighbors for coming to celebrate the birth of our Lord. The children of Dry Creek have worked hard to prepare for this pageant, and so have the adults." Elmer paused. "We may as well get to it." He bent his head over a Bible and began to read. "'And it came to pass in those days, that there went out a decree from Caesar Augustus, that all the world should be taxed....'"

Glory smiled. Elmer's grandfatherly voice was perfect for the reading.

The band's sound system must have been more than a microphone, because the sound of a symphony filled the barn as Joseph started to walk the length of the barn leading a young heifer that was carrying a very pregnant Mary. The girl's long robe fell against the heifer's side and the heifer kept swishing its tail trying to get rid of the annoyance.

"'And Joseph also went up from Galilee, out of the city of Nazareth, into Judea, unto the city of David, which is called Bethlehem.'"

The heifer stopped in front of the wooden storefront that said Bethlehem Inn. A boy wearing a white butcher's apron came out of a door in the storefront. He was carrying a chicken under one arm and a No Vacancy sign under the other. The chicken was squawking indignantly at being carried, and when the boy went to hang the No Vacancy sign on the larger sign, the chicken escaped and flew to a perch on the very top of the stable. The boy stood watching the chicken with his mouth open.

There was silence. Mrs. Hargrove cleared her throat loudly. There was more silence.

Finally Mary spoke from her position on top of the heifer. "Does that—" she pointed to the sign the boy still held "—mean there's no room in the inn?"

"No…" The boy regained his lines. He repeated loudly, "No room in the inn."

Mary nodded, satisfied. "I thought so. We'll stay in the stable." And then she slid to the floor, took the heifer's rope and said with an unmistakable tone of command, "Joseph, you bring the bags. And don't forget the baby things."

Slack jawed with surprise, Joseph watched her leave and then hurried to catch up.

A choir of children's voices started singing "Away in the Manger."

In the hayloft Matthew had finally stopped checking equipment and sat down on the hay bale across from Glory. Glory smiled up at him and moved some of the yards of material so Matthew could move closer. "Mrs. Hargrove must have decided to use animals after all."

"Goes with the barn theme," Matthew whispered.

The carol ended and Elmer's voice continued with his reading. "'And so it was, that, while they were there, the days were accomplished that she should be delivered….'"

"We'd better get you in that swing," Matthew whispered. "The angel's coming up pretty soon."

Glory nodded, stood, and then it happened. A hiccup.

"I—can't—" Glory hiccuped again. She looked at Matthew. "I've got—the—" She hiccuped again.

Some miracles happen, Matthew decided. Others are snatched out of the possibilities of the moment, like this one. He did what he'd wanted to do ever since they climbed into the loft. He dipped his head and kissed Glory.

Matthew felt surprise ripple through Glory, so he deepened the kiss. His own surprise slugged him in the belly a second later. Who would know it would be like this? Her lips tasted like molten honey. Hot and sweet. He decided he might as well hang for the real thing as for a polite peck, so he deepened it even further. He could be dead and kissing a real angel for all he knew—or cared.

Glory stopped breathing. She half thought she might have stopped living. Everything stopped except Matthew's kiss.

Matthew pulled his lips away.

"You—k-kissed—" Glory stuttered. "Me."

"Yes." Matthew tried to stop the lightness inside him. If he wasn't careful, he'd be able to float alongside Glory even without a swing.

"The hiccups. They stopped." Glory put her hand to her cheek. She needed to stop staring. He'd think she'd never been kissed before. And she had. Not like that, of course, but she had. Only, why had he kissed her now? Of course. The hiccups. That must be it. "Is that an old remedy?"

"Remedy?"

"For the hiccups. A grandmother's remedy? Like a slap on the back?"

Matthew winced. Granted, he'd thought the hiccups were a good cover for a kiss before he began the kiss, but now… Surely she knew it meant more now. And even at that, his kisses surely weren't grandmotherly.

The microphone below crackled as Elmer read. Glory stepped onto the swing. She hooked on the material that Matthew had rigged to trail beneath her. She hoped Matthew was satisfied. No one could see her feet, let alone her legs, with all that material. She watched as Matthew fastened the safety ropes.

"'And there were in the same country shepherds abiding in the field, keeping watch over their flock by night.'" Elmer's voice continued.

The boys in bathrobes and their "sheep" walked to the center of the barn and sat down. Two of the boys even lay down.

"'And, lo,'" Elmer read. "'An angel of the lord came upon them…'"

"I'm off," Glory whispered to Matthew before she took a deep breath.

Matthew helped her push off. The swing slid off its mooring and she was free. She felt the rush of air as she swooped over the shepherds below. Maybe, she thought, it wouldn't be so bad being an angel, after all. She'd talked Mrs. Hargrove into letting the children sing instead of the angel, so she concentrated on flying.

Glory's ecstasy was short-lived. The chicken, perched on top of the stable, had not been there earlier in Glory's practice run. And when Glory had practiced, she hadn't had a long white train of angel gown following her in flight. It was Matthew's modesty veil. When the chicken saw the thick cloud of material coming straight at it, it panicked and took flight again. Unfortunately, by taking flight, the chicken only rose up higher until it was swept along in the train of angel gown as Glory swung low over the stable.

"Oh, oh," Glory whispered to herself, and then added for the benefit of the passenger she carried beneath her, "Good chickie, good chickie. Just stay calm."

The chicken didn't stay calm. It screeched indignantly as it clung with its claws and beak to the train of angel gown.

Glory reached the arc of her swing just as the dogs

decided they'd rather be dogs than sheep. They started to howl at Glory as if she was the moon. She comforted herself with the thought that maybe they were baying at the chicken.

Elmer kept reading. "'And the glory of the Lord shone round about them: and they were sore afraid.'"

Glory was sore afraid herself. The weight of the chicken began to pull even harder on the gown she wore, and she heard a slow tearing sound. She'd be lucky if the bird didn't pull the gown right off her and leave her swinging in the white long johns Matthew had insisted she wear. She could just see the headlines in the *Billings Gazette:* Chicken Strips Angel At Church Pageant. She'd probably make the tabloids with that one.

Not even looking up, Elmer kept reading. "'And the angel said unto them…'"

Glory took a deep breath. She pointed out with her white-gloved finger and shouted loudly, "'Fear not, for behold, I bring you good tidings of great joy.'"

Amazingly, Glory's words calmed the chicken. Unless— *I wonder if the poor bird finally had too much and went into shock?*

With the chicken silent, the dogs quit howling and lay down like the sheep they were meant to be. Even the shepherds looked reverent as they watched the angel swing back toward the hayloft.

Elmer took up the angel's pronouncement for her. "'For unto you is born this day in the city of David a Savior, which is Christ the Lord.'"

Glory swung back and straight into Matthew's arms. Unfortunately, she'd built up so much speed she knocked them both to the floor of the hayloft.

"Oh." Glory blinked.

Elmer's voice continued. "'And suddenly there was

with the angel a multitude of the heavenly host praising God and saying…'"

The children's choir began to sing "Glory to God."

"Oh." Glory blinked again. She was lying on top of Matthew and she couldn't seem to move. She could hear Matthew breathing beneath her. Fact is, she could feel him breathing as his chest rose and fell. He hadn't screamed, so her wings must not have jabbed him. He was all right. It was her. She couldn't move. It must be the excitement of the swing, she consoled herself. After all, look what the swing had done to that chicken—

"The chicken!" Glory exclaimed, remembering.

Matthew felt Glory lift herself up. He wanted to pull her back and try another home remedy. As far as he was concerned, he could lie right there until he died. He was singing the Hallelujah chorus and it had nothing to do with Christmas. But she was right, there was the chicken to consider.

"It looks all right," Glory whispered as she studied the chicken. They had unhooked the train to Glory's gown and unfolded the material until they freed the bird. The chicken fluffed itself up and then started hopping around looking for something to eat.

"Why don't you unhook my wings, too?" Glory asked. She was already kneeling. "I want to get them off before I do major damage."

The wise men were ready to make their entrance by the time Glory and Matthew got back to the pageant. The shepherds were surrounding the manger and the children's choir was standing in front of the inn. The dogs had decided the excitement was over for the day and were lying half-asleep at their masters' feet.

Elmer's voice continued his reading, "'When they saw the star, they rejoiced with exceeding great joy.'"

Matthew stood up to slowly pull the metal star on the pulley toward the stable. It was rigged like an old-fashioned laundry line. In fact, as Glory looked at the brackets more closely, she saw that it *was* an old-fashioned laundry line.

Solemnly the wise men followed the star until it reached the stable.

"We brought you some presents," one of the wise men announced proudly as he pulled out three prettily wrapped packages. The wise men turned to Mary. "We got receipts so you can return them if you want."

Mary nodded her thanks.

The children's choir and the shepherds began to sing "Silent Night." The pageant was drawing to a close.

Christmas truly was a time of goodwill, Glory thought as she shook the hand of another well-wisher. Everyone along the Yellowstone River was out and thanking her for being their angel. Why, there was almost a crowd in this barn, Glory decided as she looked over the people. She recognized a few of them. Linda, of course, and a couple of the hands from the Big Sheep Mountain Ranch. And then there was Sylvia and the rancher, talking animatedly in the corner of the barn. Glory decided now wasn't the time to go and say hello to her friend.

Mrs. Hargrove invited everyone over to the church for refreshments, and people began adjusting scarves for the walk over to the other building. Matthew stood talking with Deputy Wall.

Glory decided it was time to slip behind the stable and get her presents ready for the children. She'd seen Josh look her way several times, so she knew he was hopeful. Glory walked over to him and bent down to whisper in his ear, "Tell everyone the angel's giving out presents behind the stable in five minutes."

Josh's eyes lit up and he nodded.

The Bullet had let the people of Dry Creek have their pageant. But now he watched the angel make her way to the rear of the barn.

The light was dim behind the stable, but the space was completely out of sight of the other people. And there was the angel, kneeling down and sorting through one of several huge boxes of toys.

The Bullet unbuttoned his red shirt and drew out his gun.

He'd hoped the angel would not even look up, but she did. Her eyes widened as he put his arm out and aimed the gun.

Then the Bullet heard a sound behind him.

"Santa?" a small voice asked. The Bullet turned his head slightly and saw the twin boys staring at him.

Chapter Fourteen

Glory felt all the blood drain from her head when she saw the gun. She thought she'd faint. When she saw the twins, she knew she didn't have the luxury of fainting.

"Oh, boys," she called out, hoping her voice was bright and normal. "You caught us. Santa was trying out some of the toys."

Please, Lord, Glory prayed. *Have the man go along with me. Let him have a heart. If I need to die, don't take the twins, too.*

"He's not supposed to point guns at people," Josh said righteously.

"That's right," Glory agreed. "But Santa and I need a few more minutes. Go back to your dad now. And keep the other kids away, too."

Glory kept her eyes on the killer. She begged him silently to let the twins go. "No one knows what Santa looks like," she reminded him. "Not with a beard and the suit."

"Yeah, get out of here, kids," the killer finally said.

Josh turned to go, but Glory watched the indecision on Joey's face.

"Run along, Joey." Glory tried not to let her voice plead as loudly as her heart. "Go to your dad."

"I want us to go home now," Joey said softly. "We don't need more presents."

Glory wished she were a better actress. "Please, just do what I ask, sweetheart."

Joey waited a minute before finally turning to go. Glory watched him reluctantly step around the corner of the stable.

"Thank you," Glory whispered softly as she looked up at the killer.

Santa nodded as he reaimed his gun.

Glory closed her eyes.

"You going to pray, too?" the man asked incredulously.

Glory opened her eyes. "If I may." She wouldn't tell him she'd closed her eyes not to pray but so she wouldn't have to watch him pull the trigger. "Sort of my last request."

"Hit men don't do last requests. That's the feds." But he lowered his gun.

"Dear Lord," Glory whispered aloud. She wanted the hit man to know she was still praying. "I've had a good life. So much to be thankful for. My mother. The captain. Sylvia. The twins—and their father—"

"Hurry it up, lady. This isn't the Oscars," the killer interrupted. "I haven't got all day to wait while you thank the little people. Wrap it up."

"The Oscars?" Glory forced herself to laugh. "Very clever. Did you see them?"

Santa glowered at her. "No."

"Oh." Glory folded her hands together just as the twins did when they prayed. She couldn't think of what to pray when it looked as if she would see God in a few seconds anyway. Then she thought of the comforting prayer and closed her eyes to begin. "Now I lay me down to sleep. I pray the Lord my soul to keep. If I should—"

Glory heard the loud sound of a gun cocking. Odd, she thought Santa had already pulled the hammer back. Then she heard the voice.

"Hold it right there, Santa!"

Glory opened her eyes. Deputy Wall was standing with his gun aimed at Santa's belly. The only problem was that Santa still had his gun aimed at Glory. Both men seemed to realize the difficulties of that arrangement as quickly as she did.

"You shoot her, I'll get you," Deputy Wall threatened as he steadied his aim.

Santa shrugged without lowering his gun. "She'll still be dead."

"They'll put you away for murder if you kill her," the deputy promised.

"They'll put me away for murder if I give up, too," Santa countered.

Glory decided now was as good a time as any to faint. She willed herself to faint. She held her breath. In the end, she had to half fake her slide down to the barn floor.

She'd no sooner started her slide than a shot was fired. Glory's last conscious thought was that Santa swore like a sailor.

Matthew blamed himself all the way to the stable. Why had he let Mrs. Hargrove lead him off with some story about the wise men so that Josh took longer to find him? Josh had gotten only the words *Santa* and *gun* out of his mouth before Matthew was frantically looking around the barn. Where was Glory?

"I told the deputy, too," Josh was saying proudly. "He knows you shouldn't point guns at people."

Matthew saw the deputy slip behind the stable.

"Stay here, son," Matthew called down as he started toward the stable. His crutches were only slowing him down, so he tossed them away and started to lope along.

"Glory!" Matthew whispered when he rounded the corner and saw what was behind the stable wall. The air smelled like burned gunpowder. And Glory lay there so still.

"You shot her!" Matthew started to lunge toward Santa.

Deputy Wall dropped his gun and grabbed Matthew. Deputy Wall was 250 pounds of muscle, but he didn't stop Matthew easily. "I've wrestled bulls tamer than you." The deputy spit the words out after he'd steadied Matthew. "That man has a gun, for Pete's sake. Keep still."

"Don't worry. I didn't even hit her," Santa said disgustedly. He turned so the gun was now aimed at the two men. "She slid right out of my range. The bullet hit the wall."

Matthew took a deep breath. He looked at Glory carefully. In all of that white, blood would show up readily and so would the scorched mark a bullet would make in passing. There was no sign of either and she appeared to be breathing normally. Besides, there was a bullet hole in the back of the stable.

"You don't need to kill her, anyway." Matthew began to pray. *Help me, God.* "Glory already told the police about the tie-in with the rustling. The manager at the grocery store is going to turn state's evidence."

Santa grunted. "None of my concern. Not my side of the business."

It must have been twenty degrees in the barn, and Matthew's hands were sweating. *Lord, I need you. I won't ask for anything else. Just keep Glory alive.*

"If you want to shoot someone, shoot me instead," Matthew offered.

Matthew heard the surprised protest from Deputy Wall, but he didn't turn to look at the officer. Matthew kept his eyes trained on Santa.

"Nobody's paying me to shoot you," Santa snorted indignantly. "I don't just go around shooting people. I'm a professional."

"I see." Matthew did some quick arithmetic in his head. "If you're a professional, how much would it cost to unshoot someone?"

Santa just laughed. "Money won't do me any good if I don't shoot her."

"Ah, they'd come and get you?" Matthew asked to keep the killer talking. The longer Santa kept talking the longer Matthew had to think of something.

"That isn't the half of it," Santa muttered into his fake beard. "It's who else they'd get that worries me."

Matthew knew from his ministerial counseling that sometimes it was these half-muttered, throwaway lines that no one expected anyone else to listen to that were the most important in understanding a person's troubles.

"A child?" Matthew probed.

Santa shook his head and mumbled, "Girlfriend."

"Girlfriend?" the deputy wailed. "How can you get a girl when I can't?"

"Charm," Santa said without looking at the deputy.

"Aah, a girlfriend." Matthew nodded as if he understood. He kept his eyes focused on Santa's brown eyes. *Lord, Lord, be with me.*

"They've already got Millie," Santa continued, as if the worry couldn't stay trapped inside him any longer. "If I don't shoot this Beckett woman, they'll shoot my Millie."

"Aah." Matthew nodded this time because he did understand. "So we're just two men trying to protect our women."

Santa eyed Matthew skeptically. "Yeah, I suppose so."

Matthew started to breathe again. He'd made the first rung in negotiations. He'd found a common ground from which they could work. "Now all we need to do is figure out a way to keep both of them alive."

"Like what?" Santa asked.

Matthew began to pray even more earnestly. The bait was being nibbled. "Well, what happens if you couldn't kill Glory?"

"What do you mean 'couldn't' kill her?"

"What if there was a storm and Montana was cut off from the rest of the country for a month? No one in or out?"

"Well…" Santa began to think. "I suppose in unusual circumstances they wouldn't hold me to the contract. But they read the papers. They'd know about a storm."

"What about if you were arrested before you got to Glory? Like on a speeding ticket?"

"Well, I suppose if I was arrested and put in jail they couldn't complain too much," Santa agreed, and then pointed out, "But I haven't got a speeding ticket."

"The deputy here could give you one," Matthew offered.

"You want me to give him a *ticket*? A cold-blooded killer? A *speeding ticket*?"

"What do you think, Santa? We could give you a speeding ticket and fingerprint you and then find out about some past crimes."

Santa was thinking. "I work clean. You wouldn't find much. Besides, what if they found out it didn't happen that way? These guys have moles everywhere."

"They don't have any moles in Dry Creek, Montana," Deputy Wall said proudly.

"Well, that's probably true," Santa said as he lowered his gun. "Might not be a better place anywhere to cut a deal."

Matthew left the two men and went over to kneel beside Glory. He picked up her arm to feel her pulse. Her heart was certainly beating strongly.

"Now, about that ticket, what speed were you driving when you came into Dry Creek?" Deputy Wall said as he took Santa's gun.

"Hey, I thought there's no speed limit in Montana."

"There is in towns. We're posted for forty-five. We'll say you were doing eighty." The deputy unclasped his handcuffs and snapped them around Santa's hands.

"She okay?" asked Deputy Wall, turning toward Matthew.

"Seems fine. Just give her a minute."

"Aah…" Santa squirmed as the deputy started to leave. "Mind if we go out the back way? There's a lot of kids out there who don't need to see Santa in handcuffs."

"I'll settle him in my car," the deputy said as he passed Matthew. "Then I'll be back for Glory."

"Back for Glory?"

"She can't stay here now," Deputy Wall patiently explained. "There's a contract out. He—" he nodded at Santa "—he might not be the only one. We'll need to take Glory into protective custody. For her own good."

Glory wondered how long she could feign unconsciousness before someone called a doctor. She supposed she needed to open her eyes, but her world was already here. She knew Matthew held her. She smelled the aftershave and heard the soft murmur of his prayers. She would lie in his arms forever if it kept Matthew praying.

But she supposed it wasn't fair.

"Glory—" The voice that finally pulled her out of her daze was Mrs. Hargrove's. The older woman's voice was determined enough to call back the dead. Glory didn't feel as if she should resist it for something as minor as a slipping spell. Glory refused to accept that she might have fainted, just for a minute. She preferred to think she'd purposely slipped into a daze.

"Are you all right, dear?" Mrs. Hargrove was pressing something wet against Glory's forehead.

Glory opened her eyes. She supposed it was time.

"You'll need to come with me," Deputy Wall ordered Glory. "I've radioed ahead. They'll have a couple of cells ready."

"You can't put her in jail. Not on Christmas Eve." Mrs. Hargrove was horrified.

"I'm not putting her in jail," the deputy explained impatiently. "Protective custody."

"It's for the best," Glory assured the older woman.

Glory looked up at the circle of concerned people looking down at her. All of these people would be in danger if she stayed in Dry Creek before everything was settled. If one contract killer could get through, another one might not be far behind. And bullets didn't always just hit the one for whom they were intended.

"I'll go with her to jail," Matthew offered decisively. "That is, if you'll take the twins home with you tonight, Mrs. Hargrove?"

Mrs. Hargrove nodded. "They're so excited they'll probably fall right to sleep on my sofa."

Matthew didn't correct her, although he was pretty sure the reverse would be true. The boys would be up all night talking about the gunman.

"And hand out the presents," Glory added.

For the first time everyone looked at the boxes.

"That's them?" Matthew asked, and then corrected himself. "I mean, of course that's them. Glad to see they got delivered in time."

"W-well, I'll be…" Mrs. Hargrove stammered. "I'll be."

"The names are already on them," Glory said. "Sylvia saw to that in the ordering."

"Well, the children will be very pleased," Mrs. Hargrove finally managed.

Deputy Wall cleared his throat. "We better be going."

"I can't go like this." Glory looked down at herself. "Let me stop and put on some jeans."

"If you're quick about it," the deputy agreed as Glory started to stand.

The jail clanked. Metal scraped every time anyone moved. And it smelled like a closed-up basement. But, Glory thought to herself, it was safe. And Matthew was here, sitting on the cot on the other side of the cell. They were both safe. No one could shoot a bullet through those thick cement walls, and no one would even try to get in the door past the four deputies called out for special duty tonight.

"Sorry you're missing Christmas Eve with your family," Glory called out to one of the young deputies as he walked past their opened cell.

"It's okay." The deputy ducked his head. "We've never had a hit man in these cells."

"You know, he didn't seem bad for a hit man," Glory mused as she wrapped herself in the blankets she and Matthew had picked up from his house.

From the outside office the strains of the hymn "O Holy Night" reached them in the cells.

"Somebody thought to bring a CD player," Matthew noted.

"And spiced cider." The sweet apple smell began to cut through the basement smell in their cell.

Just then Sylvia stepped through the door from the deputy's office. She was wearing a red Santa's hat and carrying a big box tied up with a silver bow. Behind her came the rancher Garth Elkton, carrying a CD player and a large cup of cider.

"Merry Christmas," Sylvia shouted, and suddenly it was.

An hour later Glory folded up the metallic paper. Sylvia and the rancher had set up a coffeepot of spiced cider outside. There was unmistakable tension between the two of them, but they'd done their job of delivering Christmas cheer very well. They'd even brought a large plate of cookies, compliments of the ladies at the church. There was more than enough for all the deputies and inmates. Of course, the only inmates were Glory, Matthew and the Bullet, as he called himself. Glory shuddered at the name.

Sylvia had sat with Glory while she opened the silver

box. It contained a dozen jars of homemade jam from the booth the women of Dry Creek had set up outside the barn tonight. Chokecherry jam. Rhubarb jam. It couldn't be a more perfect gift. Every time Glory opened a jar she'd think of the people of Dry Creek. She looked across the cell at Matthew. There was one person she couldn't bear to remember only with jam.

"The twins will be sleeping now," she said.

Matthew grunted. He'd been waiting for a romantic moment and it wasn't easy to find one in a cramped cement cell in the middle of winter. When they'd stopped by his house for Glory to change to jeans and a sweatshirt, he'd picked up the gift he'd bought for her. He was waiting for the right time to give it to her, but maybe that moment wouldn't come tonight. He might as well do it now. At least they were alone—something that rarely happened, as one or the other of the deputies was always walking back to chat.

"I have a present for you." Matthew reached into the pocket of his black leather jacket and pulled out a small box wrapped in white tissue paper. "It's not much, but—"

Glory's face lit up. "I got a present for you, too, but it's at your house."

"You've already given me the best Christmas gift." Matthew handed her the box. "Being an angel in this pageant was important to my boys."

Glory opened the little box and pulled out a silver necklace charm in the shape of an angel. "It's beautiful."

"I'll always remember what you've done for me and my boys," Matthew began. He was a man accustomed to words, so he had no excuse for not being able to just spit out the words that would tell Glory what he was feeling. But those words were hard. He wished he were a better man. He knew Glory deserved someone better. Someone whose faith had not been shipwrecked. He wasn't going to ask her to settle for less than she deserved and he wasn't going to ask her to wait for him to become the man she deserved. He just wanted her to know he wished it were different.

Before Matthew could speak again, a burly barrel of a man stomped through the door.

"Captain!" Glory whispered in surprise. "What are you doing here?"

It took the captain only an hour to get Glory and Matthew out of the cell. "There's feds all over Dry Creek by now. Frank talked to that grocery-store manager and we found out the hit had been ordered by the men selling the stolen meat. They were afraid you'd put the pieces together and talk to that store manager. He cracked just like they suspected. They located you through the AP wire—that silly angel story." The captain shook his head. "You were lucky. That hit man—" The captain shook his head again. "When they ran his fingerprints, they didn't find anything. But then they checked with an informant and half the bureau headed to Dry Creek. Funny, you folks catching him here on a speeding ticket."

Glory shrugged. The best story of her police career, and she'd never be able to tell it around the water-cooler.

Glory took her time repacking her suitcase. She was upstairs at Matthew's house and the early-morning sun was just beginning to warm up the sky. The captain had insisted she return with him, and he was right. Until the business of the contract on her was settled, she didn't want to jeopardize Matthew or the boys. So, instead of thinking of excuses to stay another day, she folded her socks and laid them in the suitcase one pair at a time.

Even inside the house, Glory could feel the activity in Dry Creek. The captain was outside now talking with the federal agents who were combing through Dry Creek looking for clues. They were mildly puzzled that a pro like the Bullet would trip up on a traffic ticket, but they were so relieved to have him in custody they didn't press their questions.

Finally, Glory snapped the lid shut on her suitcase. It was time.

Glory started down the stairs for the last time, smiling slightly when she came to the step where Matthew had fallen. That one step had changed her whole life. They should put a plaque there, she mused.

Matthew was sitting on the sofa waiting for her. Glory had half expected him to be outside checking with the feds to make sure they kept her safe, but he appeared willing to let them do their jobs now that they were here in such numbers.

With each step down Glory took, she tried to think of something suitable to say to Matthew. But her mind was as empty as her heart was full. None of the words seemed right.

It wasn't until Glory reached the last step on the stairs that she realized what Matthew was doing. He was staring at the portrait of his late wife, Susie. Glory had put all of the twins' presents down under the tree so that they'd see them when they came over later this morning. She hadn't wrapped the portrait, so they could see their mother the first thing. She hadn't counted on Matthew sitting on the sofa silently weeping in front of the woman's picture.

All of the hopeful words that Glory had been trying to form died unspoken. What could she say to a man who was still so in love with his late wife that he sat there weeping?

"Take care of the twins." Glory managed the words. She focused on Matthew's back. "I'll stop at Mrs. Hargrove's to tell them goodbye."

"Goodbye?" The word seemed dragged from Matthew.

He turned to look at her. Glory meant to look away, but she couldn't. The pain and despair in Matthew's eyes struck deep inside her. His cheeks were wet with new tears and his eyes were red with unshed ones. He must still love his wife very much.

"You're not going?"

"I'll call," Glory said as she stumbled to the door. It was time for her to leave.

"But—?" Matthew protested, and then mumbled in defeat, "Maybe it is best for now. You'll call?"

Glory nodded as she opened the door. She didn't trust her voice to speak.

The Bullet waited impatiently for morning. He had one call coming, and he didn't want to waste it on the answering machine.

The Bullet punched in the numbers and held his breath. One ring. Two rings—

"Hello, Millie's place." A man's voice answered.

The Bullet almost hung up, but he needed to know. "Is Millie there?"

"Forrest, is that you?" The man's voice warmed. "It's me. Douglas from Spokane."

"Douglas?"

"Yeah, I got Millie's number off the shipping label you left and called to wish her a Merry Christmas. We got to talking and she invited me out to spend the holiday with the two of you. Only you never showed. You all right?"

"Not exactly." Relief poured through the Bullet. Douglas would take care of Millie. He'd ask him to take her back to Spokane. No one would find her there.

Chapter Fifteen

Almost two months later, Glory was sitting at her drawing board in the Seattle police station. She was spending as much time as possible at work. The captain had insisted she stay with him and her mother until the federal agents arrested the distributors in the cattle-rustling ring. Glory had given in to the captain rather than argue. Besides, she hadn't wanted to be alone. For weeks she kept expecting to hear the twins giggle, and then she'd look up from her sketching or her reading and realize she'd probably never see them again—or their father.

Being with her family helped her feel better, but she couldn't stay with them forever. The feds had arrested the distributors last week, and she had moved back into her own apartment. The distributors had squealed loud and clear, but they didn't know enough to help the feds find the actual rustlers. Still, Glory was safe.

She had thought that when she moved back into her apartment she'd feel more like her old self, but she didn't. Her life stretched forward with nothing but gray in it.

Glory laid down the black pencil she held in her hand and sighed. The face of crime never changed. All of the perpetrators were beginning to look alike. Actually, in her moments of acute honesty, she realized they all had a tendency to look like Matthew. It didn't help that today was Valentine's Day and that was the deadline she'd set for him. When she first returned to Seattle, she'd had a message on her answering machine telling her he'd call later when he had things worked out. Later was stretching into never as far as she could tell. If he hadn't called her by today, she decided that someplace deep and cold she'd bury her hopes of being with him. Like the North Pole. Or maybe Siberia.

"Anyone home?" Sylvia stood in the door of Glory's small office with her hands behind her back and a secretive smile spreading across her face.

"Come in." Glory welcomed her friend, grateful for the distraction. "What brings you here on a work day?"

"Roses," Sylvia replied as she stepped into the office. "Or should I say one rose?"

Sylvia held a vase with a yellow rose. "For you—from some of the kids."

"John and K.J.?"

Sylvia nodded as she set the vase on the corner of Glory's table. "They still feel bad about that contract business."

Glory chuckled. "Tell them thanks for the rose and for not fulfilling the contract."

Sylvia nodded as she settled into a chair. "Don't suppose you heard from anyone else on Valentine's Day? Say someone from Dry Creek?"

Glory snorted. "Of course not. It would appear the phone lines don't work between here and Dry Creek, even though Garth Elkton seems to do fine."

Sylvia blushed. "Garth only called once—and that was to ask about the kids. And you," Sylvia continued. "He asked about you. Said something about Matthew being depressed. Speaking of whom, I thought Matthew asked you to call?"

"But that was months ago. He should call. I wouldn't know what to say."

"Well, maybe he doesn't, either."

"He could send a postcard."

Sylvia winced. "Ever try to put your heart on a postcard?"

"Even that man—the Bullet—sent me a postcard from prison. To apologize. And let me know he's in a Bible study there. He managed to write."

"Well, don't be too hard on Matthew. After all—" Sylvia stood up and flung her arms wide "—he came all the way to Seattle to see you."

Glory shook her ears. She wasn't hearing right. "What?"

"He came all the way to Seattle to see you," Sylvia repeated with satisfaction in her voice. "Garth brought him."

"Oh." The pieces clicked into place now. "Garth brought him?"

Sylvia nodded. "Garth thought the two of you needed to talk."

"You don't suppose it's the other way around, do you? That Garth wanted to talk to you and Matthew is his excuse?"

"Don't be silly. Garth didn't even know where to find me. He had to hunt on foot for the center. Almost got into trouble until John rescued him. By the way, Matthew's taking you out to dinner tonight."

"I'm busy."

"I already told him you were free." Sylvia winked. "Give the guy a break. It's Valentine's Day. And he's taking you to dinner at the top of the space needle."

"He won't be able to do that," Glory protested in relief. "People had to make reservations weeks ago for Valentine's night there."

Sylvia smiled. "I know. Matthew says he made them weeks ago." She turned to leave and then said over her shoulder, "Wear your black dress—with the pearls."

"It's too short."

"No, it's not."

The dress was too short. Glory frowned at herself in the mirror. Especially to be with Matthew. She didn't want him to think she was trying to get his attention. If he wasn't interested in her in blue jeans, he wouldn't be interested in her in a black dress that showed more leg than it should.

The doorbell of her apartment rang. That must be him. She'd told Sylvia she'd meet Matthew at the foot of the needle. But Matthew was a stubborn man. He'd told Sylvia he had hired a limo to take them to dinner, and she would be picked up at six-thirty.

Glory almost walked away from the door instead of toward it. She wasn't looking forward to tonight. She expected Matthew did want to talk to her, to explain how sorry he was that he was unable to be more to her than a distant friend because of his feelings for his late wife. But Glory would just as soon skip the speech.

The doorbell rang again.

When Glory answered the door, Matthew stood there in a black tux holding a dozen red roses. She'd never realized how good he would look in a tux. His chestnut hair was brushed back in soft waves. His freshly shaven chin was set in a determined smile. His blue-green eyes looked hopeful.

It was too much. Glory almost shut the door in his face.

Matthew watched the emotions chase themselves across Glory's face. He'd held his breath until she opened the door, fearful she wouldn't come, and when he saw her he almost couldn't get his breath anyway. Glory was dazzling. Her golden-bronze hair was pulled up in the Grecian-goddess style he well remembered. She could be Venus with arms. Her eyes went from molten to icy in the space of a heartbeat. Quicksilver. That was Glory. She wore a black dress that was too sophisticated and sexy for him. He wondered if he'd even get the nerve to talk to her when she looked so polished. And then he saw it. Around her neck she wore a little silver angel charm on a chain.

Glory saw the direction Matthew's eyes were taking and stifled the impulse to hide the charm with her hand. She'd forgotten to take it off. She was so used to wearing it under everything she wore and not having it show that she'd forgotten about it. She hadn't realized the low-cut black dress would reveal that much about her.

Matthew smiled. "I'm glad you're wearing my angel."

Glory gritted her teeth and nodded. "I like silver."

Sitting in the restaurant at the top of the space needle was like sitting on top of the world. The tables were arranged in a circle on the inside rim of the revolving restaurant. Each table had a big window to view the city below. At night, the lights below sparkled clear to the ocean.

"How are the boys?" Glory asked politely as she folded the linen napkin on her lap.

"Fine. Thanks for calling them at Mrs. Hargrove's. They get so excited."

Glory nodded. "I'm fond of them."

"They like you, too," Matthew replied.

"They have really good bread here," Glory said as she took another piece of fresh sourdough from the basket.

Matthew despaired. Were they going to small-talk the night away?

"My boys aren't the only ones who like you." Matthew took a deep breath and plunged. There, he'd started it.

Glory looked at him skeptically.

Maybe, Matthew thought, he needed to be more specific. "I like you, too."

Glory smiled woodenly. "Thank you."

Silence stretched between them.

"When you went away, I felt like Job," Matthew finally said. Glory looked at him quizzically. He had her attention. "The day Job said, 'He hath taken me by my neck, and shaken me to pieces.' That was me with God. He needed to get my attention and turn me around before I could be any good to Him or anyone else. Fortunately, He did...."

Matthew had his hand lying on the table and Glory reached over to cover it with her own. "I'm so glad," she said.

"I've never prayed so much in my life. Not even in seminary. Now I know what it means to wrestle with God. You lose and win all at the same time."

Glory looked into Matthew's eyes. If she hadn't been so distracted by her own emotions earlier, she would have noticed the peace she now saw there.

"I went up to Havre for a couple of weeks and stayed with an old minister friend of mine," Matthew continued. "I never listened before when he said other ministers have gone through what I did." Matthew smiled. "I thought I was the only one who'd ever been deeply disappointed. He told me I needed to learn I wasn't in control of the world. God is. As believers, we can pray to

Him, but our job isn't to carry the world on our shoulders. Our job is to trust."

"You're going back to the ministry, aren't you?" Glory asked softly. Joy rose within her.

Matthew nodded. "In Dry Creek for now. I don't want to move the twins again, and this way I can keep working at the hardware store, too."

"Mrs. Hargrove got her wish, after all."

"Mrs. Hargrove is so pleased with me she's even watching the twins for me while I'm here."

Glory smiled. "So this is what you wanted to tell me. Sort of like the steps in Alcoholics Anonymous where you go and speak to the people you've met and tell them you've changed."

Glory gave a sigh of relief. She didn't know what she'd expected of the evening, but it wasn't this. She was happy about Matthew, though, and glad she'd come to dinner.

"No," Matthew said in alarm. "That's not it. I mean— that's part of it. But I can't stop with that."

"Oh. I haven't done something, have I? Something I need to apologize for?"

"What could you have done?" Matthew asked in astonishment.

"Then it must be you. Did you do something you need to apologize to me for?"

Matthew finally realized what she was talking about—the AA practice of asking for forgiveness. "No! This has nothing to do with AA." Matthew was starting to sweat now and it was February in Seattle. "I guess the subtle way isn't working. I'm trying to work up to asking you to marry me."

"Marry you?" Glory was dumbfounded.

Matthew grimaced. He hadn't meant to blurt it out

quite that way. "Well, now that I'm back in the ministry and..."

Glory's heart went from hot to cold. "That's why you want to marry me," she said flatly. "Because you're in the ministry and every minister needs a wife."

Just then the waiter appeared with their dinners. "Blackened chicken for the lady and grilled mahimahi for the gentleman. Will there be anything else?" The waiter beamed.

Glory found her teeth were beginning to ache from the effort to keep her jaw from clenching. "If you'll excuse me for a moment, I need to go, ah, powder my nose."

Glory stood and walked to the ladies' rest room.

Matthew stared after her in dismay. How had everything gone so wrong? He knew he wasn't a Don Juan, but he hadn't expected to chase a woman away from her dinner with his proposal.

Glory stood in front of the full-length mirror in the rest room and counted to ten. She supposed she shouldn't be so angry. At least Matthew had been honest about what he wanted. He hadn't pretended to have a feeling that he was apparently reserving for the memory of his late wife. Glory sighed. It was so hard to compete with a dead woman. But still, the marriage offer did come from Matthew.

Matthew watched Glory walk back to the table. She held her head high with pride, and he scrambled around in his mind for words to apologize with....

"All right," Glory said quite calmly as she picked up her fork. "I'll marry you."

"What?" Matthew's roar was so loud the other people in the restaurant looked at him. He didn't care.

Apparently Glory did care. "Eat your fish. It'll get cold."

Matthew was speechless.

"Well, you did ask me," Glory reminded him after a moment of silence.

"But—" Matthew looked at her. "You don't seem very happy about the idea. I don't want you to marry me out of pity." Matthew had a sudden insight. "It's the boys, isn't it? You're marrying me for the sake of the twins. You think they need a mother."

Glory's heart broke. She'd forgotten. She couldn't marry Matthew. "I can't be a mother."

"But you like the twins."

"I love the twins. But I can't have children myself. I'm sorry, I should have told you before I accepted your proposal. I, of course, withdraw my acceptance." Glory speared another bite with her fork. "Delicious chicken."

"Hang the chicken," Matthew said. The muscle along his cheek started to twitch. "Look at me. We're not going to get married for the boys or for the ministry."

Glory laid down her fork, but she couldn't look at him. Not square in the eye. She didn't want him to see the tears that waited for a moment's privacy to fall.

"You may not be able to marry me because you love me," Matthew said softly. "But please, at least marry me because I love you."

"You?" Glory lifted her eyes. "You do?"

"Of course. That's what I've been trying to tell you."

"Well, it wasn't very clear."

Matthew held her eyes steady with his. She'd never seen him look so serious. "Then let me make it clear. I love you, Glory Beckett. I love you so much it takes my breath away. It has, in fact, taken my breath away a time or two. I can't even begin to count the ways in which I love you. You own my heart."

"But what about the children I can't have?"

"We have the twins. If we want more children, we can adopt."

"And what about Susie?" Glory couldn't help asking. "On Christmas Day I saw you looking at her picture and crying."

Matthew smiled. "I was crying for all the anger toward God I've carried inside me because of Susie. Seeing that gun pointed at you that night—with me being unable to save you—brought everything back. Feeling so helpless. But it was you I was crying for. Susie doesn't make me cry anymore."

"Really?"

Matthew nodded. "Really."

They looked into each other's eyes for a minute. The restaurant was filled with candlelight and the sound of soft music.

"You're sure?" Glory asked again.

Matthew nodded. "I'm sure."

Glory studied him some more. "Really?"

Matthew grinned. "Finish your chicken so I can take you someplace and convince you I'm seriously in love with you."

Glory smiled and rose from the table. "I'm not really that hungry, after all."

"Me neither."

The waiter insisted on boxing up their dinners to go. He didn't seem surprised about their decision to leave early. He said it happened quite often on Valentine's Day.

The limousine chauffeur didn't find it odd that they returned after just twenty minutes, either. He merely suggested a drive around to look at the lights of Seattle. Matthew told him to make it a very long drive—maybe over to Puget Sound—and Glory couldn't have agreed more. After all, Matthew had promised to tell her, in detail, why he really, really loved her. And she was going to do the same.

* * * * *

Receive one
FREE

Love Inspired ®

eBook
with in-store purchase.

Enjoy a FREE eBook by following these simple instructions:

1. Visit www.Walmart.com/loveinspired.

2. Select one title from the 8 free eBook options and add it to your cart.

3. Enter your promo code LOVEINSPIRED.

4. Read your free eBook instantly on the Walmart eBooks App!

Offer valid from October 29, 2019, to March 1, 2020.

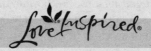
"Are the *kinder* okay?"

"Yes, they'll be fine." Uncomfortable with his small
intrusion into her family, she said, "Kevin had a bad
dream and woke us up."

"Because of the rain?"

She wanted to say that was silly but, glad she could be
honest with Michael, she said, "It's possible."

"Rebuilding a structure is easy. Rebuilding one's sense
of security isn't."

"That sounds like the voice of experience."

"My parents died when I was young, and both my
twin brother and I had to learn not to expect something
horrible was going to happen without warning."

"I'm sorry. I should have asked more about you and
the other volunteers. I've been wrapped up in my own
tragedy."

"At times like this, nobody expects you to be thinking of anything but getting a roof over your *kinder*'s heads."

He didn't reach out to touch her, but she was aware of every inch of him so close to her. His quiet strength had awed her from the beginning. As she'd come to know him better, his fundamental decency had impressed her more. He was a man she believed she could trust.

She shoved that thought aside. Trusting any man would be the worst thing she could do after seeing what Mamm had endured during her marriage and then struggling to help her sister escape her abusive husband.

"I'm glad you understand why I must focus on rebuilding a life for the children." The simple statement left no room for misinterpretation. "The flood will always be a part of us, but I want to help them learn how to live with their memories."

"I can't imagine what it was like."

"I can't forget what it was like."

Normally she would have been bothered by someone having sympathy for her, but if pitying her kept Michael from looking at her with his brown puppy-dog eyes that urged her to trust him, she'd accept it. She couldn't trust any man, because she wouldn't let the children spend their lives witnessing what she had.

Don't miss
An Amish Christmas Promise *by Jo Ann Brown,*
available December 2019 wherever
Love Inspired® *books and ebooks are sold.*

LoveInspired.com